Into the Sun

- A Novel of Africa -

JEROLD RICHERT

JLR Publishing

Into the Sun

Jerold Richert

eBook previously published as

Operation Rosie

ISBN: 978-0-9871622-4-3 (paperback

ISBN: 978-0-9871622-5-0 (eBook)

Cover design copyright 2013

JLR Publishing

This book is for all my girls
Lorna, Hayley, Karen, Taylor, Abbey, Ella and Phoebe
with all my love

Prologue

Although wary, the female rhinoceros had no fear as she approached the drying river. She had come this way many times before, following the same worn path to drink from the dark still pool, and with the dank scent of it heavy in the air she did not detect the musky sweetness of man.

Cover was thicker near the water, with many fallen branches and tangled vines, so she was not alarmed when the dry branch that she brushed aside in her passing rustled in the undergrowth, or when the vine-like object that lay in the sand over which she stepped rose to encircle her hind leg.

Only when it tightened, bringing her to a halt, did she pay it attention, turning from the path and kicking irritably to free herself of the clinging thing, but after only a short distance she was jolted to a stop once more.

With growing alarm she lunged against the restriction, shaking the stout tree to which the vine-like cable was attached, shedding brittle leaves and pods, but the grip remained firm, tightening and strangling, working through hide and flesh. And the pain began.

She twisted around to investigate the source of it, snorting at the man sweetness that clung to the cable together with the bitter scent of old fire. She hooked at it with her curved front horn, ripping at the bushes and small trees through and around which the cable snaked, flattening all within her limited reach, but to no avail. And against her violent lunging the pain grew worse.

She struggled to free herself throughout the long hot day then, with sweat darkening the deep folds in her grey hide, she stood with her prehensile upper lip brushing the trampled earth, puffing wisps of dust, searching the warm evening air for the tantalising scent of water, and when she detected its sweet moistness a long-drawn groan came from deep within her heaving belly.

Other animals came to drink, gently splashing, then departing in alarm at the snorts and crashing nearby. And in the full darkness the hyenas came to sniff and lap her splattered blood from the leaves and grass, retreating with drawn teeth from her three-legged charges to lurk restlessly in the shadows.

Throughout the long troubled night she remained standing, gaining what moisture she could from the surrounding trampled bushes and dry grass, chewing on dew-laden hairy leaves and soft branches, but it was too little to quench the burning thirst. And during the long hot day that followed it grew to surmount even the searing pain in its fiery intensity.

The hyenas returned with the dark, greater in number and ever more daring, crowding into her churned circle with weaving heads raised high, sensing her weakness, and with their foul scent intruding, her fear-driven rage exploded into red-eyed fury.

Squealing under the strength of it, she charged at their hateful presence once more, horn low and ready to kill, the pain forgotten and her great legs thrusting, and she reached the end of her circle with all of her two-ton weight driving forward at speed.

With a hollow thud that showered bark and twigs from the shaking tree, the cable snapped, breaking where the encircling loop on her leg turned sharply back on itself.

But not all of it was cast off. The loop remained embedded deep, drawn hard against the bone.

In time, after a full season had passed and her calf had been born, she learned to live with the pain, but the unravelled splayed ends of the rusted cable spiked and jabbed relentlessly, and the suppurating flesh never healed.

Part One

The yellow Tiger Moth flew low along the winding river, stirring the early mist that clung in wispy patches to the water like discarded veils, swinging from side to side in a graceful ballet of banking turns as the pilot searched for dugouts or other evidence of human encroachment into the wildlife reserve.

Tim Ryan piloted the biplane without conscious thought to the mechanics of flight, his bare feet on the cold metal of the rudder-bar working in practised harmony with his right hand on the joystick and his left on the throttle; resting there in readiness to apply instant power should startled birds rise suddenly from the green banks of reeds. His goggles were pushed to his forehead, the lenses fogged by the swiftly changing temperatures, and he squinted through watering eyes against the cold rushing air.

Only his eyes and nose were exposed, the remainder of his face protected by two green balaclavas; one inside the other. The wool covering his mouth was moister than could be expected from his condensing warm breath, for Tim liked to sing as he flew.

The Bee Gees was his current favourite, and he sang their hit song Stayin' Alive with gusto, pitching the falsetto notes above the deeper beat of the engine, timing them to suit, and hearing them resonate pleasingly in his covered ears.

Where herds of game were gathered at the larger pools he swung wide to avoid panicking them unduly, although his noisy approach and swift passing now caused only momentary confusion. They had become accustomed in some measure to the ritual morning disturbance, and had learned that it brought no harm.

When the river widened to join with the larger Sabi River on the north-eastern boundary and international border between Zimbabwe and Mozambique, he climbed the Tiger Moth above the surrounding hills, turning away from the gold orb of the rising sun to search the vast expanse of the Gona re Zhou National Park for signs of smoke. Not that he expected to see any. The new breed of poacher was too clever for that.

But Tim knew they were there. The game scouts had reported seeing their tracks and finding rhino snares, but the poachers were resourceful and cunning, doing without the comfort of cooking fires and the convenience of smoking racks. Now they simply abandoned any beast snared by accident. They were there to fill empty pockets, not empty stomachs.

With his self-appointed dawn patrol completed, Tim replaced the goggles and set a meandering course for home. Tomorrow he would do it again, even though he knew it was mostly a waste of time. The air patrols were too regular and noisy to be effective, giving too much prior warning and ample time to crouch low in bushes or stand motionless beside a tree, but it made life a little more difficult for the poachers; kept them nervous, and that, as far as Tim was concerned, was better than doing nothing.

The reserve was too big for effective ground policing, and the government too concerned with directing money into more personally rewarding areas than remote wildlife reserves. That frustrating task was left to a few men of the Lowveld, and to a handful of dedicated rangers.

Nevertheless, Tim enjoyed his early morning flights. It was his favourite time of day, and this was his favourite time of year, with the Mopani forests transforming the Lowveld into a leafy ocean of bronze that stretched from horizon to hazy horizon. Despite the tingling ears, runny nose and watering eyes, flying over it at dawn in the old Tiger Moth with its open cockpit was his idea of heaven.

Like his father and grandfather, Tim was a staunch

Mopani man. The small gnarled trees that changed color with the two seasons were as much in his blood as they were the life-blood of the Lowveld. And he felt a proprietary interest in the two thousand square mile game reserve that adjoined the family property. What affected one bled onto the other, for neither the trees, the animals, nor the poachers had respect for boundaries.

His father had flown these same hills and rivers in a Piper Taylorcraft before it was burned by terrorists in the bush war. Gara Pasi had been abandoned then, his father and stepmother almost losing their lives, but that was in the past. Now the process of rebuilding the property was well under way, although, with his father spending most of his time developing their rhino sanctuary in Australia, and against the restraints of a run-down, tourist-poor economy and largely unsympathetic Zimbabwean government, it was an uphill task.

Tim made one diversion that morning, turning to investigate what had attracted a spiral of vultures. He joined their circle low above a tree in which several of the birds had clustered in the branches, startling them into panicky flight as he searched the ground below.

The remains of a carcass lay partly concealed in bushes, making it difficult to identify, although he could tell it had been something large. It looked to be bigger than a zebra, wildebeest or impala, which were the most common species to be taken by lion in this area. It could be a buffalo or eland. They, too, could fall to the big cats, but it could also be a snare.

Widening his circle, Tim climbed the biplane to look for a suitable landmark that would pinpoint the position with more reliability than the vultures, which could easily disperse in search of better pickings before a ground patrol could be sent to investigate. But the area was flat and featureless, and a long way from Gara Pasi, at least thirty miles. It would take a ground party most of the day, and even if they found the place, it could be for nothing.

Instead, he looked for a place to land. Small clay-pans were common in the flat country, and with the dry season would be firm. He used them often, and the Moth, having a tailskid and being an old crop-duster, did not object too violently.

He found one less than a mile away from the carcass. He took a compass bearing from it to the pan, then he slipped in to land, stopping the brakeless Moth at the far end with a controlled ground loop that faced him back the way he had come in a cloud of grey dust.

Taking a water bottle and his rifle, he set off at a brisk walk, his bare feet well accustomed to rough treatment. With the vultures still circling, and further guided by the lingering smell of rotting flesh as he drew close, he managed to find the carcass a half hour later and establish that it was a buffalo. The surrounding tracks, where scavengers had not obliterated them, told that it had fallen victim to lions.

Relieved it had not been a snare, he set off back immediately. A long day lay ahead, with the stockades they were erecting in preparation for shipping the rhinos well behind schedule. Finding suitable logs had proved harder than anticipated, and he did not want to be caught short after all the bureaucratic battles they had fought, both at his father's end in Australia, and his in Zimbabwe. After stressing the urgency, he would look silly if the approval arrived before he was ready.

And he could not rely on the labourers to carry on without him. They would be sitting around yapping and waiting, no doubt recovering from hangovers, and with Juliette about to leave for her veterinary board exams in America, he still had to catch up with all the treatment details for her sick animals.

Thinking about it, Tim glanced at his watch, then broke into a jog. Maybe he should stop the dawn patrols, he thought, until the stockades were finished. Once the approval came, John Singleton would start jumping up and down, wanting to get the darting done before the rains, when his job with National Parks and Wildlife would require him elsewhere. He did not fancy the idea of darting without John's expert assistance. And, he thought cynically, if he didn't pull his finger out there would be no rhinos left to catch.

With the plane in sight, its yellow fabric clearly visible through the trees, but still busy with his thoughts, it took Tim a few moments to realize that the pounding he could hear was not all from his own two feet, and he turned to see a rhino trotting fast towards him over a stretch of barren ground. Its head was up, its tail stiffly erect, and following behind was a galloping calf.

Tim knew a lot about rhinos. He loved them, black or white, and had studied them for years in preparation for the translocation program. Books on them were stacked on the toilet floor, with Anna Merz's on top, and he believed that he, too, if given the opportunity, could understand the irascible beasts' snorting language and have them eating from his hand. And he also knew, without any doubt, that this particular rhino was not going to give him that opportunity.

Fortunately there was a nearby tree. Tim dived for it, dropping the water bottle and tossing the rifle into the branches ahead of him, hoping it would snag. It didn't, clattering down onto his head. Luckily, he managed to prevent it falling any further to what would have been its certain destruction under the heavy feet that thundered below a few seconds later.

The tree shook as the rhino hooked and butted at the trunk, shedding leaves, but not Tim, who hung on with both hands and feet, the rifle tucked precariously under his chin.

The calf arrived, blowing and mewling, trying to get between its mother's angrily driving legs, but getting knocked roughly aside. The mother gave her attention to the water bottle instead, which she attacked with grim determination, nosing it along the ground, followed by her confused calf.

She lost interest in the unaccommodating bottle and turned to glare belligerently at the tree, huffing and puffing.

'Bugger off!' Tim yelled. 'What the hell's your problem?'

It was all the incentive she needed. The second charge shook the tree to its roots, shedding more leaves and twigs, but again not Tim, who had taken advantage of the short respite to get a secure grip on the rifle.

He remained silent during the second attack on the inoffensive tree and, after giving the bottle one more go, the beast finally retreated. Favouring one hind leg it trotted haughtily away with the distressed calf cantering after it, and both of them heading directly towards the plane.

'Hey!' Tim shouted. 'Not that way!' He followed up with a piercing whistle. 'Get back here, goddamit!'

Unaccountably, this time his shouts were ignored. In desperation he fumbled with the rifle and fired a shot in the air.

The startled calf veered away, and the mother turned with it, taking them past the Moth, although still so close that Tim remained holding his breath, his finger crooked on the trigger until they were out of sight.

He waited a good minute after their departure before climbing down and going quietly to the plane. He took a long drink from the battered, but miraculously still intact bottle, then waited another few minutes to be sure before tossing the rifle and bottle into the front cockpit and setting the throttle and magneto switches.

He stood behind the propeller to swing it, stepping onto the wing, then into his seat in the rear cockpit as the Moth trundled forward under power. Dispensing with the balaclavas and goggles, Tim looked up to check ahead and stiffened.

The rhino was trotting across the pan towards him. It came in the same determined manner as before, head up with ears pricked and tail erect, and far behind it came the galloping calf in a thin haze of grey dust.

'Jesus!' Tim swore, and pushed the throttle all the way forward to the stop.

The beast was too close to think of jumping out and running for a tree again. The rhino would either get him or the plane, and neither option appealed. All he could do was carry on and hope the noise of the engine would distract it.

The Moth responded with a challenging roar, lurching forward and bouncing violently as he turned away from the oncoming animals to follow the rough edge of the pan.

The speed increased as the tail lifted, but not enough to get airborne, and Tim watched anxiously as the rhino turned with him. It too had picked up speed, lowering its head and homing in on the roaring machine with the deadly intent of a two-ton guided missile.

Tim had few options. If he increased speed too much he ran the risk of dipping the lower wing into the ground as he tried to follow the pan around, and he could not get a clear run across for a take-off while the cantankerous animal was blocking the way. Rhinos did not play games of chicken, they played for keeps.

To take-off he would have to get the beast to the side of the pan, to chase him from behind. But not too close. And he would have to slow right down, maybe even lower the tail, before turning the Moth to face across the pan.

Fortunately, like missiles, rhinos did not have the capacity to think ahead and cut him off, and the solid beasts were not built for long-distance running. It began to slow, going back to a limping trot, but still determined, and Tim eased back on the throttle with relief, enticing it closer, then accelerating with a sudden burst when it spun in behind in a cloud of dust, narrowly missing the tail with its long front horn.

'Ole!' Tim yelled, and slammed on the power as it charged after him.

The dangerous game of tag lasted for another complete, bumping, hopping and skidding circuit of the pan before the rhino lost interest and stopped, allowing Tim to lower the tail and turn for a take-off, only to see the calf standing in the middle of the pan, directly in his path.

'Get out of the bloody way!' Tim shouted.

It was the wrong thing to say. At the sound of his voice above the reduced noise of the idling engine the mother found hidden reserves. She lowered her great head and thundered in to attack once more.

'Bitch,' Tim muttered, and pushed the throttle forward hard, holding it there as if to gain every last erg from the clamouring Gypsy motor. A quick glance behind revealed only a thick cloud of dust, which must have adequately screened the plane, for the expected impact never arrived.

Tim gave his full attention to the calf, which was now running erratically across the pan, apparently wanting to escape the roaring machine coming towards it, but also anxious to join its dam that was somewhere behind it.

It chose in favour of the plane at the last instant, turning aside in panic, and Tim eased the stick back a moment later, lifting the Moth off sluggishly, and with barely enough speed as the trees raced towards him. He held it down for as long as he dared, allowing it to accelerate, then pulled up, lifting his feet instinctively as the undercarriage clipped the top branches of a Mopani tree.

Circling the pan while he regained his composure, Tim watched his adversary moving out of the dust and into the trees with her calf.

The activity must have taken its toll, for she was limping badly now, the right hind leg seeming not to touch the ground at all, and causing Tim to wonder what might have happened had she not been handicapped by the injury. By now the Moth would be scattered all over the pan and his intestines dangling from a tree to dry in the sun. He shivered at the thought, and made a silent promise that when the approval came through, she and her calf would be the first candidates for immigration.

He took a compass bearing on the distant Sibonja hills, jotting the numbers on the chalkboard tucked between his seat and the fuselage. It would be worthwhile sending a scout to keep track of the injured beast's movements, maybe to camp permanently on her trail until he could dart her and put her in one of the as-yet-to-be completed stockades. When Juliette returned from America she could attend to the injured leg. He had little doubt it had been caused by a snare. With luck the poachers wouldn't get a second chance.

Juliette was waiting for him at the airstrip, still in her short pyjamas, a coat hastily thrown around for decency, and her dark curls a tousled mop. 'Do you realize you have a branch stuck in your wheels?' she greeted him as soon as the engine had spluttered into silence. 'What happened?'

'It's a long story,' Tim replied.

'You should be more careful.'

'Absolutely.' He extricated himself from the cockpit and stepped from the wing onto the damp grass to remove the branch, tossing it aside before giving his younger half-sister a quizzical look. 'So, what brings you out so early, Jules, wet the bed?'

'Dad called from Aussie this morning.' She

seemed smugly pleased with herself, waiting for his reaction before continuing, and he supplied it reluctantly, guessing what was coming.

'Uh huh.'

'Good news. The approval has come through at last.' She beamed at him.

Tim sighed, thinking of the increased workload. 'Bloody marvelous,' he muttered despondently.

***

Nose up, and floating too high and long in the cold dense air, the Seabee alighted on the glassy surface of Puget Sound with all the weary grace of a storm-driven goose. The resulting spray all but obscured her before being swirled away in a fine plume of mist by the propeller wash.

The grey-haired man waiting on the jetty chuckled as the pilot's frustration showed in a sudden blast of power that swung the flying boat towards him. Another burst in reverse thrust at the last moment prevented the total demolition of the jetty and, with engine clanking into silence, the Seabee drifted into the buffer tyres, rocking the jetty and sending the cluster of small boats tied alongside into a jostling frenzy.

Buster 'Pop' Franz, USAF retired, caught his

balance and went forward to secure the rope tossed from the bow door, then watched appreciatively as the stooping pilot emerged backwards, denim-clad posterior prominently displayed below a hiked-up blanket jacket

'Nice tush, Kelly,' Pop Franz remarked. 'About as pretty a sight as that belly-flop.'

'Humph!' Kelly Maddock stood to wipe her palms on the seat of her jeans and smile a greeting. 'Better watch them arteries, Pop.' She stood on her toes to give him a peck on the cheek, grimacing at the rasp of stubble. 'A step closer to the razor please, Colonel. So what's that important I had to divert from my vitally important mission?' She lifted the front of her oil-stained red baseball cap to replace several strands of dark hair that had escaped, tucking them in and leaving a greasy smudge in their place. 'I have a fishing party of three to collect from Seattle in…' she tilted her head to consult the large aviation watch on the inside of her wrist, '…exactly twenty three minutes. I'm going to be late.'

'Won't keep you long, honey. I have a bit of news that will interest you. The jug's on. Hot biscuits too,' he added with a wink.

'Hmm… that'll do it I guess.'

Standing beside the potbelly in his weekender,

hands wrapped around steaming mugs and surrounded by the aroma of smoked herring and hot biscuits, they exchanged local gossip and discussed the weather - always a favourite topic in the Sound.

'So you're not planning on staying the rest of the season then,' Pop Franz said, raising his eyebrows.

'Is that what it is?' She shook her head. 'Uh, uh, I'm heading south with the birds. Thought I'd do some joy-flight work around San Diego and pick up a suntan.'

He pulled a disappointed face. 'Who's going to keep an old man company then?'

'Huh! Spare me the guilt trip, Pop. I don't see you from one month to the next anyhow. Nope, Bessie is hard enough to move when it's warm. Now she's giving me a hernia. I had to get Larry and his tractor to give me a tow this morning to bust the ice off the wheels, and the fog is becoming a pain in the ass. Sorry, I mean butt.' She paused, green eyes changing from smiling to questioning. 'Okay, Pop, so what's this news you're trying to put off telling me?'

Pop Franz frowned thoughtfully, choosing his words. 'Two bits of news, really. I had a call from Billy Steel yesterday. Seems your daddy's been raising hell again. Got drunk at Patrick and started bad-mouthing the Service, then he threatened to assault a general, for chrissakes. They had to physically throw him off the base.'

'Serves him right.'

Pop frowned. 'He's your father, Kelly. Used to be your hero. He needs help.'

'And he's your friend, Pop. You help him.' She put her mug down, ready to leave.

'You don't think he's worth it... after all he's done?'

'Oh, sure. You mean like dumping me and Mom?'

'You don't know what he went through in Vietnam.'

'Dammit, Pop. Why are you trying to put me on a charge? He wasn't the only one to have it tough over there. He's a quitter. He quit flying, quit the Air Force, and he quit on me and Mom. The only thing he hasn't quit, apparently, is drinking.'

'He's been trying. Billy said he'd booked himself into the AA a few times.'

She snorted contemptuously. 'Yeah, that sounds about right.'

'I guess he still blames himself for your Uncle Richard's death, and it takes more than the support of strangers, Kelly. He needs someone who really cares. Family... like you.'

'Well I don't care, Pop. Not any more. We tried to

help him, same as you did, and God knows how many others. Mom didn't blame him for what happened to Uncle Richard. I think he used that as an excuse.'

She took a long, deep breath and let it out in a rush of exasperation. 'No, to hell with it, Pop. He's on his own. It's what he wanted and it's what he's got. I don't need him anymore. And my mother certainly doesn't need a bad-mouth drunk within five hundred miles of her new mister-nice-guy-no-cussin'-around-here husband.'

Pop Franz hid his smile behind the mug. The bad language habit was one of the pitfalls of Service life. 'It sounds to me like you intend keeping your distance from him as well.'

She gave a non-committal shrug. 'He's okay, I guess. Takes good care of Mom. Just a bit prissy is all.'

'Okay, honey,' Pop said with resignation. 'What you decide about your father is your own business, I won't try to pressure you, although I'd appreciate you giving it some thought. And if you do decide to go...' He paused to smile. 'Which I think you will when you hear my next bit of news, I can get you a free ride on one of the Boeing test flights.'

She looked at him without answering, one eyebrow raised in suspicion, shoulders hunched and hands shoved deep into her jacket pockets.

'Billy has someone staying with him that I think you'll want to see… an old friend of yours.'

'Oh yeah, like who?'

'Do you remember that girl… the daughter of Billy's old flying buddy in Africa who owns a wildlife sanctuary?'

She frowned. 'Juliette Ryan? She's back in the States?'

'Doing her veterinary examinations in Philadelphia.'

'God, I haven't heard from her in ages…' She paused to smirk suspiciously at Pop. 'You and Billy have really been getting your heads together on this, haven't you?'

Pop shrugged, excusing himself with a smile.

'Throw one fish in to lure another, and whamo, we may hook big daddy. Is that the plan?'

'Yeah… well. If you're going there anyway, what's the harm in looking him up? Maybe you can convince him…'

'I never said I was going, Pop. You guys never give up, do you?'

'We're not all quitters, honey. Some of us like to stick by our friends… and family.'

She gave him a sharp look, but Pop had turned away to place the empty mugs in the basin.

'Well, maybe I'll give Juliette a call.' She removed her cap to ruffle her short hair, then replaced the cap and tugged on the peak 'Thanks for the warm-up, Pop.'

Pop Franz followed her down to the jetty in silence, wishing he had handled it differently, but not sure how. She was the closest thing he had to family since he had retired from the Service and moved to Boeing, and he wanted it to remain that way.

'You keep that pretty young tush out of harm's way now,' he joked as she stooped to go aboard, not wanting her to leave on a sour note.

She wriggled it provocatively, then grinned at him through the Perspex as she donned her headphones, sticking out her tongue.

Pop watched the take-off, smiling in acknowledgement at the farewell waggle of the wings. He was still watching and smiling when the Seabee disappeared from view around the dark bulk of San Juan Island.

***

Kelly Maddock, president, chief pilot, and proud owner of Sound Sea-Air and its fleet of one, trimmed for level flight at five hundred feet above the Strait of Juan de Fuca and headed south, following the ferry route to Admiralty Inlet and Seattle.

Mount Rainier showed crisp and clear above its customary blanket of early fog, the glacier-covered slopes dominating the view ahead, and glistening so brightly she was forced to squint even behind her sunglasses. More than a useful landmark, it was her favourite view, but this morning she had other things on her mind.

It was not so much her father's drunken brawling - that she had come to expect now as a matter of course - but what Pop had said about him being her hero. She hadn't thought of him like that for a long time. But he had been more than that. He had been her blueprint for all men; handsome, daring and fun to be with, and she had considered her mother to be the luckiest woman in the world and herself the luckiest child. She was his princess, and he was her shining knight of the skies. A fighter pilot in two wars with nine kills to his name - only one short of being a double ace.

He had taught her to fly when she was thirteen and needed a cushion on the seat of the Stinson so she could see the propeller. Strictly against all regulations, while on leave from Vietnam, he had hijacked the Stinson from the spares supply base at Tinker on a holiday weekend, flying it to the grass field of a friendly Oklahoma farmer where she waited with her mother.

Everybody should learn to fly in a tail-dragger, he told her, and gently put her through the paces like a horse-breaker would a wild-eyed filly, firmly coaxing, complimenting and encouraging. She went solo the same weekend after five hours flying; three touch and goes in succession, and was so shaky with pent-up exhilaration afterwards that she couldn't walk without stumbling. It had been the happiest day of her life.

Most of the technical side of flying she had done later, after he had returned from Vietnam for the last time, a changed man. From shining knight to shadowy villain in the space of two short years. He refused to fly or have anything to do with airplanes. He had quit the Air Force, moving them to California where his boyish charm and hero status helped get him a job as a realty salesman. It didn't last, although for a while he did try, spending up on flashy clothes that he didn't particularly like, and hitting the after-hours cocktail scene hard, which he did.

But a fighter pilot has little in common with selling, and after several different jobs and as many affairs, her mother filed for divorce and moved out, and she had gone with her. That was the last time she had seen him, and for Pop Franz to expect her to go back - even for a visit - was ridiculous. He was no longer her hero, and she had her own life to live.

After picking up her party of fishermen and dropping them off at Stuart Island, Kelly flew back to Friday Harbour and the dilapidated houseboat that was both office and home. It was cramped and draughty, but useful in that she could have the plane moored alongside where she could keep a watchful eye on it. And as her live aboard was linked to a jetty and not anchored out in the harbour, where it would probably sink, she also had the luxury of electricity and telephone. It was the perfect set-up for her, and the Seabee the ideal plane.

When she had seen it advertised for sale in a flying magazine while she was doing her commercial licence, and for only six thousand dollars, she knew immediately that it was the opportunity she had been waiting for. It was roomy enough to sleep in overnight, the seats reclining to make a double bed, and it even had a small galley with an alcohol stove. She could live aboard if necessary and earn money by taking people to remote wilderness lakes. America had several thousand such places, and every one was a landing place for the Seabee. And being amphibious, she could land at regular airports as well. A flying houseboat-cum-trailer.

She had bought it with part of the ten thousand dollars her mother had given her on her eighteenth birthday, and which she was supposed to have used for college.

The Bee was less appealing though when she came to fly it. Compared to the small light planes of the flying school it was a monster, and it behaved like one. Ten knots of crosswind rendered it as manoeuvrable as a barge, and she had as much chance of pushing it on the ground as she would a dead whale.

After ten hours of dual instruction, both on water and land, she still handled it like a student. It took fifty hours before she felt reasonably confident, and a hundred before she felt happy. Only then did she begin to enjoy it. Flying it over the Sound was like having a seven-hundred-square-mile airport beneath.

Kelly phoned Billy Steel in Punta Gorda and discovered that Juliette Ryan was already in Philadelphia, doing her final exams at Tufts, and would be away for the next four days. She would be staying with him for two weeks after that, until the results were known, then would return to Tufts for the graduation ceremony if she passed.

'She was hoping to see you before she went back to Zimbabwe,' Billy said. 'Did Pop say anything about getting you a free ride to Orlando?'

'He also said quite a bit about my father. It isn't going to work, Billy. I don't want to see him.'

'That's what I told Pop. Can't say I blame you,

Kel. I don't see much of him either. He kinda avoids me. Anyways, if you want to see Juliette, you can stay here. Plenty of spare bunks now that the kids have moved out.'

'Thanks, Billy, I'll see how it goes. Tell her I phoned and will get back.'

'Hey, I almost forgot,' Billy said. 'Do you remember that old fighter your daddy bought when he was still in the Service?'

Kelly had to think for a moment. Billy and her father had talked often about restoring antique planes as a hobby, and although Billy had continued with it, her father had dropped out. One more thing he had quit on. 'That old thing? I thought he had dumped it years ago.'

'No, it's been sitting here in my hangar. I got it going... sort of, in the hope it would get him interested in flying again.'

'Obviously without success.'

'Yeah... well. He said I could have it, but it's yours if you want it. I've got enough on my plate with the instructing, and I'm still trying to finish the Jenny.'

'Me? What would I do with that crock? No thanks, I have enough trouble keeping the Bee in the air. Why don't you sell it?'

'Not mine to sell. If you're down this way take a

look. You may change your mind.'

'I don't think…' she paused. 'Oh, I get it. Bribery too.'

Billy laughed. 'You're too young to be cynical, Kelly. No conditions. I'll tell Juliette you called.'

Kelly thought about it over the next few days, while she completed her dwindling charter commitments. She had got on well with Juliette Ryan. The girl was clever and friendly, and they had clicked immediately when they met at a wildlife convention in San Diego, where Juliette had been doing work with the zoo towards her doctorate. Juliette had given a talk about the sanctuary in Zimbabwe, and how they had been working towards shipping the endangered black rhinos to Australia. She had invited Kelly to visit, and she would have gone had she not only recently started the charter business. Perhaps now she could, with things slowing down, and if the offer was still open.

Still, Kelly was undecided. It was something she would love to do, but it would cost more than she had saved, and she still needed money for rent and other expenses during the quiet season, which she could earn with joy-flights around LA or San Diego, but not if she went gallivanting off to the other side of the world.

After sweating over it for another day, Kelly came up with a compromise. She would take Pop's offer of a free ride to Orlando and see Juliette. That way she would be keeping in contact personally, not by phone, and if the offer came up again she would accept for the future, when she could afford it.

With the decision made, Kelly called Pop Franz at Boeing and Billy Steel in Punta Gorda, telling them she would go, and making arrangements. She did not mention her father and, thankfully, neither did they.

***

Pop Franz had suggested Kelly leave the Seabee at the Boeing plant at Everett for the four days she intended being away. They had a secure parking area, and he would arrange for clearance. It would be more convenient than catching ferries or buses.

She arrived in the circuit precisely on time, determined to show that not all charter pilots were sloppy. Gleaming 747s were parked in a row down one side of the field. The circuit and runway were clear.

She flew the downwind and crosswind legs with textbook accuracy, so, too, the approach. No juggling with power or flaps, but as smooth and even as if the Bee had been attached to an invisible cable linking it to the threshold, setting her up for a perfect touch-down into the ten knot breeze at the second marker, and right on the painted centreline.

With flaps lowered and throttle closed, stick full back and nose rising as she held off for that perfect greaser, she was totally committed to the landing, already anticipating the rumble of the wheels as they touched, and beginning to wonder why it was taking so long and she was so close to the ground. Then the numbing realisation struck her. She had forgotten to lower the wheels.

It sounded like a collision of freight trains; a grinding, screeching, crunching and roaring that seemed never to stop. Instinctively, she tried to brake, then remembered and shut down the engine, turning off the fuel and sitting in mortified acceptance as the Bee skidded along the runway, then wincing as it slewed off on the camber to strike a runway marker and grind to a halt. A silence filled with rebuke took its place.

Resignedly, Kelly opened the door and stepped the short distance to the ground, as much concerned with her stupidity as she was by any damage she may have caused to the plane.

Within seconds a fire-tender pulled up alongside with two men, one of them Pop Franz. 'You okay, honey?' he enquired anxiously, jumping from the cab.

'I feel like a complete idiot.'

'Saw you comin' in and was wondering when you

were going to put the gear down.'

She managed a strained smile. 'I've been landing on water all week and forgot.'

He gave her a reassuring smile. 'Rather that than landing on the water with the wheels down, kid, and you're not the first member of the wheels-up club.' He detached a hose from the tender and sprayed water on the hull to cool it down, then spoke to the man with him. 'Order up the small crane and a canvas sling, Chico. We'll lift her up and lower the gear, then tow her in for a check-up.'

While the ground crew were being called, Kelly and Pop inspected the damage. For such a clamour there seemed to be remarkably little, only a dent and smear of white where the port side had struck the marker.

'These amphibian hulls are designed to take a beating,' Pop commented. 'We'll know more when we lift her up and take a closer look, but my guess is she'll have nothing but a scraped keel. A few precautionary x-rays and tests, a bit of a touch-up and she should be flying in a few weeks.'

'That long?'

'I'll have to work on her myself. Maybe get one of the apprentices to help on the weekend.'

'Sounds expensive.'

'No charge, only a favour. Go see your old man.'

'More bribery?' But she was relieved. She managed a weak smile. It could have been a lot worse

He laughed. 'No, of course not, but one good turn deserves another, so they say.'

'Okay, Pop, It's more than fair exchange, I'll do it, even though I still think it's a waste of time. And thanks.'

'He loves you, Kelly. Talked about you all the time.'

She snorted. 'Strange way he has of showing it. Maybe it was the whisky talking, heh?'

'Tell him if he stays of the juice for two weeks straight I'll get him a job here. It's only flying computers, but...' he shrugged, 'it's a whole lot better than drinking yourself to death.'

***

Other than the crew, and a dozen or so technicians monitoring an impressive array of equipment, the 747 was empty. Kelly had the first class section virtually to herself and, because they landed several times en-route to check instrument landing and other navigational systems, more time than she needed to think of what she might say to her father. Every approach had already been tried except force, and she was certainly not going to resort to that. She would simply be going through the motions anyway, she finally decided, so would play it by ear after talking to Billy Steel.

The Boeing landed at two in the morning; not an unusual time for an international airport, but awkward for catching buses to distant towns, and her budget did not extend to rental cars.

To kill time until the next Greyhound to Punta Gorda, she did the rounds of the airport, starting with an espresso bar, then browsing through the overpriced tourist boutiques and duty free shops, visiting a cocktail bar, yawning from the viewing platform, and toying with a pot of tea and a Mississippi mud cake.

Three hours, four bus changes, and a long walk with her cumbersome bag later, she arrived at the airfield where Billy rented a hangar with an attached office.

He was inside, talking to Juliette, and they broke off to look at Kelly with surprise as she appeared in the doorway.

'Hey, kid,' Billy said. 'What you doin' here? We've been waiting for you to call so we could fly up and get you.'

'Now you tell me.' She grinned at Juliette. 'Howdy, stranger.' She dumped her bag on the floor to meet Juliette's excited charge, the two hugging and exchanging breathless compliments and grins. Juliette had changed since San Diego. She was still slim and petite, her dark curls tousled, but her ready smile and open manner were the same as she remembered.

Kelly removed her cap to blow hot air up her face before submitting to Billy's kiss on her sweaty cheek.

'Juliette received notification this morning that she passed her exam,' Billy said. 'I was trying to convince her that we should go out somewhere and celebrate.'

'You did?' It was close to a shriek, and Juliette beamed happily. Kelly enveloped her in another hug. 'Congratulations, doc.'

'Can you come to the graduation?'

'Wouldn't miss it for anything. Doctor Juliette Ryan, wildlife vet. Wow!'

'It's on Monday,' Billy said. 'We'll be flying up in the Cherokee on Saturday. If you can see your father between now and then we can all go together.'

'That sounds wonderful,' Kelly said, 'except I don't know where he is.'

'He's in a trailer park over on the east coast, near Palm Bay. I'll fly you up there when you're ready.'

'Not today,' Kelly said. 'Today is old friend's day. How about tomorrow?'

Billy consulted his diary of bookings, giving Kelly

and Juliette a chance to grin at each other in anticipation of catching up on their interrupted friendship.

'Tomorrow's fine,' Billy confirmed. 'That'll give you two days with your daddy. I'll call Pop and explain. Shouldn't be a problem arranging another ride next week sometime.'

'Thanks.' Kelly would have preferred spending only one day with her father, but was in no position to object. 'Will you be coming back this way after the graduation?' she asked Juliette.

'No, I'm booked out of Kennedy on Tuesday.' She pulled a sour face. 'At four thirty in the morning.'

'It'll be just you and me on the way back,' Billy told Kelly. 'I can drop you off at either Orlando, or Palm Bay, if you want to see your father again. Now, about that drink. I have a few cold beers in the house... or would you like something more exotic?'

'I was thinking of a Coke,' Kelly said, glancing at Juliette for corroboration.

'Same for me,' Juliette gave her support.

Billy pulled a sour face. 'Okay, I can take a hint. I have work to do anyway. You'll find that junk in the machine at the Flying Club.'

***

After an hour of non-stop reminiscing, it seemed to Kelly that she had known Juliette Ryan most of her life instead of the few days they had spent together in San Diego.

Maybe it was because they came from such different backgrounds, she thought. Some of Juliette's expressions were old-world, and she spoke with an accent that Kelly could only think of as being not quite British. Combined with her animated expressions and quick wit, it made her fascinating and easy to listen to. Her mother was of French Arab extraction, she remembered, so this also may have had an influence, as it did with her looks.

She learned that Juliette's parents would be at the graduation as well.

'They're coming all the way from Australia?'

'Yes. Also my brother from Zimbabwe. You'll meet him too. I'm sure he's been hoping I'd fail so he wouldn't have to leave his precious rhino.' She paused to give Kelly a coy look. 'Come to think of it, you two should have a lot in common. He's a pilot too, you know. Flies an old crop-duster. A Tiger Moth. Who knows, you may even get a thing going together. Wouldn't that be something?' She smiled mischievously. 'I'll put in a good word for you.'

Kelly laughed. 'No you won't. He sounds great,

but I'll do my own matchmaking, thanks all the same.'

'You don't know what you'll be missing. Most of the female tourists we get at Gara Pasi don't wear knickers in case they get lucky.' She rolled her eyes seductively. 'Big white hunter stuff.'

'Jules! I'm surprised at you. And all this time I've been trying to hide my brash American ways, thinking you were the perfect lady.'

'Are you kidding? If you want brash you should try an Australian veterinary college. You'd be surprised how many crude jokes you hear when you've got your arm stuck up to the elbow in some poor cow's uterus.' She giggled. 'I've made up a few good ones myself. Want to hear them?'

Kelly grinned. 'Of course, and I'm sure they're disgusting, but save them for later. Tell me about your parents.'

'Dad's a bit of an old stick-in-the-mud these days,' Juliette confided, 'but he's done a few hair-raising things in his time. Ask Billy. They were together in Africa.'

Her father had been married previously to an Australian woman, who was Tim's mother, Kelly learned. She had been killed in a terrorist attack in Zimbabwe when he was seven. Juliette herself had been born in Australia.

'Although Tim is my half-brother, I don't think of him like that. We've always been close. Poor bloke. I boss him around a bit. Now… tell me about your family. Billy told me your dad was a fighter pilot in Vietnam. Why don't you bring him to Philly? I'm sure my folks would like to meet him. With Billy there as well it will be like old home week.'

Kelly gave an uncertain grimace. 'I don't know what to expect with my father, Jules. My mother divorced him years ago, and I haven't seen him in over four. And…' She sighed. 'I'm afraid he has a bit of a drinking problem. Don't think it would be a good idea.'

Juliette showed her concern, and Kelly explained what had occurred after his return from Vietnam, grateful to have a woman friend to confide in for a change.

'Something must have happened there, by the sound of it,' Juliette said thoughtfully. 'Maybe he needs therapy. You should try getting him into a clinic.'

'Tried that, but you can't help those who won't help themselves. I'm going to give it one more try, and that's it.' She took a deep breath. 'Anyway, enough of that. It's a pity you're going back so soon. I planned to do some flying around the lakes in California. I was hoping that after all your studying you could maybe take a break and join me. You haven't seen my Bessie

Bee. She's lots of fun.'

Juliette was wistful. 'Oh, how I wish I could. It would make a pleasant change from being stuck in the bush with only men for company, but we've just received approval to start shipping rhinos to Chipimbiri... our property in Australia, so there's heaps to do. I really need to get back as soon as possible.'

'No special men in your life?'

Juliette shook her head. 'None. Yours?'

'No. The ones I meet seem interested only in body parts.'

Juliette laughed. 'Maybe us career girls are doomed to become old maids.' She became serious. 'Look, I can't take the time off, but if you can, why don't you come to Zimbabwe? With the rhino programme getting under way you'll find it interesting, and it would be lovely to have your company. We have plenty of guest cottages. Other than the fare it won't cost you a cent... or a dime, as you say here.'

Kelly was in no doubt that the offer was genuine, and the sincerity of it confirmed her belief that Juliette thought of her as a real friend. It gave her a warm feeling. Good friends had been few and far between since she had started charter flying.

'You've no idea how much I appreciate that offer,' she said with equal sincerity. 'I'd love nothing better,

45

but right now I'm kinda broke, and I made a promise to Billy and Pop Franz to see if I could help my delinquent father. Another time though, Jules. That's also a promise.'

***

The Florida Heaven Trailer Park was more like Kelly's idea of hell than heaven. The pool at the entrance, presumably to entice potential guests, was swamp-green, the lawn surrounding it a scorched brown, and the single palm overlooking both was dead, several of its dry branches dangling forlornly. The trailers themselves looked as if they had taken root.

The caretaker was equally unattractive; a fat, gum-chewing youth with a crude slogan on his vest and, by the way he ogled, must have had Kryptonite lenses in his glasses.

'Number seventeen is down the track a ways,' he answered her query with a leer, then trotted from his pen to monitor her progress as she left. Kelly heard the office screen door squeak open but not close, and could feel his eyes burning through her stretch-jeans as she strode away. She slung her bag to the rear, where it proceeded to bounce rhythmically in time to her steps, making it worse.

The shabby surroundings did little to revive her depressed mood of the previous day, when a phone call to the Park after arriving at Palm Bay established that her father had already left for whatever work he was doing, and that he didn't normally return until late at night. She had been forced to take a cheap motel room and had spent most of the day catching up on sleep, then had been awake most of the night, her mind a turmoil of misgivings. She found some consolation in the knowledge that one day had already passed, but still resented having to be there, on what she considered was a hopeless mission anyway, when she could have been enjoying the company of Juliette.

It was a rented trailer, with a blue Ford pick-up parked in front, between two battered-looking palm trees showing traces of blue paint, apparently old enemies. The passenger door was open and the parking lights still on. The blinds covering the windows of the trailer were closed. She looked at her watch. Eight fifteen. Late enough. She dropped her bag well clear of the trashcan and pounded on the door.

Sounds of movement came from inside, the whisper of bare feet, a faint rattle from the latch, and Kelly moved back, taking a breath and arming herself with a weak smile. It had been a long time. They both would have changed.

The door opened wide enough to reveal the sleepy face of a young Hispanic woman.

'Yes?' she enquired softly, with an irritable frown, and Kelly's smile faded.

'I'm looking for Jim Maddock. Does he live here?'

'Still asleep.' She withdrew slightly to glance behind, as if concerned that the noisy question may have intruded, then she came farther out, covering her apparent nakedness with a towel held at her chin. 'You from the realty?' Then she saw the bag and her frown deepened.

'No, I'm not. Can you wake him please? Tell him his…' Kelly paused, reluctant to inform the woman, who looked not much older than herself, that she was his daughter. 'Tell him Kelly is here.'

The woman shook her head. 'No way. You want to see him, you come back later. Maybe two hours. Okay?'

Kelly held her anger in check with difficulty. 'No, I'm not coming back. You tell him his daughter was here.' She did not bother to lower her voice. 'There's a café on the next block… Coconut something or other. Tell him to meet me there. I'll wait for an hour, then I'm leaving… for good. You tell him that. For good… got it?'

The woman pulled back into the shadows without

answering, and Kelly snatched up her bag. She strode past the truck, then stopped. The keys were still in the ignition.

'To hell with it,' she muttered, and tossed her bag into the back. Her feet had taken enough. She swept an empty bottle onto the floor as she slid across to the driver's seat, wrinkling her nose at the smell of stale liquor and cigarette smoke. She twisted the key and the engine turned over sluggishly, the battery almost flat.

Kelly swore and thumped the steering wheel with her hand, then fumbled for the light switch, turning it off. She tried again, and the engine turned over once, reluctantly, then inexplicably roared into life. She grated into reverse and backed out, then skidded forward in a shower of loose gravel. The caretaker stumbled from his office to gape as she banged over the speed-bumps without slowing.

Kelly did not stop at the café. She sped past, fully intending to drive all the way back to Punta Gorda, but after a few miles she slowed and pulled over to sit and think. She knew exactly what she was doing. It was more than anger or disappointment at her father's sleazy lifestyle that was driving her. She was looking for an excuse to quit. It must run in the family, she thought, and snorted derisively. She adjusted the rear-view mirror to check for traffic behind before pulling out and caught a glimpse of her face. The expression of a petulant child. She smiled grimly to shatter the image. 'Jesus, Kelly,' she muttered, 'get a grip and stop feeling sorry for yourself .'

She turned the truck around and went back to the Coconut Grove Café.

Sitting at a table on the terrace, she didn't recognise her father at first when he arrived with ten minutes to spare. Perhaps unconsciously, she had been looking for a crew-cut fighter pilot in Air Force fatigues. The Salesman father had been a stranger, like this man was, panting up the few steps, with puffy eyes and overlong greying hair in a pony tail, wearing ridiculously long striped shorts, flowery shirt and sandals.

She was the only one there, so it was easier for him, but he still had to look twice. Kelly removed her sunglasses as he came towards her and he gave a weak smile of recognition.

'Well, that was a rude awakening,' he greeted, sounding neither angry nor pleased. 'Thought someone was stealing my truck.' He grunted. 'Hell, someone did steal my truck.'

He had put on weight, although it looked more like bloat than beef, especially around the middle, which he tried unsuccessfully to hide under the hanging-out shirt.

'My feet were sore. Anyway, you shouldn't leave the keys in it.'

'Yeah…' He made to go around the table to her, and Kelly started to rise, then he changed his mind and pulled out a chair. The smell of bourbon reached her anyway.

'Hello, Father. What's with the ponytail? You have earrings to match?' She smiled to make it a joke.

He studied her for a moment, reaching in his breast pocket for a pack of cigarettes. 'You've changed, Kelly. A grown woman.' He shook his head, either in disbelief, nostalgia or regret, she couldn't tell which. 'You look a lot like your mother.'

'That's a relief. You've changed as well.' She meant it jokingly too, but his quick scowl showed he had not taken either of her comments that way. He leaned back, looking around at the empty tables while he lit the cigarette. There was a time he would have laughed at her flippancy. And his fingers wouldn't have trembled. She tried to make amends. 'How have you been, Father?'

He shrugged. 'You sound like her too. She called me James only when she was mad.' He gave her the faint smile she had been waiting for, the crooked, restrained one she loved, when the corners of his lips turned down so it looked more like an expression of

51

gloom. 'What happened to Daddy?'

'That's what I'm here to find out.' She regretted saying that too, but the smile had triggered the response. That was how it had always been between them. But it wasn't now.

'You've obviously been talking to that nosy do-good bastard, Franz.'

'He's your best friend.' Now she didn't know what to call him. 'And Billy, too. He's been fixing up that old biplane you bought years ago, hoping to get you interested in flying again, and Pop says he can get you a job with Boeing.' She held back the part about him having to dry out first.

He laughed, scornfully. 'What the hell do they know? They've still got their heads in the clouds. There's no future in flying anymore. It's all been done. Real estate is where it's at now. No shortage of people and they all need somewhere to live.' He stubbed out his cigarette and called to the waiter. 'Hey, Armando! Bring me one of them Castro specials, pal. ' He turned to Kelly with raised eyebrows. 'Want something... a drink?'

She shook her head, feeling suddenly uncomfortable, and he continued. 'See that line of palms over there? Beyond that the land runs at around two hundred bucks a square foot. Where we're sitting right now is about ten. So what do you think that bit over there will fetch?' He pointed to a vacant stretch of land bordering the road opposite, and didn't wait for an answer. 'My guess is around a hundred, and who do you think owns it?' He leaned back to light another cigarette, not looking at her.

Kelly was surprised. 'You?'

He tried his secret boyish smile again, but it didn't quite work. 'Not yet. The woman you saw at the Park. Her daddy owns it.'

'You mean the one my age?' She found it hard not to sneer.

To her surprise he looked sheepish. 'Well, yeah, but it isn't all fun and games. Sometimes it's business. It just so happens that I know where to get the finance to develop.'

Kelly was flabbergasted. 'You mean you're using her to make a business deal?'

'Hey, nobody forced her. She happens to like me, which is more than I can say for you. And who the hell are you to judge anyway? Goddam it, you're worse than your mother.'

'Billy said you had been going to a clinic,' Kelly said, changing the subject before it went too far. 'What happened?'

'Nothing.' He was still angry, and Kelly tried once

again to smooth things over.

'No good, heh?'

'Big mistake. Not a clinic at all, just a bunch of losers. Thought I was signing up for one of those health places, where they feed you rabbit food.' He patted his stomach. 'That I could use.'

'You don't have a drinking problem?'

'Sure I do. It costs too goddam much. Isn't that right, Armando?'

The waiter, looking puzzled, placed the steaming mug of black coffee on the table. The aroma of hot rum wafted strong. 'Too much, senor?'

'Never mind, stick it on my tab, will you?' he took a cautious sip while the waiter hovered uncertainly.

'Senor… the manager…. sorry, but he say only cash...'

'For chrissakes, Armando, I came here in a hurry. I didn't bring any. Tell him…'

'Here…' Kelly interjected quickly. She paid with a ten-dollar note and the waiter gave her the change with a relieved smile.

'Thanks, kid, I'll square with you later. That's the trouble with this country. Revolves around the dollar. They should change the flags to look like hundred-dollar bills.'

'If I can find one of those health places you

mentioned,' Kelly persisted. 'Will you go? Billy and Pop said they wouldn't mind helping out if you're short.'

He snorted disdainfully. 'Those do-good bastards. All this concern for my health. And what about you? Why are you here anyway? Come to help out your poor old daddy with a few bucks as well?' He held up a hand to stop her protest. 'Okay, only kidding. If those two want to throw it away I'll take it. I could use a holiday, but no AA crap. That I don't need. So I drink too much, but who doesn't in this business? It's part of the job, and that's the only reason I do it, keeps the pressure off. If I was doing something else I'd quit in a minute.'

'So if you went to one of those health farms… say for two weeks, you wouldn't drink at all?'

'Sure, no problem.' He drained the last of his Castro Special. 'Miss that stuff though. No coffee allowed in those places.' He pulled a sour face. 'Tell you what. I'll go if you come too. We can nibble carrots together and talk. Give us a chance to catch-up.' His expression softened. 'I've missed you, Kelly. Your mother too… sometimes.'

'I used to think she was the luckiest wife in the Air Force.'

For a brief moment before he smiled, a shadow crossed his face. 'Yeah?'

She nodded. 'And I thought I was the luckiest child.'

He laughed. 'Jesus…'.

'What happened in Vietnam, Father, that made you change? You used to be so full of life… my hero. Everyone's hero. Can't you tell me about it… please?' She wanted to reach across to him, to reinforce her plea, but couldn't quite bring herself to take a stranger's hand.

His face hardened. 'Nothing to tell. I got sick of it, that's all. Sick of the war, sick of the killing. Sick of people. Heroes? Ha! That's a laugh.'

Kelly saw the chance of a breakthrough for the first time. 'Was it Uncle Richard's death?'

He suddenly looked old. 'Dick took his chances with the rest of us.' He lit another cigarette and drew deeply on it, frowning, then blew out hard. 'Anyway, that crap is all in the past. Life goes on. What are you doing with yours? I thought you'd be married by now.'

'Not yet. I'm still looking for someone like you were.'

He snorted with laughter, choking on his cigarette and lapsing into a fit of coughing. 'Jesus…'

'You should give that up, too.'

'You're much worse than your mother,' he gasped, but could not hide the pleased look her remark had caused.

Kelly told him about her small charter business and he seemed impressed, asking sensible questions, and she sensed she was still making headway. Glimpses of the old Jim Maddock were showing, and if she could get him away for a few weeks on her own the chances were good she could make the breakthrough complete. It would be hellish expensive no doubt, and she would have to repay Pop, but it would be worth it.

'I'll come with you to a health farm if you promise to behave,' she said. 'No booze. Deal?'

He laughed scornfully. 'Sounds like a barrel of fun, but yeah, what the hell.' He shrugged. 'I need a day to tie up a few loose ends though, and have to be in Miami by next Friday.'

'That soon?' Kelly showed her disappointment. 'But that will only give us a week if we leave right away. I was hoping to fly with Billy to a friend's graduation. I won't be back until Tuesday.'

'Sorry, kid, can't be helped. I've been working on this for a long time.'

'How about the week after?'

He shook his head regretfully. 'No good. If Miami comes off I'll be tied up for months.'

All that prevented Kelly from quitting right then was the knowledge she was getting somewhere. A week may be enough to complete the breakthrough, but if she left it until after Juliette's graduation they would only have two days at the most. It would be a waste of time and money. She also knew she would live to regret not taking the opportunity to help her father. She gave a sigh of defeat. It seemed she had no option but to give Juliette's graduation a miss.

'If I can find a place that will take us tomorrow, will that give you enough time to tie up the loose ends?'

He seemed uncertain for a moment, then nodded. 'Should be enough.'

'I'm serious about this, Father.'

He looked steadily at her. 'So am I, kid. Set it up.'

***

Kelly was torn between jubilance and disappointment. Everything was working out perfectly in favour of her father. A local travel agency found her a vacancy at a health ranch two hours drive north that could take them right away.

'It's very popular there,' the woman consultant informed her. 'They have a good reputation. You're lucky, they've had two cancellations… if you don't mind sharing a cabin.' She gave Kelly a pamphlet with the rates and amenities. It was expensive, but had all the facilities she could hope for, including horse riding, hiking, aerobics, and several indoor activities. Best of all, it was alcohol free. 'I'll need to take a deposit of two hundred,' the woman said. 'Drive out and have a look for yourself if you wish.'

'No, it sounds exactly what I'm looking for,' Kelly assured her. 'We'll take it.'

She called Pop Franz and he responded positively. 'Best news I've had in a long while, Kelly. No need for you to apply for a loan, I'll lend you the money myself. Hell, I'll even make it a gift if you can get the bum back here in solid form. Do you have a credit card with you?'

She gave him the details and he promised to transfer the money immediately.

'And the job offer still holds?' she asked.

'I've already cleared the way.'

Her father, perhaps knowing she would refuse because of the Hispanic woman, had not offered her a bed, which was a relief. She was already booked into the motel for another night anyway. She called the trailer park and, swallowing her pride, spoke pleasantly to the caretaker, leaving a message for her father confirming the booking, then she called Billy at the hangar, telling him what had happened and what she had planned, and that he did not have to pick her up. She also called Juliette at the house, repeating the story, and apologising for not being able to attend the graduation.

Juliette was disappointed but understanding. 'Family must come first,' she said. 'Good luck, Kelly, and let me know how you get on.'

'And the same goes for me,' Kelly replied thickly.

She felt much better after that, even a little self righteous that she was making a sacrifice to do the right thing.

With nothing left to fill in the rest of the day, she decided she would lash out on a rental car and do some sightseeing. She chose a green Mustang convertible, put the top down, turned the radio up, and cruised the beaches. She bought a bikini, and caught up on her tan, stuffed herself with ice-cream and the type of food she knew would be frowned on at the farm, and knocked back several propositions, preferring to spend the nights alone with a video.

At the end of the day she felt completely in control and ready for anything, even her father. She signed out of the motel next morning, but held onto the car until she could be sure her father's truck was reliable enough to get them to the farm.

The truck wasn't there. Neither was her father. The door of the trailer was locked, and Kelly stared at the overflowing trashcan with a premonition of worse to come.

She drove slowly back to the entrance and confronted the caretaker.

'Where's my father?' she demanded. 'Did you give him my message?'

He took his time about answering, his eyes wandering. 'Didn't know Jim was your old man. Thought you was another one of his chicky-babes.'

'Where is he?' Kelly repeated coldly.

'How the hell do I know? You think I'm his mammy or something? He's gone is all I know.' He reached under the counter and flicked an envelope across the top towards her. 'Gave him your message last night. Same time as he left you this.'

Kelly ripped it open and read the brief note: Kelly. Sorry, but it will have to be some other time. That big deal I was telling you about is coming together in Miami this week instead of next. Call me after that and we'll do it. Promise. Love you, kid. PS. Tell Freako I'll fix him up when I get back.

Kelly scrunched the note into her fist and swung out of the screen door, letting it slam behind on its spring. A few moments later she heard it slam again, and the caretaker called after her.

'Hey, chicky-babe! You tell your ol' man he owes

two weeks rent. He don't pay, he's out on his ass, you hear?'

'Up yours, dickhead.' Kelly tossed the note into the Mustang, followed it in, and scorched out of the Park in another impressive shower of gravel.

Her anger lasted for the next twenty miles, until she was pulled over by the Highway Patrol.

Tight-lipped, she had her licence ready, held up in a cleft of two fingers by the time the patrolman reached her door.

'Mornin', ma'am.' He removed the card from her fingers and flipped over his pad. 'You in an awful hurry to get somewhere?'

'Not really. I don't even know where the hell I am. I was angry. Sorry.'

'Bad day, eh?'

'The worst.'

He shook his head as he wrote. 'Don't take it out on the car, ma'am. It's too old and you're too young and pretty to die. Some good folk will miss you real bad.'

As he continued to write the details, Kelly felt her anger and disappointment wane. She took the citation he handed her without looking at it. 'Am I on the right road for Punta Gorda?'

'No, you're heading north on the interstate. Turn

left at the next interchange, then follow the Bee Line Express to interstate four and turn left again. Do it slowly, ma'am, and you have a nice day now.' He nodded pleasantly, then turned towards his patrol car; a middle-aged man with a rugged face and tired eyes that had seen too many mangled bodies.

On a sudden impulse, Kelly called out to him as he was about to open his door. 'Hey, Officer!'

He turned to scowl, defensive.

'You're not so bad yourself, you know.' She blew him a kiss and smiled, then pulled sedately back onto the road.

She watched him in the mirror, still standing there, looking after her, and she waved, hoping that he was smiling. She laughed sardonically. 'And what the hell was that all about?' she asked herself.

When the road behind was clear, Kelly scrunched the citation into a ball and tossed it in the air to be whipped away in the wind. She did the same with her father's note, then turned on the radio.

She pulled over again when she reached the interchange, and sat tapping thoughtfully on the steering wheel.

The big sign in front told her that Orlando Airport was to the left. In that direction lay home and Puget Sound; to a damaged plane and the remains of a cold winter. Behind was her father and her past, where they both belonged. If she passed the airport to interstate four, she would be going back to Punta Gorda. It was more than a crossroads. It could easily be a turning point in her life.

Then she suddenly realized there was no point in going to Punta Gorda. It was Saturday morning. Billy and Juliette would already be on their way to Philadelphia. She allowed herself a disbelieving laugh at her lapse, but could not help the bitterness that crept into it. She was too late.

The Bee Gees were on the radio again, the falsetto harmony of their new hit stayin' alive dominating the airwaves. It was a goal worth achieving, she thought, and she had another road she could choose. Straight ahead.

She hesitated for only a moment, then pulled onto the highway. It was a beautiful sunny day, she had money in her purse, music to sing along to, and a Mustang convertible. Driving a thousand miles or so to attend a friend's graduation seemed a good way to start feeling alive.

***

Tim Ryan was in a panic. With only one day

remaining before leaving for Harare and his flight to New York, the rhino stockade was still not completed. The last of the four pens had barely been started.

Once again it was the logs to blame. Searching for trees of a suitable length and thickness took the labourers far and wide. Mopani trees were plentiful, but by nature unhelpfully gnarled and twisted. Dragging those they found suitable back to the homestead with the ancient Ferguson tractor was both time consuming and frustrating, with constant delays due to breakdowns. These were invariably followed by lengthy arguments as to the cause, who was to blame, and what could be done about it.

And John Singleton wasn't much help either, with his constant mooning over Juliette, and his insistence they celebrate her phenomenal success with several crates of beer. Tim was still suffering from the hangover, and so were most of the labourers, whom John, in a more than usual sentimental lapse, had invited to join in the celebration. 'All init gether,' he had declared drunkenly. 'One frall and one frall,' and had led the chanting chorus of 'More beer for Doctor! More beer for Doctor!' with a waving bottle and a stamping foot. It had been a great thrash, but not a good example, and certainly not good timing.

Tim had tried to talk his way out of going to the

graduation, having a genuine excuse, and offering John in his place, but his father's silence on the other end of the phone, and finally his own conscience, had changed his mind.

Fortunately, as he was hastily shoving clothes into a suitcase, about to leave, John arrived to say he had taken a few days off and would stay to supervise the construction. 'Give her this, will you?' he asked, handing Tim a small, elaborately wrapped box.

'What is it?'

'Graduation present.'

'I know that, bonehead. What's inside, in case I have to declare it. See-through knickers or see-through nightie?'

John's fair complexion colored. 'None of your goddam business.'

Tim's troubles were not over. Only when he arrived in Philadelphia did he discover that he had forgotten to pack his warm jacket, his good shoes, his socks, his toothbrush, his only tie, and all of his underpants.

***

'How long do you think it will take to cool down?' Kelly asked anxiously, staring with an uncomprehending frown at the steaming engine. 'I have to be in Philly in three hours.'

The farmer sucked in through pursed lips. Not an encouraging sign. 'Well, let's see now, that's two… maybe closer to three hundred miles.' He shook his head regretfully. 'Guess you're goin' to be late.'

'What do you think is the problem?'

'Kinda hard to say with it still smokin' that way. Maybe blown a gasket, or could be you jus' run it dry comin' through them hills. Seen that happen a few times. Have to wait an' see. You been checkin' the water and oil?'

'Yes,' Kelly lied, angry with herself for not doing so. Checking the gauges in the Bee every fifteen minutes was routine.

'No offence, miss, but you gotta get in the habit of doin' it regular with these old models.'

'So, what can I do?'

'Well… closest gas station is about ten mile back. Must've passed it comin'. Telephone up at the house if you want to give 'em a call. Mind you, they ain't shy when it comes to collecting, them fellas.' He peered thoughtfully into the steam. 'Sure hope the engine ain't seized. Cost a bundle to replace one of these.'

'It's a rental,' Kelly said tiredly.

'Well now, there's a bit of luck. Only have to pay the shortfall then.'

'Do you think it could be the fan belt?'

'Hey, now there's an idea.' He went to his idling tractor and returned with a long screwdriver to poke at the fan. 'Yep, spinnin' free. That's what it is all right, a busted belt. You got a spare?'

'No, I haven't.'

He shook his head in silent reprimand. 'Me now, I always carry a spare. Never know when it could come in handy. Won't fit this though. Different size.' He straightened to look down at her bare legs. 'You have any of them pantyhose things? That might keep you going until you get to a gas station.'

'No, I don't.'

'Betty will have some. Uses them for strainin' out the cheese. And you'll need a few gallons of water for the radiator. Why don't you hop on the tractor and I'll take you up to the house? Give the engine time to cool. You had breakfast?'

'No, I...'

'Sets you up for the day, a good breakfast. I was on my way to get some when I seen you stopped by my gate... now you hold tight onto that trailer-lock there, gets kinda bumpy.'

'I must...'

' Lucky you did. Nothin' much else for a couple of miles, an' some strange folk around nowadays. Not safe for young women no more, travelin' alone… if you put your foot on that there hydraulic arm… don't mind it swingin' around.'

'Thanks, I…'

'See it all the time on the television. Young girls murdered or gone missin'. Why, only last week…'

An hour later, jolting back with a container of water wedged between her feet, a bag of home-made muffins clamped in her teeth, and two thick nylon stockings draped around her neck, he was still talking. His pleasant wife had stuffed her with porridge, eggs, muffins and coffee, while he talked about vehicles running out of gas and being completely stripped before the owner returned.

Kelly was immensely relieved to see that the Mustang was where she had left it and still had all its bits.

With a full radiator and a stocking for a temporary fan belt, the cooled engine started immediately. She drove away with his warning about checking the temperature and oil ringing in her ears. She pulled over again a few miles farther along with a flat tyre.

She spent a frantic five minutes looking for the jack, then another five trying to get it to work, all the while expecting every passing vehicle that offered assistance to contain rapists and muggers. She waved them on and changed the wheel herself, then had the flat repaired and fan belt replaced at the first gas station. Thereafter, she developed an annoying obsession for flicking her eyes down to the temperature gauge about once in every five seconds.

When she finally saw the sign: Tufts University School of Veterinary Medicine, and drove in through the gates, people were already driving out.

She parked and hurried to where a crowd of visitors and black-gowned students were milling about on the lawn behind rows of empty chairs. The banner-draped stage was already in the process of being dismantled.

She searched anxiously for either Juliette or Billy, the only two she would recognise. If they had already gone her trip would have been for nothing, for she had no idea where they were staying.

As her search widened she became more desperate, questioning anyone wearing a gown, rudely interrupting conversations to ask if anyone knew Juliette Ryan, then dashing off if they looked puzzled to ask someone else, her erratic progress marked by eloquent silence or subdued tittering.

Most seemed more interested in the way she was dressed than her question. Apparently one did not wear denim shorts and boots, grubby tee-shirts and greasy baseball caps to graduation ceremonies in Philadelphia

- or probably anywhere else for that matter. One wore long dresses and suits, ties and flowery hats, and make-up. She removed her cap and stuffed it into her hip pocket.

With failure looming, she ran back to the car park in one last, desperate gamble, positioning herself on the road out, staring intently into the departing vehicles at happy successful faces, and feeling her own despondency settle heavily as the crowd thinned and the car park emptied. Disconsolately, she walked back to the Mustang.

She would have to find her own way back to Orlando, for she didn't know where Billy had landed, and did not know the Cherokee's registration so she could find out. It seemed that she and the convertible were destined to spend a lot more time together.

Pondering gloomily over the long drive back, and whether it would not be better to pay for a flight, she opened the boot and searched through her purse, counting how much money she had left.

'Kelly!' It was screeched from the other side of the car park.

Startled, Kelly spun around, heart thumping. At first she saw nothing, then a gowned figure detached itself from a group standing by a car and ran towards her on the road, one hand clamping a tasselled mortarboard to her head, and the other clasping her rolled-up diploma like a relay baton.

Dropping her purse Kelly ran to meet her, squealing with joy and relief. She enveloped Juliette in a hug, dancing her around in a circle, the two of them hopping and shrieking with excitement.

They started talking at the same time, an incoherent babble, then both stopped.

'You first,' Juliette said breathlessly, then immediately started herself. 'What are you doing here? I couldn't believe it was you! Billy had to convince me. The car...'

'A rental. My father stood me up, so... here I am.' Kelly grinned.

'You drove all the way?'

'Uh, huh. Had a rush of blood. Couldn't miss my best friend's graduation now, could I?' She laughed. 'But I did, didn't I? Is that the certificate? Let me see!' She opened it to read, then squealed again and clasped Juliette in another hug. 'Oh, Jules, congratulations...' She sniffed, wiped her eyes and smiled. 'Way to go, doc.'

Juliette was more delicate, dabbing gently with the sleeve of her gown to save the eye make-up, then she linked Kelly's arm in hers. 'Come meet my folks.'

Kelly held back. 'Oh, God, do I have to? Look at

me, I'm a mess. The car broke down and I didn't have time to change… not that I have anything decent. And I must smell like I don't know what… '

Juliette tugged her forward. 'Who cares… of course you must. I can't believe you drove all that way just for my graduation, thank you so much.' She squeezed Kelly's arm.

'Well, I was also kind of hoping…'

She was interrupted by the arrival of a smiling but puzzled-looking Billy Steel coming to meet them.

'Goddam, Kelly, but you sure know how to spring a surprise. Everything okay?' His brow creased in a questioning frown. 'I guess Jim must have pulled out, huh?'

'Yeah, well…' She shrugged. 'I guess I should have known.'

'The bum,' Billy growled.

Behind him, wearing uncertain smiles, were what could only have been Juliette's parents and brother. The resemblance to her mother was unmistakable; the same high cheekbones and olive complexion, slender build, dark curls and bright intelligent eyes. She reminded Kelly of a foreign actress she knew, but couldn't place. A famous-looking face.

Juliette introduced them, still clinging to her right arm, which Kelly had to hastily extricate in order to shake hands, noticing as she did so that her fingers were more than a little grubby after her mechanical struggles.

'Juliette told us about you,' Zarena Ryan said. 'We must thank you for coming such a long way.'

'I'm sorry I was late,' Kelly replied. 'Had a few breakdowns... no time to shower and change.' She displayed her greasy fingers.

'No need to apologise,' Juliette's father said with a reassuring smile. He was tall and athletic-looking, with a farmer's hands and skin obviously at home in the sun.

'Kelly's not afraid to get her hands dirty,' Billy said, and Kelly threw him a grateful smile.

Unrestrained by her cap, the long strands of hair in the front kept falling in her eyes, and she had to constantly toss her head to flick them aside. It made her feel as if she had a permanent tic, and she brushed them back impatiently, tucking them ineffectually in behind her ear, and obviously leaving a streak of dirt, for Juliette licked her thumb and wiped it away. Kelly vowed silently to have the front cut as short as the back as soon as possible, and too bad if it made her look like a boy.

So far, Juliette's brother had not spoken. He stayed back and gave a polite nod in exchange for a handshake when they were introduced, the uncertain smile remaining fixed in place, although more than once Kelly saw his eyes lower towards her bare legs and boots.

He seemed ill at ease, fiddling with his tie and shifting his feet, as if his shoes were pinching. His long brown trousers were at least an inch too short. He was the only member of the family with fair hair, cropped in an overgrown crew-cut, so half stuck up and half lay down. He was the same height and build as his father, and was tanned almost as deeply. He was not at all like what she had envisioned from Juliette's description. Although not bad looking, in a confused Harrison Ford sort of way, she certainly did not feel compelled to remove her knickers.

'What say we all retire to celebrate,' Billy suggested. 'These two cheated me out of it in Florida, but not this time.'

'Will I have a chance to shower and change first?' Kelly asked.

It was Chris Ryan, Juliette's father who answered. 'We'll head back to the apartments. Do you have somewhere to stay?'

'No, I came straight here… haven't thought about it yet.'

'Good, then you can stay with us,' he said

decisively. 'We rented two apartments. You three girls can share one, and us guys will bunk in the other.'

Kelly made the suggestion that Billy travel with her to show the way, and so the family could be together. She spoke to him as soon as they passed through the gate. 'What do you think that old plane of my father's is worth?' she asked.

'The Bristol?' Billy was thoughtful. 'About ten, maybe twelve grand in its present condition. Why, what's on your mind?'

'As much as that?' Kelly showed her surprise by changing her mind about overtaking the car ahead, slowing down and falling in behind as she glanced at Billy. 'That's more than I paid for the Bee.'

'This is a rare First World War fighter we're talking about. Done up properly it could get twice that much.'

'Wow!' She slowed further. 'Does my father know that? It's a lot more than I thought.'

'Jim doesn't know what time of day it is,' Billy grated. 'Messing you about like that is something else. What are you scheming up?'

'I spoke to him about it and you're right, he isn't interested. And neither am I, so why don't we sell it?'

Billy thought for a moment before answering. 'I suppose I can put it about with the Antique Airplane Association and see what offers I get. I don't mind as long as I get reimbursed for what I've already spent on parts and repairs.'

'How about you do that and we split what's left down the middle?'

Billy chuckled. 'Last of the big time wheeler-dealers, huh?'

'It's only fair, and…' She turned to give him a charmer's smile, 'I need the money now, so how about an advance on my share?'

This time Billy laughed out loud. 'What's the hurry, you into a loan shark or something?'

'I owe Pop two hundred from the deposit I had to forfeit, and I want to go to Africa with Juliette… if her invitation is still open.'

'You sure don't mess around, do you? How long do you intend staying?'

'A few weeks. I want to see them catching rhinos, and I don't have much else to do right now.'

'Okay, if you're serious, leave it with me and I'll get the best deal I can. I'll pay Pop and your fare and we'll square up later.'

Kelly placed a kiss on her fingers and reached across to plant it on his cheek. 'I love you.'

'Yeah, sure you do.'

***

'Of course I meant it!' Juliette exclaimed. 'It will be fabulous to have you. I'm truly sorry about your dad, though,' she added gently.

'And two hundred bucks down the gurgler with him,' Kelly said, grinning at the enthusiastic response. She studied Juliette and shook her head in disbelief. 'I still can't believe I'm here, about to go to Africa. Is it for real?'

'Isn't it great? We must organise the bookings right away so we can travel together. You have your passport?'

'I always carry it with my pilot licence.'

'How long will you stay?'

'I'm not sure. Two weeks maybe, if you can put up with me for that long.'

'All that way for two weeks? Are you crazy? You have to stay a month at least.'

'I don't know, Jules, I still have a…'

'And you must come back via Australia. It doesn't cost any more to do the round trip.' She paused to grip Kelly's arm, halting her protests while she frowned in thought, then she nodded vigorously in apparent agreement with them. 'Yes, that's what we'll do. You must come with me to Cocos Island.'

Kelly stared dumbfounded at her friend for a

moment, wondering if she had missed something. 'What?'

'It's where we have to quarantine the rhinos before they're allowed into Australia. I have to stay with them.'

'But I thought…'

'If my brother gets his finger out, we can get all four rhinos in two weeks easy, then another two weeks to get them crate trained… that will make it about a month.'

Kelly laughed nervously, not sure what was going on exactly, but liking the idea of a round-the-world trip if it wasn't going to cost any more than the return, and another two weeks was not that long, really.

'Once the rhinos are on the way,' Juliette continued, 'Tim will be going on to Australia to help Dad get things organised for their arrival. I'm sure we can juggle the tickets around somehow.'

'I think,' Kelly said slowly, 'you had best start again from the beginning.'

***

'She's always grumbling about being stuck there alone,' Chris Ryan told Kelly after she had insisted on getting their approval, despite Juliette's assurance that it wasn't necessary. 'It'll do her good to have someone, and no doubt she'll enlist your help with the sick, lame and lazy Africans as well as the injured animals.'

'I'd love to help,' Kelly responded enthusiastically.

'And you're welcome to stay with us in Australia if you wish. You'll find it a lot less appealing than Gara Pasi though. Kangaroos and flies is about all we can offer at present.'

'But no poachers,' Kelly added, and Chris Ryan chuckled.

'That too.'

Juliette's brother seemed less enamoured with the idea, not objecting outright, but not supporting it either, and giving her an odd smirk as he left the room.

The unexpected look robbed Kelly of her high spirits, leaving her wondering if she was perhaps making a mistake. For some reason she couldn't fathom he seemed to dislike her, yet they had not spoken to each other except to exchange brief greetings. Maybe he was jealous of his sister or, Kelly thought with a sinking feeling, it could be that he thought she was nothing but a freeloader - which she was beginning to feel like. Her clothes certainly didn't help. All she had in her bag was jeans and a few casual tops, suitable attire for Florida. She could not remember the last time she had worn a dress.

Later that evening, after a noisy dinner at a nearby restaurant, during which Tim Ryan had continued to ignore her, she broached the subject reluctantly to Juliette, unwilling to put a damper on her friend's special evening, but needing to know.

'I don't think your brother is too keen about me coming,' she said.

'Tim?' Juliette looked surprised. 'Of course he is. We have visitors all the time. Gara Pasi is a tourist place.' Juliette paused to give her a puzzled look. 'Is that why you've been so quiet? You were worried about Tim?'

'I have feeling he doesn't like me. He hasn't spoken to me once. Do you think I may have offended him in some way?'

'Don't worry about Tim, it's probably his way of playing hard to get. If you looked like a rhino he would be all over you like a rash. He's out of his element here. He'll be different at home. You'll see.'

Kelly let it go. Maybe it was only her imagination, but she was still not convinced.

Juliette's father came early next morning from his adjoining apartment to report that Tim had managed to get an earlier flight, and that Kelly had been given his seat on the plane with Juliette. Billy had paid with his credit card, but she was to call at the airline's office to confirm and arrange the other bookings.

'It suits him better,' Chris Ryan reassured Kelly, when she expressed her concern that she was intruding. 'He's busting to get back to work. I have a feeling he's running further behind than he wants to admit.'

'He is,' Juliette said shamelessly.

Billy departed later that morning, taking the convertible, which he would leave at the airport for the rental agency. Chris and Zarena Ryan left soon after for Washington, where they had a meeting arranged with the National Geographic Society. Also on their schedule was the International Rhino Foundation in Texas, who was paying for some of the rhino translocation expenses to Australia.

Until their flight the following day, Juliette and Kelly were left to their own devices, which meant shopping, and the first items Kelly bought were a dress and a pair of strappy sandals with a short heel. The second was some make-up.

***

Sandwiched between a plump woman on the aisle who reeked of raw garlic, and a man in the window seat with a weak bladder and wayward elbows, Tim Ryan proceeded to numb his senses with Vodka and tonic. Hopefully it would also induce sleep, for he had received little during the previous night.

His father and Billy Steel had talked until after midnight, relating stories of their sanctions-busting experiences in Central and West Africa. Some were incredible, some hilarious, but after three bottles of red wine, mostly incoherent. Then, after stumbling into bed, they had tried to outdo each other with their snoring.

Getting a late cancellation had been a stroke of luck. It would mean an extra two days he hadn't counted on to complete the stockade and go after the injured rhino and her calf. John Singleton meant well, but he was too easy on the labourers. That wily bastard, Kawaseka, would manipulate him all over the place.

But now, in retrospect, perhaps he should have stayed and travelled with Juliette as originally planned. He would have had the opportunity to warn her before she found out for herself. It was going to be harder at Gara Pasi. Juliette was smart when it came to the academic stuff, but not so good with judging people.

For a while he pondered the possibility that she had somehow deceived the family all these years. Sometimes it was difficult to tell with these things, and she had spent so much time in college, away from home, where anything could have happened. And she had said nothing about the gift from John, refusing to tell him what it was, which seemed unusual.

But he finally rejected the idea. He knew her too well. Juliette was simply too friendly and trusting for her own good. Intelligent but naïve, that was all. He wouldn't mind betting that she didn't have the faintest idea her Yank friend was a lesbian.

***

The painting was of zebra drinking at a waterhole. It was the first thing Kelly saw when she woke each morning; a frieze of black and white stripes against a red ochre background. Other paintings of zebra adorned the bagged white-washed walls of the rondavel, but the big one was her favourite, its vibrant colors capturing perfectly the contrast between the harshness and beauty that was this place they called the Lowveld, as if it were a country in its own right.

Gara Pasi Wildlife Sanctuary boasted six thatched guest cottages, called rondavels, she guessed, because they were round. All had their own shower and toilet. Each was named after the animals depicted in their different paintings, and all were signed by Julia Ryan, Tim's late mother. Kelly suspected a sentimental link between the similar first names of Julia and Juliette.

Her own "Zebra Suite" was the first in the line, next to Juliette's bungalow and surgery. It overlooked flower gardens and lawn to a beautifully thatched, open-sided eating and entertaining area, complete with cocktail bar.

After three days Kelly was still finding Gara Pasi hard to accept. She had prepared herself for a rough bush camp, with makeshift toilets and round tents - which she originally thought rondavel meant - and which could easily be ripped apart by sharp claws or tusks. She had not expected this. In its stylish simplicity it rivalled any four star resort she had known.

It had been three days in paradise. Every morning she was woken at seven by Lydia, the African maid, tapping politely on the door before entering with a pot of percolated coffee, deliciously crunchy rusks, and a shy 'Goodi morningi, madam'.

Kelly had never been treated in such a subservient manner. At first, she was at a loss how to react. She watched Julia for clues, and discovered that gracious acceptance by means of a smile was all that was required. All the Africans she met treated her in the same manner. Yes, madam, no, madam, three bags full, madam. It was difficult not to develop an instant superiority complex. Tips were never given, nor expected, as they were in the States.

Three days of meals that would shame any sophisticated restaurant, cooked by an African chef by the name of Frek, who had once presided over the kitchens of a high-ranking Portuguese official in nearby Mozambique.

Breakfast was served on a table under a mahogany tree on the riverbank, above a waterhole frequented by herds of elephant, zebra, and strange antelope. Sundowners and spicy Portuguese snacks were provided in the same spot each evening. Dinner was under the thatch of the open-sided dining area, resplendent with gleaming silver and glass on white tablecloths, starched as crisply as the green tunic worn by Frek, who was also the waiter.

On her first night Kelly had feasted on guinea fowl in red wine, on the second, roast leg of warthog baked in a clay oven, which was far and away the best meat she had ever tasted. Strolling on the moonlit riverbank afterwards with Juliette, she breathed deeply on air that was filled with the sweet, peppery scent of Mopani leaves, and thought she was in heaven.

'I know it seems pretentious,' Juliette explained, almost apologetically, when Kelly expressed her astonishment at the high standard, 'but it's only show for the guests. When Mom and Dad are here in the winter it gets really flashy. If it's just me and Tim we give Frek a break and eat any old how.'

'But there aren't any guests yet,' Kelly said, and Juliette laughed. 'Of course there is. What do you think you are?'

'A friend, I hope.'

'Yes, of course, but Frek likes to show off, so we mustn't spoil his fun. If I stopped him he would think you didn't like his cooking and get the sulks.'

All that was missing was a calorie counter and bathroom scales, for which Kelly was grateful. Although she was sure that if she mentioned it Frek would quickly produce them from under his tall starched hat.

Most mornings she accompanied Juliette on her rounds of the pens containing sick, orphaned, or injured animals - the latter mainly from snares and vehicles - or those captured in populated areas that were being rehabilitated into the Park It was often sad, but also immensely gratifying work, and Kelly threw herself into it with enthusiasm, bottle-feeding antelope calves, passing instruments, and stroking velvet noses to calm terrified eyes while Juliette attended to their injuries.

They also attended to any minor ailments of the African employees and their families, which numbered about thirty in total, and Juliette took her through their village to meet them. One of them was an incredibly wizened old man with sparse white peppercorns of hair and legs like gnarled walking sticks.

Juliette greeted him respectfully, surprising Kelly by dipping her knee, and leaving her undecided if she should do the same. He grinned toothlessly at her when she followed Juliette's example, inclining his head and extending two crooked hands for her to shake.

'Mom and Dad owe Fulamani their lives,' Juliette explained later. 'They were both captured by terrorists in the war, and Fuli killed five of them with his axe. My dad got the rest. About twelve in all, I think. Come, I want to show you something.'

Juliette took her to a place a short way downriver from the complex and showed her a log bench on the bank. 'Mom's special place,' she explained. 'Whenever she visits she comes here to sit by herself. There used to be a small game-viewing hut there, and she was hiding in it when she was discovered and abducted by the terrorists.' She laughed softly. 'Had she not been busting for a pee and come out they would never have found her. She had to walk for over twenty miles barefoot, prodded by guns, beaten with sticks, and threatened with rape. Fuli and my dad rescued her as the group was about to cross the border. Dad carried her on his back for about ten miles.'

Recalling the slight, well-spoken woman she had

thought of as a pampered actress, Kelly could only marvel. 'I wish I had known all that in Philadelphia,' she murmured.

'They never talk about it to anyone,' Juliette mused. 'Not even to me. War stories are taboo.'

The only time Kelly saw Tim close enough to talk to was in the evenings. He and John Singleton had been working non-stop on the rhino stockade, which was situated out of sight on the far side of the other animal pens, where both were at a reasonable distance from delicate noses.

Tim was Kelly's one disappointment. His attitude towards her had not changed as Juliette had told her it would. He still treated her with reserved politeness, never initiating conversation, and responding briefly to her own friendly approaches. She was still of the opinion he didn't like her, and she took to ignoring him as well, directing her conversation, when not to Juliette, to John Singleton, whom she liked. He was fresh-faced and British, not her idea of a game-ranger at all, yet, like Tim, he displayed a remarkable knowledge of the bush and animals, and was obviously in love with Juliette. He was careful not to give the wrong impression by being too familiar with herself. Juliette seemed not to notice, and was never alone with him for long, which gave Kelly the impression the attraction was not mutual. She didn't raise the subject though, and neither did she mention Tim's distant attitude. If she did, Juliette would no doubt speak to him about it, and she did not want to be the cause of any unnecessary friction between them.

But it couldn't go on, and Kelly decided she would have to speak to him herself as soon as the opportunity arose. It was long overdue.

With the stockade completed, John left to collect the heavy steel cages they would need for transporting the rhinos, and Tim announced his intention of servicing the plane in preparation for the search to come. While Juliette was occupied with some paperwork, and after hearing the engine of the Moth start, then immediately shut down, indicating Tim was there and probably about to change the oil, Kelly went to the airstrip behind the complex.

The Moth had been pulled from its pole enclosure into the open, and all she could see of him was his feet. They rested one either side of the rear cockpit opening, on the padded coping, and they were waggling in time to a tuneless wailing that came from the after section of the Tiger Moth's fuselage.

Kelly recognised the sound as being vaguely familiar to a song by the Bee Gees, and she paused. She had been building up for the confrontation, but faced with the comical singing she suddenly lost her nerve. She turned to retrace her steps, convincing herself it was not the right time, but had taken only a few steps when a clatter came from the bowels of the plane and the wailing stopped abruptly. It was immediately followed by a string of crude oaths.

In all the time she had been there, Kelly had never heard any foul language, and she had made a special effort to moderate her own. Hearing it now, rattled off with such expressive fluency, caused her to turn and stare in surprise.

She was still staring when his feet disappeared and he rose up from the cockpit to inspect and suck on a finger. He didn't see her immediately, but aware that he would at any moment, Kelly had no option but to continue towards him and act as if she had not heard anything.

'Did you hurt yourself?'

He removed the finger and wiped his hands on a rag. 'It's nothing.'

'Look, we need to talk.'

'What about?'

Kelly decided there was no point in beating around the bush. The sooner it was over with and the air cleared the better.

'I get the impression that you don't like me very

much. Have I done something to offend you?'

'It's not important.'

'It is to me. Is it because Juliette invited me here without your consent, or because I'm an American?'

'Juliette can invite who she likes.'

'So what is it then?'

He climbed from the cockpit and stood wiping his hands on the rag, cleaning oil thoughtfully from between his fingers, and Kelly stood waiting for an answer, determined not to leave until she had one.

Eventually he looked up. 'I don't want Juliette hurt. She's not all that sophisticated.'

Kelly frowned, puzzled. 'I don't know what you mean. Why would I want to hurt her, she's my best friend.'

'Is that all?'

'I'm sorry, but I really don't know what you're getting at. Why don't you just come out and say it?'

He laughed disdainfully, yet at the same time looked agitated, returning his attention to the cut finger. 'Don't take it personally. I'm only trying to protect my sister. She's not used to the sort of liberal society you have in America.'

'Oh, really. And what the hell is that supposed to mean?'

'And you really shouldn't talk about your father

the way you do, you know.'

Kelly was flabbergasted. 'What's that got to do with anything? Jesus... I don't believe this.'

'I hear he's a decorated ace. That means something, don't you think?'

'And do you know something?' Kelly glared at him. 'You're the most ignorant, infuriating, arrogant bastard...' She paused, lost for further suitably insulting words, but before she could find them he walked past her, jamming the rag into his hip pocket.

Then he stopped to face her again. 'Oh, yes, one other thing. Please try controlling your bad language. It isn't feminine.'

He strode away, and Kelly could only glare after him in astonished outrage.

***

Still fuming after her confrontation with Tim, Kelly went for a walk along the riverbank to cool down. If she saw either of the Ryans in her present mood she knew she would say something she would later regret.

It seemed appropriate, when she found herself at the bench Juliette had said was her mother's special place, to also sit there to think but, unlike Zarena Ryan, she was more concerned with her immediate future than the past.

Tim's incomprehensible manner was as frustrating as it was ludicrous. Surely he couldn't dislike her simply because she had spoken disparagingly about her father, or because she was, as he had insinuated, a socially liberated American, and he certainly wasn't in the position to reprimand her over the use of bad language.

In retrospect, she realized that she had made the error of being defensive and reacting negatively to his attitude. What she should have done was to treat it as the joke it was and laughed it off. She had achieved nothing by getting angry except make the situation worse.

But it was his problem, not hers. She had no intention of changing simply to conform with his, or any other male's, idea of feminine behaviour. She was who she was, and to hell with him and what he thought.

It was not that simple though, she realized. The friction between Tim and herself could not be hidden under a veneer of politeness any longer. Sooner or later it was bound to explode, and she had no intention of living under the strain of that sort of anticipation.

With growing despondency, Kelly came to the conclusion she had no real option but to risk her friendship by putting herself between brother and sister and confiding in Juliette. Maybe she would be able to get some sense out of her brother. The only other choice was to leave.

Juliette's door was open when Kelly returned to the homestead, indicating her friend was there, and she made directly for it. The impulsive decision prompted an instant gnawing sensation in her stomach, but the sooner she got it over with the better.

Juliette looked up from her paperwork with a smile, but it quickly faded to a frown of concern. 'What is it, Kelly?'

'Your brother,' Kelly answered, her breath short. 'I'm sorry, Jules, I was hoping to avoid this.' She paused, fighting to maintain her resolve. 'I don't want to come between you. I think it would be best for all concerned if I left. Sorry.' She stepped out before she was tempted to say more.

'Kelly...?'

She heard Juliette's chair scrape back but kept going. Her room was not far. She went in and closed the door, leaning back against it, her body taught and jittery. It was done. She moved to sit on her bed, fully expecting Juliette to follow after her, to question, and she attempted to prepare herself, to suppress the nervous anger and despair that threatened to intrude on her reason.

But Juliette didn't follow her. Kelly heard the office door close, then Juliette's footsteps crunching on the gravel path, going away. She rose to look out the window and saw Juliette striding purposefully on the path to the airstrip. *Now I've really done it,* she thought sombrely.

Not wanting to closet herself in her room as if she were sulking, she wandered around the sick pens for the remainder of the afternoon, giving reassurance and advice to the animals and trying not to dwell on her own situation. A long walk would have suited her mood better, but she had been warned about wandering too far from the complex. 'Probably nowhere near as risky as downtown LA around here,' Juliette had cautioned, 'but we do get the odd lion snooping around. Best not to take any chances.' Kelly had no intention of doing so. She had heard them once during the night, and the deep resonating grunts, sounding as if they were directly beneath her window, had been warning enough.

Back at her room, Kelly showered then pondered over what to wear. Despite the fancy dinners, everyone dressed casually, mostly in shorts and loose shirts, and often with bare feet as well, for it stayed warm until late.

Tonight though, she decided on the green dress and lacy sandals she had bought in Philadelphia, and which she had not had a chance to wear. No doubt she would be overdressed, but she also felt it would give her an advantage and perhaps boost her morale.

She was applying make-up sparingly when the door opened and Juliette poked her head in. 'Ready?' Then she saw the dress and entered. 'Wow! That ought to knock their socks off. You look gorgeous.' She smiled her approval. 'Good move.'

'Jules, look, about what I said. I…'

'Don't worry, it's been sorted out. The idiot. And if you think you're leaving, forget it. Your passport is in the safe, remember, and I seem to have misplaced the keys.'

Kelly laughed, feeling a wave of relief. 'My friend the saboteur.'

'Come on, the show is about to start, and you don't want to miss this. Give me a head start then follow me over.' She left quickly, before Kelly had a chance to protest.

Walking towards the table under the tree, wondering what was about to transpire, Kelly was relieved to see that John Singleton had returned. It would even things up and help thin the atmosphere.

She was wrong. It was so thick an axe would have made no impression. Tim had a strange, fixed smile on his face, as if waiting for the end of an embarrassing joke he had heard before, and John, after smiling a strained greeting, developed an intense interest in the foam on his beer.

Tight-lipped, Juliette waited until Kelly was seated then, still standing, she launched an attack.

'Something has been going on around her,' she said, looking at Tim, who refused to meet her eyes, 'and you all know what it is.' She glared at each of them in turn before continuing. 'I want you to know, Kelly, that I'm very disappointed in my brother for insulting you, and I'm also upset that you didn't tell me sooner. I had a feeling something was wrong between you, but didn't realize it was so pathetic.'

Kelly was as nonplussed as she was astounded. This was a side of Juliette she had never seen before. 'Really, Jules, it's nothing…'

'Yes, it is, and before this evening is over he's going to apologise or I'll never speak to him again. I've already had it out with him and he knows I mean it. Isn't that right, Tim?'

Tim remained silent, glancing at John for support with a strained smile, but John's attention remained fixed on his beer, apparently not wanting to get involved.

'Isn't that right, Tim?' Juliette repeated, placing both hands on the table to lean forward and glare menacingly at him and, fearing it was getting out of hand, Kelly hastily intervened again.

'It's all right, Jules. I was also rude. For which I apologise.' She looked at Tim with a smile as strained as his own, but he too had developed an intense interest in the contents of his glass. 'My language does tend to get a little colorful at times.'

'No, he insulted me as well. Tim?'

He sighed with resignation. 'Okay, okay. Goddamit, Jules. No need to make such a bloody issue of it. Like I said, it was just a misunderstanding, and I apologise.'

'That's not good enough. You can be a little more gracious that that, don't you think? How about a real apology?'

Groaning in resignation, Tim put down his glass to stand and come around the table to offer a stunned Kelly his hand. 'Sorry if I hurt your feelings, Kelly. Had it all wrong.' He smiled disarmingly. 'You look great, by the way.'

Kelly felt the blood rush into her cheeks. 'Thank you,' she mumbled. He gave her naked shoulder a reassuring touch then returned to his seat.

Juliette smiled approvingly. 'That's better.' She turned her attention to John Singleton. 'John?'

He looked up, startled. 'Me? I never thought that

at all.'

'Of course you did. Do you think I haven't noticed the way you two have been acting? Now, are you please going to do as I say so we can forget the whole stupid business and start again?'

His fair complexion darkening with embarrassment, John threw Tim an accusing scowl and rose to follow his example. 'Didn't believe it for a minute, Kelly,' he said with sincerity, then retreated hastily.

'Believe what?' Kelly asked with a puzzled smile, but he didn't answer.

'Good,' Juliette applauded. 'Now that's over with, which of you two louts is going to pour us refined ladies a drink?'

Feeling intensely uncomfortable, and more bewildered, Kelly wanted to raise her voice; to demand to know what was going on. What misunderstanding? And what exactly was it that John didn't believe? Had she missed something?

But she suppressed the urge, accepting a glass of wine from John instead, nodding her thanks, and listening distractedly to his joke about a tourist and a lion. She joined dutifully with the laughter, aware that he was trying to put her at ease, to make amends for whatever it was he did not believe he had done to offend her.

She considered taking Juliette aside to ask what was going on, but didn't get the chance. The atmosphere had changed dramatically, and suddenly she found herself the centre of attention, being forced to respond to questions from John about the orcas in Puget, and Tim about flying the Seabee, which itself was distracting. It was the first time he had spoken to her directly.

It continued during dinner. Both men's attitudes towards her were so different it was unsettling but, surprised to discover that she was enjoying herself - and the attention - Kelly decided to leave things as they were for the moment, and to bring it up with Juliette at a more opportune time.

Tim in particular, was showing a different set of colors. Once during a lull in the conversation, she glanced at him, sensing that he was looking at her. He was, his attention fixed on the low swoop of the dress. He met her glance without smiling, holding them, and leaving no doubt in her mind as to what he was thinking.

Kelly kept her own expression bland and looked away. He may have improved his manners, but if he thought she was going to become another of his hunting trophies he was mistaken. Apology not withstanding, her own feelings towards him had not changed. He was still arrogant, and she still felt unnecessarily wronged. The whole thing was a confusing farce.

***

Elliot Gumbo always took his men across the Sabi during the night, several miles east of the Zimbabwe border. It was there that the great river widened, spreading itself over the flood plain in a complex network of channels like the veins and capillaries of an artery. In the dry season the crossing was simple, although it still required two dugout canoes for the deeper sections where crocodiles were a constant threat.

Once they were through, they concealed the slim unstable craft by turning them over and covering them with flood debris. For the remaining half-mile of densely packed reed islands and swampy ground, they relied mainly on blind faith and good luck, and tried to avoid the paths of foraging hippos.

The river provided many easier places to cross, but none so isolated, and Elliot was a cautious man. Totalling four in number, he and his men were all former freedom fighters of the Rhodesian bush war, and all were armed. Three still carried the same weapons they had been issued with in that long-gone but not forgotten conflict; the Russian Kalashnikov assault rifle, or AK- 47 as it was known to all who read newspapers or terrorist manuals.

Like many others, they had not handed in their rifles at the end of the war as they had been instructed to do under United Nations mandate. Suspicious of the transition and the promises made to them by the politicians, they had cached their weapons in the bush, sealing them in plastic bags and burying them along with as much ammunition as they could steal.

And their cynicism had been proved well founded, for the promises had been no more forthcoming than the several months back pay they were owed.

While their more fortunate comrades had been absorbed into the new Zimbabwe army, and their leaders into high office or politics, many like themselves had simply been disbanded and forgotten. After fighting for their freedom, they now found themselves fighting hunger. In many respects they were worse off than before.

Disillusioned with a system that allowed their former leaders to purchase hotels in Geneva while they starved in the bush, Elliot and his men set about getting their share in the only way they knew how. They unearthed the weapons and, for the past five years, had made a modest living by robbing stores and buses. Then they stumbled over the poachers and their fortunes changed.

It happened by chance, as they were returning to their bush camp in Mozambique after an abortive attempt at waylaying a tourist bus. The driver had ignored their brandished weapons and urgent signals to pull over, swerving instead towards them, and they had been forced to dive out of the way or be run down. They did not have time to fire even a single shot. And because the tourist buses were equipped with two-way radios, which could quickly link them to the police, they had no option but to flee the scene as swiftly as possible.

Inconveniently, the spot they had chosen was an isolated stretch of road leading to a national park, so they had to abandon their usual procedure of heading for the nearest town and losing themselves amongst the local population. In this instance, it was over fifty miles away. They made directly for the border, which was only fifteen miles if they cut through the park.

Running silently through the bush, as they had on more than a hundred occasions in the past, both during and after the war, they took the two poachers by surprise.

Foolishly, the two men had also ignored their shouts and urgent signals to stop, jumping away like startled impala and staying close together as they jinxed through the trees. But they were not as fast as the bus. Both were cut down in a heavy spray of automatic fire before they had gone fifty yards.

The reason for their unsociability became apparent as soon as Elliot removed a canvas carry-bag from one of the bullet-shredded bodies and emptied it onto the ground. It was a rhino horn.

They were naturally delighted with the find. They knew about rhino horn. It was worth a considerable amount of money. Exactly how much money, neither Elliot nor any of his men had any idea, but certainly it was worth more than could be expected from a mini-bus half full of tourists with nothing but worthless traveller's cheques, mobile phones, and cameras in their bags.

But they still had to sell the horn. Being caught with it was almost as serious an offence as being caught robbing a bus. Both would incur long goal sentences at the very least. No doubt the poachers could have told them where to sell it, but their silence was now guaranteed, and a search through their meagre belongings produced no clue as to who they were or where they came from.

'What of Ebrahim?' one of the men suggested, and Elliot was reluctantly forced to agree. He had sold stolen goods to the Indian in Masvingo on several occasions, but only after much haggling and, it seemed to Elliot, never to his own advantage.

This time, when he approached him a week later at his Islamic Butchery, the Indian would not even give him the price of a stolen goat.

'Bad news, my friend,' Ebrahim told him with a sombre shake of his head after glancing in the bag then shutting it hastily, as if afraid its contents may escape. 'Very bad news. Much worse even than traveller's cheques. You must take it away please. Quickly! I have not seen it.'

It took a further month of cautious enquiry, and may have taken Elliot much longer, had not he himself been approached.

He was sitting alone at a table outside his favourite cantina in Chimoio late one morning, sipping morosely on a warm coke and contemplating the unfairness of life, when an Asian man he had never seen before pulled out the chair opposite and sat down.

'I hear you have something to sell,' the man said.

Elliot glanced quickly around the cantina garden, but only one other table was occupied, and by two old men who were deeply involved in a card game.

'Something very interesting,' the man continued, looking up at the branches of a nearby tree and smiling secretively, and Elliot frowned. The man was younger and smaller than himself by a good six inches, but even so, had he not been in his own stamping ground, Elliot may well have run. The intruder had the same look as the Korean combat instructors he had come up against in the war, and their small stature had never prevented them from demolishing larger persons than himself in a whirl of hands and feet.

'I do not think I have anything very interesting to sell,' Elliot hedged, frowning thoughtfully, as if trying to remember.

'Ah, then I must be mistaken. Please excuse my interruption.' He made to get up.

'What is it did you think I had to sell?'

'I thought perhaps some part of an animal.'

'Meat?'

'Not meat... from a chipimbiri.'

Elliot laughed. 'Ah! Then you must speak of the horn.'

'So you have one.' It was not a question.

'Uh! I did not say I had one.'

To give himself time to think, Elliot drank from the bottle, tipping it high as he studied the man. The Korean could easily be a police informer trying to trick him. He had not told anyone about the horn, so how was it possible for him to know of it? Unless one of his stupid men…

'Maybe I heard of one,' Elliot said vaguely, taking a chance. Money was getting scarce again, and if the fellow was genuine he could be missing a good opportunity. 'A friend of mine found one… I think. For myself, I have not seen it, but I can look for him, and if he has one, I will tell him you wish to buy it. May I tell him for how much?'

Elliot sprawled comfortably back in his chair, glancing around and sipping at his coke with an air of casual indifference, pleased with his quick thinking. Koreans were very tricky people, to be sure, but so was he, Elliot Gumbo, a tricky fellow.

The Korean laughed, but without sound, nodding his head like a small monkey. 'I see you are a man who likes to be careful. That is good, but I cannot say how much until I see how big the horn is.'

'It is a…' Elliot caught himself quickly. 'I mean to say, it is a long way to my friend's village… two days walking. You wish for me to make such a long journey for no pay?' He laughed disdainfully.

'We can go together. I have a four-wheel-drive, and if your friend has a horn he will be rich. I'm sure he will pay you a good commission.'

'Rich?'

'Even if the horn is small I can guarantee two

hundred dollars American.'

'Ah! American.' Elliot took a swig at his bottle, only to find it was empty. He replaced it hastily on the table and fished a crumpled cigarette from his pocket.

'Please,' said the Korean, 'have one of mine.' He pulled a packet from his shirt pocket and slid it across the table, following it with a gold lighter, and Elliot lit one thoughtfully. It was a Madison, his own preferred brand, and they were not made in Mozambique.

'Are you from the Zimbabwe police?' Elliot asked bluntly, putting on a fierce scowl.

The Korean laughed silently, shaking his head. 'No, my friend, but I go there quite often on business. I am with the Agricultural Aid Program. It was clever of you to ask.'

'I see. North Korea.'

'China.'

'Yes, of course, that is what I mean. China. You have a name?'

'You may call me Wang.'

It took another hour of hedging, veiled promises and obscure denials, before Elliot felt sufficiently confident to admit that his friend did indeed have a horn, and that it was not a two-day walk, but only a five minute drive, and providing Mister Wang allowed him to search his body and vehicle for weapons, he would take him there immediately.

'It is a pleasure to do business with such a cautious man as yourself,' Wang answered. 'But I am the same, and it would be foolish in this part of Mozambique to go unarmed. I have two weapons. One is in my belt… a pistol, which I will give to you, without bullets, as soon as we leave here. I also have an Uzi in the Toyota.'

The remainder of that day was one Elliot would not soon forget. After Wang submitted to the search and handed over the weapons, he drove him close to the large baobab tree in which Elliot had concealed the horn; placing it in a watertight plastic bag before lowering it on the end of a line beneath the slimy black water trapped far down in the hollow trunk.

Using a small tape measure, Wang measured the horn's length and circumference at the base, then he did some quick calculations on a pocket calculator. 'Two hundred and fifty dollars,' he declared.

Elliot could only grin vacuously, already involved in some hazy calculations of his own. He did not know the exchange rate for American to Zimbabwe dollars, but knew it had to be a lot. Of course, he would have to share with the others. Not all of it though. He was the leader, so should get more… maybe half, which meant…

'I can pay in traveller's cheques,' Wang said, 'or

we can go to the bank, but they will only exchange for escudos. I have a better idea, but first we must talk business.'

'I see,' Elliot replied, but all he could see was himself losing all control over the situation. Money and business were not his strong points. Escudos were hopeless, not even the cantina liked taking them, preferring Zimbabwe dollars. As for traveller's cheques...

'Maybe we should go back to the cantina and talk,' Wang suggested. 'Leave the horn in the tree until we have agreement.'

Elliot nodded dejectedly. He could think of no other way. He replaced the horn in the bag and climbed the tree, but when he lowered the bag, he did not tuck the string into the small crevice at the top as before. He let it fall as well. It would be much more difficult to retrieve now, but the same would apply to Mister Wang if he tried to be tricky.

Wang drove him back to a different restaurant, one that served expensive food - the first Chinese food that Elliot had ever tasted, and which he didn't particularly enjoy - but, happily, they also had cold beer and, after the first one, Elliot's good spirits returned. Wang also gave him a new packet of Madison, saying he could keep the gold lighter as a token of trust for their new business venture - of which Elliot was still ignorant - explaining that the embossed head of the dragon would bring him good fortune.

He was introduced to the owner of the restaurant, a Mister Zhu, and informed that any future transactions should be conducted with him personally, and that he would arrange for the payment in cash, in the equivalent amount of Zimbabwe dollars, so long as he gave three days notice.

Elliot was sceptical at first. Mister Zhu was an ancient, wrinkled man, with a smile that remained even when he was chewing, which he somehow seemed to accomplish without the aid of teeth.

At this point a discussion took place between the two Chinese, during which, Wang produced his calculator, then the old man left and returned a short while later with a plastic take-away box filled with Zimbabwean fifty dollar notes.

'Six thousand,' Wang said, and pushed it towards Elliot. 'Take it. Bring the horn in three days and Mister Zhu will give you another twenty thousand. We must have trust in business. Do you agree?'

Elliot could only answer by grinning as he stuffed the box down the front of his shirt. Already he could see the car he was going to buy. Or maybe a small truck.

But that was only the beginning, and for the next

hour, Elliot listened to the details of his new business with an open mouth. The instructions were simple, but the reasons behind them so strange - almost foolish - that he could not bring himself to ask questions for fear of having misunderstood and appearing a fool also.

First he was given a territory, like a salesman, and was astonished to learn that he was not the only new poacher to be involved. That was why he must stick to his own territory, Wang explained. His area included all the national parks, reserves, game ranches and sanctuaries in the Zimbabwe Lowveld, from the Limpopo to the Chimanimani Mountains in the eastern highlands, and inland for as far as he cared to venture. In it, he was to kill all the rhino he came across, regardless of size, or even if they had been de-horned. In addition to the amount he received for the horns, he would get an extra twenty dollars for every tail, even if it came from the same beast as the horn.

It all seemed too good to be true - like the promises given by Mugabe's government - but he had nothing to lose, and money already in his pocket.

By the end of the evening, Elliot could see more than a second-hand truck on the horizon. He could also see a hotel in Geneva.

***

Shen Hui Ping stooped to unleash his white poodle as soon as they entered Yu gardens, remaining with hands between his knees and smiling as the dog trotted haphazardly away, following some alluring scent.

It was a morning ritual they both enjoyed; a leisurely gambol around the tranquil acres of lawns, ponds, and pavilions of the park, while beyond its ancient boundaries roared the toiling giant of Shanghai.

Although he owned a significant portion of that steaming city, the novelty of owning a dog had still not worn off for Shen. For an old man with a full memory, it did not seem all that long ago when, in the Cultural Revolution, dogs were shot on sight by the police. Now Cha-Cha had his ears scratched by them, and could urinate on the statue of Pushkin with impunity.

The change in thinking by the communist government, the ironies, and the unprecedented boom in Shanghai, including his own business, occupied much of Shen's thoughts as he strolled the curving paths. Most of the changes were for the better, but new thinking had a tendency to overshadow old values, and the speed at which it was all happening left him in some doubt as to where it would end. His granddaughter now wore a leather mini-skirt from Paris, his son drove an Italian Ferrari, and even the French poodle - a gift from his son, and which he suspected was designed to keep him occupied and away from the business - was named after a Latin American dance. It was now a indeed multicultural revolution.

It was hard to keep up, and harder still to change old habits. Shen continued to wear his faded but comfortable Mao jacket, although the right pocket now bulged with a mobile phone - another ploy to keep him at a distance - and he had relented with the footwear, exchanging his heavy black shoes for a pair of blue and white Reeboks.

Shen stopped to chat with four acquaintances of his own age sitting on a bench by an old ginkgo tree, their caged birds singing from its branches. The birds stopped when Cha-Cha came to investigate, and Shen apologised for the intrusion, then had to apologise again when the phone suddenly shrilled from his pocket, startling both the birds and the men. He withdrew hastily to answer it, fumbling and pressing three wrong buttons before finding the right one.

'Yes, yes… what is it?' he demanded loudly. The fact not every call on the miniature contraption was an emergency was something else he could not adjust to. He listened for a while, then gave a few terse instructions. He switched off, listening to be sure he had pushed the correct button, shaking his head and mumbling to himself as he returned the phone to his pocket. It was not an emergency after all, simply a message to inform him that the expected shipment from Africa had arrived. It could wait.

He called Cha-Cha and they made their way over the Bridge of Nine Turnings to the teahouse, where he ordered Long-jing tea for himself and a bowl of quail's eggs for Cha-Cha, then he sat outside in consideration of the other customers should the phone ring again. Were it not for the freedom it gave him he would be happy to see it disappear under the emerald water of the lotus pond.

He fed the tiny eggs to Cha-Cha one at a time, making him dance in a circle on his hind legs for each one. Skipping and hopping and twirling. A fine Latin American dance.

***

It was panting hot. Fighting the urge to gulp, Kelly tipped the plastic army water bottle high, allowing the blood-warm liquid to trickle slowly into her mouth and down her parched throat. She held a mouthful, swirling it around before spitting it onto her leg and smearing it over the scratches. It stung, but she had become immune to such petty irritations, and shorts were cooler than jeans. Much worse was the sweat that gushed from her pores in torrents, and to which the myriad swarms of tiny mopani flies seemed addicted.

After first glancing around to see no one was watching, Kelly poured some of the precious liquid into the cup of her palm and smeared it over her perspiring face, neck, and behind her ears. The more you drink, the more you want, Tim had cautioned her, but it was futile advice. It was only midday, and she was already on her second bottle - given to her surreptitiously in exchange for the empty bottle by one of the Africans. It irritated her that no one else seemed as badly affected by thirst.

Tim's khaki tee shirt remained almost dry, although she did note that five of the nine Africans looked to be in worse shape than she was, sweating effusively, and one even vomiting behind a bush. It gave her a measure of guilty satisfaction, until she learned that they had been on a beer-drink the night before and were suffering hangovers.

They had stopped in the shade of a small copse of scrub. Not to rest - which was a word that apparently did not exist in Tim's vocabulary - but to wait while the trackers circled in search of the lost rhino spoor they had been following since dawn.

She had been warned it would be hard going, but

despite the heat and exhaustion, Kelly did not regret her decision to join the hunt for a moment. This was Africa at its wildest. Harsh and ruggedly beautiful, and around her was every species of big game imaginable, unrestrained by fences or bars. Few people of her background, especially women, could share the privilege of such an experience.

She would have liked Juliette to have been there, so she could have asked and learned more, and Juliette would have, but for a cow on an adjoining ranch becoming entangled in a barbed-wire fence. The Africans didn't understand her questions, and Tim was too involved with tracking.

Seeing him now in his natural element, Kelly could understand his obvious discomfort in Philadelphia. No doubt a New York banker would feel the same if he suddenly found himself stuck in the bush following rhinos. She smiled ruefully at the thought. No need to go that far. A Puget Sound pilot was already suffering that unlikely experience.

Despite her suspicions, Tim had made no further advances towards her, remaining friendly but not flirtatious, and for a while she had wondered if he was doing it on purpose to first gain her confidence. She had put the suspicion aside though, trusting her instincts, which told her he was not really the conniving type.

And she had not found the opportunity to question Juliette about her confusing lecture. With an early start looming she had retired early, leaving Juliette in the hopeful company of John, and deciding that, for the moment at least, she could live with things as they were.

A low whistle, relayed from a ridge some two hundred yards away, signalled the finding of the spoor and they moved on again, Kelly groaning under the strain of stiffening muscles.

'Are you sure it is the same one with the calf?' Tim asked Kawaseka, his lead tracker, once they had climbed the ridge.

The man seemed to consider the question beneath him. A wiry African of indeterminate age and sporting the smell of a brewery, he adopted the aloof, long-suffering expression of a master with a pupil who continually failed to note the obvious, even though it stared him in the face. He waved casually with his tracking-stick in the direction of some stony ground as he moved off, not bothering to point out the obvious detail.

Kelly looked carefully, but saw only pebbles. However, a short while later two separate piles of dung; one small and watery, the other large and glistening with mucus, proved he had been right.

They walked in ragged single file, Kawaseka leading, followed by Tim and the man who carried the radio. Kelly came next, and behind her, two armed African game scouts - in case of meeting up with armed poachers, she had been informed - and the remaining four labourers with their loads of ropes and other gear, including the medical pack containing darts and drugs.

The Africans' names were mostly unpronounceable to Kelly, except for Kawaseka, and Mathias - one of the uniformed scouts who spoke some English. She had assumed that the one with the radio was called Roger - usually repeated - until she realized with amusement that it was the name given to the radio and, presumably, to the one who carried it.

They came upon the rhinoceros and her calf late in the afternoon, when Tim was on the point of giving up for the day.

The first knowledge Kelly had of it was when, in a state of glazed exhaustion, she bumped into Roger-Roger who had stopped suddenly in front of her. Mathias caught her arm to steady her, and indicated with hand movements that she must stand still and be quiet and, with heart thumping, Kelly peered round the radio man to see what was happening.

She saw nothing unusual, only more of the open stony ground, sparsely dotted with bronze-leafed bushes and trees. Kawaseka was some distance ahead, standing in the shade beside one of the trees, and Tim was crouched beside him, holding the dart gun in one hand while removing his shoes with the other.

Barefoot, and standing erect with the butt of the gun tucked under his arm, ready for raising into the firing position, Tim moved slowly forward towards a thicket of scrub some hundred yards away. Kelly stared hard into the grey tangle, but could see nothing there either.

Tim stopped to lower himself slowly, lifting something in his left hand, then straightened with arm raised to allowed a thin trickle of dust to fall, and Kelly realized he was testing the direction of the wind, which was non-existent as far as she could tell. Apparently she was mistaken though, for Tim changed direction slightly, edging several yards to the side before once again moving stealthily forward.

Kelly started when Mathias suddenly plucked at her arm and pointed to a nearby tree. Kelly stared at him, uncomprehending, until he made running signals with two fingers and pointed up with a grin. Then Kelly remembered what John Singleton had told her the night before when she had asked about the darting and if it was dangerous. 'Not really, provided you can do a hundred yards in under seven seconds. Black rhino are cantankerous and bloody-minded. They object strongly to having a three-inch spike fired into their backsides. They usually retaliate by attempting to throw you on top of the nearest tree, so it's best to get there voluntarily while you still have your guts tucked safely away in your belly.' He had given her one of his gentle, understated smiles. 'Good at tree-climbing, are you, Kelly?'

She had laughed, thinking it was a joke. Now she knew it wasn't. She studied the tree carefully to see exactly what branches to grab and how she could get to the tree in the shortest possible time. She hoped Mathias didn't choose the same one.

No trees existed where Tim was. It was completely open, with bushes no higher than his waist. The nearest cover was the thicket in which the rhino and calf were supposedly lurking. Even there, Kelly could see nothing that looked even remotely suitable for protection against a large angry beast, and she recalled what Juliette had said in Philadelphia about the chances Tim took.

Watching him, Kelly breathed in the hot air in short, shallow breaths. Her senses seemed to have concentrated themselves in her head, as if it alone was her entire being, and her body nothing but a numb lump somewhere below.

Small sounds and smells seemed amplified in the stillness; the mournful cooing of a dove somewhere in the distance, Mathias's harsh and irregular breathing close behind, the smell of him powerful and cloying.

A trickle of sweat ran from her temple and down the side of her cheek, scorching its way to her neck, where it suddenly cooled in a soft, barely discernible wafting of breeze, and she jerked with fright as the rhino exploded from the thicket with an alarmed snort.

Tim had his left hand held high in the air, about to test the breeze again, and he froze in that position with the rhino barely twenty paces away, trotting towards him, and Kelly gasped, then covered her mouth to stifle the warning cry that threatened to escape her lips.

Then another snort came, a fluttery, horsy sound, but this time from Tim, and the rhino stopped. It sniffed the ground, blowing a puff of dust, and Tim remained with his arm raised and the gun tucked, standing as still as a tree.

The alarmed calf followed after its mother, trotting about in confusion before reassuring itself by getting on its knees to suckle. The cow turned quickly, dislodging it, and it mewled in protest then tried again. She let it have its way while she sniffed the air and snorted into the dust.

And still Tim seemed unmoving, yet his raised

arm was lower than before, and one bare foot had shifted slightly forward, turning his body to face the beast squarely. It was a moment thick with tension. Kelly could feel it hanging in the hot air, sense it in the African labourers' heavy silence, in Mathias's halted breathing, and in the constricting of her own chest and breath.

It was a chilling display of cool courage, as arrogant as it was foolhardy. She could see no good reason for him taking such a risk. He was gambling his life on the vagaries of an uncertain breeze and the whims of a dangerous beast. There had to be other ways to dart. Could it be that he enjoyed the danger? Was he trying to prove something… maybe trying to impress them all… impress her? The thought sent a shiver up her spine. Men did stupid things like that. And if that was what he intended he had succeeded. She was impressed. She was filled with awe, and she also felt a stab of resentment that he was putting them all at risk. She flicked her eyes to the tree, getting its position marked in her mind.

Suddenly the rhino swung away. Favouring one hind leg, it trotted several paces to the side, and once again the calf was dislodged. It trotted after its mother then, inexplicably, it changed direction and came directly towards Tim.

It ran past him, no more than three paces away, then must have scented him, for it wheeled suddenly in an about turn that was so hasty it almost fell. It scampered back with its ears flattened, emitting a series of short, panicky squeaks, running past its mother in the direction of the thicket and, as she turned to follow it, Tim lifted the rifle into his shoulder in one swift movement, took quick aim, and fired.

The red and white flighted dart struck her far back in the right rump, and she spun in that direction with a wheezy bellow. She charged blindly away and kept going, her run taking her within yards of where Tim had been standing.

But he was no longer there. A moment after firing he had disappeared, collapsing silently onto the ground beside a bush.

So intense had Kelly's attention been fixed on the unfolding drama that the flat explosion of the cartridge barely caused her to flinch. Other sounds erupted around her as the labourers dropped their bundles and scrambled for the trees, but she barely heard them. She stood frozen as the rhino, either seeing movement or catching a scent, suddenly veered and, with head lowered, huffing and puffing like a steam engine, and with the calf galloping erratically alongside, thundered in her direction.

'Get up that bloody tree!'

Tim's yell pierced into Kelly's frozen awareness, but seemed to come from a great distance, and it failed to move her. She stood transfixed, her body refusing to respond to the urgent messages from her brain, watching as the outraged beast swerved again to attack a tree up which a pair of black legs were fast disappearing, hooking and ripping at the twisted trunk with her horn while the calf scampered around uncertainly.

Shouted abuse and laughter was hurled down from other trees nearby and, distracted from her murderous task, the rhino careered away with her calf into the bush.

'Kawaseka, get down and follow,' Tim shouted. 'Come on, you lot! Get a move on or we'll lose her.'

With the disappearance of the rhino, Kelly's legs finally found some feeling, but not enough to support her, and she sank, trembling, to sit on the ground.

Tim stopped beside her and sat to put on his veldskoen boots. 'Are you okay?'

Kelly nodded. She felt light-headed, as if all the blood had been drained from it.

'Sorry about that. Damned stupid of me to tell you to climb a tree when it was too bloody late. You would never have made it. Just as well you had the presence of mind to stay where you were and keep still.'

Kelly looked dazedly at him, expecting a sarcastic smirk, but he was monitoring the voluble progress of the Africans while tying the laces of his boots, his fingers quick and nimble, and Kelly removed her own trembling ones from her face. She could never be sure with Tim Ryan.

'You're a crazy person,' she said hoarsely, and he grinned at her.

He picked up the empty dart gun and stood, offering her a hand up. 'You all right to keep on? We'll have to move fast now or we'll lose her in the dark. In twenty minutes she'll be down, and the rate she was going she could be five miles away in that time. Without her protection the hyenas or lions will get the calf. If you like I can leave you with Mathias to follow behind.'

'No,' Kelly answered, shaking her head. 'I'm fine. I could sure use a drink though.'

Tim gave her his bottle. It was still full.

The sun had dropped below the ridge ahead, showing only a fiery tip, when Kawaseka lost the spoor again.

'Find it! Find it!' Tim shouted. 'Everyone spread out and look. Move!' He ranted at them in Shona, and the Africans scattered hastily to search, their excitement after the tree-climbing episode long since abated.

'She'll be out for at least five hours with the dose I gave her,' an exasperated Tim said to Kelly.

He did not have to explain further. 'Anything I can do?' she asked anxiously, knowing there wasn't.

'Pray that we find the spoor,' he answered, and left her to go looking himself.

Kelly tried as well, stooped over and peering hard, but she did not even know what she was supposed to be looking for. She fixed the image of a pile of dung in her mind and searched for that, but with the stony ground and long shadows getting longer with every second, finding even that obvious a sign was becoming impossible.

The sun was completely behind the ridge now, leaving only a golden glow, and throwing the whole valley they were searching into deepening purple shadow.

'Kawaseka!' Tim bellowed.

'Mambo?'

'It is too dark. Have everyone spread out in a line and keep going in the same direction as when you lost the spoor. And by Christ you had better hope we find it or I'll kick your arse all the way back to Gara Pasi.'

They set off with the glow of the sun on their right, Kelly walking behind Tim now, the encroaching dark and talk of lions keeping her close on his heels.

She shivered as she imagined what it must be like to be alone in this wild place, with no gun for protection, and no vehicle in which to escape the hungry predators. Tree climbing would soon become second nature.

Kelly quickened her pace. 'Please, God, keep them safe,' she murmured, and glanced entreatingly towards the dying sun, as if to halt its swift demise.

Night seemed to come more suddenly in Africa. Below the ridge was almost black now, its jagged outline showing every bush and tree and rounded boulder starkly etched against the fading yellow glow, and Kelly was sure that one of the boulders had moved.

Her steps slowed and stopped. 'Tim?'

'What is it?' He was quickly at her side. 'You okay?'

'Up there... on the ridge.' Kelly pointed. 'I'm not sure, but I think I saw something...'

The uncertainty in her voice made her wish she had held her tongue. She could see no movement now, although she stared hard. A foolish woman with an overactive imagination seeing mysterious things in the dark, and she waited for his scornful response to follow.

She received a firm grip on her arm instead. 'Well, I'll be buggered. That's her! Well done.' He raised his voice. 'Kawaseka!'

'Mambo?'

'Get your arse over here… and everyone else's too. The madam has found what you and your drunken comrades have failed to see. Missus Chipimbiri is sleeping up there on the rocks by the sun. Chop-chop, let's move it.' He turned to face her with a wide grin. 'Good work, Kelly.' He gave her arm another hard squeeze. 'Bloody excellent.'

He took off for the ridge and Kelly ran after him with heart racing, her feet no longer feeling like lead weights, and her weary legs suddenly revitalised. She had been right! She, Kelly Maddock, dumb Yank, had saved the rhino and the day. And also poor Kawaseka's arse from being kicked all the way back to Gara Pasi. Tim's words kept running through her head, repeating themselves in time to her strides. Bloody excellent. Bloody excellent. Never had she felt so fit in her life.

They scrambled up the slope, Kelly falling behind, stumbling over rocks and through bushes, feeling no pain, gasping her way to the top, and there was Missus Chipimbiri, collapsed on her belly between the boulders, snoring peacefully, with the calf on its knees, trying to reach her dugs.

'Catch it!' Tim shouted, as the frightened calf scampered about in confusion, its instincts in conflict, not knowing whether to run or stay with its dam, and the sweating, laughing, yelling Africans threw themselves after it with renewed enthusiasm. No arse-kicking tonight, only beer.

'Fix the ropes and light a fire,' Tim ordered, the jubilation showing in his voice too. 'Over there between those rocks, so I can see what the hell's going on. And where's that bloody Roger-Roger?'

'Here, suh.'

While Tim called John Singleton to bring the truck, giving lengthy directions on how to reach them, Kelly took a closer look at their prehistoric captives. The bound calf struggled and squealed pitifully, eyes wild, and she spoke to it soothingly, but her close presence seemed only to make it worse, so she left it, to inspect the mother.

She was awesome. Two tons of concentrated belligerence. Kelly tentatively extended an exploratory hand to feel the hide and was surprised to discover it was wet. The dart had gone, no doubt ripped away in her crashing flight. A small jagged hole in her rump, and a dark stream of dusted, drying blood showed where it had been.

She was not the only one impressed. The Africans too, gaped and shook heads, ah-ing and hey -heying, laughing and slapping each other's hands in mutual congratulations.

One hind leg was tucked beneath her, the other stuck awkwardly out behind, revealing the suppurating wound that caused her to limp, and Kelly growled low in angry dismay at the pain she must have suffered in the name of ignorance and greed. 'At least they didn't get your horn,' she murmured in consolation.

One of the labourers filled a sack with clumps of grass ready for putting under the great head as soon as she was rolled over, and Kelly moved to take a closer look.

It alone must have weighed more than she did. The eyes were open and glazed from the drug, the eyelashes long and dark and glistening. She felt the horn. It was coarse and gouged, the tip as rounded as her thumb, and the thought that she could easily have been impaled on that blunt, legendary scimitar, gave her a shiver.

Tim appeared beside her. 'Impressive, isn't she?'

'She's wonderful.'

'Don't get too close,' he cautioned. 'If she builds up enough oxygen it can temporarily overpower the drug and she could wake up.' He laughed at her expression. 'Don't worry, she may thrash around for a bit, but she'll soon go back to sleep.' He yelled to the men. 'Okay, stop the yapping and fix the ropes. Also fill the sack with grass and cover her eyes.' He explained to Kelly. 'We have to turn her over to get the weight off her brisket, blindfold her, and give her a cushion so she doesn't damage her head or an eye on the rocks. I want her ready for sledding onto the truck as soon as it arrives.'

'Will she be all right?'

'She'll be fine,' he said confidently. 'Why don't you give her a name?'

'Me?'

'We always name the rhinos we catch. Makes them easier to identify, and but for you I don't think we would have found her.' He laughed disdainfully. 'We were going in the wrong bloody direction. You've earned the right.'

Kelly flushed with pleasure. 'I'd love to.'

Looking at her there, her great belly heaving, sweating hide bathed and glistening in the glow of the fire, Kelly recalled her prayer and the dying red golden sunset she had turned towards at the last possible moment.

'I think I'll name her Rosie,' she said.

**

Wedged on the seat of the truck between John and Tim, Kelly inhaled the musky residue of their day's exertions sparingly. Her eyes refused to stay open, although sleep itself was impossible with the constant thumping of the gear lever against her leg, and the lurching, twisting and jolting as they cautiously negotiated the rough terrain.

Only Rosie slept - lashed in a web of ropes like Gulliver to the sled on the back, her great bulk further restrained by the jovial crew, to whom she provided convenient seating.

For the first half hour Kelly had sat bolt upright, like a child in the first row at a circus, peering hard through the dusty windscreen into the darkness beyond the reach of the headlights, at the ghostly shapes she saw there, and the reflecting eyes; bright as stars, and often as numerous.

Twice they had been forced to detour around herds of browsing elephants, and once had to weave through them when they suddenly found themselves surrounded. It was like negotiating huge grey moving boulders. John had laughed, a little nervously, she thought, and even the labourers in the back had fallen silent.

Once they were through, the Africans began singing. Not the bawdy, drunken-sounding songs of soldiers, but melodic harmonies rich in nostalgia; lone falsettos followed by deep, group basses. Songs sung from the heart. African songs.

Kelly listened to them with a wistful smile. She was tired and hungry, hot and thirsty, sweaty and smelly, blistered, scratched and itchy, and wonderfully contented. Her sense of wellbeing came from what she had seen, experienced, and accomplished. Nothing she had ever heard or read about could have prepared her for this, and even now she had to remind herself that it was real. She was in Africa. She had saved a rhino. Rosie. It was a wonderful feeling. With her eyes closed, her smile broadened as she remembered and corrected herself. It was more than that. It was a bloody excellent feeling

***

'I think Rosie is a bit fed-up,' John commented, lifting the hurricane lantern clear of the posts as Rosie crashed into them, shaking the entire wall.

The mild understatement drew a derisive chorus from the others standing with him on the pole observation rail that encircled the upper section of the stockade.

'I think I'd be the same if I'd been through what she has,' Juliette said. She had joined them as soon as the truck had roared into the holding compound with lights blazing and the jubilant labourers shouting to no one in particular that they had a chipimbiri and soon would have beer too.

She had administered the antidote while Rosie still lay bound to her sled, after the cumbersome contraption had been noisily sweated and cursed and winched off the truck and down the slide-rails into the boma that was to be Rosie's temporary new home. Juliette had also given Rosie a dose of penicillin as the sled was being dragged from beneath her, then had scrambled up the wall to safety while Tim had remained to remove the last of the restraints.

'Hold on, here she comes again...'

Snorting and puffing with rage, Rosie hooked at the poles with her long horn, slashing and goring them, and raising a whirling storm of choking dust. The pestering calf scampered around after her, adding to the confusion.

'Don't be an old sorehead, Rosie,' Juliette scolded. 'Go get a drink. And let your calf have one too.'

'Silly bitch is going to stand on him in a minute.'

John called to his assistant watching from the other side with the labourers. 'Mathias! Get a branch and splash the water.'

Mathias climbed down to poke a branch through a gap between the poles, beating the surface of the water, and Rosie spun around with a wail of fury, bowling over the calf. She ripped and swiped at the branch, killing it, and the water too, tossing it high and hurling spray and mud over the group of Africans.

Their exclamations and laughter only caused Rosie to redouble her efforts.

'Keep the bloody racket down!' John bellowed at them. 'Mathias, get those clowns off there and throw in some more branches.'

'Maybe we should leave too,' Kelly suggested. Her concern was as much for herself as for Rosie. It was after midnight, and she was so exhausted she felt in danger of falling off before she had a chance to descend more gracefully.

'Good idea,' John agreed. 'I don't know about you lot, but I'm pooped.'

When everyone had been moved away, Tim remained alone to encourage Rosie to drink, using a hose to trickle water into the muddy pond from a height so she would hear the sound. She attacked that too, but eventually the smell or taste got to her and she slurped greedily, her great flanks heaving like bellows, and the calf took the opportunity to scramble beneath her to get his own drink.

'Good girl,' Tim said.

Standing behind, Kelly heaved a proprietary sigh

of relief, then yawned.

***

The spectators began arriving at Gara Pasi shortly after dawn. Some had walked from villages as far away as ten miles. Several unkempt and quick-eyed strangers came from even farther afield, from over the Mozambique border. It was not every day that an open invitation was extended to witness an operation of any kind, never mind one on such a dangerous beast as a chipimbiri. And especially not one that was to be conducted by a doctor who was also a woman.

John Singleton gave them all a lecture.

With Mathias acting as interpreter, he told them that because of a few greedy individuals, all the chipimbiri would soon be gone. None would be left for their children to see, and the tourists would not come with their dollars. That is why the government had given orders that all poachers were to be shot on sight. This included anyone helping them, he added, pausing to scowl furiously at the ring of black faces. Those caught with snares, he told them, would themselves be snared in handcuffs and spend a long time in the stocks.

This ominous warning caused some uneasy

shuffling in some quarters, and a mild stirring generally, for no one wished to be shot, but neither did one wish to starve. It brought a sombre note to the occasion.

The mood changed however, when they learned that four chipimbiri, including the injured one they had come to see, were going to a new home in Australia, and that they were being flown there in an aeroplane. This brought exclamations of disbelief. Even a few derisive sniggers. Everyone knew this was impossible. Chipimbiris were too dangerous to go in flying machines, and Australia was too far, even farther away than South Africa.

When Tim poked his dart-gun through a gap in the poles of Rosie's stockade and shot a large dose of M99 cocktail into her left rump - the opposite side to where she had received the previous dose - a murmur of astonishment rustled through the crowd, and Mathias had a hard time keeping them at a respectable distance for the twenty minutes it took for Rosie to succumb.

When she finally went down and John reluctantly gave them the long-awaited nod, the audience scrambled for the best vantage points along the rail of the stockade, jostling, squirming and giggling with suppressed excitement. The show was about to begin.

First came the preliminaries. The four upright poles comprising the gate were removed and a crate hauled into the gap. After first checking that Rosie was breathing satisfactorily, Tim threw a rope over the calf and, with the enthusiastic assistance of several experienced clowns, and much encouragement from the gallery, manhandled the protesting calf into the crate.

If Rosie was the main event, Juliette Ryan was undoubtedly the star performer, and her entrance into the boma with her case of magical instruments was greeted with hushed expectancy.

Looking the part in a white clinic-coat, her dark curls restrained with a yellow scrunchy, she went into quiet consultation with Tim for a few minutes, who then passed on her orders. The area was to be shovelled free of dung and hosed down to settle the dust.

When this was completed, Rosie herself was washed down, and her lower half sprayed with disinfectant. This was obviously to chase away any evil spirits that may be lurking, and all around the top rail, breaths were cautiously held to avoid breathing them in.

More comic relief was provided when Tim called on several labourers to tie Rosie's forelegs and sit on her in the event she came around, which was not that uncommon, yet they obeyed with alacrity, for the audience contained several giggling and impressed young females. Mathias and Kawaseka claimed the most dangerous, and therefore the most prized position, for themselves; the great head with its two-foot front horn.

The tittering stopped when Juliette spread a rubber sheet on the ground and laid out her shining instruments.

A sack was placed under Rosie's head to keep her eye clear of the dust, and the uppermost eye, which remained open, was shielded by Kelly's red cap to prevent the mucus membrane from drying in the sun.

Tim removed the dart then cleaned and dusted the wound thickly with disinfectant powder, then he held his hand below Rosie's warm nostrils to time her breathing rate; relaying the information to John Singleton, who sat on Rosie's shoulder with a pad on his knee to record her vital statistics.

Considering what she had been through, Rosie was in reasonable shape. Her temperature - the taking of which caused more restrained sniggering - was below a hundred, and her breathing was regular at six deep breaths per minute. Juliette recorded the heartbeat at fifteen, then removed her stethoscope and picked up a large scalpel.

Grasping it like a dagger in her small fist, she cut deep into and across the suppurating wound, the sharp blade grating on the stiff wire strands of the steel cable. Tim pulled the flesh apart to expose it, and also the muscles and tendons, which were swollen and oozing pus.

'Poor thing,' Juliette murmured, swabbing at the mess. 'The wires are rusty all the way down... look at the yukky color of that flesh.' She probed for the splayed strands with her forceps. 'I'll hold them up... if you use the wire cutters...'

They removed the strands one at a time, pushing and nipping them as far down as possible, lifting them out smeared pink with blood and pus; all sixteen of them.

Juliette swabbed and probed some more, then looked up with a sigh. 'It's worse than I thought. The cable's gone into the bone.'

'Into it?'

'The whole noose. It was pulled so tight the bone has grown over it.'

'Damn!' John Singleton shook his head.'

'What are you going to do?' Tim asked.

Juliette pondered the problem as she inspected the bone closely. 'We can chisel it out, but it would take too long.' She consulted her watch. 'It's been an hour already, and we won't have enough time before she comes around. And I don't think it would be good for her to be under for too long. Anyway, we could damage the muscles and tendons.'

'You mean it has to stay?'

'She's lived with the pain for a few years, by the look of that bone,' Juliette said. 'It won't be as bad now without the ends poking out. I think it will be best if I chisel carefully around the cable where it goes in, then cut the strands off below the surface where it won't damage the leg tissue. Eventually the bone will grow over and the wound should heal. I'll have to get all the chips out though,' she added thoughtfully.

It took another two gruelling hours with all of them sweating under the beat of the climbing sun, including Rosie, who had been given a booster dose of drugs when she showed signs of restlessness, twice thrashing out against her restraints and causing Juliette to retreat hastily with her precious instruments. Fortunately no harm was done, and with eight bodies sitting and lying astride her, three holding her massive head, Rosie quietened down with a long groan and resumed her gentle snoring.

Kelly sat with her hand on the soft leathery nostrils to monitor the breathing, with instructions to call out if it changed. Her fingers explored the jutting prehensile lip, which was also surprisingly soft; not unlike that of a horse. Each breath Rosie took was long and slightly wheezing, as if she had a cold, and Kelly counted them. 'Eight per minute,' she called in an efficient nurse's voice.

'Uh, huh.' Juliette swabbed the wound clean, using forceps to get deep down, then packed the wound with antibiotic powder before stitching it closed, using a leather sail maker's thimble and glove to force the big needle through the tough hide, tying and snipping the thick gut after each stitch.

'You'll have to finish off,' she informed Tim, flexing her slender fingers. 'My hand won't take any more.'

'Weakling,' he said, and gave her a brotherly pat on the behind by way of congratulation.

At her instructions he sprayed the exterior wound with terramycin spray, enveloped it with lint, and bound it in place with several layers of adhesive plaster.

'Okay, show's over,' John Singleton said to Mathias. 'Untie the ropes. And you can tell that lot to bugger off now so Rosie can wake up in peace and quiet.'

John cut a two-inch notch out of Rosie's left ear, while Tim jabbed a needle into her rump and pumped in a dose of penicillin. The dart wound and ear were treated, then John administered the antidote, pinching a vein in the undamaged ear and injecting the nalorphine directly into it.

'Everybody out,' he ordered, and they gathered all the equipment and padded ropes, scrambling up the poles to sit on the top and wait for Rosie to come awake.

She was in no hurry. She kicked spasmodically, lifted her head a short distance, then collapsed again with a deep groan.

'Oi! Wake up, Rosie!' John shouted, and Rosie's ears twitched.

Tim clapped his hands and Rosie lifted her head again, then clambered slowly to her feet, swaying unsteadily and holding up her leg.

'Don't worry, Rosie, it's going to be better,' Kelly called out, and Rosie turned quickly at the sound of her voice. She glared malevolently in her direction, then lumbered forward drunkenly, stepping high with the after-effects of the drug, but still able to attack the poles below Kelly's feet with determination, poking her horn through a gap and hooking violently, losing her balance and, as she stumbled to the side with the full weight of her massive body twisting the horn, it snapped off at the base with a dull thud.

'Oh, no!' Kelly cried. 'What did you do that for?'

Unable to fit completely through the gap, the horn fell into the pen. Rosie sniffed it suspiciously. It failed to meet with her approval. She hooked it with her bleeding stump, following it into the centre of the boma, then lost interest. She stood there, looking decidedly the worse for wear with her drooping head, her bandaged leg, and her ear and nose dripping blood.

'As if the poor thing hasn't suffered enough,' Kelly whispered. 'I should have kept my big mouth shut. I'm sorry.'

'Not your fault,' Tim reassured her. 'Maybe now she won't be such a damned pest. We'll give her an hour or so for the drug to wear off then give her some glucose and water.'

'How do we get the horn out?'

'We're going to have to put her under in another four days to give her a shot of penicillin,' Juliette said quietly. 'We'll get it then.'

'She's not going to like that one bit.' John remarked. 'I think Rosie is going to be fed up with the human race for a very long time.'

***

Elliot Gumbo watched the operation with the same bemused detachment a bank robber might have adopted after being invited in to witness repairs to the vault.

Like the majority of Africans his age, he had spent much of his childhood in and around the cities and adjoining African townships, and had little contact with the more isolated Tribal Trust Lands, particularly those of the remote Lowveld. Until joining the Freedom Fighters he had seen few wild animals, and even these had been limited mainly to hippos, zebra, and the shy antelope. Only recently had he seen elephant, and he had never seen a rhino.

Its size and apparent ferocity chastened him, gnawing at his enthusiasm, and allowing nagging doubts as to his ability to get rich by hunting them. Using AK's against such a beast, even on automatic, seemed futile.

Some of Elliot's resolve returned after the rhino had been rendered unconscious and was being sat on by several joking labourers, but he determined that as soon as he returned to Mozambique he would see the Chinese and arrange for the purchase of a much larger weapon.

Once the operation on the animal was well underway, Elliot turned his attention to the pole enclosures. There were four, joined together to form a square, so it seemed it was expected that more than one rhino would be held there at the same time.

This was confirmed by listening and talking to

the other spectators, and especially the local labourers of the property, who were only too willing to boast of their knowledge, especially after he told them he was a schoolteacher from Masvingo. His students must learn of such an important event, he told them, and the deception was made convincing in that he also looked the part by being smartly dressed and wearing borrowed glasses.

Having four animals securely penned in one place, Elliot thought, seemed too good an opportunity to miss. Especially so, as they were destined for Australia. Every one taken meant one less for him, and they were hard enough to find as it was.

But he could see no way to take advantage of the situation. Shooting the chipimbiris in the pens would be safe and easy, but the place was well guarded by armed game scouts. Even with his three men and surprise on his side, it would be risky. They could not hit and run, as they had been taught in the war, but would have to spend a long time hacking off the horns, and the firing would alert everyone for miles around.

The only solution Elliot could think of was to wait in the vicinity and see what happened. At the moment only one rhino was caught. It would not take so long for a man to cut off one animal's horns while the other three engaged the guards, and they could do it after dark, when they would have the whole night to escape without fear of being tracked. By morning they would be over the border and their tracks lost amongst the villages. It would mean losing the opportunity to return for other captured animals, but there was little choice.

And he did not want to kill anyone. Simple robbing was one thing, but the war was over, and killing game scouts could have the entire Zimbabwe army after them.

When the operation was over and the crowd began leaving, Elliot sent his men away then approached one of the labourers he had become acquainted with, asking if he could pay him to share his hut for the night, and the man agreed. It proved a fortuitous decision, for later that evening, on the pretence of having to relieve himself, he was not only able to learn that the pens were unguarded, but heard the news that the chipimbiri had lost one of its horns while attacking the poles. At first he was disbelieving, but was able to see it for himself next morning. It lay in the middle of the pen, its base a mess of congealed blood and dust, and the nose of the animal was much the same.

It would have to be left there, he heard, until the beast was darted again in four days, when it was due for some medicine. Then he heard even better news. The game scouts and most of the labourers would be leaving before then on another expedition, leaving the place almost totally unguarded.

Elliot left Gara Pasi with several other visitors, then slipped away to double back to where his three men were camped and waiting in thick bush outside the sanctuary's high game fences.

'We are soon to get another horn,' he told them jubilantly, explaining what he had seen. 'It is bigger than the one from before, so each of us will receive at least one thousand dollars.' He always gave them the amounts in Zimbabwe currency. They did not understand exchange rates. It would only confuse them. Anyway, a thousand sounded so much more generous than twenty.

***

Kelly accepted her first invitation from Tim to go flying.

Since Rosie's capture and operation the improved situation between them had become even better. Perhaps it was her own change in attitude that made it so, she thought with some amusement, for the role she had played in finding Rosie had boosted her confidence, making her feel less like an outsider and more like a member of a team. She could even crack the odd joke with him now, and he had continued his exemplary behaviour.

He had come to treat her much the same as he did Juliette, and with even more amusement at the self-inflicted irony, Kelly found herself wondering if it was because he found her unattractive. Although she still felt no urge to go around without her knickers, as Juliette called them, neither did she want to be treated like his sister.

The Tiger Moth had already been pulled from its thorny enclosure when Kelly arrived at the airstrip. Her hands were clasped around a mug of hot coffee, much of which had spilled along the way. Three African youths stood nearby, shivering and hugging bare arms as they watched Tim doing the pre-flight inspection.

'Goodi morningi, madam,' they chorused in practiced unison, as if welcoming the teacher to the classroom.

Greetings in their language, she had discovered, seemed always to end with an 'i', so they invariably tagged it onto the English ones as well. She had learned a few African words in the past week. She now knew that Gara Pasi meant sit down, or more correctly, sit down and rest. Gona re Zhou meant place of the elephants, and chipimbiri was the name for rhino. She even knew how to say good morning in Shona. She tried it out on them now, slowly, and with an accompanying smile. 'Mang-wan-ani.'

They didn't laugh, so she guessed she had got it right. She wondered why it had been necessary to get them up so early when she could easily have helped move the plane.

Tim paused to also wish her a cheery good morning, grinning, and she tried to respond too quickly, gulping, and choking on her coffee. She waved a hand in front of her steaming mouth. 'Hi…'

He still had the knack of catching her unawares.

Not wanting to follow Tim around like a student pilot as he finished the checks, Kelly waited to the side with the three youths, listening as they spoke to each other loudly in English, obviously trying to impress her. And that is what they did, but not in the way they would have expected.

She was charmed by their simple innocence, as she was by that of their elders. Life seemed to swing to a different beat in this part of the world. Hardship, tragedy and bitter war had been part of that life, yet she saw no animosity, only smiling faces and politeness. The only frowns she had seen were ones of puzzlement as they tried to understand what she was saying.

The puzzling presence of the three youths was answered as soon as Tim had finished his checks. He joked with them in their language, asking a question, which seemed to provoke an argument between the three. They began jostling each other for position, as if wanting to be first in a queue. Tim pointed to one with a shaved scalp, only a small square patch left in the front. The unsophisticated version of a punk rocker, Kelly surmised. The other two youths fell silent immediately, looking disappointed, and Tim smiled at Kelly, shaking his head.

'They know damn well whose turn it is to spin the prop, but always have to squabble about it.'

Kelly laughed. Where else in the world, she wondered, would three teenage boys leave their beds at dawn, braving the cold in short pants, sleeveless shirts and bare feet to compete with each other for the dubious honour of spinning a propeller.

Tim glanced at her odd assemblage of warm clothing with a critical eye; a striped rugby jersey on top of a blue tracksuit, and a woollen beanie, all loaned to her by Juliette.

'Better put this on as well,' he said, pulling a green balaclava from his anorak. 'It gets a bit chilly around the ears. Goggles are on the seat.'

Like the youths, Tim was barefoot and wearing shorts.

'Why aren't you wearing shoes?' Kelly asked.

'Aren't your feet cold?'

'Frozen, but that's how I like to fly.'

'Oh? Any particular reason?'

'Don't know, really. I suppose it's a bit like having your finger on a pulse when you're wearing gloves. Can't feel it.'

Kelly looked at her own feet encased in a pair of Juliette's Australian sheepskin boots, and felt privileged to the point of embarrassment. She wished she had the courage to remove them.

'Ready?'

She swallowed the last of her coffee and nodded.

'Take the rear cockpit, if you like,' Tim said, and she gave him a startled look.

'You expect me to fly it?'

'Sure, why not? Or you can have a go from the front. I replaced the dual stick last night. I usually take it off when one of the scouts comes along.' He grinned. 'They tend to use it as a panic handle, which makes things interesting, especially when you're trying to land.'

Kelly returned the smile distractedly, feeling a sudden rush of adrenalin, as nervous as if she had just been asked to do her first solo. But she was an experienced pilot - a professional, whereas Tim only had a private licence. 'I wouldn't mind a feel, but it's a long time since I've flown a real tail-dragger, and I'm not used to a joystick.'

'Same principle, and after a Seabee you won't find this a problem, I'll follow you through on the controls. Ever swung a prop?'

She shook her head, and he explained briefly, showing her the magneto switch on the outside of the fuselage. 'Throttle on the left. Just crack it to start. Hop in.'

Kelly stepped into the front, passenger cockpit and Tim helped her into the shoulder harness, adjusting the worn-looking webbing with quick fingers, the back of his lean brown hand pressing without intent against her left breast.

'How do we communicate?' she asked, her voice sounding a little forced and unsteady in her ears.

'Hand signals. If it's important, there's a blackboard down the right side of your seat.'

Kelly pulled on the balaclava, and slipped her feet into the straps of the rudder-bar as Tim climbed into the rear cockpit. She felt his movements on the dual controls, and heard the squeak of the fuel plunger, and almost immediately smelled the fuel as it dripped on the grass beneath the engine.

The youth whose turn it was to spin the wooden propeller pulled it slowly back twice, each turn counted aloud by all three boys. He aligned it carefully, then, with an enthusiastic chorus of 'Fire!' from his companions, swung it down quickly with a flourish.

The engine caught with a roar, then settled into a reassuringly steady burble, and the boy ran off laughing to receive the high-fives and handshakes of his friends.

After a short warm-up, one of the other youths, who had been waiting anxiously for the signal, pulled on the long string attached to the chocks, and the Moth began to move forward.

'Okay, you've got her,' Tim shouted from behind. 'Just concentrate on the flying, I'll check the mags as we go. Don't forget we have no brakes.'

'Thanks for telling me,' Kelly muttered, and hastily fumbled on her goggles. She eased the throttle forward and they weaved across the wet grass.

Tim leaned over her shoulder to give some last minute advice. 'If I need to take over I'll jiggle the stick like this...' he gave it a quick shake to demonstrate, 'then you can follow me through. Okay, you can give it the gun now.'

'What about take-off checks?' she shouted back louder than she intended. 'And what's the lift-off speed?'

'Rotate at around sixty and reduce power at two hundred feet. Level out at five hundred.'

'Now he tells me.' Kelly eased the throttle forward, forgetting in her nervousness to put on right rudder to counteract the gyroscopic effect as she applied full power and the tail lifted. She felt the rudder bar move under her feet and realized Tim was controlling it. She clamped her lips in frustration. She had to do the same thing every time she took-off in the Bee, so how could she forget? Fly the damned plane, you silly bitch, she told herself, and kicked firmly on the bar to let him know she had control.

When the airspeed indicator passed the sixty mark she eased firmly back on the stick and the Moth leaped willingly into the air.

Now that she was airborne and fully committed, her confidence returned. Flying was what she loved and did best, and this was flying as she had never experienced it before. The rushing wind was cold, but not as strong as she had thought it might be from the combination of propeller and speed. No more than the Mustang convertible, but infinitely more exhilarating.

She reduced power and levelled out, turning towards some distant hills in response to Tim's tap on the shoulder and pointing finger, and after each adjustment the wind sang a different tune. She did some lazy turns, getting the feel of the controls and the response, and her confidence increased. The Moth was sluggish, but compared to the Bee it was like driving a sports car, and despite the numbing cold she revelled in the unique experience.

A tapping on her leg signalled the arrival of the chalkboard, and the shaky message: lower to river.

She reduced power and descended sedately towards the winding silver thread below. The sun was on the horizon, bathing the yellow wings in light, but the landscape was still in mist and shadow, an ocean of mauve and white for as far as she could see all around.

Tim took over by waggling the stick, and the Moth suddenly became a different airplane. No longer was it like a docile sports car, now it was more like a high performance rally machine, and Kelly caught her breath as he dived low above the trees, skimming through wispy pockets of damp mist that fogged her goggles, weaving above the river from one side to the other with smooth yet decisive crispness. Showing off again, she thought uncharitably, and immediately corrected herself. No. This was flying

With her feet now resting lightly on the rudder-bar, she could feel its movement coinciding smoothly with each banking turn, and her eyes were drawn almost against her will to the ball in the turn and bank indicator, checking what her body was already telling her, but her mind was finding hard to accept.

The ball was not moving. She had expected to see some movement either side, to show they were either slipping or sliding in the turns, but it remained fixed in the centre of its tube as if stuck there with glue.

Kelly considered herself a good pilot, one who could fly on the basic instruments as well as anyone, but never had she been able to hold the ball so still and, even more incredible, he didn't look at it once. She could see him in the small rear-view mirror, peering over the side at the river below, flying by instinct alone, and the Moth seemed to know its controls were now in the hands of a master and not an amateur. It was a humbling experience for Kelly.

She followed his movements carefully on the stick and rudder, trying to imagine it was she who was flying, attempting to transfer this magic control into herself, but knowing it was more than brain and nerves and muscles that did it. Tim was a born flyer, a natural, like her father had been and, she realized with dull acceptance, like she would never be, no matter how determined she was, or how much she loved it.

The unfairness of it struck Kelly like a bucket of cold water, dampening her enthusiasm, so that she almost gave up trying to follow Tim's movements. She felt an almost overwhelming anger that her father could squander such a gift that she would give anything to possess.

They flew over a herd of elephant, circling them, and she watched one of the great beasts following their progress with raised trunk, lumbering after them, and she laughed at the sheer splendour of it all, her despair forgotten.

The banks of the river steepened as they entered a range of hills and they climbed above them, going higher, and the chalkboard tapped at her leg: hold on, going over.

Suddenly the nose pitched sharply down, lifting her off her seat. They dived, picking up speed, the wind shrieking and snatching at her breath, then a sinking, heavy feeling as the nose lifted, going higher, passing through the horizon, nothing but icy blue, and Kelly let go of the stick to clutch at her seat when she realized she was going upside down.

With the engine gone quiet the wind took on another tone as it rustled and thrummed over the fabric of the fuselage and played through the wires; an eerie moaning, and she felt as if she was floating weightless. The thought crossed her mind that she was hanging there only by the thin fabric of her pants, flying by the seat of them, and she laughed. Thin, shrieking laughter, like that of a mad woman, the sound resonating in her head against the woollen helmet covering her ears.

She lifted her hands to wave them above her head, tempting the gods, but they only sang and left her there - dangling by the seat of her pants and the laws of physics. The sun appeared, shining full in her eyes, then a glimpse of the horizon. She felt movement on the right rudder, then once again the steady roar of the engine as they came out of the dive and climbed.

Breathless, she turned in her seat to grin at Tim, nodding vigorously to signify her approval, and the wool of his balaclava distorted around the area of his mouth as he grinned back. He shouted something that she couldn't hear, and when she raised her hands in a shrug of puzzlement, he scribbled on the board and held it up.

Your turn.

Kelly shook her head. 'No way!'

But she was not to be let off so easily. Tim wrote again on the board and held up a sketchy drawing of a chicken and a question mark.

Kelly glared back at him, shaking her head again, but he only shrugged and grinned back behind the wool, hands clasped unconcernedly behind his head, and Kelly turned back with a gnawing in her suddenly empty stomach, knowing she would have to go through with the stupid stunt or hate herself afterwards.

'Right, you arrogant bastard,' she muttered, and

took a deep breath. She pushed the throttle and stick forward, conquering her fear by closing her mind to everything except the mechanics of the exercise, much as she did when having to eat Brussel sprouts or turnips at a dinner party.

The speed increased rapidly. The engine seeming to scream louder and the plane to vibrate more than when Tim had done it, and for a moment she almost lost her nerve, her imagination intruding, but she had reached the speed, was passing it, and had to act.

Staring straight ahead at the sun, she pulled back on the stick and the Moth swooped up. The horizon disappeared. She could see only a blue void that seemed to go on forever. With no idea where she was, she held the stick firmly back, left hand frozen on the throttle, staring fixedly ahead and willing the earth to reappear.

It finally came, a dark line drawing closer to the solid bulk of the upper wing, joining with it and, almost reluctantly, she pulled back the throttle, half expecting to fall out of the sky.

No more blue now, only the dark bush filling the void, rushing up to meet her, and she pulled out of the dive and applied the power. She sat staring at the horizon in a euphoric trance, unable to believe she had done it.

The board tapped at her leg. Bloody excellent!

Kelly shrieked with laughter, pumping the air with a fist. So she had forgotten the rudder, and had come off the line. So what? She had done a loop. And in a biplane! The most wonderful plane she had ever flown.

She was still filled with the wonder of it a half hour later when Tim landed on a clay-pan and shut down the engine.

He stood to remove his anorak, then produced a thermos flask. 'How about some coffee? We have to wait for a game scout, so I thought we'd sit in the sun for a while and warm up.' His voice sounded unnaturally loud in the sudden quiet.

Kelly removed the balaclava and shook her hair free, undoing her harness with trembling fingers. She held them up to inspect and giggled. 'Wow! I haven't felt like this since I went solo. That was fantastic!'

Tim climbed out and jumped to the ground, then waited, offering a steadying hand as she stepped from the wing.

'My head is still up there,' she said breathlessly. 'The wind… and the sound, the feeling of being free, and that loop… '

'You did it well.'

'It was the most…' Still intoxicated with her experience, Kelly glanced up at him and stopped. He was standing close, still holding her hand, the secretive smile on his lips, and the look in his eyes was unmistakeable.

She tried to step back, but was still too close to the wing, which pressed into the back of her legs, stopping her. She tried to remove her hand, but he came with it, pushing close, jamming her between the wing and the fuselage, and he bent to kiss her.

'No,' she said sternly, and twisted away, but he placed a hand behind her back, sliding it up to her head, entwining his fingers and holding her firm.

Had his lips been hard and demanding Kelly would have fought him off, maybe even used a knee, but his kiss was surprisingly gentle and, with the breathless exultation of the flight still in control of her senses, Kelly found herself not wanting to resist.

Cautiously at first, then more eagerly when she realized what she was doing and that it was too late to stop, she clung to him, then gasped at her own sudden urgency when he placed both his hands on her buttocks and pulled her against him.

She pushed away to breath, panting against his ear as his fingers pressed into her flesh, his hardness pressing, and she found her own hands wandering as if by their own volition, slipping beneath the elasticised waistband of his rugby shorts, sliding over smooth flesh.

With a tug on her loose tracksuit bottoms he jerked them down, taking the panties with them, and then there was nothing between them but the hot smooth flesh and the urgency.

'On the wing,' he breathed, and lowered her, shoving up her two cumbersome tops to quickly fondle her breasts with his cold hands as he followed her down, then removing one to hurriedly guide himself.

Kelly looked up at the pale sky and abandoned herself to the exquisitely painful sensation, surprised at her readiness, her almost frantic willingness. She wanted to keep her eyes open, to look at the sky, and it was like going through the loop all over again.

'Yes…' she gasped, and he covered her open mouth with his, filling it with warmth as he panted, and Kelly could no longer keep her eyes open.

They lay spent and exhausted, clinging together for a full minute before he slid down between her knees and collapsed onto the ground, lying back against the fuselage.

Still breathless, Kelly sat to pull up her pants. So much for keeping them on, she thought. She looked down on him, lying back with his eyes closed, and wondered if it had really happened.

His lips twitched in a smile. 'That was rather good. We should do it again sometime.'

She smiled. 'Not excellent?'

'Bloody oath. I take back everything I ever said or thought about you.'

'Which is what, exactly?'

He placed a hand on her thigh, caressing. 'Come down her and I'll show you.'

She gently removed his hand. 'I don't think so, Tim. I'm still trying to make up my mind if I was raped or not.'

He laughed, opening one eye to squint up at her, but said nothing.

'There is no game scout, is there? You planned all this.'

He sat forward to pick up the flask. 'Coffee?'

'You really are an arrogant bastard, Tim.'

'Do you blame me? You're gorgeous. How could I resist.' He poured her a mug and she took it gratefully.

'You seem to have done all right up to now. But no, I suppose I can't blame you. I didn't exactly resist, did I?'

'Sorry, I didn't mean to rush. Couldn't help it. Guess I needed it more than I thought.'

'Is that it? A quick screw to satisfy your lust and ego?'

'Absolutely. But also because you're irresistible and have balls... if you know what I mean.' He grinned, pleased with his joke, and Kelly could not resist smiling back.

'I suppose that's a compliment of sorts. By the way, that was rather irresponsible of us, you know.'

'Oh, yeah, why?' He grinned. 'Haven't got Aids, have you?'

'Not unless you just gave it to me. I'm not on the pill.'

'Oh, shit…'

Kelly let it go. The possibility was too remote to make an issue of it, and it was as much her fault. Besides, there was nothing they could do about it now. She changed the subject.

'You know, I shouldn't be telling you this, your ego is big enough already, but up there…' Kelly looked up, squinting into the sun, 'I got quite resentful watching you fly. I've only known one other person who was a born pilot, and that was my father. You really are good.'

Kelly could not be sure why she felt compelled to tell him, especially now. Maybe it was because she wanted to share something more meaningful than what they had just experienced together, something that would bring them closer emotionally, and the only thing they shared in common was flying. It was no idle compliment, it came from the heart, and he would know it. Whatever the reason, she was glad she did, for it took him by surprise and, astonishingly, turned the top of his ears pink.

He shrugged modestly, then grinned. 'I like you, too. Now, if you're really sure you don't want to make love again, how about we go find us a rhino?'

***

Kelly telephoned Billy Steel that same night, asking if he had sold the Bristol yet, and when he said he hadn't but had a few interested buyers, she breathed a sigh of relief.

'Can you put them off,' she asked.

'What are you cooking up now?' Billy countered.

'I'd like to buy it myself, if you can wait until I get back to organise a loan. I flew a Tiger Moth today, Billy, and did a loop. I'm hooked.'

Billy chuckled. 'Okay, kid, we'll work something out. What's happening there?'

She raved for the next five minutes, giving Billy no chance to speak, and ended by giving him several noisy kisses in the ear. 'Love you.'

She replaced the receiver and sat for several moments in a daze, hoping she had done the right thing, and wondering where she was going to find the money.

***

As much as she would have liked to, Kelly demurred when invited by Tim to go on the next rhino expedition.

'I'll only hold you up again,' she excused. 'The way my legs are feeling after the last hike I don't think I could walk more than a mile even with a gun at my head. Maybe I can help Juliette around here. Do something for Rosie. She looks so dejected with her raw nose.'

'Nothing we can do except leave her alone until she gets used to her pen and realizes no one is out to harm her or her calf.' Tim answered. 'Her nose will be sore, but the horn is only a mass of glutinous fibre, a bit like losing a fingernail.'

Kelly winced. 'That's bad enough.'

'Juliette will dose it with antibiotic cream or terramycin spray when we put her under for her shot.' He paused, taking her hand. 'Seeing as how I won't have the pleasure of your company tomorrow, how about tonight, after dinner…in my room?' He grinned. 'I have protection.'

Kelly responded with a half-smile. 'That's not exactly the most romantic proposition I've had. No thanks, Tim. What we did was a one-off. I don't make a habit of sleeping around.'

'Not around. Just with me. I'll bring roses.'

'Sorry.'

He sighed theatrically. 'Okay, Kelly, if that's how it is I'll suffer in silence, but if anytime you're feeling lonely…'

***

Kelly did find something she could do while the men were away.

Browsing through the books, she discovered that a woman in Kenya had read aloud to her rhinos, to get them used to the sound of human voices, which Rosie seemed to respond to angrily. If she did the same, it could only be of benefit to all concerned, especially Rosie.

After she had completed her daily round with Juliette, she took the book with her to Rosie's boma. She could read aloud and learn at the same time.

As expected, Rosie welcomed her with an angry snort and few menacing charges that lasted for only a few steps. She was learning already. Remembering how Tim had snorted in return, Kelly tried the same, making the blubbering horsey sound between slack lips. Rosie glared balefully, unimpressed.

The horn was still lying in the dust near the middle. Such an insignificant-looking object, Kelly thought, and a terrible irony that what was designed for the rhinos protection was the cause of its destruction.

A steel crate had been fitted into the entrance, lashed securely in place with stout rope. It was the same crate in which she would travel to Australia, and essential that she get used to its presence. The front was raised so she could enter, and all her food was provided there; tasty acacia branches, horse pellets, vegetable scraps, and a mix of lucerne and hay.

Kelly made herself comfortable on the ground beside it and, after a furtive look around to ensure nobody was within hearing range, opened her book.

She paused often in her reading to see what reaction she was getting, and to break the monotony so Rosie would get the benefit of stops and starts. Sometimes she spoke loudly, and Rosie would snort and back away with ears erect, as if readying herself to charge, but she never did, remaining at the far end of the boma, even when Kelly mimicked her snorts with damp ones of her own.

The calf was more forthcoming, making several brief excursions towards the cage before losing courage and retreating.

Kelly stopped when her throat was dry, her tongue

furry, and she had read a good half of the book.

'And there endeth the first lesson,' she said, getting stiffly to her feet. 'If you promise to be a good girl we'll do it again this afternoon.'

***

Elliot Gumbo watched from behind a tree across the river as the woman finally left the boma. Why she had been guarding the chipimbiri without having a gun was a mystery, but he had long since given up trying to understand the odd behaviour of whites when it came to animals. Of more importance was that he had seen the big Isuzu truck pull out of Gara Pasi earlier, with the raft-like thing on its back for loading the chipimbiri, and seven men, including the two uniformed scouts with their guns.

Once again Elliot congratulated himself for keeping the binoculars he had taken from the German tourist, and not attempting to sell them to that thief, Ebrahim. Being able to put your eyes so close without danger was worth a hundred times what the Indian would have paid.

With only a handful of servants and the two white women left to guard the rhino, it was going to be easy. He would plan for midnight, two hours after the diesel engine with its generator had been switched off. Everyone should be asleep then, and it would still give them five hours of darkness in which to reach the border. More than enough time.

It was too bad they would only get the one horn, but without risk. One already in the hand was worth more than trying to hunt for two in the bush. Even so, he may still be able to think of a plan to get the other three rhinos yet to come. Having them all in one place would make life so much easier.

He rubbed his eyes then focused the binoculars again on the cage that had been fitted into the gate of the boma, trying to think how such a heavy thing could be moved by only four men.

***

Kelly sat up quickly in her bed. It was still dark in the room, but pale light showed at the window. The knocking that had woken her came again.

'Kelly! Are you awake?' Juliette's voice was quietly anxious, and Kelly threw aside the blankets to pad swiftly across the cold slate to unlatch the door.

'Jules? What is it… something wrong?'

Juliette was standing against the wall in the shadows, dressed in her tracksuit and holding a shotgun. She came into the room quickly, closing the door behind and going to the window. 'It's Rosie. She's gone.'

'What?' Kelly stared at her in confusion, 'gone where?'

'Her boma is empty. Frek noticed when he went to light the fire for the hot water.'

'But how? Surely she couldn't have escaped.'

'Someone must have let her out.'

'Who… I mean why would somebody…?' She stopped, baffled. 'The gun… you think it's poachers?'

'I don't know, but I feel better having it.' Juliette turned away from the window and returned to the door. 'It looks quiet. I'm going down to have a look.'

'Wait for me…' Kelly scrambled into her jeans and borrowed slippers, pulling on a top as she hurried through the door.

It was light enough to see a small gathering already at the rhino enclosure, inspecting the shifted cage and the open gate. The front of the cage had been lowered and the securing ropes cut.

'They take the horn, madam,' Frek informed Juliette as they arrived. 'No spoor to see. All wearing bare feet only.'

'And nobody heard anything?'

Her question brought only silence.

'Obviously not,' Juliette said grimly.

Kelly observed the moved cage in dismay. 'Who would do such a thing?'

'Who knows? A hundred locals must have seen it lying there. It could be anyone.'

'She was just beginning to get used to it, and quietening down, too.'

'I'll try to get a message to Tim and John. They're going to be mad as hell.'

'I suppose they'll have to go after her again. Goddamit, Jules. I feel so bad about this. It's my fault she lost the horn.'

'Nonsense, it wasn't your fault. Come on, let's get on the phone. The base at Chiredzi may be able to get a message to them on the radio.'

But the phone was dead.

'Bastards!' Juliette slammed down the receiver. 'They've cut the line. We'll have to go fix it.' She went to the door of the office and yelled for Frek, and when he came running from the kitchen, white apron flapping, Juliette fired a list of instructions at him. 'We need to fix the telephone. Bring the wire and the pliers, and tell your youngest son I need him to climb the pole. Also tell those two friends of his to start following the tracks of the chipimbiri. And tell them to be careful. Is the coffee ready?'

'Yes, madam, you want I should bring it?'

'No, put it in a flask and in the Jeep.' She came back in to gather a handful of shotgun shells from the desk drawer and stuff them into her pockets, then she turned to face Kelly, all efficiency and determination. 'Let's go bundu bashing.'

'We're going to fix the lines? Isn't that dangerous?'

'It's quite safe, the wires aren't alive unless someone is ringing, we do it all the time. The elephants keep pushing the poles over. If we had to wait for the linesmen we may as well not have a phone.'

They followed the cut-line beneath the wires and found the break less than a mile away. The two wires had been cut close to the insulators. Both were lying on the ground.

Juliette jerked to a stop alongside the pole and Frek's son, whom Kelly recognised as one of the propeller trio, jumped on the bonnet of the Jeep and shinned up the leaning pole with the pliers in hand. He cut the wires on the other side of the insulator, dropping them to the ground as well.

It was a simple matter then to join the wires using pieces cut from the coil they had brought, Kelly and the boy, Tandai, pulling on each in turn while Juliette twisted them together with the pliers. Then Tandai climbed the pole again with the sagging wires and hooked them onto the insulators.

'A bit saggy, but that should do it for now,' Juliette declared, and Kelly wiped her palms on the seat of her jeans with relief, wondering what new hair-raising experiences awaited her in this do-it-yourself country.

The Isuzu truck with its full complement of men and a comatose rhino strapped to the sled, roared into Gara Pasi late in the afternoon, closely followed by a dusty John Singleton in his Landrover. It was dusk by the time the rhino - a male - had been offloaded, treated, and given the antidote. He was much calmer than Rosie, sniffing and snorting, but not attacking the poles of his new home.

John and Tim stood with hands on hips, shaking their heads in angry frustration as they inspected the empty boma that had housed Rosie. Meanwhile, Mathias and the other scout hurriedly followed in the tracks of Rosie and the two boys. Fortunately they had dragged a stick behind them, so were not difficult to track in the fading light.

Kawaseka stalked around outside the boma, trying to make sense of the multitude of bare footprints, remonstrating to no one in particular that some stupid people had stupidly walked all over the signs.

It was not only Kelly who felt responsible for Rosie's release.

'It was my fault for allowing so many strangers in to watch,' Tim insisted. 'I thought it would send a message.' He laughed sardonically. 'It did that all right.'

'No way,' John said. 'It was a good idea. I should have posted a scout as a guard.'

'Probably a good thing you didn't,' Tim said. 'Kawaseka is sure there were four of them, and I agree. It would have taken that many at least to move the cage, even levering it like they did with poles. They would have been armed.'

'Well, we can forget about tracking them, they'll be long gone.'

'And Rosie, too, I wouldn't mind betting,'

'Even with her sore leg?' Kelly ventured.

'That won't stop her. But let's wait and see what Mathias and the two boys have to say. I could be wrong and she's holed-up in a thicket somewhere.'

But Tim wasn't wrong. When Mathias and the boys returned in the dark, they reported that Rosie had been walking steadily north, stopping only once for a drink, then following the river, as if wanting to put as much distance between herself and Gara Pasi as possible.

'She'll be thirty miles away by now,' Tim said tiredly.

'So, what's the plan?' John asked.

'It's fairly open country up there,' Tim answered. 'I'll see if I can spot her with the plane first thing in the morning. If you take the Isuzu with the crew and follow the track to Sibonja Hills, and then across to the river, you should pick up her spoor. Seki knows the way.'

'I'll follow in the Landrover,' Juliette said, 'in case there's a problem getting through.'

Tim agreed. 'We'll leave at first light. If I spot her, I'll try to head her off and talk you in on the two-way.'

'I can go with you, if you like,' Kelly offered. 'If you think another pair of eyes will be of help. That is, unless you are taking one of the scouts.'

'No, I can do without their puke blowing all over me. Your eyes will do just fine… thanks.'

It was a sombre evening, which not even hot showers, cold beer and a roast dinner could revive. And the gloomy news John heard from his head-office in Harare when he called on the scratchy phone to report, did nothing to improve it. There had been a meeting at which two men from the South African Endangered Species Protection Unit had been present, and it seemed that Rhino poaching was on the increase, not only in South Africa and Zimbabwe, but also north of the Zambezi as far as Kenya and Tanzania. Beyond that, rhinos probably no longer existed, not even the white ones.

Even more disturbing was the manner in which it was increasing. In many areas, traditional poachers were being threatened and muscled out by well-trained organised gangs using sophisticated equipment. High-powered rifles with telescopic sights had replaced cable snares, and VHF radios tuned to police and ranger frequencies allowed them to elude capture.

'It's almost like a drug operation,' Tim said.

'That's exactly what the ESPU believes. They think it's being organised by a Chinese multi-national company called Golden Horn in Shanghai. Many of the old Indian middlemen have disappeared from the scene.'

'So much ignorance and greed in the world,' Kelly remarked dejectedly. 'The whales, the elephants, the rhinos… it makes me want to cry.'

'Phuh!' Juliette snorted. 'It makes me want to kill someone.'

'The thing is,' John continued, 'there appears to be something even more sinister behind it all.'

'Do tell,' Tim muttered. 'I can't wait to be cheered up some more.'

'They don't seem to be as interested in getting the horn as they are in simply killing off the rhino. De-horned animals have been killed, and one was even shot in a sanctuary, for Godsakes, by the guard who was paid to protect it.'

Kelly was aghast. 'The damned traitor.'

'And another strange thing. They have been taking tails as well.'

'Bounty hunting,' Tim said. 'Like they used to do with baboons.'

'The ESPU thinks that this Golden Horn is out to corner the market. Stockpile the product, kill off the supply, and you can ask whatever price you like.'

'God...'

'Five years from now we can turn our stockade into goat pens,' Tim said. There won't be a single bloody rhino left in the wild.'

'Try two years,' said John. 'When black politicians are smuggling horns out in diplomatic pouches, how long do you think they can last?'

'Jesus Christ...'

'It makes our own operation even more important,' Juliette said grimly. 'So let's not give up just yet, shall we?'

***

John's disturbing news, plus graphic images of

Rosie's calf being eaten alive by hyenas, its bones crunching as it squealed pitifully, held Kelly suspended in a fitful doze for much of the night. She could not escape the feeling she was somehow responsible, not only for their welfare, but also for the certain fate of all rhinos, yet she could do nothing but wallow in helplessness. She fell into a deep sleep towards dawn, only to be woken a short while later, first by the diesel motor on the generator starting, then by the truck as it left the complex with its noisy crew. She was still lying in bed when Juliette came in with a mug of coffee.

'No rush,' Juliette greeted brightly. 'We wanted to make an early start with the vehicles. You have half an hour.' She placed the mug on the bedside table and switched on the light. 'Frek has made you some sandwiches to take along. It could be a long day.'

They took off from the airstrip as soon as the trees at the end became visible.

From the air the lights of the two vehicles could be seen clearly a few miles away, weaving and dipping along the rough track. Tim flew low over the top to let them know he was airborne before climbing and heading north.

Encumbered with a large Thermos flask, a packet of sandwiches, a rifle, and the metal box containing darts and drugs, Kelly had little room to move in the front cockpit. By the time she had reorganised herself the stars had disappeared and the sky was grey. Within a few minutes she could see the individual trees clearly, but her view was obstructed by the lower wing. Only by sitting upright on the box and craning forward into the full blast of the icy wind could she hope to see anything smaller. She was relieved when, a short time after the sun had cleared the horizon, Tim landed on a clay-pan not far from the river they had been following.

'Rosie was headed this way,' he explained. 'Have some coffee while I take a quick look for her spoor. Maybe I can pick it up between here and the river.' He took the rifle, loaded a round into the chamber, then handed it back to her. 'Ever fired one of these?'

'Yes, my father taught me when he was still in the Air Force. Am I going to need it?'

'No, but it'll make you feel better. If you see anyone… or if an inquisitive elephant looks like it's going to give you a problem, fire a shot in the air and I'll come running.' He gave a reassuring smile. 'To save the damsel in distress.'

He showed her the safety-catch, then left, and she sat on the coping with the rifle propped alongside, sipping coffee and peering around at the silent bush, wondering what it concealed. Never a dull moment in Africa, she thought, but it made life exciting. The constant state of nervous awareness when alone in the bush sharpened the senses to every small sound that could herald danger. A constant adrenaline rush, then a sense of euphoric achievement afterwards.

Tim was back in twenty minutes, coughing and making plenty of noise, no doubt so she wouldn't take a nervous shot at him.

'Rosie passed close to the other side of the pan,' he reported. 'I think she's slowing down, although she doesn't seem to be browsing much. Maybe the calf is lagging. Not surprising. It's at least fifteen miles from here to Gara Pasi.'

'What do we do if we see her?' she asked, relieved that her nightmares about the calf being eaten alive had been in vain.

'We'll circle around in the plane and hope she'll be so confused about where the noise is coming from that she'll stay where she is.' He pulled a hopeful face. 'It works with sheep, but Rosie ain't no lamb. I may have to try turning her back.'

More alert now, and sitting on the drug box to get a better view ahead, it was Kelly who spotted Rosie less than a minute after taking off. She was trotting briskly, although with a heavy limp, the white Elastoplast encircling her leg a clear marker. The calf loped clumsily at her heels.

Kelly almost lost her goggles in her excitement. She knocked them from her forehead as she waved and pointed, then did lose them when Tim banked quickly to avoid flying directly over the top of the fleeing animals and she had to grab for the coping. Fortunately, the goggles landed in Tim's lap.

Rosie slowed down after they had circled her three times, turning and trotting aimlessly in several directions, ears forward and tail erect. Then she entered a thick tangle of bushes and disappeared from view.

Tim widened his circle and gained altitude, revealing the clay-pan they had recently left. Kelly noticed it was only about half a mile from where Rosie and her calf had gone to cover. It was a useful reference point, enabling her to keep Rosie's hiding place in sight.

They passed over the far edge of the pan, flying slowly with reduced power, and she heard Tim talking on the two-way, no doubt giving their position to John in the truck. It seemed as if it was not going to be such a long day after all.

Kelly was rewarding herself with a sandwich when the engine suddenly quit. The propeller, after windmilling for a few moments, stopped. She turned quickly to look at Tim in alarm, but he seemed unconcerned. He leaned forward to speak without shouting, his voice clear in the unnerving silence. 'Don't panic, I did it on purpose. I want to put down on the pan without chasing them off.'

With her mouth still full, Kelly nodded in understanding. What he was doing made good sense. The last place Rosie would have heard the sound of the plane was where they didn't want her to go. If they could land silently behind her, the chances were she would stay where she was. And power-off landings were a part of every pilot's basic training. They were perfectly positioned for gliding in to land on the pan. Still, she was relieved it wasn't an engine failure. She removed the box and settled onto her seat, tightening the harness, ready for a rough landing.

Tim side-slipped the last few hundred feet, reducing their speed further, and did a wheel landing on the far side, lowering the tail last to reduce the grinding noise made by the skid, then stopping close to the trees in one of his expertly controlled ground-loops. It was a masterly display of judgement and technique, and one she was reluctantly forced to admit she could not have done half as well. It made her more determined than ever to learn to fly like him if it was the last thing she did.

'What now?' she asked, after they had pulled the Moth tail first into the trees.

He stepped onto the wing and lifted out the drug box and rifle. 'Now we move. I want to get after Rosie before the truck arrives.'

'We're not going to wait?'

'No. John's only about ten miles away. He should be here in less than an hour. When Rosie hears the truck she'll run. I'm going to try getting a dart into her first.' He quickly replaced the bullet he had loaded earlier with another, shorter one, then placed a dart into the barrel extension, putting two spares in his breast pocket.

'What do you want me to do?' she asked.

'You can wait here if you like.'

'Don't you need me to carry the box of drugs?'

He observed her with the hint of a smile. 'Nervous?'

'Damn right.'

He chuckled. 'Okay, that may be a good idea, but first take off that red anorak, and stay well behind and keep quiet. Watch for my hand signals... and be ready to climb a tree if she comes your way.'

She did as he asked, thankful for the sleeveless denim shirt she wore under the anorak that matched her shorts. The temperature was already climbing with the sun. She replaced the balaclavas with the army jungle hat Juliette had given her.

They stayed with the trees, moving swiftly as they circled the pan, then slowly as they left it to approach the thick tangle of bushes where Rosie had concealed herself and the calf.

Hardly daring to breathe for fear that Rosie would hear the harsh, unsteady sound of it, or the beating of her heart, Kelly watched every step she took carefully, her eyes constantly moving from the ground to Tim and back.

When the fluttery alarm snort sounded from the dense thicket ahead, there was no need for a hand signal. Kelly stopped breathing altogether and jerked to a halt as if reaching the end of a tether. She stood frozen with heart thumping, glancing around for the nearest tree. She chose one of the gnarled ones within easy reach that had stout branches.

Tim had also stopped, but after a short pause began moving forward again, the rifle raised with the butt tucked into his shoulder, and Kelly edged closer to her tree.

With her eyes fixed on Tim, she did not feel the thin end of the dead branch underfoot, and when the other end suddenly shot up behind her with a rustle of dry leaves, she was taken by surprise. Half believing it was a snake, she jumped and spun around with a stifled gasp, her arm swinging wide, and the metal drug box in her hand smashed into the tree with a tinny clatter.

A furious snort followed, then a split second later came the dull explosion of the dart gun. Kelly turned again to see Rosie erupting from the thicket, her great bulk crashing through the tangle of bushes like a huge runaway boulder, charging directly at Tim, who stood only a few yards away with the gun still at his shoulder. He made to leap aside, but was too late.

Rosie struck him with her great head low, catching him on the legs and tossing him up and over her back as easily as if he were a sack of straw. She turned quickly to jab and poke and toss him again with her hornless raw nose, the red and white dart dangling from where it had lodged high on her head, flapping and bouncing as she hurled and ploughed Tim through the crackling grey bushes, crashing after him, and Kelly could only watch in helpless, silent horror, her scream locked in her throat.

With a furious squeal that chilled Kelly all the way through, Rosie threw Tim once more, arms and legs flailing, into a small tree, where he hung, limp and silent for several long moments before the slender branches finally gave way, depositing him on the ground.

Rosie's crashing departure and the alarmed calling of her calf had faded into silence before Kelly found the will to move.

Mortified by what she had done, and fearful of what she would find, she went reluctantly at first, then gave an anguished cry and ran to where he had fallen.

She stopped a few paces from him, shocked by what confronted her.

Tim lay on his back, one blood-splattered arm outflung, the other hidden beneath him. One leg was raised, his bare foot wedged between the forked trunk of the tree, while the other was twisted at an acute angle below the knee, broken.

Blood smeared nearly all of his exposed skin. It trickled from his mouth and nose, oozed from a gash on his neck, saturating his ripped shirt, which had been pulled up to his armpits to expose a lacerated, bloodied stomach

Glistening blood also coated much his legs, the raised one in particular, where gore from a wound on his thigh spread in a delta of crimson to his shorts, saturating them too.

He lay inert, with his mouth open and his eyes closed. And she could not see him breathing.

A croaking sound, half moan, half wail, escaped Kelly's lips. She took a faltering step forward, then threw herself on her knees beside him. 'Oh, God, Tim... I'm sorry.' She lifted her hands, wanting, needing to take control, to do something, but didn't know where to start. So much blood. Her mind whirled, causing a moment of dizziness, and she closed her eyes, clamping them tight until the moment passed, then she searched her brain for the emergency first aid procedure she had once known by heart.

The alphabet. That was it. A for airway, B for breathing… or was it bleeding? C for chest? Breathing, it had to be that first. Oh, Godrichardmackenziedirect. com…

She placed her hand lightly on his bared chest and lowered her head to listen at his mouth, but heard and felt nothing above the sound of her own harsh breathing and thudding in her ears. She held her breath and pressed closer, and her ear suddenly filled with warmth.

Relief flooded through her. 'Thank God, Tim, you're alive.' She said it louder, as if to reassure him as well as herself. 'You're going to be all right, darling. Jules will soon be here. You're going to be okay. Do you hear?'

What to do next? Make the patient comfortable was all she could think of.

She scrambled to her feet and lifted his foot carefully from the tree, placing it alongside the other, broken one, which she dared not move.

On her knees again, she rolled his body slightly to free the trapped arm, then pulled the other close until both rested at his sides. She lifted his head gently to brush away a clear spot for it, and noticed that one side, close to his temple, was red and swollen, his fair hair matted with blood.

Bleeding. She had to stop the bleeding. She surveyed his battered body in dismay. 'Oh, God, where... how?'

His chest was sticky with blood, some of it a different color, almost dry, and a large patch on his stomach was slimy with mucus, which puzzled her for a moment, then she realized it must have come from Rosie.

His entire torso was lacerated from sticks and thorns, and nearly all the cuts were bleeding, but the most blood came from the one on the side of his neck and the wound on the outside of his thigh. Both needed stitches, but for now she must stem the flow.

She ran back for the drug box, but all it contained was spare darts, bottles, tins and tubes with obscure labels, and two large veterinary syringes. No bandages, dressings, or anything suitable for use as a tourniquet. Bark string came to mind. She had watched one of the propeller boys making it to repair a catapult, rolling strands of the pale inner bark together on his hairless thigh, but she could see no similar saplings here, only the thorny bushes and twisted Mopani trees.

Tim's shirt was already ripped, but it was dusty and stained with both his and Rosie's blood. It could cause infection if she used it. She looked down at her own shirt.

She pulled it over her head and tried to rip it, but the denim was too tough. Feverishly, for Tim was still bleeding, she sought for a way. The tree. She pulled the hem of the garment taut and rubbed it furiously against the rough trunk until it frayed then, using a foot, she tugged and jerked until it ripped. She repeated the procedure several times, until she had torn it roughly into strips.

She did not have enough to make a compression bandage. She placed one strip loosely around his thigh above the wound and knotted it, then tightened it by placing a stick through the slack and winding it tight, and she was relieved to see the oozing blood slow and almost stop.

She hooked the end of the stick under the makeshift tourniquet to hold it in position, then turned her attention to his neck, placing a thick wad over the cut and holding it in position with another strip tied around his neck.

The remaining scraps of shirt she used for wiping

away the excess blood, searching for more wounds but, thankfully, most were superficial.

Water would have been useful, especially for cleaning the dirt from the wounds, but it was in the plane, almost half a mile away, and even if she dared leave him, she was not sure if she could find it. She knew the rough direction, but the area was flat, with every tree looking the same. If she became lost they could both perish.

Thinking about that brought other fears. But the truck could not be that far away now. It was their only hope, although how could she expect John to find them? She may hear the vehicle, but what could she do to attract their attention in return? Then she remembered the rifle. She could fire a shot. That would do it.

She found the two spare darts that had been in Tim's pocket, their red and white flights making them easy to see, but the rifle, when she saw it lying under a trampled bush, made her heart sink. Rosie must have stood on it. The stock had splintered and the barrel was bent where it joined the breech.

Seeing it lying there, useless, brought yet another fear. It was their only protection, and hyenas, she had heard, could smell blood a mile away. A pack of them, John had told her, would chase a pride of lions off a kill if they were hungry enough, and they would eat practically anything, including sealed cans of meat.

The only other solution she could think of was fire, and she searched through Tim's pockets, but they revealed no matches or lighter.

In desperation, she gathered the darts and arranged them, along with the open drug box, within easy reach. If hyenas came she would throw the darts. If that didn't work she would throw them the bottles and tubes. Maybe they would eat them and poison themselves.

With nothing more she could do but wait, Kelly cleared a spot for herself beside Tim and gently lifted his head to rest on her lap. She aligned her body to shield his face from the sun, which had now risen above the short vegetation, and even at this early hour she could feel its warmth on the exposed skin of her back.

Tim groaned as she moved him, and she studied his face for further signs of awakening. He could tell her what to do. But his eyes remained closed, his breathing soft but steady.

He looked so young lying there, his nose scant inches from her naked breasts. So helpless, yet strangely, she still felt protected by his presence. She removed her hat and placed it over the wound on his thigh, then looked around at the ominously silent bush. She began to sing quietly, to buoy her spirits, and in the hope her voice would penetrate the darkness and bring him around. 'Oh, oh, oh, oh, stayin' alive, stayin' alive…' She stopped. That didn't seem appropriate somehow. She began again, croakily. 'If you're going… to San Fran… cisco, be sure to wear some flowers in your hair…' She stopped again. 'Oh, God, Tim…'

She plucked fragments of dry leaf and twigs from his blood-matted hair, then licked her thumb and wiped away the remaining dried blood from the corner of his lip and his nose. She did the same for his brow and, more tenderly, his temple, which began to worry her. The swelling had increased.

She glanced at her watch. Eight thirty five. The hour Tim had estimated it would take the truck to reach them had come and gone, and almost another half on top of that.

But the truck would find them, she was sure. They would reach the clay-pan and see the plane. They had a truckload of experienced trackers. Kawaseka would follow and find them… or she didn't know what she would do.

***

Kawaseka thumped urgently on the roof of the cab and John Singleton braked the Isuzu quickly. 'What is it?' he called, poking his head from the open window.

'Spoor of the chipimbiri, mambo.'

Kawaseka jumped from the rear of the truck and walked a short distance back along the road, holding up an officious palm to halt Juliette in the Landrover trailing behind. He stooped to examine the signs they had passed over, then followed them into the scrub before stopping to break a small branch from a bush.

He returned with it to where John and Juliette waited near the vehicles. 'Gazi, blood,' he reported, pointing out several dark streaks on the leaves. He smeared them with his thumb to show it was still fresh. 'from the head of the chipimbiri. It must to come from the dart.'

'Are you sure?' John queried.

Kawaseka face took on an expression of bemused disbelief. 'Did not the Nkosi Tim call with the roger-roger from the flying machine to report a meeting with the chipimbiri?'

'Yes, but…'

'Also, I think to hear a sound of the gun when we make a short-cut by the hill, only the truck she is making too much noise to be sure. Best I follow.'

John was thoughtful. 'And you are sure the blood is from the head?'

'Ndio, yes. Less than one hour, I think so.'

'It is from the same chipimbiri we are looking for?'

Kawaseka turned his head aside so as not to give the question too much importance. He waved his hand vaguely in the direction he had checked. 'The small spoor of the umfaan chipimbiri is there also.'

John opened his mouth to say something, then changed his mind.

'Maybe if we backtrack,' Juliette suggested. 'If Tim darted her he may be following and we should meet up with him.'

John demurred. 'I think he'd be more likely to get in the plane and contact us on the two-way.'

'Can't we call him instead and find out?'

'We can give it a go, but if he's still on the ground it will be switched off.'

After trying for several minutes to raise Tim on the radio, John gave up. 'Either he's following, or he's waiting.'

Juliette frowned thoughtfully. 'I can't see Tim waiting around for too long.' She paused for a moment. 'Look, why don't you go on, like Kawaseka suggests, and leave me here to wait. If he's right and she has been darted, she could be down already, so you need to get to her as soon as possible. And if she hasn't, you have the other rifle and enough darts with you, so you can keep on her trail.'

John nodded. 'Just as well someone around here has brains. I'll leave Mathias with you. Keep your ears open. If I find her down I'll fire off three spaced rounds, and when you meet up with Tim, get Mathias to do the same.' He turned to Kawaseka. 'Okay, hotshot, away you go.'

Juliette began doubting the wisdom of her plan not long after the slowly grinding Isuzu was out of sight. Mathias was not the most competent of trackers, and the previously sandy ground had become hard and shaly. While he meandered back and forth with his head down, shaking it negatively and all too frequently, she idled slowly behind in first gear, stopping often, and she worried that Mathias may wander too far off the spoor and that Tim and Kelly would pass by unnoticed.

After nearly an hour had elapsed and they still had not progressed more than five hundred yards, Juliette switched off the engine and went to look for herself, but she was an even worse tracker than Mathias, seeing nothing but ants.

'Where is the last place that you were sure?' she asked, and when Mathias pointed sheepishly to a fallen tree some two hundred yards back, Juliette made another decision. 'I'm going back to wait there,' she told him. 'When you are certain you have found something, give me a whistle. I'll beep the horn every ten minutes.' She gave two short blasts to demonstrate, then turned the vehicle around and returned to park in the shade close to the fallen tree. With the engine off, she would hear John's signal shots, and beeping the horn periodically would also alert Tim and Kelly if they were anywhere in the vicinity.

Satisfied she was doing the right thing, and that no one was likely to get lost, and after verifying for herself that Rosie had indeed left tracks where Mathias had said they were, Juliette settled back in her seat to wait.

***

Elliot Gumbo removed his boot to inspect the swollen ankle in disgust. It did not seem fair that so many bad things could happen in so short a time. First the gold lighter, then two of his stupid men getting lost, which had forced him to change his plan. Then the aeroplane, which he was sure had been searching for him with its special instruments that could see in the dark, followed soon after by the truck he had assumed was full of soldiers or police, and from which he had run, sliding down the steep hill and twisting his stupid ankle on the even more stupid log. The only good thing of the night was that he, and not any of his men, had the horn.

Elliot consoled himself with that thought while he massaged his aching foot. His plan had been so brilliant that he had even surprised himself. It had been as easy as letting goats out of a pen. Easier, for the chipimbiri had needed no chasing or enticing. It had charged into the door of the cage as soon as they had cut the ropes and lowered it, moving the cage back several inches and making it easier for them to shift it some more with the poles.

And the beast had continued to help them all the way until it had pushed through. That must have been when he lost the lighter, hurrying to climb the poles and get out of the way. Now he had a half packet of Madison with nothing to light them.

Elliot removed his other boot, tied the laces of both together, then slung them around his neck. 'Give me a push,' he ordered Sibanda, his one remaining man, holding out the strong stick he had been using for a crutch.

When he had been hauled to his feet, Elliot took a few experimental steps, wincing at each one. It was going to be a long and painful walk, even going directly to the border, which he had hoped to avoid. This park was his territory now, and he did not want to leave his footprints all over it. He needed to be cautious.

With his rifle on one shoulder, and the bag containing the horn slung on the other, Elliot was about to take his third step when the sudden blast of a car horn made him jump with alarm. He stumbled forward onto his hands and knees.

'Uh! Jesus…'

His companion threw himself down in a defensive position, cocking his rifle with a loud metallic clatter and pointing it in the direction from which the sound had come.

'Be quiet!' Elliot hissed.

Faintly in the silence, they heard an engine start, then listened as it drove away slowly. It stopped again, and they stared at each other in puzzlement.

'Is it the police?' Sibanda asked anxiously.

Elliot shrugged. 'Must I be the one to know everything? We must wait and listen.'

When the horn sounded twice again, but with no sound of an engine, Elliot's bewilderment turned to impatience. The more he delayed, the greater the chance someone would find their tracks.

'You must go carefully to see what is it,' he instructed Sibanda. 'I will stay here with my foot for fear of making a noise with it.'

Sibanda looked at him in alarm. 'Myself?'

'Of course. Were you not a soldier? If you are seen you can run.'

'Yes. I am not afraid for me. But what of you?'

'If you must run, then you must not come here. You must go...' Elliot looked up at the sun for confirmation, '... that way.' He pointed to the southeast, a direction well away from his own intended escape route.

With a droop to his lower lip suspiciously reminiscent of a pout, Sibanda removed his hockey boots and, after some deliberation, tied them together and looped them around his neck in the same manner as Elliot. He began moving stealthily, only to fall flat again when the horn sounded for the third time.

'Go, go,' Elliot encouraged.

The horn sounded once more before Sibanda returned.

'A white woman by herself in a Landrover of the rangers,' he reported, looking pleased with himself. 'She looks to be waiting for a person to come.'

'I see.' Elliot smiled with relief. 'And you did not think to catch her? Anyway,' he continued quickly, not sure that would have been a good idea. 'If she is only one by herself, we can order a lift.' He ignored Sibanda's surprised look and waved him on before he could object. 'Show me.'

They approached the green Landrover from a

slightly different direction than the one previously taken by Sibanda, being sure to keep out of view of the woman sitting in the driver's seat, and it was pure luck that caused Elliot to glance to the side and see the game scout not fifty yards away, coming slowly towards them with his head down.

'Psst!' Elliot caught Sibanda by the sleeve and pulled him low, pointing to the scout, who seemed to be following something. It could not be them, Elliot realized with relief, for they had not come that way, but still they were in danger of being seen very soon. And the scout had a rifle resting on his shoulder, holding it by the barrel. The same kind as those the Rhodesian soldiers had used in the war. A big, high-powered semi-automatic with a long barrel. The sort of weapon with which one could more easily kill chipimbiri than the short AK he carried. The calibre was the same, but the bullets were much longer, which meant he would be able to shoot more cautiously from twice the distance. It would be a nice prize, such a weapon.

'We can kill him easily by shooting,' Sibanda whispered close to Elliot's ear.

Elliot shook his head vehemently. 'The shooting will be heard by the woman and she will drive away. We must wait and catch him.'

It was even easier than letting the chipimbiri out of

the boma. With his eyes lowered, looking at the ground and concentrating on what was there, the scout did not see them until Elliot stood from behind the bush and pointed his rifle directly at the man's head from only a few paces away. The scout jerked back as if he had been poked in the stomach with it.

'Fall down quickly on the ground!' Elliot commanded in a harsh whisper and, as the shocked scout lowered himself slowly, Elliot stepped forward to relieve him of the prize. 'Thank you,' he said politely. 'Whose spoor is it you follow?'

The scout cleared his throat before answering huskily. 'Chipimbiri.'

'I see. And who is it in the Landrover?'

The man took a while longer to answer, glancing warily at Sibanda, who stood looking down aggressively at him with his gun pointed at his nose. 'The doctor from Gara Pasi.'

'I see. And why does she make noise on the hooter?'

'To tell me where she is.'

Elliot sniggered. 'You don't know the place where you are?'

The scout shrugged, remaining silent, and Elliot ordered him up with his new rifle. 'Come, we must see the doctor. Walk in front.'

'What are you going to do?'

Elliot cocked his weapon with a flourish and chuckled. 'Who can tell? Maybe I have some practise with my new gun.'

***

Kelly listened hard, waiting for the foreign sound that had penetrated her drowsiness to repeat itself. But heard nothing above the cooing of the doves. It was also hard to concentrate. The aching in her legs had subsided into numbness, but the stinging on her naked back from the relentless beat of the sun was becoming unbearable. She tried to avoid looking at the shade on the other side of the tree. It may as well have been on the other side of Africa.

She could not move Tim, but she could move herself, she thought, and began edging her way around his head, lifting it with each small shift until she was facing into the sun. He groaned twice during the exercise, his eyelids fluttering, and each time she paused hopefully, but they remained closed.

She placed her hat over his face to protect it, then cautiously straightened her legs to ease the cramps, lying back on her elbows with eyes closed to enjoy, for a few moments at least, the sun on her front.

For the next ten minutes - which she monitored carefully on her watch bezel so as not to miss the deadline for the next loosening of the tourniquet - she tried to imagine she was sunbathing nude on the top of the Seabee, as she had so often during the Californian summer, flying into an isolated cove and anchoring there with fishing lines out, novel in hand, and ice-box full of goodies at her side.

She could be there now had she not weakened and gone to see her father. Of course, then she would have missed Africa, and she wouldn't have missed it for anything, so perhaps she had done the right thing. Except for this experience. This bit she could well have done without.

When the time was up, Kelly shifted aside the small leafy branches she had gathered to shade the thigh wound and keep the fat, ugly blue flies at bay, then removed the useless scrap of blood saturated denim covering the gash. It needed to be replaced, or to have some clean padding beneath it.

She pondered the problem for a few moments, then removed her boots to inspect her socks. They were not exactly clean, and were also damp with sweat. She could think of only one other article of clothing.

Carefully, she extricated her legs from under Tim's head, then stood to unbutton and lower her shorts, permitting herself an ironical smile as she stepped out of them. Removing her knickers for Tim was becoming a habit.

Folded into a pad, the red cotton panties were ideal. She replaced her shorts then tentatively loosened the tourniquet, allowing the wound to bleed. It began to ooze dark blood immediately, and she waited for it to run clear, giving it a full minute before re-tightening then binding on the new pad.

His leg worried her the most. She didn't like the swelling, both at the wound, and around the break lower down. If the truck didn't come soon she would have to do something about it. The swelling was only going to get worse, and she wondered if it wouldn't be a good idea to try and straighten the leg and splint it somehow while he was still unconscious and wouldn't feel the pain.

Or would he? Maybe it would bring him around. She decided she would do it if the truck didn't come in the next twenty minutes, which was another two loosenings of the tourniquet.

The neck wound was not so bad, the blood beginning to congeal under the wad of cloth, sticking to it as she carefully lifted the corner, so she left it in place.

She put on her boots, replaced the branches

and checked her watch again to mark the time, then removed the hat from his face and leaned forward to shield it with her body, using her hands to further screen it from the flies, and also to protect her breasts from sunburn. It brought her left nipple close to his nose, almost touching it. If he woke now it would give him a shock, and she smiled at the thought.

It came again, two faint, but unmistakable beeps from a car horn, as clear in the still morning as the sounding of a distant bugle, and Kelly sat up quickly, alert and certain. Thank God! They were here! Wonderful Doctor Juliette was close, letting her know she was coming.

Kelly's fears evaporated instantly, tired blood pumping furiously. No more worries about wild animals or having to straighten his leg. The cavalry was about to arrive.

***

'We wish very much for you to help us with a lift to the border,' Elliot said to the surprised woman. He smiled politely, not threatening too much, and shifted the AK slung on his shoulder farther to his back, keeping most of it hidden, and pleased now that he had thought to return the scout's rifle - minus its ammunition, which now weighed comfortingly in his trouser pocket.

He did not want to alarm the woman unnecessarily. Too many repercussions could follow, but it was also important that she feel threatened enough not to refuse his reasonable request. 'As you can see of my foot. It is very bad for walking such a long way.'

She took a while to answer, her eyes moving slowly over his body, including his foot, missing nothing, and Elliot began to fidget nervously, wondering if she recognised him, as he did her, from the day of the operation on the chipimbiri. Maybe a more direct approach was going to be necessary.

'Where is the scout?' she asked finally.

'He is there, talking with my friend.' Elliot replied, indicating to where he had left Sibanda in charge of the scout, well out of her view. 'We find him on the spoor of the chipimbiri and ask for help in finding our way. We become lost and wish to return to Mozambique.' She did not look too convinced, perhaps because of the guns, and Elliot had a flash of inspiration. 'We search for some very dangerous men who are also poachers.'

'Oh?'

'Will you not help me?'

She hesitated, and Elliot shifted impatiently on his sore foot, scowling, then she nodded. 'Very well, I will take you as far as I can, but Mathias must sit in the front. It will be best for you to lie in the back with your injured foot raised.'

Elliot grinned. 'Thank you, madam, we are very happy for your help.'

'Don't mention it,' she responded quietly.

***

The soft, barely discernible breeze that cooled the perspiration on Kelly's skin, brought relief of another kind; the sound of a moving vehicle. The cavalry had taken longer than expected, and she disentangled herself from Tim once again to stand and welcome it, stretching and flexing her stiff limbs in readiness as she peered hopefully through the trees for the first glimpse, preparing herself to run towards it and show the way.

It took some while, long after the sound had dwindled and she had screamed herself hoarse trying to call it back, before she was able to accept that they were not coming.

Somehow, they had managed, even with two vehicles, several trackers, and the knowledge of where to go, to have taken the wrong direction. Had they only gone to the clay-pan behind her, which they were supposed to do, they could not have failed.

Kelly's disappointment turned to anger and frustration. She hurled her hat, which she had been holding in preparation for covering herself as she ran, onto the ground. 'Stupid! Stupid! Stupid!' She stomped, then kicked the hat into the bushes, preparing to follow it up with further, more colorful abuse, when the sound of three rifle shots stopped her foot in mid-swing, causing her to stumble noisily as she tried to listen.

They had sounded distant - miles away - and in the wrong direction, but were unmistakable. She listened for more, but none came, and she wondered at the reason for them as she strode around in agitation. It made no sense.

She retrieved her hat and returned to look down at Tim. 'It seems as if we're on our own,' she told him grimly. She glanced at her watch. 'We'll give them ten more minutes, then I'm going to splint that leg, okay?'

She placed her hat under his head, then searched for more leafy branches to shield him, jerking on them angrily until they ripped free.

She was going to need binding for the splints. Thankfully, his khaki shirt buttoned down the front, so it was not too difficult to remove. She eased a few of the smaller, more leafy branches, beneath his naked back, then ripped the shirt into strips as she had done with her own. Finally, she searched for three short sticks that were straight and strong.

Twenty minutes had elapsed by the time she was ready. She eased the tourniquet again, then stood above the broken leg, observing it with the same uncertainty she would a stunned but very much alive snake.

But she had to do it. If no one came she would have to move him, even if it meant dragging him on a makeshift litter. She had no intention of spending the night there, and to move him with his leg dangling loose could cause irreparable damage.

'Get on with it, Kelly,' she muttered. She knelt astride the leg, her sticks and strips of cloth ready at her side.

The break was halfway between the ankle and knee, so at least she had space either side to tie the splint. That would be the easy bit. Aligning the break was going to be more difficult. The lower part of the leg was not only turned, but also jutted out at an angle. She would have to twist and straighten at the same time. And also pull down a little, she reminded herself, as if it was on an elastic and needed to be stretched before it would spring back into place.

Wishing she had done it earlier, before the swelling, and praying she was doing the right thing and was not about to cause more damage, she placed her hands on his leg, moving them into several different locations before she was satisfied. She took three deep breaths, then, biting on her lip, she straightened, pulled and twisted the leg roughly back into place.

She held it there against the jerking spasms of muscles and the twitching of nerves, both hands clasped firmly around his calf, as if it were a writhing snake she was restraining, feeling the live heat of it, and she closed her eyes against the reality, against the cold sweat that prickled on her forehead, and she gnawed on her lip as Tim gave several long, anguished groans.

Her fingers felt like miniature wooden extensions of the splints as she fixed them in position, placing as many of the small unusable scraps, including her socks, between the rough timber and his skin before binding the sticks in place.

She straightened to inspect her work and wipe sweat from her brow with the back of a shaky hand. 'Thank God that's over,' she breathed, and was about to move when more firing sounded in the distance and she stopped to listen. It was not the same as before. This was automatic fire, several short bursts, followed by one long one, then silence. Even the doves had paused to listen.

When no further shots came she returned her attention to the more urgent problem of Tim.

Speculating was a waste of time.

His breathing had changed. From steady and shallow, it had become quick and rasping, interspersed with short groans, and his tanned face had taken on a flat, grey color. 'Sorry, Tim, you felt that, didn't you?'

Leaning over him to block the sun, she wiped clammy beads of sweat from his brow, and his eyes fluttered open.

For a few moments they were unseeing, flickering, rolling and blinking, and she put a hand to his cheek, turning his face towards her. The blinking stopped and his eyes narrowed, focusing, and she saw her shadowy image in them. 'Hi,' she said, smiling.

He blinked some more, the tip of his tongue appearing to moisten his dry lips, and he croaked something unintelligible. His lids came down and he drew in several shuddering breaths, a pained expression on his face. 'What...?' He opened his eyes again, alarm showing in them, and he tried to move his head to look around, but she held it firm.

'It's all right. You're okay, just keep still. You have a few cuts and a broken leg.'

He swallowed and moistened his lips again. 'My stomach...' He coughed dryly, his face screwing in pain. 'It hurts...'

'Your stomach?' She turned her head to inspect

it. Apart from smeared dry blood and a few blotches, she could see no major problem. 'It looks okay on the outside. Maybe a little bruised. How about your head? You have a bit of a bump on the side.'

He raised himself onto his elbows. 'Have to get up...' He shook his head groggily. Bloody hell...'

'Maybe you shouldn't.' He struggled to sit, and she placed a hand behind his shoulders to help. 'Be careful of your neck, you have a cut, but I think the bleeding has stopped now.'

He felt it gingerly. Then he saw his leg; the splints and the tourniquet. 'Oh, shit...'

'I had to,' she said, 'you were bleeding... still are. I'll have to loosen it soon. And your leg was bent. Sorry if it hurt.'

He grimaced, then looked at her with a puzzled frown. 'How long have I...? He stopped. 'I thought I'd had it... that bloody rhino.'

'God, Tim, I was petrified. I'm sorry for what happened. I didn't know...'

'No. I was closer than I thought. She scented me... the bitch. Lucky she didn't have her front horn.' He glanced at the sun, squinting. 'How long was I out?'

Kelly studied her watch. 'About two hours. I've been waiting for the truck. It hasn't come.'

He looked at her, intently, with a puzzled frown,

his eyes lowering briefly before turning again to the splints and denim strips binding his wound, and Kelly folded her arms across her naked breasts, suddenly conscious of them, although she had promised herself she would try to act natural. It was not as though she had a choice.

'You used your shirt,' he said matter-of-factly.

'And yours. There was nothing else.'

He looked at her again with a small smile. 'You did well, Kelly. Thanks.'

The smile and the compliment, the relief of seeing him awake and taking control of her uncertainty and fears was too much for Kelly. It began as a returning smile, but something went wrong in the forming of it. Without warning, it suddenly turned inwards, caught in her throat, and exploded from her nose in a mixture between a sob and a snort. She covered her face with both hands. 'Oh, goddam it, Tim... I thought you were dead.'

'Not me, Kelly.' He laid a consoling hand on her bowed head, caressing. 'Come on, we have to get in the shade, you're getting burnt to hell. If you take the weight of my leg I'll pull myself along.'

It took much less time than she had expected. He grimaced and grunted, panting with the pain, but within two minutes it was over.

When she had made him comfortable with his back against the tree, and he had caught his breath, she sat to whisk at flies with her leafy branch, and told him all that had happened while he had been unconscious, and he listened without interruption until she mentioned the three shots and the bursts of automatic firing.

'Automatic?' He frowned. 'Are you sure?'

'Absolutely. Sounds just like on TV.'

'The three shots I can understand. It was a signal. It's what we usually do when trying to locate each other. Turn around twice out here and you're lost. But the automatic, I don't know. None of the game scouts would dare fire in rock and roll mode. John would have their skins tanned and nailed to a wall.'

'What about the beeping horn? It had the same tinny sound as the Landrover, and was much closer than the shots.'

'It's anybody's guess, but I'm hoping it was not a contact with poachers. And that bloody Rosie… she'll be well and truly under by now.'

'So what do we do? We can't wait around here. You need attention.'

He thought about it for a while. 'You're right. Sitting around here is getting us nowhere. John and Jules could have their hands full. You'll have to fly me out.'

She nodded. 'I thought of that, but how do we get to the plane? Must I whistle for it, or just click my fingers?'

'Sorry… you'll have to be my crutch.'

Kelly observed him silently. She could think of several strong objections to the idea, but they had no choice. 'I think you'll need a stick as well.'

She went to get the strong one she had kept beside her for protection, then stood before him, adopting a lifting stance and holding the stick so he could grip with both hands. 'Ready when you are,' she said.

He rose unsteadily, hopping to keep his balance, tottering, and she let go of the stick to support him, staggering against his weight, clinging to him with both arms clasped around, and acutely aware of her naked breasts pressing firmly against his bare chest. 'I didn't know you cared,' he joked.

'Never mind about that.' She placed an arm around his waist, trying to avoid the scrapes and bruises. 'Ready?'

With the stick in one hand, his other arm across her back and gripping her shoulder, he took a few deep breaths and nodded. 'Let's do it.'

They hobbled forward, awkwardly at first, then gradually finding a rhythm, but it was slow and agonising for them both.

'It's getting to be a thing… this, isn't it?'

'What is?'

'Taking our clothes off in the bush.' He tried to laugh, but the pain was too much, turning it into a silent grimace.

'Don't you ever give up?'

'Today… I will…'

Tim's hand on her scorched shoulder felt like it was gloved in sandpaper, but it must have been as nothing compared to his own agony, and her heart went out to him.

They divided the ordeal into segments of twenty steps, resting briefly after each one, and thinking only of achieving the next. Tim gasped and grunted, every muscle trembling with strain but, as before, he made no complaint, and Kelly wondered how she could ever have been so wrong. Perhaps next time she would not refuse.

He tried to make light conversation, asking inane questions about her past, to take his mind off the pain, she surmised, but they were so broken and interspersed with heavy grunts and panting that they made little sense, and she eventually had to order him to be quiet and save his breath.

He knew exactly where they were. Kelly saw the occasional footprint they had left on the way in, then he pointed out a new direction, a shortcut, he explained. No need to circle the pan now, they could cut straight across.

When they reached it she suggested he wait there while she brought the plane. Blood from his thigh wound covered most of his lower leg now, saturating the splint and even running between his toes, but he refused. 'Just getting the hang of it,' he wheezed. 'Can't feel much anyway… now. May as well… finish.'

Getting him into the rear cockpit the right way up was like trying to thread frayed rope through a needle. Luckily, she had flown the Moth from the front passenger cockpit, and not the rear, which was closer, and therefore that much easier to get him into.

She had to climb in first so she could support and guide his injured leg over the seat, while he sat on the coping and tried to lower himself down, but his tired arms wouldn't support the angle and he eventually had to let go and fall.

Forced to release his leg, it slipped down between her own and crashed to the floor, and she suddenly found herself on his lap, straddling, and trying to prevent him from slipping all the way down.

With his face smothered between her breasts, she hoisted him up by lifting under his arms, gaining leverage from her knees. If only they could see us now, she thought, and released him to push herself back and look down at him.

'Are you okay?' she asked anxiously.

He squinted back at her with a weak grin. 'Can we save it for later... when I'm feeling more up to it?'

'Only if you're a good boy and do as you're told. Hold on, we're almost there... just get you strapped in... somehow.'

'They tho nithen... thoft,' he mumbled incoherently, and passed out.

'Goddam it, Tim, not now! How the hell... what direction do I go... Tim?' She shook him gently, but he did not respond, his head lolling.

Kelly disentangled herself and made him as comfortable as possible, then climbed from the cockpit to lean into hers for the water bottle. She splashed some of the lukewarm liquid into her cupped hand and washed his face, then dribbled some between his lips before taking a few long gulps herself.

He groaned and came to groggily as she was putting on the anorak. 'Thank God,' she breathed. 'Tim... can you hear me? Where do I go... what direction?'

He stared woozily at her for a moment, then mumbled something she couldn't understand before closing his eyes again, apparently going back to sleep. His lethargy worried her. He had lost too much blood.

About all she knew of their position was that it was close to the eastern boundary, so she had to fly west to find civilisation. She hoped it wasn't so far that they'd run out of fuel before reaching it. The two-way radio was bolted into the rear cockpit, the microphone cord not long enough to reach the front. She tried calling on it several times, even resorting to the emergency mayday procedure, but received only static in return.

Thankfully, the Moth was already facing into the pan, so she did not have to lift the tail and turn it around with Tim's weight in the back. She gave the primer two pumps and cracked open the throttle, then ran around the wing to the propeller, standing behind it as she had seen Tim doing it. The engine roared into life on the second swing, but didn't settle to a reassuring idle as she had expected. The roar continued, and the Moth trundled forward, the lower wing catching her unexpectedly behind the legs and toppling her backwards. She grabbed at the stay wires, missing them, and slid over the wing on her back, falling off the trailing edge to land awkwardly on her naked shoulders with her legs in the air.

She scrambled hastily to her feet, losing one boot in the process, and attempted to halt the plane by putting her weight on the tail, but the only result was to make the Moth turn, swinging it towards a tree.

She pushed hard sideways, turning it around in almost a full circle, until it was moving once more into the open pan. She kicked the other boot off and sprinted to catch up, hoisting herself on and leaning in to pull back the throttle, which must have been knocked forward during her struggles with Tim.

The Moth slowed and she scrambled, panting, into the front cockpit, wrestling with harness as she taxied around in a circle, looking at the rising dust for a clue to the wind direction, but it revealed nothing, swirling around in the propeller wash.

Trusting to luck, she lined up with the longest stretch of pan and pushed the throttle all the way forward to the stop.

***

When Juliette heard the first of John's anxiously awaited signal shots, she reacted instantly, allowing the foot she had resting on the partly depressed clutch to slide off so the pedal banged against the stop. At the same time she revved the engine and grated the gears, steering towards the branches of a fallen Mopani tree, bumping over them to raise a clatter in the rear and further distract her two unwelcome passengers.

'Sorry,' she yelled, 'this vehicle needs repairing.

The gears keep jumping out and the steering is faulty.'

Only a series of surprised exclamations consistent with soft flesh coming in sudden contact with hard metal answered, reassuring her that, like herself, they had not heard the other two shots, and were unaware that she was now heading in the approximate direction they had sounded. Juliette relaxed, steering away from the rough ground and weaving between the trees.

She had not believed the ridiculous story for a moment. The leader was too smarmy, and his companion too sullen. And Mathias's attitude was disturbing. He sat rigidly with his rifle clamped between his knees, staring straight ahead and not talking to the men as he would normally have done.

Also, she was positive that Mozambique had no anti-poaching force on the border or she would have heard about it. They were either bandits or two of the new breed of poachers John had been talking about, and she believed the second of the two possibilities more likely.

The bag the leader clung to as if it contained the crown jewels had a familiar carrion stench about it. They could well be part of the group that had freed Rosie and stolen her horn. If so, she was determined they were not going to get away with it. If she was wrong and they were legitimate, no harm would be done. She'd simply make up some story and give them a lift to the border as requested.

Juliette further occupied her passengers with a barrage of trivial chatter, talking about the poor rains and crops, the famine in Mozambique, and the high cost of spare parts and petrol. She refrained from the touchy subjects of politics and poaching, and she kept a sharp lookout through the dusty windscreen for the first glimpse of the Isuzu.

When she saw the green cab glinting ahead and a little off to the left, she veered slightly to block any view from the rear. She glanced at Mathias to see if he had also noticed, but his gaze was still fixed stonily ahead. Juliette moved her foot across to nudge him on the ankle. He started nervously, turning to stare at her, and she spoke quietly without looking at him. 'Get ready.'

A small but fairly dense grove provided the opportunity Juliette had been waiting for. With her right hand already on the door handle, she swung the vehicle towards the nearest tree, gave a blast on the horn, and jumped out.

The Landrover struck the tree and came to a shuddering halt, stalling, and hurling its startled passengers forward in a tangle. Their surprised shouts followed Juliette as she ran, crouched low, around the front of the truck towards the grove, with Mathias close on her heels.

She sprawled behind a bush. 'Quick, Mathias,' she gasped. 'Fire a shot over their heads... order them to stay where they are.'

'No, madam!' Mathias grabbed her by the upper arm and pulled her roughly to her feet. 'We must run. I have no bullets.'

'What...?'

'They take them.' He shoved her forward. 'Please... keep running.'

'God almighty...'

More shouts, then a burst of automatic fire that crackled overhead and showered them with leaves and bark was all the further persuading Juliette needed. She ran towards the Isuzu on feet that barely touched the ground, leaping over logs and bushes, swerving around the trees, and Mathias pounded close behind with his useless rifle.

A second volley came from behind, then shouts from ahead, and Juliette's racing heart rejoiced at the sight of John running towards her with his rifle. Behind him came the other scout, also with a weapon. She stumbled to a halt and flung herself down behind a tree to wait for them, and Mathias did the same, sitting on the ground with his head resting on raised knees.

'What the hell's going on?' John demanded, falling beside Juliette and placing a protective arm around her shoulders. 'Are you okay, sweetie? What happened?'

'Two... two of them,' Juliette panted, 'hijacked us... back there... where I was waiting.'

'The bastards! Come on, you two,' he ordered the scouts, 'let's go get them.' He jumped up to go, but Juliette stopped him.

'No, wait! Mathias has no bullets.'

'No What?' John lowered himself to glare at the sheepish Mathias, but Juliette again intervened, explaining breathlessly what had occurred and what she suspected, and a shattered Mathias filled in the gaps.

As they spoke, John studied the stretch of bush between them and the vehicle, expecting a follow-up attack, but it remained silent and empty.

'I think they've buggered off,' he said.

By then, most of the crew had arrived to add their questions, and John allowed them a few minutes of noisy conjecture before sending them back to continue loading Rosie on the sled. The other scout gave Mathias a full magazine and John ordered him to stay with Juliette.

'They won't get far if one has a sprained ankle,'

he said to Juliette. 'I'll check the Landrover on the way past. I'll have to leave you to supervise the loading of Rosie and her calf, if you're feeling up to it...'

She nodded, and he explained quickly what still needed to be done, anxious to be gone. 'Be careful,' she called after him.

The only visible damage to the vehicle was a slight dent in the front bumper where it had collided with the tree. John started and reversed it while Kawaseka and the scout picked up the tracks of the two men.

One of them, Kawaseka explained, had been running, and the other limping with a stick, not travelling together. It was good news. At least they were certain to get the crippled one.

They saw him only a few minutes later, standing in the open, but close enough to a tree to dive for cover. His hands were raised in surrender and, as John drew nearer, his rifle at the ready, he saw the AK lying on the ground at the man's feet.

'Move back,' he ordered, and when the man had hobbled away, he picked up the weapon and inspected it, removing the plug of four-by-two from the barrel to sniff. It had not been fired. 'Well, that's something in your favour at least,' John said.

'Yes, of course!' the hijacker answered indignantly. 'You think I am the one to shoot a woman? Uh! Not me, sir. It is the stupid person who runned away. He is the one, for sure.'

'Who are you and what are you doing here?' John demanded.

'I am a patrol for the Mozambique poaching, sir. We become lost and ask the kind lady for a lift because of my foot.' He lifted it for inspection. 'I think it is broken, for sure.'

'Don't give me any of your bullshit. Mozambique doesn't have a poaching patrol. Where is the bag?'

'Sir?' He looked more startled than puzzled.

'The bag you were carrying,' John repeated menacingly.

'Uh! The bag. Of course, I think it is taken by the one who runned away.'

'Oh, really.' John turned to Kawaseka. 'Have a look around, Seki, see if you can find it.'

It took only a few minutes to locate the bag where it had been hastily concealed under a rotten log.

'Runned away, hey? Didn't get very far, did it?' John emptied the bag to reveal the horn. 'You're in big trouble, my friend.'

Faking surprise, the man bent over to inspect it, shaking his head and clicking his tongue. 'That is not my bag, sir. This thing is not belonging to me.'

'At least you got that part right,' John said.

With their sulking captive once more resting his foot in the rear of the Landrover, John drove back to the Isuzu. Having recovered the horn, he had decided against going after the other, trigger-happy, poacher. It could have taken hours, and Rosie needed to be moved quickly, before more booster drugging was required. She had been given more than he was happy with already. And he was also concerned that they had not seen or heard anything from Tim and Kelly.

After the curious crew had inspected and commented scathingly on the captive, and Mathias had berated him angrily for the threats he had received and the stealing of his ammunition, which had since been recovered from the thief's pocket, the hauling of Rosie onto the truck was completed quickly, with much noisy joking. It had been a successful and highly entertaining day. They had captured the chipimbiri and also a scabenga, and tonight there would be beer. Not the African that looked and tasted like sour goat's milk, but real beer, with bubbles to tingle the blood.

The captive was transferred to the back of the truck as well, where he would be under the watchful eyes of the crew and, no doubt, where he would also keep them amused on the ride home.

'What have you decided to do with him?' Juliette asked John as they were preparing to leave. He had been walking around in one of his thoughtful circles, and she assumed it was because he was trying to plan his movements over the next few days. They were not really geared for housing prisoners at Gara Pasi. 'If we phone them from home, I'm sure the police will send a truck to fetch him. It will save you having to make the trip.'

John continued walking for a moment, nodding as if agreeing, then he stopped. 'No,' he said finally. 'I think I have a much better idea.'

He refused to explain further, telling her he still wanted to think it through, and she didn't persist, knowing how thorough he was, and that she would get the full story when he was ready.

They had gone only a few hundred yards, with Juliette following in the Landrover, when banging on the roof of the Isuzu brought it to a halt.

'What now?' John shouted as he leaped from the cab.

'Nkosi Timi!' came a chorus from the rear.

John looked up to see the yellow Tiger Moth a few miles ahead, climbing slowly and flying in a westerly direction. He pointed it out to Juliette who had pulled up alongside.

'I'll see if I can get him on the radio,' he said, leaning in to drag it out. But he received no answer.

'Damn thing must have packed up again,' he said in disgust.

They watched until it disappeared, then John climbed back into the truck. 'They'll let me know from the peanut gallery if Tim comes back,' he said, hooking a thumb over his shoulder. 'And if he's looking for us it's best to be moving so we can raise some dust.'

Juliette nodded in agreement. 'It's a relief to know they're all right,' she said. 'I was beginning to worry that something may have happened to them.'

**

In the past three hours and forty minutes that she had been waiting in the hospital outpatients wing, Kelly estimated that she had stopped to stare at the AIDS poster on the wall easily as often as she had consulted her watch. She turned irritably away to continue her aimless meandering. In her present mood it was not something she wanted to be reminded of.

She left the crowded room and wandered outside to wait for Juliette and John in the almost fresh air. Even there it was crowded, with every patch of shade accommodating at least four hopeful African patients.

Despite the number, the two African doctors she had seen wandering around seemed in no hurry, stopping to exchange lengthy pleasantries and limpid handshakes with practically everyone but herself. She was thankful it was not she that needed attention. The place looked and smelled anything but sterile. Over half the black population in the country was reported to be afflicted with Aids, she had learned. One in every three fifteen-year-olds wouldn't reach the age of forty.

Her despondency deepened. The only person she had spoken to was the matron, a buxom black woman whose orders reverberated through the corridors like a bugle. All she knew was that Tim had been placed in an emergency ward, his leg x-rayed, and he had been put on a drip until Juliette arrived to cross-match her own blood, which was in the same group. He was one of the lucky ones. Were it not for a friend of the Ryans, who had driven them from the airstrip and barged his way in, Kelly was sure Tim would still be lingering on the lawn with all the other hopefuls.

With nothing to do but wait and think, dejection had settled on Kelly like a wet blanket. The hospital, the patients, the poverty, the graft, the plight of the animals - of the whole stinking world - depressed her immeasurably, but nothing dismayed her so much as her own gullibility.

At first she had been elated at finding the town airstrip and landing safely. Then finding a friend of

Tim's there to help had been another stroke of luck. He had quickly summoned several willing Africans to help remove Tim from the plane, and she had sat with him while waiting for the friend to fetch his car. Although groggy, he had regained consciousness, and taken her hand as she knelt over him to wipe his face with a damp cloth.

'You're a shtar, Kelly,' he had mumbled drowsily. 'Don't know why I thought you wash a leshbian.'

'What?' She had stared down at his closed eyes in disbelief. 'What did you say?'

'Best...' his voice had faded to a murmur, 'not leshbian... are you...?'

She sat looking blankly over his head for a long time, unseeing, but in her mind everything came sharply into focus. The past flicking across her memory like the flashbacks of an old movie; his attitude towards her when they first met, his obscure comments and knowing smirks, what Juliette's lecture had really been all about, and the dozens of other clues, none of which she had picked up. Suddenly it was all perfectly clear. He had believed she was a lesbian.

He must have told Juliette that, and Juliette had probably assumed that she knew as well, or she would have said something. The misunderstanding they had mentioned had never been explained, and now it was too late to bring it up. She would only look a bigger fool than she was already.

His comment about bad language not being feminine and, oh, God, the sex. He had taken her… all but forced her… for no other reason than to prove she was not a dyke with designs on his sister.

That he now thought differently was irrelevant. It had gone far beyond a simple misunderstanding. He had deliberately manipulated her. All his phoney charm and concern, his seeming change of attitude, even the naming of Rosie and the flying, had all been a sham, designed to lull her into the belief he genuinely liked her. He had even admitted taking her to the pan under false pretences.

She found it difficult to accept that she could have made such an impression, but she obviously had, and it was disturbing to think how many other people she had affected that way. She had never considered herself in that light. Tomboyish perhaps, with a practical approach to things, as Billy had intimated with his remark that she was not afraid of getting her hands dirty. That was something she had inherited with her love of flying and airplanes. It had nothing to do with being a woman, yet he obviously thought differently. Maybe he believed that flying was strictly for the boys.

Her being there had become a farce. She felt used,

but could feel no anger, only profound disappointment that what she had believed was the experience of a lifetime should end in such an unsavoury manner.

She accepted that she had been attracted to him. No other man she had known came anywhere close to igniting her senses the way he had. But she had also accepted that he was not for her - or rather, she admitted with brutal self-effacement, that she was not for him. Their lives travelled on paths that were too far apart and, despite the way she now felt about him, his was the more important. Her own seemed to be going nowhere.

It was too much, Kelly thought. She did not belong here. It was too close to the real thing. She belonged in the pristine, enlightened wilderness of the Sound, where she could sit on the wing of the Bee and contemplate life with all its uncertainties from a safe distance.

She had not been looking forward to her departure, but suddenly the days couldn't go fast enough.

Kelly returned to the waiting room, only to be confronted once again by the poster. Practise Safe Sex, it cautioned, and she turned away tiredly. Too bad she had not followed such good advice, she thought gloomily.

***

Elliot Gumbo did not believe what he was hearing. The two white men could only be playing a joke on him, and he laughed to placate them, but without humour, for such a joke was not to his liking. In fact, it was so unfunny as to bring fear instead of laughter.

'Would you rather go to prison?' the big South African policeman asked, and Elliot clamped his jaw on the smile. 'That can very easily be arranged, you know.'

'Maybe he doesn't believe us,' the ranger who had captured him said.

'Ja, I think you're right, but how can we convince the silly bugger?'

'Maybe he's just frightened. Can't say I blame him.'

'True, but we'll have to get him back over the border soon or the whole thing will be a non-starter. Then he will have good reason to be afraid. So what do you say, Elliot? Do you want to be free and make some money, or would you rather go to the stocks?'

Elliot tried hard to comprehend what was taking place. Until a few minutes ago he had been treated like a bandit. Now they were saying he could not only leave, but must take the horn with him. And all he had to do in return was to sell it to the Chinese, which was what he had intended doing in the first place. Had they asked for a share of the money it would have made some sense, but they had not.

'I'm sorry to be a such a confused person, sirs,' Elliot said, putting on a bewildered expression that needed little enhancing, 'but I do not understand too well what it is you ask of me. To be free would be a happy thing, of course, but I fear only that you wish to trick me.' He gulped, looking earnestly at each of the men in turn, afraid that he had gone too far.

'No trick, Elliot. We want to stop this poaching, and you can help us. If you do, you will be rewarded with the money you get from the horn, which we will allow you to keep so long as you stay in line. Otherwise…' He drew his finger across his throat and made a gurgling sound.

'Setting a thief to catch a thief,' said the ranger.

'Sir?'

'Never mind. You will be one of us, Elliot. An undercover agent like James Bond.'

'Ja, we'll even give you a bloody licence to kill,' the South African said with a chuckle.

Elliot tried to make his smile look not too disbelieving, going along with the joke and playing it safe. 'You will give me permission to kill the chipimbiri?' White men had very strange humours.

'No, man…' The South African shook his head sadly. 'Jesus, John, are you sure you've got the right man here?'

'Doesn't catch on too quick, does he?'

'I see. Is it then that I must kill my friends?'

'That's up to you, but it's not exactly what I had in mind either. Mind you, it wouldn't be a bad idea to act alone. You can't trust anyone these days.'

'I see,' Elliot said, nodding sagely. 'But I fail to understand why you will allow me the horn of the chipimbiri and also to keep the money for its sale. Do you not wish to share?'

'Christ, Elliot, I thought you said you had been a schoolteacher.'

'Yes, sir.'

'Primary school, I bet,' said the ranger.

'I think we're wasting our time,' the South African said, shifting restlessly on his seat. 'This is one spy that will never find his way in out of the cold.'

'Ah!' Elliot exclaimed with sudden understanding. 'Is it that you wish me to be a spy?'

The two men stared at him in surprise, then roared with laughter, slapping the table, and Elliot grinned weakly.

'Top marks for that, Elliot,' said the South African,

still chuckling. 'That's exactly what we want you to do. Now, let's start again, shall we? From the beginning.'

When, an hour and a half later, Elliot was returned to the shed in which he had been kept prisoner, he could not resist a small dance of happiness that such good fortune had come his way after all the bad things that had happened. He sipped on the cold beer his captors had given him, and smoked two cigarettes in succession, lighting them with the gold dragon lighter that had been returned, and shaking his head continuously in disbelief. It was all very strange. Even more strange than what the Chinese had wanted him to do.

He did not mind being locked in. It was all part of being a spy, as would be the handcuffs early tomorrow when he was taken away in the Landrover, as if going to the police. He must remember to look sad. No one other than himself and the white men must know he was a spy, and this was something he understood.

He would be a good spy, he promised himself. No need for the South African to take his picture and threaten him with being tracked down and killed by other agents if he tried to be tricky, or if he killed even one chipimbiri. Why would he do such a dangerous thing when there was no need? They would give him horns taken from other poachers that he was to claim as his own. No searching, and no danger. It was dreaming coming true.

Elliot lit another cigarette and gave some thought to getting rid of his men. It would not be too difficult. The ones who had run away must already be expecting punishment, and would receive it by being excluded. They were too stupid to be the friends of a spy. He would pay them off with a small share of the horn, then simply tell them he preferred to work with only Sibanda from now on. And he must tell the Chinese the same if asked.

With the problems out of the way, Elliot sprawled on the blanket and gave himself over to daydreaming about what he would do with all the money. Maybe the hotel was not such a good idea. He had heard that it was cold in Geneva, and was visited by too many politicians, some of whom may know him and who would ask questions. They could be very tricky people, and spies had to be cautious about such things. Maybe he would just start with a new truck.

***

Shen Hui Ping listened with two hearts and two minds to the discussion taking place between his son, Lan, the politician from Zimbabwe, and the banker from Taiwan.

While one mind struggled with the complexities of the unfamiliar terminology they used for the business he had once thought was so simple, the other sought understanding for the changes they had made to it.

In one heart he felt pride in the achievements of his firstborn, with his business degrees from Western universities, but there was also sadness for the passing of the old ways. Golden Horn Company was no longer a small distributor of traditional herbal medicines. Now it had multi-national interests and distributed money, mostly in American dollars, and in such amounts as to numb the brain

Trusted friends with whom he had often dealt personally had given way to faceless agents, contacts and representatives. Loans had become financing, and debts were now liabilities that somehow resulted in acquisitions.

Sitting at the long polished table with its red folders and glasses of cold water instead of iced tea, Shen fondled Cha-Cha's ear as he dozed on his lap. Lan had insisted he sit at the head of the table in the place of honour, but he was seldom consulted, and then only out of politeness. He may just as well be sleeping himself.

The man from Zimbabwe was complaining about

the Hong Kong & Shanghai Bank. He had removed the ivory toothpick from his mouth so he could talk more loudly. Shen had met many such bad mannered people in his time, but never one who kept a toothpick in his hair.

It seemed that not all the money promised in the Malaysian deal for purchasing the majority share of his country's main power generating plant had been forthcoming. It was ten million dollars short, and because of that, newspapers were now asking questions as to why the deal had been agreed before the other interested parties had submitted their tenders.

What one had to do with the other made no sense to Shen, but little the man said made sense.

'My president is very angry about it,' the African said, adopting an aggressive attitude as if it were he who was the injured party. 'The board has resigned and the price of electricity has doubled.' He paused to look at them with his mouth open, as if astonished that such a thing could occur. 'This was not part of the agreement. Our poor people cannot afford such increases. Your bank is to blame for making the company start repaying the loan before the agreed time.'

'We sympathise, of course,' Lan said. 'We gave much assistance to your president in liberating your country from the racist imperialists. It is unfortunate that your people continue to struggle without electricity… as people do all the time in China, but please, Mister Marufu, we are the Golden Horn Company, not the Hong Kong and Shanghai Bank.'

'But you are major shareholders, not so?'

'We have no say in matters of policy,' Lan answered obliquely.

'Perhaps it would have been wiser,' the snakehead banker from Taiwan said with a barely concealed sneer, 'if your president had not sold the majority share.'

'I am not aware of the exact details,' Lan continued, 'but the ten million dollars you speak of. Was it not goodwill money to be paid off against the interest until the bank made arrangements to transfer the same amount into the Swiss account? I believe six months was the arrangement. Could not your president have waited that long?'

The politician lounged back in his chair with his expression of outrage changing to one of petulance. 'Well, you see, I know nothing of that, only what I have been told.'

'Ah, yes, Of course,' Lan said. 'I will pass on your concerns to the bank. I am sure they will look into them carefully. Now, if you are willing, we can discuss the other matter. You expect no trouble shipping the horns?'

The politician answered with a question of his own, his expression changing yet again to one of casual indifference, almost of boredom. 'Do you agree to meet the price offered by Yemen?'

'It is very high. Almost double what we have been paying.'

The politician gave an unconcerned shrug. 'It is what the president said.'

'You have confirmation?'

Without disturbing Cha-Cha, Shen opened the red file before him. It was a three- page list of countries in Africa, and the names of the agents representing them, including that of Wang, his second born, with five columns of numbers on the right, each column depicting one year. The first four were already filled with numbers, although many of the northern countries showed blanks.

Each year the amounts were progressively less, until the last year, where the column entitled "The Year Of The Golden Horn" was blank.

Only those countries in the south had numbers exceeding two digits. Three had only one, and five had none. Zimbabwe and South Africa had the greatest number. Prices were listed as well, and Shen glanced up to see if the black politician had the same file. It would not be wise for him to have such bargaining ammunition.

He did not. The toothpick was back between his teeth and he was rummaging worriedly through his elephant-hide briefcase.

Shen smiled inwardly at his foolish doubts. Lan would never make such an obvious mistake, and was more than able to handle the black buffoon without his help. He lowered Cha-Cha to the floor and excused himself.

It was also an area of the business he disliked. Not a day went by that he did not receive at least two phone calls from old friends asking why they were no longer receiving the horn they had requested, and Shen could think of no way to tell them without losing face.

He could not say it was merely because of insurance. Most were simple men who would not understand the insecurity of bullion standards and economic trends. He did not even fully understand them himself. Certainly, he did not understand why ancient horn carvings and cups - some a thousand years old - had to be collected and stored as well.

On his way out, as he and Cha-Cha waited impatiently for the security guard to fit his key in the lock of the lift, Shen slipped the mobile telephone from his pocket and placed it carefully inside the Ming vase that stood on the table nearby.

***

In the past week, since her recapture, Rosie had behaved with admirable restraint, bruising only one labourer when he was too slow climbing the fence, and bloodying her nose only twice on the poles trying to attack the docile Rupert in his adjoining pen. The third boma held the most recent arrival, another female they had named Maggie, who was almost as cantankerous as Rosie. The fourth was due in another few days; the last black rhino they believed still existing in the area, although there were a few of the white remaining. They too, would eventually be darted and moved to sanctuaries.

Now, as Kelly and Juliette climbed the stockade wall to look down on them, Rosie restricted herself to a few intimidating snorts, the effect spoiled by her having a leafy branch as thick as pick-handle protruding from her mouth.

'Hi, Rosie,' Juliette greeted.

Rosie glared, munching reflectively, and her calf, which had been dozing peacefully alongside, ducked his head under to suck, only to be bowled over by an irritably swung, plastered hind leg.

'Isn't she something else? What gruesome stories

have you been reading her?'

'She's wonderful,' Kelly said. 'Real motherly.'

'You'll have to visit her in Australia sometime,' Juliette said. 'And me too. I'll be spending more time there once this operation is over. You can stay with us at Chipimbiri.'

'What about Tim? I suppose he'll be coming back once they've settled in to look after things here.'

'He has the National Geographic people coming in January to film the white rhino darting, and we have quite a few photographic safaris booked for the winter. It's the best time, you'd love it.'

'I love it now. What are you going to do for two months on Cocos Island?'

'God knows. Go mad I suppose. I hope you feel guilty about leaving me there on my own.'

'I do, Jules, really. I was looking forward to a few weeks there, but you'll have the other vet and his wife, and the two handlers. It won't be so bad. I'll think of you snorkelling around the coral reefs while I'm freezing my ass off in the Sound.'

'Serves you right.'

Kelly did feel guilty. She had not told Juliette the real reason, and the delay in shipping the rhinos made her excuse that it was too long a time away from her business feasible. And with Tim being in hospital for a week it had not been difficult to hide her feelings. Now he was back it was not so easy, but he still spent much of his time away with John, disobeying doctors orders by driving the truck while John did the darting.

He obviously had not remembered saying anything to her, and acted as if she was the heroine in the episode, turning on the charm, but she saw him with different eyes now, and his compliments seemed merely patronising.

'What do you think of this spy the men are so interested in?' Kelly asked.

'Elliot Gumbo? Huh! He's a former terrorist, and not the sharpest knife in the drawer. Anything can happen.'

'I'm sure the South African knows what he's doing, but him allowing Rosie's horn to be sold to the Chinese seems a bit like defeating the object, don't you think?'

'Perhaps, but it's what the ESPU have to do occasionally. Hansie Joubert is hoping to get to the source eventually. Personally, I think he's wasting his time.'

Kelly was inclined to agree. It made little difference where the horns were going. Shanghai, Taiwan, Hong Kong. It was still China, with a hundred trillion people. Not even the CIA would be able to do anything about it, let alone the small Endangered Species Protection Unit and a harmless-looking African that reminded her of Forest Gump. She smiled at the thought. Mind you, he hadn't done such a bad job of accomplishing the impossible.

But Rosie's horn was personal. She hoped that whoever swallowed its powder would get violently ill.

***

Elliot Gumbo shifted uncomfortably in his cramped hiding place amidst the stacked crates of empty bottles. He had been there since shortly before the last customers and kitchen staff had left the Chinese restaurant at midnight, and now it was approaching dawn.

After three nights of maintaining his vigil he had become immune to the stench of beer and wine dregs, rotting prawn heads, and the constant rustle of cockroaches. A spy must expect to endure such discomforts in the course of his duty, he kept telling himself, although he had come close to giving himself away the previous night.

One of the customers, either too drunk or lazy to negotiate the few remaining yards to the outside toilet, had paused to relieve himself on the crates, splattering him with steaming urine. Since then, Elliot had taken the precaution of equipping himself with a sheet of cardboard to use as a shield.

It was his first assignment. The South African policeman had told him he must find out where the horns were kept and, if possible, how they left the town. Elliot was beginning to think that poaching must be easier.

He sincerely hoped his discomfort was not in vain. He had very little to go on, only his belief that the horns were being kept somewhere in the restaurant. After he had sold the one given him by the men at Gara Pasi to the old Chinese man, both he and Sibanda had been watching constantly, and he was sure it had not been taken elsewhere.

While Elliot had entered the front of the restaurant with the red and white sports bag containing the horn and received payment for it as arranged by Wang, Sibanda had watched the back through the binoculars, and had assured him that no one had left carrying anything. The old Chinese had crossed the open service yard behind the restaurant several times, going to his adjoining house, but on each occasion had been empty-handed.

The only other thing Elliot had to go on was what the old man himself had told him when he had asked to see Wang personally, saying he had some important news. Wang had been away for the past week. He would be back soon, was all the old man had been willing to say, although, when Elliot had pressed for more details, with the excuse he had to see him before he went back to the bush, the old Chinese had let slip the fact Wang couldn't be late because he had an important meeting before the weekend. Since then, Elliot had maintained his night vigil from the crates, and Sibanda had watched during the day while Elliot slept.

Wang had finally returned earlier that evening. While Elliot had been watching the back, where he wouldn't be seen and recognised, Sibanda had been waiting in his place across the street from the restaurant, and had seen Wang arrive in the company of another Chinese-looking man.

'He looks to be like the Korean instructors we had in the war,' Sibanda had informed Elliot. 'I think he has a gun, although I did not see it.'

While Wang went inside, the man had waited by the Toyota Land Cruiser, looking about suspiciously, even staring at Sibanda, which had caused him to withdraw into the nearest shop and pretend to be looking at women's shoes while peering around the posters on the window. He had been about to go out the back entrance and run through the sanitary lane to inform Elliot, when he had seen Wang come out again with two African waiters to remove a large steel trunk from the back of the vehicle and carry it inside. The other man had remained in the doorway for some minutes, looking out, then had also gone inside.

After reporting to Elliot, Sibanda had returned to his post and, as soon as it became dark, Elliot had crawled into his own hiding place, pulling the crates in after himself to close the gap.

It was Friday night, so if the old man had been correct, it must be the night of the meeting. With whom, Elliot had no way of knowing, but he had instructed Sibanda to write down the registration numbers of all the vehicles that came to the restaurant, and make note of any suspicious-looking characters. It was the best he could do in the circumstances. One thing he was certain of though. The steel trunk had not been taken out again.

Wang had left the restaurant early by the back entrance, crossing the service yard to the old man's house, and his stocky companion had driven the Land Cruiser around to the front of the house and parked it, then he too had disappeared inside. An hour later the lights in the house had gone out.

At midnight the staff had departed as usual,

followed shortly thereafter by the old Chinese, who had gone to the house, leaving Elliot in the dark with the cockroaches.

He waited impatiently for the stars to disappear and the sky to lighten, vowing that this was definitely the last night he would spend there. Cramped, cold and desperately in need of a cigarette, he finally succumbed to the craving and lit one, hunching down low to conceal the flame, but had taken only one delicious draw when he heard a vehicle turn off the road into the service lane and he hastily stamped the cigarette out.

Grinding in first gear, the vehicle bounced slowly past the crates, flooding the yard with light, and he clearly heard men talking, discussing where they should stop. It too, was a Toyota Land Cruiser. It pulled up alongside the kitchen entrance, presenting Elliot with a clear view of the lit rear number plate, and he quickly reached into his pocket for his notebook and ball-point, managing to scribble the number down only moments before the lights went out. It was a Zimbabwe registration.

The car doors opened and three men got out to stretch and talk quietly. All three were Africans. The driver wore a safari suit, but the other two were in camouflage fatigues, and both had AK's slung on their shoulders, which caused Elliot's hand to tremble more than a little as he replaced the notebook in his breast pocket.

They talked quietly amongst themselves, waiting, then a light went on in the house and, a short while later, Wang, his suspicious companion, and the old Chinese man came out. The recent arrivals went forward to meet them.

After shaking hands and exchanging greetings, all six moved to the kitchen entrance of the restaurant, where the old man unlocked the door and switched on a light. They filed in, all except for Wang's companion, who remained outside, looking around furtively. Elliot sank lower, tensing as the man came towards the crates, but he passed by to stand in the lane a few yards away, presumably where he would have a view of the street.

The two men in camouflage reappeared carrying the steel trunk, which they loaded into the back of the Toyota. They went back in to come out again with a second trunk identical to the first. After they had loaded it in as well, one of the men rubbed his hands and blew on them, as if they were cold, and the other laughed, likewise rubbing his hands, and making some joke about how he would soon be able to warm them on his woman's body.

The other three men appeared and the man guarding the lane went to join them. Hands were shaken once more, then the man in the safari suit climbed into the driver's seat, followed on the other side by the two soldiers.

Wang and his two companions waited until the Land Cruiser, with only its parking lights on, had driven away before going back to the house. The lights remained on inside, and Elliot gave it another ten minutes before cautiously extricating himself from the crates.

He lit a Madison as soon as he was out of sight in the lane, inhaling deeply on it, allowing himself a few moments to luxuriate with eyes closed before going to join his friend.

***

'Obviously,' John Singleton stated in his usual quiet manner, although anger had firmed his jaw, 'the poor blighter has run out of pocket money. He needs a few rhino horns to keep him going. Maybe the Cypriots didn't pay him enough to rip-off the country for forty million bucks by pushing through the air terminal.'

'Goddam it, John, there has to be something we can do.' More agitated than he had been in a long while, Tim lowered his plastered leg to the floor with a thump, getting up to hobble around the dining room, unable to keep still.

'There is. We can pray that some kind person will scribble the bastard.'

'I'd do it myself,' Tim growled, 'if I thought I could get away with it.'

They were discussing their unlikely spy's surprising success in Mozambique. It had allowed them, with the added assistance of a sympathetic friend in vehicle registration, to trace the number Elliot had jotted down, to one of President Mugabe's relatives; one of many family members and friends to benefit directly due to roughshod presidential sanction. Either because of arrogance or lack of wit, he had not bothered to change the plates, or use one of the many company or government vehicles at his disposal.

'I wonder if Mugabe is aware that his precious relative is breaking the law,' John mused, 'or if he even gives a damn.'

'If he doesn't he soon will,' Tim replied. 'I'm going to call the Standard and give them the story. They'd love it.'

'Do you think so? The editor will probably land himself in detention again, and we have Elliot to consider. The poor sod is sitting on a bomb and doesn't know it. I think it would be better to let Joubert at ESPU handle it. Meanwhile, I might whisper in a few trusted ears at the Department and see if we can stir something up.'

'Can we be sure it was horns that were in the trunks? Maybe Elliot was mistaken.'

'It must be. Horns are frequently frozen to hide the smell, and what else would they keep in the cold room that needed guarding with armed soldiers... frozen chicken?'

'I'd break the other leg to know where they are right now.'

'Probably in another freezer, waiting to be flown out under diplomatic seals.'

'Which reminds me,' Tim said. 'What's the latest on the seven-three-seven?'

'Still next week, as far as I know. They promised to confirm tomorrow, so I'll give you a call. The guys at Chete are also having a problem, but in their case it's cold feet. Their informant is still saying an ambush is planned once the rhinos are caged and leave the camp. They've organised a police escort and the volunteer guards from the wildlife association will follow as well, all the way to the airport.'

'At least we don't have a hijacking problem here,' Tim said. 'Our friend Elliot is proving himself to be a regular little godsend.'

***

Elliot removed the two horns, one long and one short, from the red and white sports bag, and laid them on the ground next to Wang's Toyota. 'Very good ones,' he said, launching into his new sales pitch. 'Also very hard to get. The chipimbiri almost kill one of my men. He now demands more money.'

'You have done well,' Wang replied, squatting to inspect the horns more closely. 'I did not expect you to bring more so soon.'

'I am a very good hunter,' Elliot said. 'Even as we speak, my men are following another chipimbiri. In two weeks for sure, I will bring the horns.'

'Mister Chu told me you brought only one horn while I was away, and also that you had something to tell me.'

Elliot had considered both these points at length. He was certain that the old man would have told Wang he had asked to see him personally, but had hoped he would not mention the single horn. On that issue he had been unable to come up with a reasonable explanation. Rhinos had two horns, so how could he explain having just one? The white men at Gara Pasi should have thought of that, and it had given him some satisfaction to inform them of their lapse. In future they would give him both the long front horn and the shorter back one, they had promised, which of course meant more money, but he had not mentioned that to them.

Pondering the problem earlier, it had occurred to Elliot that he could link the two awkward questions together, which he did now.

'You see,' he began, adopting a concerned air, 'it happened that one of my men stole one of the horns and ran away. That is why I now have only three men.' That too was a lie, but Wang was not to know. 'I wished to warn you of this man if he comes to you for selling the horn. He is very dangerous and not to be trusted. However...' Elliot paused to give a reassuring smile. 'I have heard from a friend that he has run to Beira, so no cause now for worry.'

'Wang mumbled something Elliot couldn't quite hear, then picked up one of the horns, turning it around in his hands. 'These do not look so fresh. Are they old ones?'

The question took Elliot by surprise. It was something else neither he nor the white men had thought of. He coughed to cover his hesitation, thinking furiously. They did look old, and they had hardly any smell compared to the other horns he had brought. The bases were dry, almost bleached, as if they had been salted and left for a long time in the sun.

'They are not old. Of course not. I wash them because of the smell and leave in the sun.' It sounded so good an answer that Elliot laughed with relief. He was getting to be rather a good spy, he thought.

Wang went through his usual procedure of examining the bases with a magnifying glass and running his metal detector over them then, while Elliot leaned over his shoulder to see for himself, he weighed them on a spring scale suspended from the rear door of the truck and entered the results on his pocket calculator.

'Four hundred and sixty dollars,' Wang announced. 'Mister Chu will pay you the money.'

'I see,' Elliot said, a little disappointed. He had expected more. Nevertheless, after all the tricky questions he felt relieved to have it all over and done with.

Having taken care of business, and feeling more confident, Elliot thought now would be a good time to do some more spying. He could not be sure when he would see Wang again, and the South African had said he must try to find out how many poachers were working for the Chinese, and where they were based.

'You had a good journey?' he asked politely. How far was it?'

'Too far, and very rough.'

'I see.' Elliot clicked his tongue in sympathy. 'And the other poachers found you many horns? How many would you say?'

Wang ignored the question, asking one of his own. 'When will you be going back to join your men in the bush?'

'The bus for Massangena is leaving one day from tomorrow. For sure, I will go with it.'

'I will be going past there myself tomorrow,' Wang said. 'Maybe I can give you a lift.'

Elliot accepted with alacrity. The bus took all day, and frequently longer, depending on the length of the breakdowns, which occurred with monotonous regularity. In the Toyota they would be there in four or five hours, and he would have the opportunity of questioning Wang along the way. It would mean Sibanda would have to catch the bus on his own, and for a while Elliot considered asking Wang if he would give him a lift as well, but he rejected the idea. Wang had never met Sibanda, and it was best it should remain that way.

Elliot had rented a hut on a more or less permanent basis from a local headman whose small village lay on the outskirts of the town, and he informed Sibanda of the change in plans when he met him there later that evening.

With bundles of crisp new Zimbabwe twenty-dollar notes bulging reassuringly in three of his pockets, and a litre of beer residing pleasantly in his belly, Elliot was in a jovial mood. He gave Sibanda one of the bundles of cash, and produced two more beers to get him in the right mood before telling him the news. Sibanda was inclined to be nervous on his own.

'I will wait for you at Massangena,' Elliot reassured him. 'Then we will go to Gara Pasi together.'

Surprisingly, Sibanda did not seem to mind. After drinking the beer and counting his money, he was almost tearfully grateful. 'I am very happy to be working with such an honest man as yourself,' he said thickly. 'Three thousand dollars is much money. Anyway, tomorrow I will buy my new girlfriend some shoes and she will travel to Massangena with me.'

'Don't forget your gun,' Elliot reminded him, then laughed. 'I mean to say, the long one with the bullets.'

***

Suffering a mild hangover, Elliot presented himself at the Chinese restaurant next morning at the appointed time, and was dismayed to learn that he and Wang would not be travelling alone.

'I have offered to give another man a lift as far as

the border,' Wang explained.

Elliot was alarmed. 'We are going into Zimbabwe? But I have no passport.'

Wang laughed. 'Do not worry, Mister Gumbo, you will not be needing one. I am not going through the border. From there we can take another road to Massangena that is shorter.'

Elliot's relief was short-lived, his alarm returning when the extra passenger turned out to be the stocky man who looked like a Korean instructor, the same one he had seen standing guard when the steel trunks were being loaded.

The situation was not to Elliot's liking at all. The guard had the same arrogant manner as the instructors had, which disturbed him. The man gave no greeting, and his face remained expressionless as he held open the passenger door and indicated with a slight inclination of his head that Elliot should get in first.

It was too late to change his mind. He climbed reluctantly into the centre and sat with his red and white bag on his knees, only mildly reassured by the feel and weight of his AK resting on the bottom.

'We should put that in the back to give more room,' Wang suggested, and took the bag from Elliot. 'It is very heavy,' he remarked, dropping it behind with a solid thunk. 'Do you have your gun inside?' He laughed before Elliot could think of an answer. A quiet laugh, with only a hissing sound, and glanced at his Korean friend as if sharing a private joke.

As they bumped out of the service yard, Elliot noticed that the crates of empty bottles had gone, probably now replaced by full ones that would be kept inside. He had been lucky.

Elliot sat rigidly erect between Wang and the unpleasant man, becoming more and more convinced that he was a Korean. He took up more than his share of room, sprawling with one arm hanging out of the window, and the other resting on the back of Elliot's seat, uncomfortably close to his neck.

They travelled the forty minutes it took to get to the border mostly in silence, Wang and his companion exchanging a few words in Chinese, but saying nothing to Elliot, and his discomfort increased with every minute, his senses, sharpened by years of living with danger, telling him that something was not quite right, although he didn't know what. He badly needed a cigarette, but they were in his bag, and to get them he would have to reach over the Korean's seemingly immovable arm.

He was relieved when they finally drove through the small village of Machipanda and stopped at the pole barricade of the border post. They were not stopped for long though, and the Korean did not get out as Elliot expected. A uniformed African ran out of the building to raise the pole and wave them through, and they drove past the Mozambique customs and immigration building.

'Do we not have to stop?' Elliot enquired anxiously.

'Only at the Zimbabwe side,' Wang said. 'Then we turn back.'

When they arrived a few minutes later at the Zimbabwean customs building, Wang turned the Toyota around and stopped opposite one of the side doors some distance from the main entrance. He beeped on the horn, peering through the window at the door as if expecting someone to come out. He said something in Chinese and beeped again, impatiently, and the Korean laughed scornfully, shaking his head.

The door finally opened and three soldiers came out, one of them yawning. All three wore the red berets of the fifth brigade, and Elliot's stomach instantly tied itself in a knot.

'Goodbye, Mister Gumbo,' said Wang.

Elliot had no time to react. The Korean clamped his head in an arm lock and dragged him from the vehicle. A knee in the stomach took all his wind, and a moment after his head was released a rabbit punch knocked him to the ground. A boot struck him painfully in the ribs, then another caught his knee. His arms were wrenched behind his back and he was handcuffed.

Writhing in agony, Elliot was only vaguely aware of the Land Cruiser starting and driving away.

***

'Listen up, Rosie,' Kelly called out from her place beside the training cage. 'It says here that if I make a squeaking sound, holding the last note steady, you should come to me. It goes something like this...' She cleared her throat, then took a sip of water from the glass on the small table at her elbow, which, along with a camp-stool, Frek had provided for her. She bared her teeth in a grimace and made what she thought was the noise described in the book. 'Eeeak...' She took a breath. 'Well? Are you coming yet?'

Rosie's only response was to glare balefully and continue munching on the leafy combretum branch Kelly had brought for her.

'It also says,' Kelly continued, undaunted, 'that if I end on a high-pitched note, sort of like it was a question, it means who, or what the hell is that? Like this...' She held her mouth a little differently this time, teeth not so clenched. 'Eeeeak...?' It sounded much better, not so strangled, and Rosie must have thought so too, for she stopped chewing momentarily and flicked one ear.

The response from her calf, which Juliette had named Bamba Zonke - a Shona phrase for "grab everything" - was more encouraging. He had been facing the other way, dozing in his mother's shade, and he scrambled to his feet with ears pricked. Still facing away, he made almost the identical squeaking sound.

Kelly stared at Bamba Zonke's plump backside in surprise. 'Well, I'll be damned,' she murmured. 'I think I've just spoken in rhino.'

'Congratulations,' Tim said from behind, and Kelly twisted around to see him observing her from behind the cage, leaning forward on it with his chin resting on his hands. He grinned at her.

'How long have you been there?' Kelly asked.

'About five pages or so. Please carry on. You're doing great. Better than I ever did.'

'You've been reading to her as well?'

'Not to Rosie, but I have tried with a few others. I didn't persevere because I couldn't stand the sound of my voice. Made me feel like an idiot.'

'A bit like I'm feeling right now. Why didn't you say something?'

'Then you'd have stopped, and I was enjoying it.

You have a nice voice… lots of expression, and look what you've achieved. Talking to rhinos. Nothing idiotic about that.'

Kelly laughed, pleased and flattered. 'I did, didn't I?'

Tim stooped to pick up a bag at his feet, then hobbled around with it. 'I brought some horse cubes and vegetable scraps for the calf. Juliette wants to supplement his diet and get him used to eating the sort of stuff he'll get on the trip. Why don't you try that calling sound again? See if you can handfeed him.'

'I will… as soon as you've gone.'

He laughed. 'Okay, I'll get out of your hair. Keep up the good work.' He swung away on his crutches, then stopped to turn awkwardly and face her again. 'You know… I'm going to miss you when you're gone.'

'Thanks. I'm going to miss you, too… all of you, and Gara Pasi as well. It's been terrific.'

'Are you sure there's no chance of us…' he paused, 'you know… getting together again? I don't mean just sex.'

'We never were together, Tim.'

'Oh?' He raised his eyebrows. 'Was I dreaming?'

'That doesn't count. It just happened.'

'It counts with me, Kelly. And after the accident.

That counts too. I thought we were doing pretty good. Is it something I said or did?'

Kelly had been expecting him to bring it up. In the past week he had been on his best behaviour, attentive and polite, trying to woo her, but it was too late for that. In a few days she would be gone, and giving in now - which at one point she had seriously considered - would only make her leaving more difficult. Still, his earnest expression, and her own confused feelings compelled her to say something.

'Well...' she began, but stopped when she saw Kawaseka hurrying towards them with a stranger in his wake, a scruffy-looking African with tangled woolly hair and an anxious expression.

'This man wishes to speak with you alone by yourself,' Kawaseka said to Tim. 'I ask his reason, but he refuse to tell me the nature of it.' He glared disdainfully at the stranger, as if personally insulted. 'You wish I should stay?'

'No, it's all right, Seki.' Tim tilted his chin at the stranger. 'Yes?'

The man glanced hesitantly at both Kelly and Kawaseka, obviously ill at ease, and Tim adjusted his crutches and moved off to the side, indicating with his head that the man should follow. Kawaseka left and, out of earshot, the stranger went into a lengthy explanation.

Kelly watched curiously. Tim said little, nodding his head and asking terse questions, which the man answered in an animated manner. He was nervous and agitated, and Kelly wondered what had happened to cause such obvious distress.

At the end of it, Tim pointed with his crutch towards a tree and the man left to sit in its shade.

'Is something wrong?' Kelly asked when Tim returned, and he nodded, his expression grim.

'I'll have to get hold of John. It seems our spy has disappeared.'

***

It was definitely blood on the walls, Elliot decided. Old blood and new blood.

When first he had seen it, he had been reluctant to admit to himself that was what it was. He had tried to think of other explanations. Perhaps that was the color the room was meant to be, and the white patches was simply old paint showing through, or stains from a leak somewhere. There was too much for it to be blood, he had told himself. It would have to be from many people to be so much.

But now he no longer tried to fool himself. It was

definitely blood. And some of it - the new blood - was his own.

It showed below the high barred window, from where they had smashed his face against the wall. Several times, they had done that, holding the back of his neck and grinding his face against the rough plaster. Blood from his nose and lip had run down the wall in rivers.

It was on the floor too, but most had been washed away. They did not like to get it under their boots to be walked outside, so buckets of water were thrown on it, and on him too, and he was made to sweep it out through the hole in the corner using his hands.

The pain was bad. He could not say which place on his body hurt the most, for it seemed that all of it was one single wound. Both eyes had swollen almost shut, so he could not see to examine his injuries too closely. His lips were also swollen and some teeth were broken. He was sure his nose must be broken too, and also some ribs. He had been punched in the groin, his toes and fingers crushed under metal-tipped heels, and both knees kicked. Perhaps that was the worst pain.

Then there was the fear. They came every few hours to threaten and inflict some further pain or indignity on him.

'We have orders to kill you,' they said once,

making him kneel while holding a pistol to his head. They had argued jokingly amongst themselves about where was the best place to shoot him. In the back of the head, or behind the ear? And they moved the barrel each time to prod the suggested location. 'No. We will leave him to think about dying until after we have eaten. Then we will do it for certain.'

They even brought a woman soldier in to taunt him, and to have some fun. A flat-faced woman with the stupid eyes of a cow. Already naked, he was held on the floor with a boot on his throat while the woman played with his genitals and joked about the small size. Other soldiers crowded in through the door to gape and snigger. When she failed to get it erect they goaded her on, and she lowered her fatigues to her ankles and squatted on him, rubbing, and when that also failed and the men jeered, she became angry. She pulled up her trousers, spat on his crotch, then stood on them with her army boot.

They did not ask many questions. It was mostly accusations and threats.

'You are a spy and must be killed. You are a criminal and must be killed. We know you are working for enemies of the government. It is against the law to have an AK if you are not a soldier, so why did you have it? Are you a soldier?'

'I was a soldier. A freedom fighter.'

'No, you are a spy.'

Had they asked sensible questions Elliot would have answered them truthfully, for he had no wish to suffer unnecessarily, and he no longer considered himself a criminal. He was on the right side now, and tried to tell them, but they would not listen.

'So, you admit spying against our friends the Chinese?'

'No. That one who tricked me is a criminal. He buys horns from poachers.'

'Are you a poacher?'

'No. I wish to stop the poachers who are stealing horns from Zimbabwe. It is not me who is a criminal. Why do you not wish to stop the stealing?'

That had earned him another beating.

Not once did they ask him who he was spying for, and it began to dawn on Elliot that his Fifth Brigade captors knew very little about him, and were not really interested in knowing anything. If he told them what he had witnessed, it would be like asking to be killed, for the men he had seen from the crates at the restaurant must also have been Fifth Brigade. It was either themselves who were dealing with horns, or they were working for the man in the safari suit. It was a pity he had not been able to recognise him. Whoever he was he must be very important.

Elliot could not think how it was that he had been discovered. He was sure he had not been seen in the crates, or he would have been caught right then. And he was equally sure it was not Sibanda or the men from Gara Pasi who had betrayed him. It could only be that he had betrayed himself to Wang - perhaps with his questions or the old horns - or that his footprints had been seen inside his hiding place when the crates had been moved. Maybe, he thought despondently, he had not been such a good spy after all.

As the days passed Elliot began to think less and worry more about surviving. He had been given no food, and the only water he drank was what he could scrape up in his palms from the puddles on floor after a bucket of water had been thrown in for him to wash out the filth. It was slimy and salty.

After a few days the hunger no longer bothered him. He had been hungry before. And the fear left him too, for that was also something he had experienced many times in the past. During the long cold nights he huddled in a corner, sleeping fitfully, and thought about his childhood. That had been a good time, with no hunger or fear. That had only come with the war. The war in which he had fought for freedom but found none.

He thought much about his father. He had been a religious man, of the Apostolic faith, as was his mother. He himself had never liked it much, especially having his head shaved, but didn't mind the white robes on Sundays, the preaching, or the singing under the trees. Sometimes people shook their heads until they became dizzy and fell over in a trance. When he was older he used to laugh when he thought about it, but it was not funny at the time, and it was not funny when he thought about it now.

His father had been very strict and stubborn, but also kind and fair and, thinking about him in the darkness, Elliot sought for some of his father's strengths, and remembered long-forgotten words. 'Fear only God and good men, and try to be one with them. Do not fear the devil or evil men, for they can only harm you if you allow it. To be killed is only death, and all must die. To live with shame is worse, for you will suffer many times over.'

Elliot wept when he recalled those words; the first tears since the happy days of his childhood. He had lived with shame, as he had lived with fear, and he had spurned God and worshipped evil. But no more. People had died in this room, as he would, but they could give him no more pain than he had already suffered.

That night, naked in his corner, Elliot prayed

sincerely for the first time in his life. He did not pray for freedom, or even for forgiveness. He prayed only for the strength and courage of his dead father.

***

The assistant editor of The Standard was aghast. 'But, Mister Ryan, we could never print such a thing.'

'Even if it's true? I thought your paper was against government corruption.'

'Yes, we are, but even with proof we could not do it. We know of many such crimes, even worse than what you speak of, but there is nothing we can do. The President would like nothing better than another excuse to arrest the editor for treason. Me too,' he added.

It was the reaction Tim had expected, but he was not there to have a blatant accusation of the favourite relative's criminal activities exposed. That would be tantamount to suicide for the paper. It was already treading a thin line by giving support to the growing opposition party, and there was no doubt that Mugabe was getting twitchy. Simply remaining in business was the best way for the Sunday paper to help oust Mugabe and his corrupt government.

Having put the editor on the defensive, Tim gave a theatrical sigh. 'Well, if you can't print it, can you at least ask some of your contacts to help find our man? All we know is that he was taken from the border by three soldiers of the Fifth Brigade.'

On the principle that if you can't beat them you can join them, Tim had borrowed one of John's National Park uniforms and obtained the information from the barrier attendant at the border post, on the pretext that he wanted to speak to the arrested man about poaching. Knowing almost the exact time of the arrest had helped. So too, had the hundred dollars.

'I will see what I can do, Mister Ryan,' the Assistant Editor said tiredly. 'But if the Fifth Brigade is involved, there is little hope. Those men are killers. I doubt they would have taken him to Army Headquarters. They would take him to their barracks, and we get little information out of there.' He smiled sardonically. 'You whites must be laughing at us now for what we've done to the country. Fifty-three percent inflation, over half the people unemployed, aid money going into the pockets of the ruling party officials, and a president who calls the judges impudent when they don't agree with him. I think we are close to having another Idi Amin.'

'No one is laughing, Mister Chivuku. And there are still plenty of people like yourself working to make it better. You probably have more support than you realize. All I can do is wish you luck.'

Tim discussed the impending transportation of the rhinos with the editor, then left. It was all he could do. And he was all too aware that even if he did manage to discover where his spy had been taken, there was no chance of helping him. Although there were still members of the police who were honest, he had nothing to give them except guesses. The North Korean trained Fifth Brigade was, to all intents and purposes, President Mugabe's private army, and was above the law. And Elliot Gumbo was a nobody in a country bursting at the seams with nobodies. He was simply another statistic that would not be missed.

With only two days left before Kelly departed, she and Juliette had accompanied Tim to Harare, all of them squeezing into John's Land Rover. As it was also only ten days before Juliette flew out with the rhinos, it was not time wasted. She had taken the opportunity to double-check all the arrangements, especially those concerning the Ilyushin cargo plane that would fly the rhinos from Cocos to Australia after quarantining, and she could use the more reliable telephone in the two-bedroom flat - accommodation the Ryan family had owned for the past twenty years.

It was there, the day after Tim had spoken to the Assistant Editor, as they were introducing Kelly to the novel experience of Zimbabwe television, that the call Tim had been waiting for finally came.

He answered it himself, listening and saying little, but his demeanour said much.

'What the hell's the problem now?' John asked, the moment Tim had replaced the receiver.

'Our spy... Elliot,' Tim answered dispiritedly. 'The bastards had him at their barracks all right. They buried him this morning.'

***

From her window seat on the right side of the Quantas 747, Kelly looked out to the hazy landscape below. They were still climbing, flying almost due east, according to the route progress screen, so somewhere down there Rosie would be standing in her boma with her calf, no doubt munching on one of the branches that seemed to protrude permanently from her mouth. Bamba Zonke would be sleeping, as he usually did at this time of day. She wondered if they would miss her reading to them.

The thought probed nostalgically, but so did many others, all competing for a share of her emotions, until she no longer knew how she felt. Overwhelmed by them, she simply stared out through the window, her mind suspended along with her body in the small world of the aircraft.

'I don't know about you,' the man sitting beside her said, 'but a large part of me is being left behind down there.'

Kelly turned to smile at him. 'Would you like to sit here?' she asked. He had already introduced himself as a former tobacco farmer who was immigrating to Australia. His wife sat on the other side of him, and his two children sat across the aisle, already involved with headphones and channel switching.

'No thanks, love, it's all yours. The less I see of it now the better. I was born there, and the good parts are stored in here.' He tapped his head with a blunt finger. 'Mugabe can take my land, but he can't take my memories. I just feel bad about leaving so many good people behind to fend for themselves. But…' he sighed, 'that's the new Africa, and my kids deserve a future.'

Kelly wondered how many of the other passengers were leaving their homeland behind for a new life in Australia. She guessed quite a few, not only from Zimbabwe, but also from South Africa, where this particular flight had originated. It was a mixed load, with few blacks, the majority of passengers being Asian or Europeans of one kind or another. Although she knew a group of four Africans were travelling in First Class.

Tim had seen them as he, Juliette and John were standing with her in the check in queue. She was trying to get them to leave her, not wanting to drag out the emotional farewells.

'No way,' Tim said, laughing. 'We're going to stay and make you miserable right to the end.' Then, looking past her, his expression suddenly changed. 'Well, well, look who you will be having for company.'

They all turned. The four Africans - three men and a woman - were standing at the separated, uncrowded area reserved for First Class passengers, talking and smoking, while three porters unloaded trolleys of luggage and a uniformed chauffeur lounged on the counter, waiting as the check in clerk applied labels and flipped through documents.

'Who are they?' Juliette asked, and it was John who answered.

'That overfed little slob in the Saville Row safari jacket and gold chains is one of Mugabe's relatives. I don't know who the others are. Probably bodyguards or friends tagging along for a free holiday at the taxpayers expense.'

'The bastard,' Tim growled. 'Bodyguards or not, I've a good mind to go over there and slug him with a crutch.'

'That would be immensely satisfying, but woefully unproductive,' John said. 'We need you around for a bit longer. However, if we were anywhere else but Zimbabwe I'd be borrowing the other crutch.'

'I wonder where they're going,' Juliette mused.

'Somewhere in Asia, most likely. They'll change in Sydney, like Kelly is doing.'

'Do you mean I'll have to travel in the same plane with that criminal? If I'd known that I would have changed flights on principle.'

'Don't worry about it, Kel, you won't see them. They'll be up front getting pampered while you'll be squashed in with all the peasants at the back.'

'Thanks for reminding me.'

'If they're going to Asia,' Tim said thoughtfully, 'I wouldn't mind betting that I know the reason.'

They all looked at him expectantly, then John laughed. 'Wouldn't that be something. But I don't see any steel trunks anywhere.'

'No, they would have gone through earlier as bonded cargo. Probably under diplomatic seal direct to their embassy in Taiwan...or wherever. Isn't that what Joubert at the ESPU said he thought was happening?'

'Can't the Australians do anything about it?' Kelly asked. 'They're pretty hot on that sort of thing, and if the horns are in their country...'

'They won't know that, and even if they did, I doubt they could do anything.'

Juliette had been right. After the group had been ushered through to the VIP lounge, Kelly had not seen them again. It didn't help though. She knew they were there, wallowing in ill-gotten gains, and one of them at least was responsible, even if indirectly, for the death of Elliot Gumbo, the unlikely spy who had reminded her of Forest Gump. His death, and her knowledge of the circumstances surrounding it, brought her closer to the tragedy and political chicanery than she felt comfortable with.

Another disturbing thought plagued her. It was quite likely that somewhere on the plane, maybe even directly below her feet, in the cargo hold, were two metal trunks full of rhino horns. It was also quite possible that Rosie's was amongst them. And there was not a damn thing she could do about it.

Brooding and without appetite, Kelly picked sparingly at her lunch when it arrived, passing much of it on untouched to the farmer beside her.

The farewells had been as traumatic as she had expected them to be, with Juliette bright-eyed and sniffing, and Tim holding her close for a long time before ignoring her slightly turned cheek and kissing her on the mouth. 'I'll miss you,' had been his parting words.

That had disturbed her more than she would have guessed.

On the screen the flight progress line reached the coast and, looking out, Kelly could see the dark expanse of the Indian Ocean far below. 'Goodbye, my Rosie,' she murmured.

'Sorry, did you say something?' the farmer asked, leaning towards her, and Kelly shook her head. Like him, she was leaving a large part of herself behind, but she too, had her memories, both good and bad.

And she also had a growing suspicion that she may be taking something away with her that was more than merely a lasting memory. For the first time ever, she had missed her monthly cycle.

***

After seeing Kelly off at the airport, and before leaving Harare, Tim, in response to a previous request by his father, invested in a Satellite phone. Only Tonga and a remote province in Southern Russia had a worse land communication system than Zimbabwe, and with so much going on, reliable contact was vital, not only locally, but internationally.

He would have invested in one much earlier, but for the fact Robert Mugabe's nephew was involved in the mobile network. Since then, the courts had restored the rights of the original applicant - whose licence had been arbitrarily cancelled by Mugabe in favour of his nephew - and Tim was able to buy one of the new Iridium services with a clear conscience.

Standing on the balcony of the flat that evening, where he had a clear view of the heavens and, presumably, one of the many accommodating satellites, and feeling as tentative as an astronaut about to venture into space for the first time, he inserted the cellular cassette and called his parents in Australia. After a few seconds delay he was mildly surprised to hear the ringing tone. He was also surprised to learn, once his mother had answered with sleepy concern, that it was after two in the morning there. Nevertheless, he gave her the number, and spoke guardedly about what had occurred, telling her he had changed his mind about going to Cocos with Juliette. He would fly directly to Australia two weeks before the rhinos were due to arrive there, to help receive and settle them in. Impressed with the instrument, it became a regular fixture on his person.

Without Elliot Gumbo to pass information on what was happening with poaching in the area, Tim had decided it would be prudent to remain as long as possible at Gara Pasi. From information obtained by the game scouts, John Singleton had estimated there were at least three white rhino still existing in the Park, and they would be vulnerable. As soon as the captured black rhinos left for Australia the bomas would be free, and John suggested they fill them as soon as possible. It would not take the Chinese man long to find a replacement for Elliot.

Juliette was sceptical. 'The whole idea of spending that time on the island,' she argued, 'was to give your leg a chance to heal. You're not supposed to be bouncing it around all over the place.'

'I'm not going, Jules, and that's all there is to it. I can't just sit around with my leg up while John does all the work. And the bomas will need to be guarded twenty- four hours a day.'

'All right then,' Juliette had relented. 'But no flying, and definitely no darting.'

'Absolutely not,' Tim agreed.

***

The Australian Customs official looked startled. 'I beg your pardon? Did you say rhino horns?'

'Like I said,' Kelly repeated. 'Two metal trunks

full of them. I'm almost certain they're on the plane, and this is Australian soil, isn't it? Exporting horn is prohibited by international law. Can't you check with a sniffer dog or something?'

The Customs Officer looked about helplessly, as if in search of assistance, then fixed Kelly with a perplexed smile. 'I doubt if our dogs would know what a rhino horn smells like. What did you say your name was?'

Kelly handed him her American passport. 'I've just come from a wildlife sanctuary in Zimbabwe, helping to catch black rhinos that are coming to Australia before people like that creep in First Class kills them all.'

'Would you mind waiting here for a minute please?'

He hurried away, and Kelly paced aimlessly about in small circles, trying to revive muscles that were stiff from sitting for long hours on the plane. She was tired and irritable from lack of sleep, and now regretted not accepting the Ryan's offer of breaking her journey and spending a few days with them in Australia.

The Customs Officer returned. 'Will you come with me please?'

Kelly followed him to an office at the end of the customs hall, also beginning to regret her accusations.

She had no proof the trunks were aboard, and even if they were she doubted anything would come of it. But she felt she had to try.

She was introduced to another, apparently more senior man, who stood from behind a cluttered desk to offer her a chair.

'I believe there's some problem,' he said. 'Would you mind telling me?'

Kelly repeated her story, going into more detail now that she had a more sympathetic ear, and he listened without interruption. 'I know it's not going to do any good,' she finished lamely, 'but I just had to do something. Somebody has to make an effort to stop these people.'

'I agree with you whole-heartedly, Miss Maddock. And I read about the rhinos coming to Australia. It's good news. However, we've checked, and these people you mention are travelling on diplomatic passports, and are also in transit. All we can do is notify our counterparts in Malaysia, but I doubt that will achieve anything positive either. If it was drugs it may be different, but many of our Asian neighbours don't consider rhino horn a prohibited substance. I appreciate your concern though, and for telling us.'

Getting back on the plane, Kelly seethed with frustrated anger. It was all so hopeless. Nobody cared, and those who did were so few in number that their efforts went practically unnoticed.

Kelly was one of the last to board. As she passed the two welcoming flight attendants standing in the doorway, she glanced to the left, past the screen to the stairs leading up to the First Class section.

Without conscious thought, spurred on by her anger and frustration, Kelly swung aside and swiftly climbed the stairs before the receiving flight attendant could prevent her. She saw the four Africans immediately - three men and a woman - lounging in their exclusive seats, and stopped to glare down at the one in the safari suit.

'You goddam criminal,' she said loudly, wanting everyone to hear. 'I want you to know that I've just reported to the Customs that you have rhino horns aboard.'

The three men gaped up at her in astonishment. The woman covered her mouth with a hand, concealing a stupefied smile. Kelly glanced around quickly and was pleased to note that she had everyone's attention, including a male flight attendant, who took her gently by the arm. 'Excuse me...'

Kelly shrugged his hand away and continued. 'You think because you're related to the President of Zimbabwe that you can get away with anything. Well, you're wrong. We're not in Zimbabwe now, and we know all about you. I'm going to make sure the whole world knows what a slimy creep you are.'

'Please,' the flight attendant persisted, 'I must ask you to return to your seat immediately.'

'He's also a murderer,' Kelly shouted. 'He had one of our agents killed only two days ago. His name was Elliot Gumbo.' She glared down at the one in the safari suit. 'You swine! You need to be locked away for good.'

He finally found his voice. 'What?'

'Please, lady...' The attendant tugged on her arm, pulling her back.

One of the Africans stood to help, shoving her roughly on the shoulder. 'Get away, get away, white bitch.'

'No need for that, mate,' the attendant said. 'We can handle it. Take your seat please. Come on, lady.'

The door of the flight deck opened and a junior officer appeared. 'What's going on?'

The man who had shoved her turned to the officer in appeal. 'We demand that you arrest this racist woman.'

'Ignorant bastard,' Kelly fumed, but allowed herself to be led away.

'Christ, love,' the attendant said quietly, 'what the

hell are you trying to do, get yourself thrown off the bloody plane?'

'It's okay, I'll be good now,' Kelly reassured him. 'I just wanted everyone to know what bastards they are.'

'Well you certainly did that.'

The truth of his words was shown a few moments later as they began to descend the stairs. A ruddy-faced man beamed up at her as she passed. 'Good on ya, Love,' he said, and winked.

Subdued, but still flushed from her efforts, Kelly managed to raise a satisfied smile as she was escorted to her seat past the rows of curious upturned faces. Her regard for Australians had risen by several points.

It was only a small, petty thing she had done, she realized, but it would give them something to think about, and she felt much better for having done it. She thought Elliot Gumbo would have approved.

***

They had left the black plastic bag in the room with him; to remind him, they said, that he was already dead, and would soon be placed inside it and buried. They even told him where that would be. In the same place they buried all the other rubbish. And he believed them.

He had used the bag during the night to keep warm. The smooth feel of the dry plastic covering his nakedness gave him a small measure of comfort, and was a welcome relief from the chill of the wet cement. For a few brief hours he was able to think of other things besides his misery.

He had come to accept that he would never leave the place alive. He was not an important person. No one would even know he had gone except those who killed him, and why they had not done that already was a mystery. They were visiting less than before, asking no questions, only the sticks and the threats, not even the bucket. It would happen tomorrow, for sure.

How the idea came to him he could not say. His mind played many tricks on him during the night, going from one thing to another like a sniffing dog, sometimes going back for another brief inspection before wandering off again in another direction. Maybe it was thinking about his dead father that had sparked the idea, but whatever it was, as soon as it came, his mind stuck to it, following the new trail carefully with suppressed excitement, examining its potential without digression to its hopeful conclusion.

But after the idea had come the doubts. It was foolish and bound to fail. He had seen dead people.

They were cold and stiff, and did not breathe. They looked dead. It would not fool his tormentors for a minute. They too, would have seen dead people. Many more than himself.

When dawn arrived he was loath to leave the bag. It felt warm and secure inside, while outside he would again be cold and exposed. He sat unmoving for a long time, delaying the inevitable, listening without interest to the muted sounds of the awakening camp. Another day was beginning. It would be his last, he was certain.

Only when he heard the sergeant major bellowing for the men to fall-in, did he crawl with a groan from the plastic. If they saw him in it they would beat him. He stood for a moment undecided, wrapped in his arms, then, because he had nothing else to do, he lay on the floor to experiment with several different poses, twisting his limbs into awkward positions, both face down and lying on his back, putting into practise the plan he had conceived during the night. He went through it mechanically, as if by rote, his mind occupied not with what he was doing so much as the futility of it.

Nothing seemed the least bit convincing, especially the bag. It would not work, yet he knew he would do it anyway. It was as if his plan had developed a mind of its own and was ignoring common sense.

His other mind finally settled for him lying in the

centre on his back. In that position they would not have to turn him over, and once the bag was removed would immediately see his gaping mouth. The swelling around his eyes and mouth would be a help. And he must not forget the tongue. It was important that it be sticking out a little to the side.

With that decided, he adopted his position and practised holding his breath. That was the hardest part, and he soon discovered it would be impossible for even half a minute without giving himself away. He tried slow, shallow breathing through his open mouth, and that proved more successful. With his eyes partly open he would be able to see when anyone was looking and, if necessary, hold his breath accordingly. If a doctor examined him, or they tried to feel his heart or pulse, it would fail, but those were chances he had to take. All they could do was kill him, and they would do that anyway.

They came later than usual, and by then Elliot did not have to worry about his body being cold, only about the shivering and the goose bumps showing. The scraping sound of the lock being taken off was one he had constantly dreaded, but never so much as now. With the bag already wrapped around his head, he pulled it tight and froze into position, stiffening his limbs, bending one arm and hooking the fingers into a claw-like pose.

A short silence came after the door opened, then the sound of the full bucket being set down and the scuff of approaching boots, and Elliot caught his breath, trying in the dark to make his half-opened eyes look blank and unfocused, sticking his tongue out the side of his mouth and playing dead for all his worth.

The plastic was unwrapped and wrenched free, bumping his head on the cement.

'Huh! Jesus! He kill hisself!'

A boot pressed on Elliot's chest and rocked his stiffened body, then another kicked his partly out flung arm in towards his side. He allowed it to spring back just a little.

'Must we tell the captain?'

'No, Sergeant Juku first.'

Then they left, leaving the door open, and Elliot took several deep breaths. He heard talking at the end of a short corridor, some of it questioning, then a few moments later the sound of approaching boots, and Elliot stopped breathing once again, but the boots stopped at the door. After a short silence the sergeant spoke.

'Get three men on detention to bury him.'

They were the most welcome words Elliot had heard in his life.

The footsteps departed, and he was left to wonder if perhaps he was still dreaming. It was too simple. But it was not yet over. He still had to be taken away and buried, and that would be even more dangerous.

When the three men from detention arrived they quickly bundled him into the body bag and zipped it closed and, in the relative security of the darkness, Elliot was finally able to close his dry mouth and take a few cautious breaths.

His stiffened limbs made him easy to carry, with two holding his upper body and the other his feet, but he hoped it was not a long way, for his muscles soon began to ache with keeping them tense, and the air was rapidly becoming hot and stuffy.

As soon as they were away from the building the three men, who so far had remained silent, began to talk, making jokes about how they wished it was the sergeant major or one of the Military Police they carried. There was also some speculation as to who it was they were burying, but mostly they complained to each other about the bad things that were happening to them on detention.

When Elliot thought he would pass out, either from lack of air or the pain in his knee, they reached their destination and dropped him on the ground. They seemed to be in no hurry to complete their task, discussing at length who would fetch the shovel, and if it was possible to borrow some cigarettes without being caught.

Lying in the full sun under the thick black plastic, Elliot was becoming desperate. Sweat stung his lacerated body, and his breath came in tight, unsatisfying gulps, which he had to subdue for fear of being seen or heard.

Finally two of the men left, presumably for the shovel and cigarettes, and the third remained to move about restlessly, and when Elliot heard his steps going away, he took a chance. He cautiously lifted his hands to take some slack in the bag near his head and gnawed furiously on it with his broken teeth, ripping a small hole in the tough plastic no larger than the thickness of his finger. Holding his mouth to it he sucked in deep breaths of air that was heavy with the cloying stench of rotting garbage, but he savoured every lungful.

When the dizziness had abated, Elliot considered pushing his hand through the hole to unfasten the zip. Maybe even get out of his sweltering cocoon to run, but he knew he did not have the strength. He could only wait and hope they did not bury him too deep, and that enough air would remain in the bag to breath for as long as it took them to finish.

Then he heard the sound of an approaching tractor

and stiffened with alarm.

For a horrifying moment he thought it was going to drive over him, but it stopped close and the driver's voice sounded above the rumbling engine, giving some instruction he couldn't make out.

Elliot made himself rigid again as he was lifted a short distance and dumped onto something hard and vibrating, then the tractor moved over rough ground that jostled him so much there was no longer any need to try and remain still. It stopped again and he had the sensation of being lifted. With a squeaking noise his platform suddenly tilted and he slid off, falling through dark, unknown, terrifying space.

His fall ended abruptly, but with remarkable softness, and a new sensation, one of tumbling, spinning and sliding, came to whirl his brain into confusion. Finally, that too, ended in a soft, mushy halt, depositing him face down, disoriented, but remarkably unhurt.

He lay still, listening to the clatter and squeak of the tractor, at first becoming fainter, then louder again as it returned, and a few moments later the bag rattled and pressed down around him, burying him under the weight of more mushy garbage.

That was enough for Elliot. Arching his back against it, he scrabbled desperately in search of the opening he had made and ripped feverishly at the stubborn plastic with his bruised but unfeeling fingers, forcing his arm through in search of the zip tag, bending his knees and thrusting himself up and out of it, at the same time as his clumsy fingers dragged at the zip, pulling it only a short way down before his urgency took control and he fought his way out in rising panic, pushing and kicking as if it were some vile thing attempting to swallow him alive.

He lunged away through the evil smelling morass of slimy bags and kitchen slop, clawing his way through it to the far edge of the trench, then he turned with his back against the vertical earth wall in time to see the bucket of the tractor appear above with another load.

It buried him up to his neck, but he did not attempt to move it. As the tractor withdrew from the ledge he reached for a cardboard carton and placed it over his head, then, with each load that came down he eased his way up through the mess, until finally the tractor departed and he was left only with the raucous squabbling of the crows and the buzzing flies.

He remained there until dark, dozing fitfully under his box, wallowing in the rubbish, and in his unexpected success.

***

The insistent ringing of the office telephone finally stirred Tim enough to switch on his bedside torch and squint at his watch. It was after midnight. He flung the blanket aside and stumbled to the door. Then the ringing stopped. He turned and went back to bed, only to be summoned a few minutes later by Juliette pounding on his door.

'What?' he shouted irritably. They had arrived back late from Harare, and he and John had an early start and a busy day planned.

'Hurry up. It's the exchange wanting to know if you'll accept an urgent person-to-person reverse charge call from a Mister Bond in Harare.'

Tim followed her back to the office, fully awake now and puzzling over what could have happened. He didn't know anyone named Bond in Harare.

'Yes,' he told the operator. 'I'll accept the call.' He waited anxiously, listening as she told the caller he was through, then an African voice spoke tentatively.

'Hello? Is that Mister Tim?'

'Yes, this is Tim Ryan… who's that?'

'Thank you, sir, for answering,' relief sounded in the voice. 'It is me, sir.'

'Who's me?' Tim asked, more puzzled than ever. 'Can you speak louder?'

'I am afraid to be heard, also to speak my name,

but it is me, sir, the one who is like James Bond. You know this person?'

'James Bond?' Tim raised his eyebrows at Juliette, shrugging and pulling a confused face, and she returned a questioning frown.

'Please, sir, I am very much needing your help. I have no clothes and no money, and the place I am is very dangerous. I search for a long time to find the call box, and walking is very painful. If you do not come the soldiers will take me, for sure.'

Tim's suspicion that it was some sort of a hoax began to fade. The voice sounded too genuine and too desperate, and there was something about it he thought he recognised. He searched his memory, recalling names and faces of Africans he knew in Harare. There were not that many.

'Sir?'

'Yes, I am still here, but I don't recognise your voice. What is your real name?'

It came after a hesitant pause, with a hint of resignation. 'It is Elliot, sir.'

'Elliot?' Tim gave Juliette a startled look and received a stunned one in return. 'The same Elliot who knows chipimbiri?'

'Please, sir, you must be careful of the phone. Those people are very tricky.'

Any remaining doubts Tim had vanished with those words. Now he recognised the voice clearly. 'Well I'll be buggered. It is you. Christ, Elliot, we thought you were dead.'

'Yes, sir. They think I am dead also, but I am here. Please, sir, you must help, I have no trouser and many injuries.'

'No trousers?'

'No, sir, they take everything. I hide in the bush until there are no people to see.'

'Shit... okay, Elliot... let me think... where are you? There should be an address above the phone... and a number. Give them to me.'

Tim nodded to Juliette, and she hastily searched for a pen and wrote down the details as he repeated them.

'That's on the way to the airport. Can you get there?'

'No, sir, I think my knee is broken. Also, I don't eat for five days.'

'Okay then, I think I know where you are. Is the call box on the main road?'

'Yes, sir.'

'Good. Stay close to it. If you hear it ringing, try to answer. I'll be there in the aeroplane as soon as it's light, so watch out for it. I'll fly down the road. When you see it coming stand by the call box and wave both hands... got that?'

'Thank you, sir. I am very happy you are helping me. God is with the good people, for sure.'

Tim replaced the receiver, staring thoughtfully at it. 'Well I'll be damned.'

'What happened... how did he get away?' Juliette asked.

'I don't know, but I'd better get his naked arse out of there quick smart before he gets spotted.'

'You're going to fly there with a leg in plaster?'

'You got any better ideas? I'll have to be there at first light and find a place to land that isn't too far away. He can't walk.' He gave Juliette a speculative look. 'He's going to need a doctor, so guess who that's going to be?'

Juliette raised her hands in surrender. 'I guess we have no choice, but please be careful, Tim.'

He grinned at her. 'Absolutely. Now, if you would like to organise some sandwiches and a flask, I'll get the generator going and sort out the plane. I'll need to take extra fuel so I don't have to worry about finding a place on the way back and...' he consulted his watch, mentally calculating. 'I'll have to be away in forty minutes.'

It was closer to fifty. By then the entire camp

had been aroused and had assembled at the airstrip to witness the exciting event. At the last moment Tim remembered that Elliot had no clothes, so one of the propeller boys was hastily dispatched to get some blankets and a pair of overalls.

A bemused John Singleton drove the Landrover along the strip to chase away any browsing animals, then parked at the far end with his headlights illuminating the trees to give Tim a point of reference.

It was a three-hour flight, but the stars were bright, with no wind to speak of, and he knew the route well. It was also cold. Once he was airborne, Tim set his compass course, then chose a group of stars to steer by, allowing him to slide well down in his seat below the main blast of the wind. From there he only needed an occasional glance at the altimeter, and an even less frequent look over the side at the lights of villages and towns, mainly to check that the wind wasn't blowing him too radically off course.

He remained huddled down, trying not to fall asleep, until the glow from the lights of Harare showed ahead and it was time to reduce altitude and pay attention. What he was doing was not only dangerous but also highly illegal. The Moth was not rated for night flying, and neither was he. He was also entering controlled airspace without clearance or radio contact.

The Moth did not even have navigation lights. If caught he would lose his licence and face a heavy fine.

Well before reaching the outskirts of the city, he descended to a few hundred feet above the ground, where he hoped he would not be picked up by the radar, then concentrated on finding his way.

It was not easy with being so low, and not having flown over the city before at night, he only had two reliable reference points. One was the city centre, with its tall buildings and neon lights, and the other was the international airport itself, with its runway lights and flashing beacon. The road on which Elliot waited linked the two, but he was much closer to the airport than the city - only a few miles away. At this hour, with so little traffic noise, they may even hear the Moth at the airport.

The arrival of an incoming flight and one departure made it easier. Seeing the flight paths, he was able to steer well clear, going close to the city before turning towards the airport.

Finding the road was easy. Only one major highway ran in that direction, the last few miles passing through a dark, sparsely populated area with only industrial premises and the barracks. It ran straight, and was lined on both sides with street lights, much like a runway, Tim thought, and descended lower, skimming a hundred feet above the tall street lights and passing over a truck. He kept a wary eye open for crossing transmission lines.

He almost missed the call box. He was still looking back at the barracks on the other side, wondering if his passing so low and close would cause alarm there. It was something he had not considered, and being fired on by a bunch of trigger-happy soldiers was definitely not part of his plan. It was only when he looked back on the other side that he caught a glimpse of the small booth passing under the wing.

It was much closer to the barracks than he had anticipated, barely half a mile. He banked quickly to get a better look. It was on the corner of a small intersection, in front of a small group of shops and a used-car yard. All were in darkness except for a few dim security lights. He could see no sign of anyone.

Still concerned about the barracks, Tim went into a steep turn, taking a chance. He looked directly down on the box, yet still saw no one, and was beginning to sweat when he saw a dark figure detach itself from the shadows of a building, waving frantically.

Tim levelled out with relief and considered his next problem, which was where to land. Either he had miscalculated the time, or he had enjoyed a tailwind, for although the sky was beginning to pale in the east, first light was still a good twenty minutes away. It was a semi-rural area, and bound to have fields or some other suitable place to land nearby, but he could not risk waiting around that long.

He looked up the highway towards the airport and saw the headlights of several cars, obviously returning after picking up passengers. The road going in showed only two vehicles, still some distance away. It was going to be a tight squeeze.

Tim hesitated only a moment. He had no choice, and little time to ponder the risk he was taking. Turning again steeply, he reduced power and glided down between the streetlights towards the road, searching anxiously for the glint of light on crossing wires.

The wheels touched the smooth bitumen a few hundred yards short of the intersection as the first vehicle topped a gentle rise and bathed the Moth in its headlights. Tim held the tail off the ground until he was almost at the intersection, than cut the power right back and turned into it, slewing dangerously on loose gravel, but the Moth straightened, trundling a short distance up the side road before Tim was able to make a wide swinging turn and face back towards the highway.

The leading vehicle in the line - a freight truck - slowed down, its occupants no doubt startled, but

Tim had no time to worry about what they might do. He was occupied with weaving the unstoppable Moth from one side of the road to the other at the same time as he searched the deserted buildings and tried to avoid the deep rainwater culverts.

Elliot finally appeared, hobbling slowly from his alley, a plastic shopping bag held modestly between his legs. As he came closer, seeming undecided, Tim signalled urgently, directing him towards the rear of the port wing, and Elliot began hopping to increase his speed. Tim extended his arm to give him something to pull on.

'On there,' he shouted, leaning out and pointing to the black-lettered sign on the wing, and clasped Elliot's feverishly searching fingers to hoist him up. 'Get in the front.' He shrugged out of his harness to stand and help Elliot in. 'Don't touch anything,' he warned. 'Especially that.' He pointed to the stick. There was no time for harness and other niceties. One of the vehicles had stopped at the intersection and partly turned in to catch them in its lights. 'Get down and cover yourself with the blanket.'

Tim sat and steered the Moth towards the car, causing it to reverse hastily onto the verge, where it stopped once more. Approaching the intersection, Tim could see more vehicles coming along the highway, at least a dozen sets of headlights, and no doubt there would be more behind them, he guessed, including buses.

Three vehicles were well ahead of those following and, as they passed without slowing, Tim gritted his teeth and pushed the throttle forward, swinging onto the highway behind them and showering the stopped vehicle of the curious onlookers with dust and gravel.

He was not concerned about catching the vehicles ahead. Despite the speed limit, he guessed they would still be travelling faster than his take-off speed, but the increasing light from those behind told they were catching up fast. He hoped they would see the yellow Moth and use their brakes, and they must have done, for the lights stayed at a respectable distance until the Moth was safely airborne.

At first light the city was out of view, and Tim greeted the dawn with huge relief. The whole exercise had taken less than ten minutes, but it felt like ten years. He hoped no one had seen the registration.

A short while later he landed again, at the deserted airstrip of a small mine, to refuel from the twenty-litre can sharing the front cockpit with Elliot, and to have some well-earned coffee.

Elliot did not emerged from under his blanket until they stopped, and Tim was shocked at his appearance.

His face was so battered he would not have recognised him. His body looked as if it had been towed behind a galloping horse. Nevertheless, he managed to give Tim a beaming, if somewhat lopsided, grin.

'I am very, very happy you come for me, sir,' he said, exchanging the grin for a frown of sincerity. 'God has listened.'

'Hell, Elliot, you smell terrible.'

'Yes, sir, I hide in the rubbish.'

'I can't wait to hear, but first we'll get you home and checked over. I suppose you're hungry.'

'More even than a lion.'

'Chew on these, then,' Tim said, giving him the parcel of sandwiches Frek had prepared. He also handed him the bottle of water. 'Sorry, but the coffee is badly needed by the captain.'

Elliot didn't answer, his mouth already stuffed full, and his eyes fixed hungrily on where he was going to take the next bite.

***

Kelly nibbled tentatively on the spicy satay. She had bought the skewered chunks of unidentifiable meat from the young street vendor more out of sympathy than appetite, and wondered exactly what it was she was eating, and what unpleasant results she could expect. And the solid press of humanity, complete with its associated smells, was hardly conducive to alfresco dining. She dropped the food into a nearby bin and continued her aimless wandering through the busy market.

Having a one night stopover in Kuala Lumpur instead of taking a direct flight from Sydney to LA had seemed a good idea when she had booked from Philadelphia. It didn't cost any extra except for the price of a hotel room, and she had thought she would enjoy the break in an exotic location, and probably would have, had she had company, but shopping alone was no fun, and she was not in the mood for sightseeing. Other than the quaint Moorish arches and turnip-topped towers, Kuala Lumpur was like any other big city; full of people.

Also, she had been forced to endure being on the same flight again as the unpleasant Africans. Thankfully, they had now departed.

To kill time until her flight that evening, Kelly returned to her hotel and spent the afternoon swimming and dozing by the pool, then caught the courtesy bus to the airport. She checked in and surrendered her single bag, bought a magazine, and was sitting in the departure lounge, engrossed in it, when an authoritarian voice intruded.

'Kelly Maddock?'

'Yes?' She looked up to see two uniformed men confronting her.

'Come with us, please.' The one who spoke took her officiously by the upper arm.

Alarmed, Kelly jerked away. 'Leave me alone. Who are you?'

'Police. You must come please. We have some questions to ask.'

'What questions? What's all this about?'

She received no answer. One man nodded to the other and suddenly Kelly found herself being hoisted bodily from her chair. Her arms were pulled behind and her wrists swiftly cuffed.

'What the hell do you think you're doing?' Kelly protested, too shocked to even think of struggling. 'I have a plane to catch.'

'No plane,' said one, gripping her arm firmly. The other picked up her purse and tucked it under his arm. They pushed her forward.

Kelly resisted. 'Let me go, damn you! I'm an American citizen. You can't do this. I haven't done anything.'

They didn't reply. Flanking her, they used their bodies to move her. People were staring. Many looked like fellow Americans, waiting to board the same flight, and Kelly appealed to them, twisting around to call out. 'If any of you are Americans... will you contact the embassy and tell them what has happened... please?'

She barely had time to call out her name before being taken round a corner and along a passage, out of view. 'You've got this all wrong,' she told the two policemen, trying to keep her voice even and reasonable. 'Why are you arresting me?'

They continued to ignore her questions, and she gave up resisting, walking quickly, wanting now to get to someone who would listen.

After passing through several service doors, descending in an elevator, and passing along another corridor, Kelly was ushered into what looked to be some sort of rest or first-aid room. It contained a high, rubber-sheeted examining bed, a washbasin and a stool. On a table against the wall sat her large canvas holdall with all its luggage tags and stickers. The man with her purse and small travel bag dumped them on the table beside it while the other removed the handcuffs. Then they left, closing the door.

Kelly rubbed distractedly at her wrists. Uncertainty and a growing nervousness had replaced her initial shock and outrage. Her spinning mind sought for practical answers, but found none. This can't be happening, she thought.

Her passport was in order and she knew it hadn't expired. She had her ticket and boarding pass. They were in her purse with her few remaining dollars. She snatched up the purse to check. It was all there. Then she noticed the zip on her holdall was open, and she dropped the purse to look closer. Her clothes inside were in disarray, as if everything had been removed then carelessly replaced.

She was staring at it, trying to fathom the reason, when the door opened and a man wearing a white coat with a stethoscope dangling from the breast pocket entered. Close behind came two women in khaki and blue uniforms, similar to that worn by the policemen.

The doctor acknowledged Kelly with a nod. 'Remove your clothes please.'

Kelly stared at him.

The doctor said something to the women in Malaysian, then one of them spoke to Kelly. 'You must be examined by the doctor. If you do not remove your clothes we will have to do it. It will be easier if you do as he says.'

'Why? There's nothing wrong with me. I don't need a doctor. Don't you see you have the wrong person?'

'You are to be searched for drugs.'

'Drugs?' Kelly laughed scornfully. 'You've definitely got the wrong person. I don't do drugs.'

The women spoke to each other again, then to the doctor, who gave a helpless shrug then glanced at his watch, as if in a hurry to go somewhere. One of the women went to the door and partly opened it. She leaned out, spoke briefly to someone outside, then turned back, holding the handcuffs. Both women advanced on Kelly with determined expressions.

She stepped back. 'All right, damn you. I'll take them off myself.' Angrily, Kelly kicked off her shoes and unbuttoned her jeans, dropping them to the floor. She stepped out of them, then caught the bottom of her tee shirt and pulled it over her head, dropping it on top of the jeans. She stood with her arms folded across her naked breasts. 'There! Satisfied?'

'Also them,' said one of the women, indicating to her briefs.

Kelly hesitated, then hooked her thumbs into the elastic and pushed her pants down, standing on them to free one foot at a time. 'I don't know what the hell you expect me to hide in there,' she said. 'You people are really something, you know that?'

One of the women picked up her clothes and searched through them quickly before laying them neatly on the table. The doctor stepped forward to stand close, and Kelly glared at him as he looked carefully into each of her eyes in turn. He stepped back to lift her arms and examine the insides, presumably for needle bruises, then he did the same with her thighs and buttocks.

'Stand here, please,' he said, taking her arm and leading her to the bed. He left her to open a cupboard and remove a sealed packet, which he ripped open to withdraw a pair of surgical gloves.

'What now?' Kelly asked, guessing what was intended and horrified at the thought of it.

He stretched on one of the gloves then, from an open jar in the cupboard, scooped a glob of gel. 'Bend over and spread your legs.'

'No,' Kelly said, determined. 'I don't have to submit to that. You can see I'm not hiding anything. Please, why don't you believe me?'

She was given no time to protest further. The women stepped forward to each take one of her arms and twist them up behind her back at the same time as her head was forcibly pushed down onto the thin mattress.

Kelly relaxed her legs to slump on the bed and pull her knees up underneath it, but the women each hooked one of their own legs around hers and pulled them apart. They had obviously done it before.

Kelly had no option but to submit to the indignity of the probing fingers. They were finally withdrawn without comment, but still she was held down. She heard the distinctive sound of the rubber glove being removed, then the equally recognisable sound of another one being snapped on.

The fingers returned to explore again, this time where no finger had ever been, and Kelly tried to blank her mind to the unpleasant sensation. After it was withdrawn, tissues were used to wipe her clean, as if she was a helpless child, and that small condescension was, to Kelly, far worse than what had preceded it.

The women released her and she was allowed to dress. She did so silently, humiliated beyond thought or words. With her clothes back on she still felt naked and shamed.

The doctor left, but the women remained, and a short while later another two men came in. One was older and wore a different uniform to the police. His companion was in plain clothes. The man in uniform held a book that Kelly recognised instantly. It was the photo album she had bought in Harare. It had a picture of a giraffe on the cover, and she had spent the last afternoon there filling it with the photographs she had taken at Gara Pasi with Juliette's camera. Most were of Rosie. She remembered having placed the album in the bottom of her holdall where it would lie flat.

'Miss Maddock,' the man said, placing it on the table. 'How can you explain that we found this in your possession?' He opened the album to reveal a clear plastic bag containing a white substance. It was flattened from being pressed between the pages.

Kelly stared at it in shock, a numb feeling coming over her. She had seen the bizarre warning posters that had been placed strategically around the airport for the benefit of would-be drug smugglers. It could not be happening to her.

'We look very seriously on the illegal taking of drugs in or out of our country,' the official continued. 'Especially heroin.' He tapped eloquently on the packet with his finger to indicate that is what it was. 'Are you not aware that we have the death penalty here for those who are caught with it and convicted?'

***

Mystery plane on airport road.

It would have received greater coverage had it not been too late to make the daily newspaper, and had not the looming food riots and politics dominated the morning news on radio and television. Even so, in some circles, it caused quite a stir.

Although two of the several motorists who had witnessed the incident agreed the aircraft was a yellow one, others gave conflicting reports as to both color and type. One said it was a crop-sprayer that had landed with engine problems on its way to work, another that it had not landed, but had been dive-bombing the traffic, and still another that swore it had been an army helicopter landing at the barracks. The Ministry of Defence had declined to comment, and the Department of Civil Aviation was investigating the incident.

Tim accepted his notoriety with remarkable aplomb. A few local residents and friends who knew the plane, telephoned him to find out what he had been up to, and he assured them it was not his plane, that he would never pull such a crazy stunt, and that he could not fly anyway because of his broken leg.

. 'Maybe I should go paint the Moth a different color,' he suggested to Juliette. 'How about purple?'

'You won't think it so funny if you lose your licence,' she rebuked him, still angry at the risk he had taken, and because he had not told her exactly what had occurred, leaving her to hear about it on the news. 'It's a miracle you weren't killed.'

'Yeah, well, like I said. I got him into it so I had to get him out. No choice.'

'You could have waited until it got light.' She

321

changed the subject. 'What are you going to do with him?'

'They took all his belongings and money, so I suppose we'll have to give him a job. He says that now he is experienced, he should be the one to guard the rhinos in Australia. I guess he's feeling a bit nervous.' Tim chuckled. 'He's even shaved his head. Maybe he thinks it will make him invisible.'

'He won't go with John to have his knee x-rayed either,' Juliette said. 'Mind you, after what those swines did to him I can't say I blame him for wanting to keep a low profile.'

The subject under discussion had himself achieved some measure of celebrity status amongst the staff and their families. They had known him only as the poacher who had been tricked by the Madam Juliette, and whom they believed had been handed over to the police to be put in prison. So it was not surprising that his return to Gara Pasi in the plane, after its exciting departure in the dark several hours before, had been the cause of much confused speculation. Especially after it was seen in what condition he was in, and how well he was now being treated.

It was left to Elliot to explain and, no longer gagged by a spy's code of silence, he was quick to reassure them that he was not an escaped prisoner or poacher, but a famous undercover agent who worked for ESPU and knew James Bond personally. The fact no one except Mathias had heard either of those names before did little to detract from their importance. His battered appearance, and the fact he had tricked the despised Fifth Brigade, was more than enough.

The majority of the staff, being of the Shangaan tribe, had little love for the Mashona as a whole, of whom the Brigade was mainly comprised. Neither did they care much for the Matabele, but all had heard of the atrocities carried out by Mugabe's army on that tribe, and none put it past the Fifth Brigade to do the same to them if given the opportunity. To have escaped from inside their own barracks was to be a hero.

Pretending to be dead, Elliot warned the enthralled propeller boys, pitching his voice to reach the sister of the eldest one, whose pretty ear was turned in his direction, was very dangerous work, and could only be done after much special training. It was not something they should try.

When asked what he was going to do now that he was no longer a spy, Elliot was obscure, saying only that a dead spy was the best disguise, and that he was going to teach the man who had betrayed him how to be dead for real.

Still harbouring some resentment and loss of

face from his earlier experience with Elliot, Mathias reported what he heard to Tim, perhaps hoping to get some of his own back, and Tim confronted Elliot, asking him exactly what he meant.

'When my leg is good I will cross the border and kill the Chinese one called Wang, sir,' Elliot admitted candidly. 'Is that not what you wish also?'

'We are not like Mugabe's thugs, Elliot. We will leave that to the law.'

'Uh!' Elliot laughed disdainfully, shaking his bald head, which Tim still found disconcerting. On top of his battered face it gave him the look of a third rate prize-fighter. 'Even so,' Elliot persisted, 'I will kill him, for sure.'

Tim was somewhat taken aback by this uncharacteristic show of defiance, the more so because he believed Elliot was serious. In truth, he did not mind in the least if the Chinese buyer was taken out. Certainly, he could not see the law doing anything, and Elliot had good reason for revenge, but he could not openly condone such a drastic solution.

'We have already informed the ESPU about him, Elliot, so maybe you should just leave it. They may want to use him to get more information on who is behind this killing of the chipimbiris.'

'I will ask him, sir. He will tell me, for sure.'

'You mean with a gun pointing at him?'

'I will do what God says,' Elliot answered, then frowned. 'Do you think the madam doctor will have some ointments for to put on my head? The mosquito, he like it too much.'

***

It was two days before the American Embassy sent a man to see her, and by then Kelly was beginning to believe her message had not been received and was destined to be incarcerated forever - or until they hanged her without anyone knowing.

They had brought her to the prison and locked her in a cell shortly after the unpleasant body search. As far as she knew, she had not been charged, but she had been questioned at length on three separate occasions, the questions mainly concerned with where she had obtained the heroin, how much she had paid, who were her accomplices, and was it for her own use or to sell for profit. All of her own questions, denials, protests and demands, had been ignored with typical Asian equanimity, which she found even more frustrating than their dumb questions. It was like talking to deaf parrots.

Thankfully, she had not suffered any of the nasty

experiences she had heard took place in prisons, and which she had been dreading. She had not been abused, raped, or molested in communal showers. She shared one shower with three terrified Asian women who spoke no English, and looked upon her as some sort of threat, made worse by her friendly approaches. Although her clothes badly needed washing, she was at least allowed to wear them - minus her watch - and not the drab prison smocks. Food consisted mainly of stodgy noodles and rice combined with obscure vegetables, none of which she could bring herself to eat.

When the man from the embassy finally arrived, sporting a flowery shirt, and in the company of a plump Asian man wearing a suit flecked with silver threads and no tie, Kelly's heart sank.

'What took you so long?' she demanded irritably. 'I thought you people were supposed to be efficient. Didn't you know I was here?'

The Asian man smiled expansively, and the embassy official - who looked not much older than herself - appeared flustered and nervous, as if not used to this sort of assignment. 'Yes, sorry about that, Miss er... do you mind if I call you Kelly? No, we didn't. That is, we did, but not where... exactly.' He frowned. 'The authorities haven't been very helpful.' Then he gave what he must have thought was an encouraging smile. 'Have you been treated well?'

'No, I've been stuck in prison, and I want to get out. I shouldn't be here.'

'Yes... of course.' Then he suddenly remembered his companion. 'Ah, yes... this is Mister Willie Rama, a lawyer who will represent you.'

'Why do I need a lawyer? I haven't done anything. This whole thing is a stupid mistake.'

'You are to be charged with drug trafficking,' Mister Rama explained. 'The amount you had exceeded what is considered adequate for personal use.'

'Peddling drugs?' Kelly gave a disgusted laugh. 'You've got to be joking. I hate people who sell drugs. I hate drugs, period. That stuff was planted on me. I never saw them find it. It could have come from anywhere.'

'Nevertheless, it is a very serious charge in this country,' the embassy man said.

'Very,' the Indian lawyer agreed, nodding sombrely. 'It would be better if we could convince them you were a heavy user. Even though the amount you had exceeds the limit, we may be able to argue for life imprisonment instead of the mandatory death penalty.'

The same feeling of bizarre unreality swept over

Kelly that she had experienced at the airport, but this time also accompanied by a heavy, disembodied sensation, as if her blood had suddenly thickened to double its normal consistency. It could not be her standing here, accused and listening to threats of the death penalty. It had to be someone else. Someone with whom she shared the same body, but who had a different life.

It began to dawn on her that getting out of the prison was not the foregone conclusion she had anticipated. Her being there was a mistake, but the drug had been in her bag - perhaps placed there by someone with the intention of retrieving it once safely in the US. These two men were her only hope. She had to convince them. If they didn't believe her, who would?

'Look,' Kelly appealed wearily. 'There's no point in discussing what penalty I might get. You have to work on how the drug got in my bag. If it was mine I would tell you, but it's not. I'm completely innocent and that's what I'm sticking with. You have to believe me.' She looked sincerely at each of them in turn, suddenly feeling the full effects of no food and little sleep.

'Very well, Miss Kelly,' the lawyer said. 'If that is what you wish. Where did you keep the bag?'

'In my hotel room.'

'Did you meet anyone at the hotel who, in any way, was suspicious... a fellow traveller perhaps?'

'No. I saw tourists there, but I never spoke to anyone, and no one approached me. Nothing suspicious that I can think of, except...' Kelly hesitated, not sure if she should mention her little episode with the African diplomats. It was hardly relevant, but she had threatened them... had even mentioned reporting them to the Customs. Could she have given them enough reason to get their own back? In her anger she had given away more than she had intended, even accusing them of murder. Being imprisoned was certainly an effective way of keeping her out of their hair. They would not know she had been bluffing.

The two men were waiting expectantly for her to explain, and she decided she had nothing to lose and, as far-fetched as it seemed, it may even be true.

She told them from the beginning, and the more she explained, the more convinced she became that she was on the right track. The Africans had also disembarked here. It would have been simple to follow her to the hotel and plant the drugs. They had the money, the opportunity, and the motive.

'I'm sure I'm right,' Kelly ended positively. 'If they can arrange for a man to be killed, they can also arrange for a person to be arrested. All it takes is money, and they have plenty.'

To her surprise, Willie Rama agreed with her. 'The horn is a very powerful currency here. Worth even more than gold. It will be very difficult to prove such a thing though. Can you describe these people?'

'Only that they were well dressed and African. I think the woman was wearing a wig.'

'I see. Well, anyway, I will talk with the staff and see what I can find out.'

'Is there anyone you would like us to contact on your behalf in the States?' the embassy man asked.

Kelly gave him both Pop Franz's and Billy Steel's details. 'You'll find their telephone numbers in my purse... wherever that is.'

'How about toothpaste, shampoo, uhm... women's things?'

'Toothpaste and shampoo... thanks. What happens now? Will I get bail?'

Willie Rama shook his head. 'Not in these cases, Miss Kelly. I think after today you will be moved to another prison to await trial.' He paused in thought for a moment. 'It will probably be in three or four months. But don't worry,' he added hastily. 'I am sure we will be coming to visit you often.'

***

Standing on the apron at Harare Airport in the company of John and several other National Parks men, reporters and sundry officials, Tim watched the departure of the Boeing 737 and felt as if the precious load it carried aloft had been removed directly from his own shoulders. It had taken two years to achieve this moment. Years of wrangling, politicking, threatening, and even the odd bit of bribery, yet he felt no sense of achievement, only nagging doubts that he had missed or forgotten something.

But everything had gone remarkably smoothly, without the expected last minute hitches, and Juliette had seemed well in control of the situation aboard the aircraft, administering mild tranquillisers to her eight charges and assigning responsibilities to the Australian handlers with the calm assurance of a seasoned veteran. All without his assistance.

Still, the nagging sensation persisted. He told himself it was simply the anti-climax. A reaction after the weeks of hectic activity and worry, and that he was tired and needed a break, but it didn't help. The feeling prevailed all the way back to Gara Pasi, and was still with him next morning when he left on his dawn patrol.

Drawn by some nostalgic magnet, he flew over the pan where he had landed with Kelly after her loop, where they had made love, and his eyes were drawn by an even stronger force to the trailing edge of the port wing where it had taken place. He smiled as he recalled the incident, but with more derision than wistfulness. It was not a conquest he was particularly proud of. He had taken advantage of her while she was still on a high from the flying, all but forced her, yet, despite that, he was still pleased that he had. It had broken the ice, brought them closer, although not nearly as close as he had hoped.

Looking back on it now that he had little else to occupy his mind, Tim found it hard to believe that he could have been so wrong about her. She was definitely all woman, and the few minutes of passion they shared returned more than once to stir his blood and disturb his sleep. He wished he had acted differently, but he had not, sticking stubbornly to his male ego, and now it was too late to make amends. By now she would be back in her familiar life, and had probably forgotten him. It came as a surprise to realize how much he missed her.

Back at Gara Pasi after his patrol, Tim threw himself into work to keep himself occupied. Normally happy with his own company, now he felt agitated, and he would be on his own for the next two weeks, until John had finished with his reports and other duties at his head-office.

Tim had plenty to do. The stockade needed cleaning and some poles replaced where angry horns had ripped and loosened them, and several miles of game fence had to be patrolled and repaired.

'Where the hell is Elliot?' he demanded irritably of Kawaseka. 'He was supposed to be here to help.'

Kawaseka took his time about answering, emptying his loaded shovel into the wheelbarrow and methodically scraping it free of the sticky dung before putting it down. As with following spoor on rocky ground, some signs needed careful consideration before committing oneself, or one could easily take the wrong path. 'I think he has gone to church,' he ventured warily.

'What?' Tim laughed, but with a resigned shake of his head. Elliot's recent preoccupation with religion was understandable after what he had experienced, but it was also an inconvenience.

'Yes, mambo.' Then, in further explanation. 'Tomorrow is Sunday.'

Tim groaned. He had forgotten it was the weekend. Except for Frek, who took his day off on Mondays, the staff finished the week at midday on Saturday, which a quick glance at his watch informed him had passed close to two hours ago, yet no one had said anything, no doubt aware of his mood, for he had done little to conceal it.

'Okay, Seki,' Tim capitulated. 'Tell the men to knock off now. I'll pay them overtime.'

'Yes, mambo.'

Tim walked away and Kawaseka stooped to take the handles of the barrow, then he hesitated. 'I think he has gone to the church in Chimoio where also lives his friend, Sibanda,' he said.

Tim stopped and turned round, alarm bells tinkling. 'Oh? How do you know?'

'I hear it from Lydia.'

'Did she say anything else?' Chimoio was also where the Chinese man, Wang, was based.

'No, mambo, she say only that he must go there to take a message from God.'

The bells began to clang. It could be nothing, but recalling the quietly determined manner in which Elliot had threatened to kill the Chinese agent, and knowing the former terrorist was fully capable of doing it - if he wasn't killed first - gave him an uneasy feeling to add to his growing collection of misgivings.

And the worst of it was that he could do nothing about any of them. His leg would not be free of its cast for at least another five weeks. He could drive and fly, but walking any distance was out of the question.

Elliot would have to fend for himself.

***

With the aid of a pair of tweezers, a small piece of broken mirror propped in the fork of a tree, and a reasonably steady hand, Elliot carefully positioned the tuft of hairs on his chin, holding it in place for a few moments to allow the sticky glob on the end to grip onto the much shorter hairs that sprouted naturally.

It had taken the better part of the previous day to assemble them. Each tuft comprised at least six long, crinkly black strands, selected from amongst those he had shaved from his scalp, and which he had bonded together at the base with transparent glue stolen from the office at Gara Pasi.

When all the tufts stored in the empty cigarette box had been fixed to the point of his chin, Elliot examined the result with a critical eye, shaking his head and waggling his chin to see if they remained in place. They did, and he gave a grunt of satisfaction. It had been a good idea to use the fruit of the gomarangwa tree to stick them. He had used it many times in his youth to trap birds, chewing the fruit into a sticky mass and smearing it on branches, or on the long grass by a river where the birds came to eat the seeds. And, unlike the shiny office glue used to make the tufts, it did not dry and shrivel the skin.

To conceal the shiny globs, he powdered them with fine grey dust he had collected from a clay-pan. Although the result looked more dusty than grey, it was still very impressive, and the hairy chin contrasted well with his bald head, giving him exactly the religious look he was after. He must remember to frown though, he told himself, and not laugh to often. Frowning would make him look more wise.

Satisfied, Elliot removed the white robe from the plastic bag and put it on over his shirt and shorts, being careful not to scrape his chin. Made from coarse sheeting by Lydia, the hem reached to his ankles and the wide sleeves to his wrists. She had done a good job, even embroidering a design in red cotton around the neck.

Sibanda was going to be shocked to see him, and Elliot smiled at the thought. He only hoped the fool's new girlfriend had been accommodating enough to keep him in the village, and that he had not become frightened after the betrayal by the Chinese, and run away with all the money buried under the floor of the hut.

Elliot removed his boots and put them into the bag, which he then concealed under a bush. It was only a short distance from there to the road where he would wait for the bus to Chimoio. The bag could be retrieved on his return.

Ready to leave, he had a quick look around to be sure he had not left any signs, then picked up his tall staff. Made from a dry mahogany branch that he had scorched in ashes and polished to an aged sheen, it was perhaps not as impressive as his father's staff had been, and which he remembered well, but it was stout, straight and heavy, and more than adequate for the task. A bonus was that it helped support his still painful knee, and the limp would add an authentic touch.

Who could dispute, he asked himself as he took a final look in the piece of mirror, holding it at arm's length to try and fit all of himself in, that he was anything but a suffering apostle bent on spreading the good word of Jesus?

Sibanda came hastily when summoned urgently by his girlfriend to confront the white-robed figure beckoning from across the swept area of the huts. He pulled her protectively behind him. 'What does he want of me? Do you know him?'

"I do not know him, my soon husband,' she

answered shyly. 'He speaks only your name, and will not allow others to approach. I think he is a ma'postle.'

'Stay here,' he cautioned her, then walked confidently towards the ma'postle. Religious men were not to be feared, and he could see no weapon other than a stick.

As he approached, the man ambled away, going farther back into the sparse shade of the trees, where he laid down his staff and sat cross-legged beside it, bunching the robe modestly into his crutch. When Sibanda stopped a short distance away, he looked up and grinned. 'Do not be afraid, my friend, it is only a dead man coming to visit you.'

'Jesus!' Sibanda exclaimed, then grinned widely, stepping forward to shake the proffered hand reverently in both of his. 'You are not dead.'

'Exactly,' Elliot replied, 'although it is what I wish to be, so I did not want to be seen alive by the people who know me. Do you understand?'

'Of course,' Sibanda replied with a confused frown, 'but I am happy to see that you are not. We heard from the cousin of a man who works for the Customs that you were taken by the Brigade. Is it so?'

Elliot patted the ground beside him in invitation. 'Sit, and I will tell you. But first you must tell me of our money.'

They spoke for most of the afternoon, interrupted only by the arrival of food and water, delivered by Sibanda's girlfriend, who coyly averted eyes. Even had she happened to glance in the stranger's direction, which she may have done once or twice purely by accident, she could only have seen the unrecognisable rear of a bald head.

As the shade lengthened, she brought welcome mashesh beer in clay jars, and after the third such delivery, Elliot finally decided she must be taken into their confidence. He would have to spend the night with her and Sibanda in their hut, where it would be impossible not to give himself away. She responded with gratifying shock to the discovery, giving them much amusement, and after being sternly sworn to secrecy, was permitted to sit at a respectful distance, where she could see but not hear.

It was for her own good that she did not know too much, Elliot explained to a proud Sibanda. A woman of such youth and innocence should only be concerned with pleasing her man, and not be troubled with thoughts of revenge and death.

**

It was late on Sunday night when the chirping of

Tim's Iridium phone jerked him awake. He snatched it up from his bedside table, squinting at the display screen, then fumbling with the antenna as he threw aside the blanket and crashed out through the door, hopping about erratically on his good leg. He jabbed at the OK button. 'Yes... hello?'

'Tim? It's me.' Juliette's voice came through strongly, but not happily, and Tim's already pounding heart took another leap.

'Jules? What's happened... is everything okay?'

'Everything is fine here, no problems. It's Kelly, Tim. I've just had a call from Dad. Billy Steel contacted him a few hours ago to say that she's been arrested in Kuala Lumpur.'

'What?'

'She's in prison, Tim...' Juliette's voice cracked with emotion.

'Kelly? What for? Take it easy, Jules. Tell me...'

'...don't know too much... accused of smuggling drugs.'

'What?' Tim gripped hard on the instrument, grinding it against his ear. 'What did she do a stupid thing like that for?'

'She didn't, Tim.' Juliette's voice took on a stronger, even admonishing tone. 'Do you really believe she would do such a thing?'

'No… I guess not…'

'There's something else… something that happened on the plane, but I'm a bit concerned talking about it on a mobile, you never…'

'To hell with that. Tell me. It's the middle of the night here.'

'Okay, listen… you're not going to believe this…'

But Tim did believe it. Every word, and after Juliette had clicked off he stood naked in the moonlight with the instrument clenched in his fist and his head pounding with the force of his anger. Juliette was right, Kelly didn't do drugs. But Mugabe's relatives and their friends were not beyond it, and this had their grubby paws all over it.

Tim became aware of whispering beside his rondavel, then Frek materialised from the deep shadow. 'The madam, she has a problem with chipimbiris, suh?'

It took Tim a few moments before he realized what Frek was talking about. 'No, Frek, all is well. Who is with you?'

'My wife, suh. She wake me when she hear you shouting. You want coffee?'

Tim hesitated, but sleep was out of the question. 'Good idea, but first I had better put on some clothes, hadn't I? I'll come to the kitchen, then we must talk. Ask your wife to wake Lydia. I want to speak to her as well.'

Tim dressed hurriedly, his mind in turmoil, Juliette's words still ringing in his ears. While Frek was occupied in the kitchen, he remained outside to call John, as much to share the disturbing news as to feel he was doing something positive.

'What are you going to do?' John asked, the shock still evident in his voice. 'Do you want me there? I can say I'm sick, or have toothache or something…'

'No I haven't a clue. Can't even phone her.'

'I'll think on it. Keep in touch. Those bastards…'

By now the entire compound was awake and wanting to see what all the fuss was about. Tim sent them back to their huts, except for Lydia, whom he questioned as to the exact whereabouts of Elliot. A desperate plan was beginning to form.

After some confused discussion with Frek, who was familiar with the area, having worked there before the war, she eventually managed to impart sufficient information for Frek to fix the locality of the village where Sibanda's girlfriend lived.

'It is on the other side of Chimoio,' he explained to Tim. 'close by the school.'

'A big school?'

'Yes, suh. You know it?'

'No. Does it have a soccer field?' Practically every

school in Africa had one.

Frek was quick to catch on, his face creasing into a concerned frown. 'You wish to go there in the flying machine?'

'I don't know.' Tim observed him thoughtfully, drumming his fingernails on the table. 'Maybe.' Then, after several moments, during which only his drumming and the hissing of the kettle on the stove and the lamp could be heard. 'Do you still have your bicycle?'

Frek was shocked. 'Uh! You wish me to go there with my push-bike?'

'Not from here,' Tim answered with a smile. It was all of three hundred miles by road. 'Only from the Chimoio school. If you are sure you can find the village from there.'

'Suh?' Frek's puzzled look showed he had completely lost the tenuous thread, and Tim made signals towards the spluttering kettle and set about enlightening him, and also himself, the hazy idea beginning to take substance in his own mind as he spoke. Before he had finished it had become a concrete plan, something tangible to cling to in place of the uncertainty. Action instead of frustration.

He stood quickly. 'Leave that, Frek. Go wake Kawaseka and the gang. Wake everyone. Start the generator and open the storeroom. I want that drum of green paint we use for the fence taken to the airstrip. Also all the paintbrushes and all the lamps. Chop-chop, Freki boy. In three hours the sun will be here.'

Frek rushed to the door.

'And don't forget you bicycle!' Tim yelled after him.

***

It was not the prettiest paint-job in the world. Viewed in the garish light of the hissing hurricane lamps, the Moth looked as if it had suffered a virulent attack of green measles over yellow jaundice. Only the fuselage and underneath surfaces of the wings had been painted, including the registration, so from below at least, the Moth would defy recognition.

The twelve painters had enjoyed themselves immensely. Given a brush and free reign to express their artistic abilities on such an interesting canvas as an aeroplane, they had swiftly produced a work that Salvador Dali himself might have been proud of. Especially, he would have approved the inclusion of Frek's bicycle lashed to the fuselage and upper wing struts beside the front cockpit.

Standing outside the circle of light, sipping his

third coffee, and waiting for the paint to dry, Tim observed the completed masterpiece with some regret. He had liked the gay yellow, and it was not going to be easy to get rid of the green, but it had needed repainting anyway, and he had been toying with the idea of bright red.

'Excuse, sir,' one of the paint-splattered propeller boys said at his side. 'Old Father wishes to speak with you.'

Tim was surprised. Fulamani seldom left his huts these days. The boy's raised arm showed him where the old man was sitting on the ground with his two wives and he went over. 'Mangwanani, Old Father,' he greeted, shaking the gnarled hand that protruded from the blanket.

'Your machine now has the face of a soldier, Nkosi Timi. Is it that you wish for it to hide in the bush?'

Tim laughed. Very little escaped the old man. 'Something like that.'

'Is it a time of war?' Fulamani gestured to his oldest wife and she held out his snuff tin, and Tim shifted impatiently as the old man sniffed a pinch into each nostril in turn. Taking snuff was usually the precursor to protracted reminiscing or a lecture, and he did not have time for either. The sky was already beginning to pale in the east.

'Today it is the war of the chipimbiri,' he answered.

'You are much like your father,' Fulamani said, changing the subject. 'He also make war with the flying machine. Did he speak to you of the time he throw the bombs on the houses of the man who put gasoline in the waterholes?'

'Was that the same man you tried to shoot?' Tim countered, and Fulamani cackled with delight, looking modestly pleased with himself, then he became serious.

'There will be snakes on this path that you travel.'

It was not a question, and Tim nodded soberly, glancing at the lightening sky. 'Yes, there are snakes.'

'Famba gashle, Timi, walk carefully.' Fulamani signalled for another pinch of snuff then shrugged closer into his skin blanket. The audience had ended.

Accompanied by much shouted advice from the propeller boys, a nervously grinning Frek settled himself into the front cockpit and pulled on his balaclavas and goggles. Tim did the same, and one of the boys rushed forward at his signal to spin the propeller. Kawaseka had already run to the end of the airstrip with one of the hurricane lamps to clear away any grazing animals, and Tim thundered towards him on full throttle, cheered on by the enthusiastic propeller boys.

Once airborne and on course, Tim's dark thoughts returned. Despite the festive mood of the past two hours, it was no joy-flight he was embarking on, and the old man's sobering words were well founded, his reference to snakes prophetic. The African diplomats could not have arranged Kelly's arrest in an Asian country alone. They would have needed local assistance, and who better to provide it than the Golden Horn snakeheads with whom they must be involved?

The illegal flight into Mozambique itself did not worry him overmuch. It would still be early morning when he arrived over the school, which probably would have been deserted even if it weren't a Sunday. And anyone hearing the Moth would naturally assume he was going to or from the local airfield, which was only a few miles away on the opposite side of the small town. If he was quick, and glided in, no one would be any the wiser.

His main concern was the unpredictable Elliot. He needed him to get to the Chinese buyer, who was his only link to Kelly. If Elliot was not at the village where Lydia said he had gone to visit his friend Sibanda, or if he had already killed Wang as he had threatened, then his hastily conceived plan was doomed.

***

It was close to dawn when Elliot left the village

347

and strode purposefully along the path to Chimoio. Like Moses descending from the mount, he too, was filled with righteousness determination. Not only had he been betrayed and sent off to a certain death, but the Chinese had not paid for the horn, and had also stolen the one hundred emergency dollars that had been in his red bag.

Trailing some distance behind Elliot came his faithful followers, Sibanda and his girlfriend, Miriam, holding hands. She had been a last minute inclusion, mainly because she had refused to remain behind while her soon-to-be husband went to town on a Sunday and, as she didn't know the true reason for the journey, Elliot had been unable to think of a likely explanation as to why she should not accompany them. In any event, he rationalised, she could prove useful in that she knew the town well, and her presence made them look less suspicious.

During his days with the freedom fighters, they had invariably launched an attack at, or shortly before, dawn, and Elliot had decided to carry on the tradition. His enemy would be asleep and unsuspecting, although Elliot intended to wake him first. It was important that Wang know who was killing him.

Beyond that, Elliot had no definite plan to speak of, and none, he believed, was necessary. He would simply walk in through the alley behind the restaurant, into the back of the house, stick his bayonet into Wang, then walk out again. Providing he was not seen, no one would suspect a dead man of being the killer.

Elliot's only concern was that he would meet Wang's Korean companion unexpectedly and be forced to use Sibanda's rifle, which presently bumped reassuringly against his hip beneath the robe. He had even been in two minds about taking it. Unlike the rusty bayonet, which could easily be replaced if necessary, he could not leave their one remaining weapon at the scene after firing it, and neither could he risk being caught with it on his person.

But that, Elliot decided, was less of a problem than not being able to defend himself, and if he had to shoot the Korean, or anyone else that came between himself and Wang, he would.

Dawn had broken by the time they reached the outskirts of the still sleeping town, and Elliot shepherded his followers into the shadows of a convenient tree while he affected some minor repairs to his itchy beard, which had a disconcerting habit of dislodging itself every time he forgot it was not real and scratched. Thankfully, he would not be needing it for much longer.

'Much of it is still there,' Sibanda observed,

peering closely at Elliot's chin in the gloom. 'Does it matter if some look to be pointing up?'

Elliot pushed aside his friend's probing finger impatiently, his nerves beginning to twitch now they had arrived. 'Leave it. Do you remember what it is you must do?'

'I must walk with Miriam past the house,' Sibanda answered. 'To look for the Land Cruiser. If not there I must...' He stopped, head tilted as if listening.

'It is only an aeroplane,' Elliot said. 'If the Land Cruiser is not there you must send Miriam to look at the back, then you...'

'The engine has stopped.'

'Maybe the pilot does not want to wake the sleeping people,' Elliot said sarcastically. 'It is going to land, you fool. Now what will Miriam do if she is seen?'

'It is going the wrong way for the airport.'

They all stared up at the dark silent shape now directly overhead and descending rapidly to the north of them. It made a sudden turn, showing a flash of yellow in the brightening sky.

'It has four wings,' Sibanda observed. 'Does not the aeroplane belonging to...'

'Eh!' Miriam interjected. 'It looks to be crashing by the school!' Her voice rose excitedly.

'Be quiet,' Elliot hissed. Then he drew himself up with aloof resignation. 'He has come for me,' he stated, a hint of pride, maybe even relief, showing in his stoical sigh. He retrieved his staff and adjusted the unseen rifle on his hip. 'For sure, God has sent him.'

***

The sun was already shining yellow on the trees when the returning Elliot and his disciples met a perspiring Frek peddling fast towards them on his bicycle. They were forced to step hastily into the long wet grass beside the path to avoid collision, and Frek skidded to a halt well past them.

After lengthy greetings and introductions to Miriam, during which time Frek's eyes turned more than once to the point of Elliot's chin, he informed him that he had already been to Miriam's huts to look for Elliot. Mister Tim wanted to see him urgently at the school, he said, where he was waiting in the aeroplane, even as they spoke

'Better we go quickly,' he advised. 'He fears to be seen.'

Elliot handed him the staff. 'I will take the bicycle,' he declared loftily and, straddling it before Frek could protest, he set off along the path.

'Uh! Be careful of the dress,' Frek called after him, but too late. Elliot's wet robe caught in the chain and he was brought to a sudden and undignified halt.

The three ran to assist, and a few minutes later Elliot was on his way once more, this time with the mangled hem hoisted safely clear, but with the barrel of the AK dangling dangerously close to the spokes. He wobbled precariously as he shifted the rifle to his front, then straightened and proceeded without further mishap.

Tim stopped his nervous pacing to stare intently when he saw the strange cyclist approaching along the perimeter of the soccer field. The area was still deserted and quiet, but the surrounding countryside was too open for his liking, with too many huts and small farms. Africans were early risers, and the Moth could easily have been seen, even if not heard.

He relaxed only after the cyclist gave him a cheery wave and, as he drew closer, a welcoming grin.

'Bloody hell, Elliot, I didn't recognise you. What's with the robe? And your chin… is that supposed to be a beard?'

Elliot ignored the questions and stated positively. 'You came for me, sir.'

'What the hell are you doing taking chances by coming here? Dammit, Elliot, I told you to leave the

Chinese alone. You were supposed to be at work...' He paused to fix Elliot with a stern frown. 'You haven't done anything stupid... like killed him, have you?'

'Not yet, sir. God sent you to stop me, I think.'

'Well...' Tim blew a sigh of relief. 'Thank God for that. I need to speak with Wang.'

Elliot swept away beads of sweat from his bald pate, pondering the implications of the surprising statement with an expression of amused disbelief. 'But for sure, he is a very dangerous person. How can it be that you will see him without trouble?'

'That is something I still have to figure out, Elliot, but see him I will, and that's for sure. Where is Frek?'

'Coming, sir,' Elliot dismounted and propped the bicycle against the tree next to the Moth. 'Also Sibanda and Miriam.'

'Who?'

'She is Sibanda's girlfriend.'

Tim scowled. A party was not exactly what he had in mind, but not much could be done about it now. 'Okay, but we had better talk before they get here. I want you to tell me everything you know about this Chinese man. How he looks, what he wears, the way he talks, where he's living... everything. And can you please remove that ridiculous beard? It's distracting as hell.'

But Elliot could add little to what he had already told them in his debriefings with Joubert of the ESPU. Nevertheless, Tim prodded him until Frek and the other two arrived some twenty minutes later. He needed to build a picture in his mind of Wang, to have an idea of what to expect before he met him.

How to accomplish that eventuality, Tim thought, was going to be the next problem he hadn't given much prior consideration. Maybe he had been around Elliot too long.

Surprisingly though, it was Elliot himself who came up with the basics of a plan.

'We should first send Sibanda to see him,' he suggested. 'He can say to the Chinese that he has a horn in the bushes that he wishes to sell very cheap. He will come, for sure, then we will catch him.'

'Uh!' Sibanda looked startled. 'Myself? I don't think that is such a good plan.' He laughed nervously and appealed to Tim. 'He is very tricky, sir. He will know I am lying.'

'He does not know you,' Elliot scoffed, 'so of what are you afraid?'

'Of course!' Sibanda replied heatedly. 'It is true. He does not know me. So how is it that I must know of him, eh? Does he have a big sign that says he buys the horns? Does he speak of it on the television? No. I can't do it. The plan is very stupid.'

'He has a good point,' Tim intervened. 'The idea is good, but we have to change it somehow. Maybe if Sibanda admits to the Chinese that he was employed by you, Elliot, and that you had told him where you were selling the horns.'

'I do not think he will believe such a thing,' Sibanda said, his lip beginning to droop. 'He will see it is a trick. I am not a good one for making lies.'

Elliot snorted derisively, but made no comment.

'I can do it,' Miriam said.

Tim looked at her in surprise. So far, she had been silent and withdrawn, as African women usually were in the exclusive company of men, and perhaps even more so with himself being there. He had been averse to having her present, not wanting, for a variety of reasons, to get her involved, and had only agreed reluctantly after being informed that she already knew about the horns and Elliot's spying.

'No,' Sibanda objected again, but this time with a shake of his head and a condescending smile.

'Yes, I can do it,' Miriam argued, perhaps spurred to disagreement by his smirk. 'A woman will not cause suspicion. I will say to him that my boyfriend told me of the place.' She glanced apologetically at Sibanda, who scowled in return. He opened his mouth to protest, but Elliot was quicker.

'You will make a very excellent spy,' he complimented. 'Sibanda is a stranger, so will be person who is seen with suspicion, but who can be afraid of a woman? The Chinese will believe you, for sure. Heh!' He gave her a patronising smile. 'Sibanda is lucky to have such a woman as you.'

With his face saved, Sibanda bowed out gracefully. 'She wishes to be a teacher,' he announced proudly.

Tim refined the plan further. Miriam was to go to the restaurant when it opened and speak to the old Chinese owner, telling him about the horns hidden in the bush. That would give the impression she did not know of Wang, and knew only that her former boyfriend - who she was to say had deserted her - had sold them at the restaurant.

To save time, Sibanda would give her a lift there on Frek's bicycle, then wait in hiding to see what eventuated. If she accompanied Wang in the Land Cruiser - as they expected and hoped would be the case - he was to race back along the path to the school and inform Tim and Elliot. As Wang would have to take the much longer route around by road, then walk for a short distance to reach the proposed ambush site, they would have ample time.

They dragged the Moth farther back into the trees

and Elliot used his rusty bayonet to hack off a few branches, which Tim used to further conceal the plane. As an added precaution, Frek would remain with the plane to discourage any visitors.

With the others following on foot, Tim had Frek give him a lift on the bicycle to the thicker bush a few hundred yards away, where they selected an ambush site on an overgrown anthill.

Using the bayonet, Elliot dug a shallow hole beside the mound, then filled it in again, covering it over with dead leaves and grass to give the impression, if inspected closely, that something was buried there.

With everything set, Miriam arranged herself comfortably on the crossbar of the bicycle and, with Sibanda's knee bumping against her overhanging buttocks with each rise of the pedal, they set off for the restaurant.

***

It was past noon when Sibanda finally returned. Miriam had almost not gone through with it, he informed them breathlessly. The Land Cruiser had been there, but they had not seen Wang until only a short while ago. The old Chinese owner had said nothing to Miriam, telling her only to wait outside. After two hours of waiting she had become nervous, expecting the police or soldiers to arrive at any moment.

'With many people by the restaurant I see the opportunity to speak with her,' Sibanda explained.

'Yes, yes,' Elliot said impatiently, 'but what of the Chinese?'

'I think he is coming,' Sibanda replied. 'I see Miriam get inside the Toyota with him. Then she get out again when the Korean wish to come also. I think she refuse to allow it. Only after the Chinese speaks to the Korean and he goes away does she get in again.'

'Clever girl,' Tim said with relief. The possibility of the Korean joining in was something he had overlooked. 'Hide the bicycle and let's get into position. And better let me have that, Elliot,' he said, reaching for the AK. With only one weapon between them, other than the rusty bayonet, and with the likelihood of the Chinese man being armed, he was not willing to gamble on Elliot's expertise - or his restraint.

'No, sir,' Elliot said apologetically, moving the weapon out of reach. 'I must do it. You have a broken foot.'

'Oh yes, I forgot about that. Okay, Elliot, but for God's sake don't shoot him.'

Miriam had already been instructed on what direction she was to approach the ambush, and when they saw her blue dress flashing through the trees a short time after hearing the Toyota, Tim was not the only one to give a grunt of relief.

'You two keep your heads down and out of sight until I tell you,' he cautioned.

Followed by the Chinese man, Miriam strode confidently to where they had dug the shallow hole on the other side of the anthill, then she stopped to point down. 'It is here,' she said, much louder than was necessary.

'Only one?' the agent queried. 'You told me four.'

'Yes. I mean to say this is the place. I will show you now…' She kneeled and began to scrape away the leaves with her hands.

Tim had not been given much time to assess the man, and much of that had been taken by his searching for Wang's pistol, which Elliot had told him was usually tucked into his belt at the back, concealed under his shirt. He believed he had located the slight bulge there, and hoped Elliot hadn't forgotten. Other than that, Wang appeared relatively harmless. He had the typical short stature of the Chinese, with his black hair cropped, and was younger than Tim had expected, perhaps no more than twenty-five.

Tim prodded Elliot gently in the ribs, giving the signal.

They had told Miriam to face towards the anthill as she scraped at the hole, so Wang would be more likely to stand with his back to them as he watched, and that was how it was. But they had not told her what to do if Wang resisted, and that is what he did, with astonishing speed, the moment Elliot opened his mouth and delivered his rehearsed ultimatum of: 'Don't move or I must shoot!'

Wang dived over the top of the still crouching Miriam, catching her around the neck with one arm at the same time as the other went to his back for the pistol. He jerked it free and held it to Miriam's head, dragging her back on top of him as a shield, and it was only then that he had an opportunity to look at his assailant.

'Ai-ya!' He squirmed back, digging with his heels and dragging Miriam with him, obviously shaken, but was quick to recover. 'Put down the gun or I kill her!' His voice was pitched high with impending panic.

To Elliot's credit he did not shoot at Wang. He kept the AK pointed and stepped closer. 'You think I am afraid of such a small gun?' he sneered. 'If you kill her, do you think I will not kill you also?' He thrust the rifle forward threateningly.

It was too much for Sibanda. Already on his feet and about to follow after Elliot, he called out before

Tim could stop him.

'No! You must not shoot her, I beg you.'

'Get away!' Wang yelled. 'Tell your friend to put down his gun or I will kill her.'

'No! You must let her go.'

'I will let her go only if you put down the gun and go away.'

'I think you are very much a liar,' Elliot stated calmly.

'No, he is not a liar,' Sibanda cried. 'Please, my friend, put away the gun so he will let her go'

'Yes,' Wang said, his voice now steadier. 'Listen to your friend, I am not a liar. I will let her go.'

Miriam had been silent to that point, now she began to wail, and Wang dragged her up until they were both standing, his arm tightening on her throat and choking her cry to a whimper. 'Stay where you are,' he warned Elliot and Sibanda. 'I will let her go when I reach my truck.' He began pulling the terrified Miriam backwards with him, the pistol still pressed hard against her head.

Restricted by his leg, and to avoid further complicating what was already a volatile situation, Tim had remained hidden, but now, with Wang coming backwards towards him, obviously intent on making use of the cover of the anthill, he saw his opportunity.

He did not even have to move too far. He simply waited until Wang was within range, then took one hop forward and struck the pistol from Wang's hand with his reversed metal crutch. He followed with a backhand that caught the surprised Wang behind the ear as he attempted to turn, and he slumped to the ground.

Fortunately, the end of the crutch was padded, or it would have shattered his skull. Miriam scrambled away to be comforted by Sibanda, and Tim scooped up the pistol.

'You forgot the safety catch,' he said, clicking it over and pointing the nine millimetre at Wang. 'That was pretty dumb, don't you think?'

A grinning Elliot added his support with a none-too gentle kick in the ribs. 'For sure, God has delivered you unto us,' he happily informed the groaning Wang.

'Okay, let's leave the sermon for later,' Tim said. 'Find something to tie him up. We have to get out of here.' He searched through Wang's pockets and found a keyring with a Toyota tag and two keys. 'Can any of you drive?'

'Last year I get myself a learner permit,' Elliot confessed after a short silence.

'Is that it... only a permit?'

'Yes, sir. After one lesson I have no opportunity for driving.'

Tim grimaced with dismay, but he had no choice. He tossed the keys to Elliot. 'Well, now you have. See if you can get the Land Cruiser over here... use the big key... and leave your AK with Sibanda.'

Twenty minutes later, Elliot had still not moved the Toyota, although he had managed to start it, and Tim was forced to suffer another uncomfortable lift on the bicycle to help him.

'The first thing you must do,' he told the harassed Elliot after he had seen what the problem was, 'is to release the handbrake.'

Once that was accomplished, and with some further basic instruction and urgent intervention by Tim to avoid demolishing the goal posts, Elliot managed to jerk the vehicle around the perimeter of the field and, with more good luck than judgement, manoeuvre it through the trees and stall it beside their prisoner.

A search through the rear of the vehicle revealed nothing of interest, only basic and well-used camping equipment, including a narrow felt mattress, a sleeping bag and an empty fuel drum. The front was more rewarding. In a leather document case under the seat Tim discovered a cheap address book. Most of the pages were blank, but several contained Chinese characters and long numbers, presumably telephone numbers. The glove box surrendered an almost full carton of

Madison cigarettes, one of the gold lighters with the snake-like dragon, several road maps of Mozambique and Zimbabwe, a wallet containing a little over three hundred American dollars and, surprisingly, a satellite phone.

The thick antenna gave it away. It was a different brand to his own, and not as modern, Tim noted with satisfaction, but finding it, along with the numbers in the book, provided distinct possibilities.

Elliot pounced eagerly on the cigarettes and lighter as Tim was counting the money, swearing that he recognised the lighter as the one Wang had originally given him, then he eyed the money with a similar proprietary glint in his eye. As Wang had stolen Elliot's money, Tim gave him half, but with conditions attached.

'Use it for petrol,' he said, then, after a thoughtful pause. 'That is, if you think you can drive this thing all the way to Massangena without crashing it.'

Elliot laughed, confident. 'For sure. No problem. I go the same way as the bus.'

'How about from there to Gara Pasi, going through Mavue?'

Elliot looked doubtful. 'It is not a good way, sir. We can be easily seen unless walking. Better I take the road to Vila Salazar, but leave the road at the border to go by the bush.' He grinned slyly. 'This way I know very well.'

'Okay, but fill the drum and make sure the petrol tank is full as well.'

Wang was silent and unresisting as they lifted him, first into his sleeping bag - which Elliot referred to as his body bag - then into the back of the vehicle. Only his eyes showed any emotion; a sullen obstinacy that worried Tim. It was not going to be easy to get him to co-operate.

Tim put the truck into four-wheel-drive, then instructed Elliot on the use of high and low range, demonstrating both on the short drive back to the plane. He also instructed him not to drive at night, and to use side roads after leaving the school to avoid going through the town, and to this end, Miriam again made herself useful as a guide, telling them where they could get petrol on the outskirts.

She had refused the suggestion that she return alone to her village. The Korean had seen her, she argued, and people she knew had seen her waiting at the restaurant. It would not take too many questions to find her.

Before Tim sent them off, he switched on his phone in the plane and dialled its number with Wang's instrument, and was relieved to hear a warbling response.

He gave the phone to Elliot with his number and yet more instructions on its operation then, with a final warning to keep Wang zipped up and hidden in his sleeping bag, and with more misgivings than he cared to think about, he bade them a safe journey.

He gave Elliot an hour start then, with Frek and his bicycle safely aboard, he took-off, giving the town a wide berth before swinging back to intercept the rough track to Massangena. It was not a busy road, and not long before he saw the white top of the Land Cruiser inching its way south ahead of a thin plume of dust.

Relieved, he dived low over the vehicle to be sure, hoping he wouldn't startle the novice into driving off the road, then waggled the Moth's wings and climbed, setting a rough course for home.

Although messy, the operation had been a success, but many questions still nagged Tim, not the least of which, was what the Korean would do when Wang didn't return.

And he would have preferred staying close to Wang, but taking him in the Moth had not been an option. Even bound hand and foot, and without the rear joystick - which he had removed again after Kelly's departure - the exposed cables made sabotage too simple. It would be suicidal, but Wang's unhesitant response when threatened by Elliot, and the look he had seen in the dark eyes, suggested to Tim that Wang could well possess a kamikaze mentality as well as a murderous one.

***

Tim had the Moth in the air at first light. That the time coincided with his usual morning patrol was fortuitous. It would allay any suspicious mind that he was involved with anything out of the ordinary. Which, he had reminded himself often during the night, abduction certainly was.

After seeing Elliot on his way and flying back to Gara Pasi, he had considered refuelling and returning immediately to oversee the Land Cruiser's progress from the air, but resisted the temptation. It would only distract Elliot and draw attention to both the plane and the vehicle. Instead, he had spent the remaining hours of daylight preparing suitable accommodation for his guest.

He had few choices in this regard. A rondavel could not be used because they could not be made secure without major alterations, and the shed in which Elliot had been held after his capture would be too obvious if anyone came looking. Wang had friends in the government who may hear about his disappearance, or be informed of it by the Korean, and he could not take the chance that his own involvement had remained secret.

The only place he could think of that would be suitable for the short time he expected Wang to be with him was a rhino cage. It was definitely secure, and would be well out of the way.

With the help of Kawaseka, Frek and the tractor, the cage was dragged into the centre of Rosie's old boma, a short length of chain and a padlock attached to the heavy drop-down gate, and a tarpaulin draped over for privacy and protection from the weather.

As he flew towards the border, Tim's main concern, besides Elliot having an accident, was that he would get lost or hit a landmine. Crossing by foot in the remote area was one thing, but following the road was another. Many of the tracks in the proximity of the boundary had been mined during the war, and despite the long time that had elapsed, they were still exploding with alarming regularity under vehicles, people and animals. Elliot would no doubt be aware of this though, Tim reasoned. The former terrorist had probably been responsible for laying a few of them himself.

The track Elliot said he was taking turned sharply

once it crossed into Zimbabwe, following the border, and was unmarked except for the few rotted posts of a fence, the wire of which had been removed for snares almost on the same day it had been erected. Ultimately, the track led to the old border villages of Vila Salazar and Malvernia.

A more reliable indicator of the international boundary was the prominent transmission lines a few miles to the east, and when Tim saw the glint of the silver pylons, he turned north and flew parallel to them as far as the Sibonja Hills, climbing to three thousand feet then spiralling down like a descending vulture to land on a large pan, hoping that Elliot was in the vicinity and had seen the plane and marked his position.

He waited impatiently in the silence until six - the time he had arranged with Elliot to switch on the phone - then dialled the number. To his surprise, Elliot answered immediately.

'Where are you?' Tim asked.

'We are here, sir.' Elliot sounded bright and chirpy.

'Where is "here?"'

'Gara Pasi.'

'What... already? But...' Tim took a deep breath. To reach Gara Pasi, Elliot must have ignored his orders and driven through the night, but reprimanding him would serve no purpose, and relief swiftly overcame his flash of irritation. At least he was there. 'Is everything all right… your passenger?'

'Yes, sir. We have only some few accidents with the trees because of going with no lights, but my driving is good. We arrive as you leave. We wait now by the landing place. Must we go to the house?'

Tim sighed. So much for his elaborate security arrangements. By now the entire labour force would have seen the vehicle arrive with their captive. Elliot would not have missed such an opportunity. 'No, just wait there until I come,' he said. 'Ask Frek to find you some food.'

Elliot, and the remarkably intact Land Cruiser, were still surrounded by a group of admiring fans when Tim arrived a half hour later. He sent them away and peered in. Wang's eyes were closed, but with all the excited chattering and laughter, Tim doubted that he was asleep. The bag had been unzipped to expose his bound hands, undeniably to further enhance Elliot's status in the compound, but Wang seemed none the worse for his hazardous journey.

Tim dispatched both Frek and Kawaseka to instruct the people not to talk about the prisoner to anyone, and to inform them that no one was to leave Gara Pasi until further notice.

While they were carrying out his orders he

inspected the vehicle, somewhat bewildered as to how Elliot had managed to negotiate the rugged tracks and open bush in the dark, ford the many dry rivers without getting bogged in the sand, and arrive with only a few minor dents and scratches. It was not a journey he himself would have undertaken lightly.

Elliot's explanation, when he asked, was simple. He had not been able to find the intended track, so had stayed on the road, crossing the border at Vila Salazar. The two men on duty had been asleep, so he had simply driven through without waking them. And knowing that Tim was expecting him to come from another direction, he had continued on to Gara Pasi, hoping to reach it before Tim left.

'But we go too slowly because of using only one gear,' he explained apologetically. 'For sure, not more than twenty-five on the clock.'

He also informed Tim that the mobile phone had rung a short time after leaving Chimoio and that he had answered it, thinking it was Tim, but the man had spoken Chinese to him and he had switched off. He thought it was the Korean, and Tim was inclined to agree.

Wang was untied and ushered into his cage with his mattress and sleeping bag. He complied in silence, ignoring the food given him by Frek, but drinking the water, and his sullen attitude gave Tim strong misgivings about the man's willingness to be reasonable without threats of violence. Or even with them, for that matter. Deprivation of freedom was his limit. Torture was a bit beyond it.

Tim's resolve strengthened, however, when he thought of Kelly. She too, had been deprived of her freedom, and if the threat of being hanged in a Malaysian prison was not a form of torture, it came close enough in his view. The only difference between her situation and Wang's was that she was innocent. Tim sent Kawaseka and Frek outside the boma, to keep any curious staff at bay, but kept Elliot with him in the hope that his glowering presence would intimidate Wang.

'Do you speak English?' he asked Wang, and when he received no reply, Elliot answered for him.

'Yes, sir, he speaks English.'

'Good. In that case,' he told Wang, 'you had better listen carefully. Elliot here was going to kill you for what you did to him, and the only reason he didn't is because I stopped him.'

Wang remained aloof, and Elliot growled. 'Heh! You think I don't do it?' He produced his rusty bayonet and thrust it through the bars close to Wang's face. 'I put it inside your neck, for sure.'

Wang didn't even flinch, and Tim's misgivings increased. 'Take it easy, Elliot,' he cautioned, then spoke to Wang. 'Because of you, a girl I know has been arrested in Kuala Lumpur. She was framed by your politician friends because she knew they were smuggling horns and threatened to expose them.'

For the first time, Wang showed some interest. He looked at Tim with a frown, obviously puzzled, but said nothing, and Tim continued in his reasonable tone. If he could do it without threats it would make things much easier all round. He told Wang that he knew about the Golden Horn Company, and that he believed only they could have arranged the arrest, then issued his ultimatum.

'I want you to phone the Golden Horn and tell them to have the woman released in exchange for your own freedom. You understand?'

Wang put on a surprised look that seemed a little overdone to Tim. 'You think you can call to Shanghai from here?' He laughed, shaking his head. 'It is not possible. Anyway, I know nothing of such a company or the arrest of a woman.'

'Really? Then how do you know it is in Shanghai?'

Wang's expression became bland. 'You waste your time. I don't know who you are or what you are talking about. But you are right about my friends in government. For now we will call it a misunderstanding, but if you do not release me immediately you will be asking for big trouble. What you do is illegal.'

'So is dealing in rhino horn,' Tim responded coldly. Being reasonable was not working. It was time to get tough. 'You are going nowhere unless you cooperate. Maybe I'll put a rhino in here with you to keep you amused. One with a big horn.'

Wang's face remained expressionless, and Elliot spat on the ground in disgust. 'Sir, if you feel like some cup of tea, I can stay with him to talk about my bayonet.'

'First we will try calling a few numbers,' Tim said. He observed Wang closely as he removed the book from inside his shirt, and his own new satellite phone from its leather case on his belt. The man was not as immutable as he thought he was. He had made two slips already. Perhaps he would go for three. 'I think the first call we should make is to your father,' he continued conversationally, and was gratified to see Wang stiffen, proving him right. 'Yes,' Tim went on. 'You made a mistake by writing it in English next to the number. As for the ones in Chinese, it doesn't matter. I know a Chinese man who will translate for me.'

He dialled the number in the book. 'It's ringing,'

he reported. 'How about that?' After several long moments, during which he fully expected to hear a recorded message, there came an answering click followed by a cacophony of sound; shouting in Chinese, the noise of heavy traffic, the ringing of what sounded like bicycle bells, then, clearly, the words "Cha-Cha!" shouted in alarm.

Before dialling, Tim had positioned himself closer to Wang with the intention of handing him the instrument should he receive a reply in Chinese, but with the odd sounds he held on to it, compromising by lifting it a short distance from his ear and turning the receiver so Wang could hear as well. At the shouted words, Wang reacted by staring at the phone. A loud clatter followed the words, then scraping sounds and the squealing of brakes.

'Hello?' Tim enquired tentatively. More scraping and clattering noises came in reply, then suddenly a querying voice in Chinese, and Tim spoke quickly. 'Who is that please? Can you speak English?'

When he was answered by a further rapid babble of Chinese, Tim passed the instrument through the bars with a puzzled look, and Wang took it reluctantly. He spoke a few words in Chinese, but obviously got no reply, for he repeated himself a few times then simply listened with a look of puzzlement.

'What's happening?' Tim asked, but Wang ignored him, continuing to listen, although he appeared not to be hearing much. He thumped the instrument several times against his palm, putting it back to his ear and frowning with concentration, then finally he gave up. He went to pass the instrument back, then stopped. He gave Tim a venomous look then began smashing the phone against the steel bars on the other side of the cage, shattering the plastic with a satisfied smirk before calmly dropping the remnants into the half-filled jug of water.

Although Tim was tempted to reach through and strangle him, he forced a laugh. 'It is you who is going to buy me another one,' he said. 'From the money you left in the wallet, and I still have your phone in the truck.'

While he waited for Elliot to fetch the instrument, Tim took the time to stretch his legs and reflect on his luck in keeping Wang's phone secure. Its number could be traced, but not the caller or exact locality. It was something he had not taken into account before, and an added bonus was that he would not be charged for the calls.

When Elliot returned, Tim held the instrument up for Wang to inspect. 'Shall we try again?' He dialled the same number, but it was engaged. 'Not to worry, it's a free call so I'll keep trying. Bound to get through sooner or later. Meanwhile, I'll leave you alone to think about it.' He inclined his head at Elliot, indicating he must leave too, then looked down at Wang. 'By the way, what does Cha-Cha mean?'

Wang did not respond, turning his face away, and Tim followed thoughtfully after Elliot. It sounded more to him like a dance than a Chinese name.

***

For several moments Shen Hui Ping tried to ignore the mobile phone. It was a new one, bright red, and played Chinese music instead of the irritating treble of the previous instrument. It was no less annoying though, and he had again told Lan not to call except in emergency, but it seemed his words were even less important than himself. Finally, he jabbed his finger on the button.

'Who is it?' he answered shortly, wanting to convey his displeasure by the tone of his voice. He knew very well who it was. Only his sons and a few old friends had the number, and none of his friends would call him at such an inconsiderate time.

'Please forgive the interruption, Father,' his eldest son, Lan, apologised, 'but we have an emergency. You should return to the office.'

'Why?'

Lan was slow to answer, and Shen's annoyance eased. It was not like Lan to be hesitant about anything. 'We have received a message from Mozambique...'

'Wang?'

'No, Father, from Koh. He reports that Wang is missing. He went to meet with a seller and did not return. He believes he has been abducted or arrested.'

'Ai!' the sharp exclamation caused Cha-Cha to lift up and stare at his master with ears cocked.

'Father?'

Shen gazed blankly at Cha-Cha. He had feared for a long time that something like this should happen to his second born. Wang was a rebellious young fool. It had not been necessary for him to go to Africa. Any number of employees could have done his work there, many of them more qualified in negotiating with people who were little more than peasant bandits, but Wang had insisted, and probably for no other reason than that his brother had opposed the idea. That is how it had always been between them.

'Father?'

'Why does Koh believe that... is he not certain?'

'Yes, he is sure. Wang left in the morning, saying he would only be away an hour, but when he hadn't returned by evening, Koh says he called Wang on his mobile telephone and a stranger answered. An African man he couldn't understand.'

'Money? Did he ask for money?'

'No. Are you coming back to the office? We should not discuss this on the phone.'

'Yes, yes, I am coming.'

His private office at Golden Horn Company in Shanghai was seldom used by Shen. Apart from the stone building's cathedral-like dome, which now glowed in the sunset like some giant golden egg instead of blending conservatively with the smog, the former bank's exterior remained the same, but the inside had been completely renovated.

Lan had taken it upon himself to restore much of the colonial grandeur lost in the communist revolution, when the financial institutions had hastily departed. Like his Western counterparts, with whom he had studied at university, Lan believed a modern, although still conservative look, was more appropriate to conducting serious business in a burgeoning international enterprise than red lacquer and paper dragons.

The fluorescent tubes in Shen's office had been removed and a crystal chandelier similar to the previous one installed, along with period furniture, plush blue carpet and carved teak desk. Being of the old Chinese school, Shen disliked, and even felt threatened by the pretentious trappings, but never more so than that afternoon, when he sat at the desk opposite a trusted employee and attempted - or rather the clerk attempted - to contact Wang's Korean friend on his mobile phone. They also tried Wang's number, hoping to speak to the African and find out what were his intentions, but neither party answered.

The clerk tried other numbers from the list given him by Lan. For security reasons, each number had been pre-programmed into the instrument supplied by Lan and could be dialled by pressing only one key, but even this simple operation confused Shen, which is why he brought in the clerk to do it for him.

When the clerk received an answer he would pass the instrument to Shen, then hurriedly leave the room, returning only after the call was completed and Shen had summoned him back with the buzzer on his desk.

The majority of the numbers were those of Africans, and with these he had more success, but none was able to shed any light on Wang's movements or plans in response to Shen's veiled, and often confusing, questions. It was made no easier in that Shen's English was limited, and so was that of the people he spoke to.

Beyond the door waited another employee, A

Korean, who would speak to Wang's friend should they ever manage to raise him, thus eliminating any confusion that may arise with language problems there. Although mistrustful of Koreans in general, Lan was also thorough.

In particular, Lan mistrusted his brother's Korean friend, Koh. No other country, with the exception of Khartoum and Yemen, gave Lan as many headaches. Powdered horn was an essential ingredient in Chung sin hwan, medicine of the heart balls, which had become enormously popular in Seoul. Sealed in wax, each ball was covered in gold leaf and sold in a decorative box for ten dollars. The balls were swallowed whole on a daily basis to boost energy. The competition had become so intense with the pharmacists clamouring for a share of the lucrative market that the price of horn in those areas frequented by Korean agents had become ridiculously high. Much higher than the prices presently paid by Wang to his poachers, and both Lan and his father found it hard to believe that Koh was unaware of the situation, or unwilling to exploit it.

Thinking about it as the afternoon dragged tediously on without success, Shen became increasingly convinced that it was the Koreans who were involved with Wang's abduction. The poachers would not delay with their demands. That was a Korean tactic, making the opposition uncertain by giving them only the bad news, letting them have time to think and sweat before providing a way out.

So convinced was he that this was the case, that he finally dismissed the clerk and prepared to leave himself. The abductors had made contact once, so would do so again when they were ready to negotiate. Until then he could do nothing. He put Lan's satellite phone in one pocket and his own in the other, then aroused Cha-Cha from where he lay sprawled on a couch with his legs in the air.

He left the building by the rear entrance. At the front his driver would be waiting to take him home and would be disappointed when he refused. It was not that long a walk to Yu garden, and both he and the dog could use the exercise after the day's inactivity.

With Cha-Cha trotting ahead at the limit of his lead, dodging the heels of pedestrians, they were abreast the busy Zhongshan Road when Lan's mobile phone shrilled from one of his pockets and Shen stopped suddenly, jerking Cha-Cha to a halt.

At first, with being so close to the road and its noisy traffic, Shen was not sure in which pocket he had put Lan's instruments, so he gripped the lead in his teeth to free his hands so he could removed both. He returned his own and was about to remove the lead so he could talk in the other, when the leather strap was suddenly torn from between his teeth.

With his weaving progress suddenly arrested, Cha-Cha had turned back and into the path of a hurrying pedestrian, who stumbled over him, entangling his foot in the lead. Cha-Cha yelped and sprang aside, into the path of yet other pedestrians, one of whom tried to snatch up the lead, which only served to frighten the dog more. He darted away in panic, leaping off the walkway and into the path of a passing truck.

Shen stood mesmerised as the heavy vehicle passed over his pet, tumbling him along the road like a bouncing furry ball, the roar of the truck's exhausts all but drowning his terrified squeals. Then, when he saw Cha-Cha come out the back and struggle to his feet, stunned but alive, Shen called out to him, dropping the phone as he ran to his aid.

Ignoring the blast of a horn, the screeching of brakes and the yelling of abuse, Shen gathered Cha-Cha in his arms and returned with him to the walkway, where he sat and cradled him on his lap to search for injury, intoning soothing words to still the stricken animal's shaking and whimpering.

A smear of blood showed on the top of Cha-Cha's head, along with black grease and caked grime from the underside of the truck, and Shen wiped it away with his cap before parting the woolly fur to study the wound. Fortunately it was only a graze. He ran his hands cautiously over the shivering body and Cha-Cha yelped, twisting around as if to nip at the gently palpating fingers on his left hind leg. It too, was smeared with grime and grease, and the lower part of the leg was twisted awkwardly, undoubtedly broken.

A few pedestrians had stopped to watch. One of them retrieved the mobile phone from where it had been kicked into the gutter. The light was still on. He spoke into it, his rapid Mandarin questioning. He listened briefly, then handed the instrument to Shen. 'Engleesh,' he explained with an apologetic shrug.

Shen took it distractedly and, without bothering to switch it off, stuffed it into his pocket. 'I must take him to the animal doctor,' he appealed.

The man smiled and nodded sympathetically before moving on, and Shen looked helplessly about, wondering what he could do. He did not know of any animal doctor, only the man at the complex where Lan had purchased Cha-Cha. He would tell him where to go, but it was a long way to carry his injured pet. He thought of telephoning for his driver, but the rush-hour traffic was getting worse with each passing second. It would be quicker to go on foot.

With Cha-Cha cradled in his arms, Shen set off

at a brisk, shuffling trot, murmuring apologies as he barged his way through the throng, sometimes even resorting to going backwards to avoid bumping Cha-Cha against the press of bodies.

He was thus occupied when a bicycle detached itself from an equally dense stream of cyclists and stopped beside him. 'What is it, sir? May I be of help to you?' the man asked with a concerned frown. Shen saw it was the clerk with whom he had spent the afternoon, and greeted him with relief, quickly explaining the accident.

'I must take him to the animal doctor,' he said breathlessly. 'Do you know the Place of Faithful Friends?'

'Yes, I know it.'

'We can go on your cycle.' Shen indicated to the large wire basket attached to the handlebars. 'We can put Cha-Cha in there. Help remove my jacket.'

Talking consolingly to Cha-Cha, Shen arranged his blue jacket in the basket, then lay Cha-Cha gently on top. He placed a restraining hand on him and positioned himself on the crossbar. 'Be careful not to crash us,' he warned the clerk as they edged into the traffic.

Later that evening, after Cha-Cha had been thoroughly examined and his leg set in plaster, Shen removed his phone from the pocket to call his driver. He was mildly surprised to note that it wasn't working. He shrugged philosophically. It didn't matter. All that mattered was that Cha-Cha was alive.

***

Tim was becoming increasingly frustrated. Of the sixteen numbers he had called in Wang's book, only seven had answered, some in Chinese, and some in an African language he didn't recognise. The remainder had either rung-out, returned strange signals, or prompted recorded messages. Part of the reason, he believed, was the time difference. By his rough calculations, it would be night in Shanghai. But he could not even be sure it was Shanghai he was calling, as he had not once heard the name spoken. As for the other calls, he had no idea where they were going.

And Wang was being as stubborn as expected, refusing to answer even simple questions as to his needs, and responding to veiled threats with indifference. He had made no more demands or threats of his own, and Tim was left in no doubt that the ball was firmly in his own court and would remain there until he did something spectacular with it.

Elliot's contribution had been to suggest slowly

removing Wang's body parts with his bayonet, but Tim was of the opinion that even going to that extreme would fail. He suspected it had something to do with oriental loss of face, but had no idea how to get around it. Neither did he have any idea what he was going to do with Wang once he had finished with him. Handing him over to Elliot for bayonet practice was out of the question, but so too, was releasing him to report to his government friends. To all intents, Wang was proving to be nothing but a dangerous liability.

About one thing Tim was determined though. Until he had definite proof that the Golden Horn Company was not involved in Kelly's arrest, Comrade Wang was going nowhere.

Solving the language problem, Tim realized, would have to be his first priority, or he too, would be going nowhere. Not only understanding what had been written beside the numbers was essential, but also the people who answered. The trouble was, he didn't know any Chinese people. He dispatched Frek for the telephone directory and began searching, beginning with the closest towns. He could find none in nearby Chiredzi, but came across a Foo Yong Fruit and Vegetable Emporium in Masvingo, a much larger town a little over an hour away in the Moth.

Tim dialled the number and, after being passed

from one juvenile to another, finally spoke to Mister Yong. 'Do you speak Chinese?' he asked, feeling somewhat foolish.

'Yes, of course,' Yong answered, sounding puzzled.

Tim explained that he needed some Chinese writing deciphered, and when Yong agreed, he made an appointment to meet him at the shop early next morning. 'I will be needing some vegetables too,' he added for insurance. 'Do you have gem squash?' Laced with butter, pepper and salt, they were his favourite.

'Picked fresh every morning,' Yong replied.

***

Foo Yong's Emporium had been a thriving gift and artefacts shop in the Mozambique port of Beira before the Portuguese departed the colony and, having serious doubts as to the commercial sympathies of a communist regime under Samora Machel, Yong had left with them, taking his family to what was then Rhodesia. Originally from Hong Kong, carved ivory had been his speciality, but he had found little market for such items in a country sympathetic to elephant preservation, so had wisely switched to fruit and vegetables, a more traditional Chinese enterprise and, after twenty years hard work, a reasonably successful one.

A greying man with a cheerful round face, he met Tim outside his shop early the next morning. He took the list of vegetables compiled by Frek, and passed it on to one of his numerous young staff, then led the way to a minuscule desk at the rear.

Tim produced Wang's book and Foo Yong perused it swiftly, nodding his head knowingly. 'Common Mandarin character,' he announced. 'You would like me to write the names?'

'Please.'

Foo Yong pronounced them as he wrote, printing in neat letters above the characters. It took only a few minutes. Most were names like Zhong, Yao, Hua and Xin. One of them caused him to hesitate, and he screwed his face in a moment of thought. 'This one means same as place for work,' he explained. 'I put office.' He printed it in and returned the book with a cheerful grin. 'Very easy if you know how.'

Tim laughed obligingly and thanked him, but except for the office number it didn't help all that much. He still needed him to actually talk to someone there, and to get Foo Yong to do that he would have to explain the reason without giving too much away. It was a delicate situation with some risk, but he had to take it.

'Mister Yong,' he said, approaching the subject circuitously. 'I need your help and have to be honest with you. Can I talk to you in confidence?'

Yong merely frowned, waiting for him to continue, and Tim went on. 'My family owns the Gara Pasi Wildlife Sanctuary near Gona Re Zhou National Park, and this book belongs to a rhino poacher we caught in Mozambique.'

Yong's expression brightened. 'Ah, yes. You are Timmy Ryan, of course. I know your father very well, and your mother. She always buy from me. Please, you must tell me what I can do to help.'

Making a silent vow to place a weekly order with Foo Yong's Emporium, Tim went on with more confidence. 'First of all, what we need to know is if these numbers... especially the office one, are in Shanghai, and what the office is called. We think it is the Golden Horn Company. I also need to talk to someone there who speaks English. Do you think you could do that for me? If they ask, you can give them a false name.'

'You will pay for the call?'

'Yes, of course. We'll do it outside on the satellite phone.'

They got through on the second attempt, Mister

Yong signalling his success with a nod and a smile. He spoke rapidly in Chinese for a few moments, listened to a reply, spoke again in English, asking the person to please wait, then passed the instrument to Tim. 'A Mister Lan Hui Ping of Golden Horn Company in Shanghai,' he explained with a wink. 'I'll be inside if you need me.'

Tim suddenly found himself the victim of stage fright. He cleared his throat as a preliminary, then began slowly, putting on what he hoped would be recognised as an American drawl. 'Hello? Is that there the Golden Horn Company?'

'Yes. Who is speaking please?' The man's English was even better than Yong's, Tim noted with relief.

'It doesn't matter who I am, pal. I'm calling for Wang. Do you know him?'

'I know many Wangs. Where are you calling from?'

'He works for you guys in Mozambique,' Tim hedged. 'He gave me your number. He needs your help.'

The man was silent for a moment, then spoke guardedly. 'I am not sure I can help.'

Tim decided the sparring had gone on for long enough. 'Wang needs you to save his life.'

This time the pause was longer, with some muted

conversation in the background, and Tim suspected Lan was informing some other person of what was happening. 'I am not sure what you mean,' he said finally. 'Is this man you speak of... Wang, in danger?'

'Damn right. He's about to have his throat cut with a bayonet unless you do exactly what I say, so listen carefully.' Tim took a deep breath, hastily gathering thoughts. So much depended on him getting it right first time. 'About two weeks ago, some African diplomat friends of Wang arranged for a young American woman by the name of Kelly Maddock to be arrested in Kuala Lumpur. She had accused them of smuggling rhino horn in diplomatic bags and threatened to expose them. Now she has been falsely charged with drug trafficking and put in prison. I want her released immediately. Do you understand?'

'No, sir. Forgive me, but this is very confusing. It is true we have a representative in Mozambique by the name of Wang, but he is there for the agricultural program initiated by the People's Republic. Golden Horn Company supplies machinery. We have no knowledge of Zimbabwe diplomats or horns. I think you have mistaken our name.'

Tim could barely restrain a derisive chuckle. 'No, Mister Lan. I think it is you who made a mistake. I did not say the diplomats were from Zimbabwe. Obviously you know them, just as I know Wang was buying horns because I supplied them through an undercover agent. And I also know he was giving them to Zimbabwean officials to take out of the country, because my agent saw him and his Korean friend loading them into a vehicle.'

'I must have misunderstood. We do have some contact with Zimbabwe, but if our agent is involved in illegal activities with them we have no knowledge of it. However, we do not wish him to come to harm and are willing to negotiate his release once I have been permitted to speak to him. He will be returned to Shanghai and questioned further on the matter. You must give me an estimate of your expenses? Will that be a suitable arrangement?

'I'm not interested in your money, Mister Lan, only in the release of the woman.'

'Yes, I sympathise, Mister, um…'

'Smith.'

'Mister Smith. But they are very strict with drugs in Malaysia, and we are in Shanghai. We have no influence there.'

'We are talking about the death penalty, Lan. The same as your agent is facing if she is not released, so if you can't arrange it, maybe you should get President Mugabe to do something.'

'That would not be possible, Mister Smith, but if you permit me to speak to our agent, perhaps I can get more information that will be of use.'

'He's not here, so I'll have to call you back, although I don't think he's in the mood to talk to anyone.'

'I see. In that case I will not be able to help you. Goodbye, Mister Smith.'

The line went dead, and Tim frowned at the instrument in annoyance. For a while he had believed he was making progress. Now he was not sure. Lan did not seem all that concerned about his agent. Or maybe he did not believe the threat to kill him was genuine. Whatever his reasons, he had taken the initiative, and if Wang refused to talk, Tim realized he would be no better off than before. All he had achieved was confirmation of something he had already suspected.

He began thoughtfully back to the emporium, then stopped. If he could raise Wang's father again while he had Foo Yong handy to speak, he may glean a little more information. He dialled, and the moment he heard the ringing tone, waved frantically to catch Foo Yong's attention. The connection was made before the merchant arrived, and Tim spoke urgently into the transmitter in reply to the few abrupt Chinese words shouted in his ear. 'Wait! Please wait, someone is coming.' He handed the instrument to Foo Yong gratefully. 'Speak to him,' he said hurriedly. 'Ask his name… where he is….anything. Keep him on the line until I can think of something.'

Foo Yong was a good salesman. After a few terse, questioning words, he settled into an animated conversation with the person on the other end as if they were old friends. There was even some laughter and, Tim surmised, discussion about the weather, for Foo Yong took a few steps onto the road and peered up at the few clouds as if assessing the chances of rain. After several moments he signalled to Tim and broke off his conversation, holding a hand over the transmitter. 'His name is Shen Hui Ping,' he said to Tim. 'I did not ask, but he must be the father of Lan, the one you have been talking to. The names are the same. Is there anything more you want me to ask?'

Tim grunted with satisfaction. Success at last. Lan had been stringing him along, and obviously hadn't had time to inform his father of developments. 'Yes,' he replied slowly, thinking as he went, 'ask him if he is the father of Lan, and also if he knows Wang.'

The conversation changed dramatically in tone. And after a few brief words, Foo Yong had to consult Tim again. 'They are his sons. He wants to know what has happened to Wang. He sounds very worried.' Foo

Yong's expression mirrored the concern. 'What should I tell him? He is old and seems like a nice man.'

'Good. Tell him that Wang is unharmed but in danger, and that Lan has all the details. And say you are calling on Wang's mobile phone… he should have the number.'

Before leaving Masvingo for Gara Pasi, Tim visited the mobile phone agency and bought a replacement instrument for the broken one, using Wang's money. 'I hope this one can talk Chinese,' he said to the bemused assistant.

***

'Your brother, Lan, sends his regards,' Tim informed Wang untruthfully.

 The agent's inscrutable demeanour gave way to a start of surprise.

'Your father too,' Tim added conversationally. 'He's worried about you.'

Wang shifted uncomfortably, but remained silent.

Undaunted, Tim related the salient events of the morning, being careful not to mention Foo Yong's name or where he had seen him. He did not want the helpful merchant implicated in any way.

On the return flight to Gara Pasi, he had spent the

time planning what he was going to say when he called Lan back, and how he was going to get Wang to speak to his brother without giving him the reason for doing so. If Wang knew it was simply to prove he was there and alive, he was as likely to remain silent out of spite, or to save face.

Tim was still not sure how he was going to accomplish it. Threats wouldn't work, and neither, he believed, would a few healthy prods from Elliot's bayonet. He guessed that his best chance would be through Wang's father, so with that in mind, he left the sullen agent to think about what he had learned, and went outside the boma where he couldn't be heard.

Lan must have been waiting for the call. He answered immediately, in English, and gave his name, so it must also have been a private line.

'Is your father there?' Tim asked.

'Yes, but he doesn't speak English.' His tone was less polite than before.

'It doesn't matter,' Tim said in the same brusque manner. 'Put him on. Your brother is being very stubborn and refuses to talk. Tell your father to wait on the line until I tap like this...' he flicked twice on the microphone with his fingernail to demonstrate. 'Then he can start speaking to Wang. Maybe he will answer.'

Tim had been strolling slowly back as he spoke.

Now he quickened his pace until he reached the cage. Holding his hand over the transmitter he spoke to Elliot, who had been walking around in circles kicking up dust to express his boredom. 'Hold the point of your bayonet against his leg,' Tim instructed. 'If he tries to take the phone give him a jab.'

When Elliot was in position, Tim tapped twice then pushed the instrument between the bars and held it close to Wang's ear. 'It's your father,' he explained.

Tim could hear the old man's questioning voice and expectant pauses clearly, and so could Wang. His expression became anxious, yet still he remained stubbornly silent.

'The poor old man believes you are dead,' Tim said, shaking his head sadly. 'Is that what you would like him to think? Do the Chinese people have no respect for their fathers?'

Wang glared venomously, but leaned forward to speak in brief sentences with short pauses; a one-sided conversation, and it did not last long. Tim would have given much to know what was said, but Wang's tone had been reassuring, and it had served the purpose. Elliot looked disappointed when the phone was removed.

The old man was still on the line, but after Tim had asked for Lan, repeating the name a few times, Lan returned. 'Your brother does not wish to speak to you,'

Tim said misleadingly. With his face turned away, Wang would think the remark was also addressed to him. 'Now that you know he is alive, ' Tim said to Lan as he walked out of earshot. 'What are you going to do about it?'

'What you ask is impossible,' Lan answered, a touch of frustration, or maybe desperation, in his voice. 'I have no influence in Malaysia.'

'Bullshit!' Tim exploded, losing patience. 'You have twenty-four hours. After that you can tell your father that you have been responsible for your brother's death.' He switched off and strode angrily back to the cage. 'You had better start praying to Buddha that your brother does something to save your life,' he stormed at Wang. 'He has until this time tomorrow, then I'm handing you over to Elliot for bayonet practise.'

'For sure,' Elliot agreed happily.

***

It was a long twenty-four hours. By the next morning Tim was gritty-eyed from lack of sleep and short on patience. Dreams of a naked Kelly hanging suspended with a rope around her slender neck while Wang jabbed at her with a bayonet, had jerked him awake, sweating, only hours after retiring. Finishing the bottle of his father's favourite scotch - a drink he disliked - in the hope it would put him back to sleep, had only resulted in giving him a thick head as well.

While still under the influence, he had attempted to write to her, producing several pages of such sentimental rubbish that he had not even found the courage to read it before ripping it to shreds. But she would not go away, her green eyes challenging, and he had gone for a walk, prowling around the complex in the moonlight until he found himself at the rhino stockade. Wang was asleep, stretched out comfortably in his sleeping bag, snoring gently, and he had woken him by rattling the chain on the steel bars, angry that the villain should find asleep while he could not. Wang had been gratifyingly alarmed by his aggressive manner, which had prompted him to further efforts.

'You snivelling bastard. If anything happens to her, you are dead meat, do you hear me?' He rattled the chain for emphasis. 'I'll hang you from a tree like Fuli did to the terrorist that murdered his family, then watch the hyenas eat you alive.' He rattled the chain some more. 'You think I'm joking? Huh! Watch me.' The growing strength of his hate had shocked him into silence. He had meant every word.

He had prowled his way to the airstrip, but she was there too, even more so, her body reclining on the wing.

Maybe it was the whisky, but his eyes had blurred at that instant, and he had become angry with himself for losing control. A woman had never affected him in such a strange manner before. He told himself it was only because of the predicament she was in, and that he felt sorry for her, perhaps admiration for speaking out for what she believed in, even guilt that he had not done as much, but it didn't work. It went deeper than that. It was in her smile and walk, the toss of her head and the look in her eyes. In the smile that tried to hide itself, but could never quite succeed.

He did not go on the dawn patrol, and had no appetite. At seven, Frek deposited a large plate before him and removed the warming cover with the flourish of a French waiter and a murmured, 'you blekfast, suh.'

Tim peered through the steam at the loaded plate and felt his stomach clench in rebellion. 'Jesus, Frek. I said I only wanted coffee. Anyway, you gave me gem squash for dinner... four of them.'

'Yes, suh, we have plenty now.'

Tim groaned. 'Just bring me coffee.'

'You prefer I make the pumpkin fritter?'

'No.' He pushed the plate aside. 'You have it, Frek. I've got a headache. Share the vegetables out among the staff... take as much as you want, and give that tin of yellow paint I brought to Kawaseka. Tell him we're going to paint the plane and I want the brushes properly cleaned.'

Restoring the Moth to its original color and replacing the registration numbers occupied Tim for most of the morning, preventing his thoughts from straying too far into areas where they took control and colored his imagination. He stayed away from the rhino stockade, leaving Elliot to keep the prisoner awake and pondering his future. Wang's mobile phone remained within easy reach, its battery fully charged. He had considered using it during the night to call Juliette, John Singleton, and even his father, to inform them of what was happening, but had resisted the temptation. Juliette may understand, but John, and certainly his father, would be unlikely to condone his actions. In this particular exercise he was strictly on his own.

Only later in the morning, when his head had cleared sufficiently for sensible thought, had he realized how close he had come to making a foolish blunder. The destination of all mobile calls was recorded. They could easily have been traced back to him. To avoid being implicated, he could only use the instrument to call people usually contacted by Wang. For the others he must use his own.

As the deadline approached, Tim became

increasingly uneasy. He removed himself to the stockade, where good reception had already been proved, and checked the instrument frequently to confirm it was still working.

Elliot watched him expectantly as he entered the boma, and Wang could not resist casting a hasty glance in his direction as well. Tim ignored them both. He strolled with studied nonchalance around the perimeter, making a show of inspecting the timbers, but his nerves were strung as tight as the poles. His plans did not extend beyond the time limit he had set, and he now regretted making it so short. It would surely take much longer to manipulate the Malaysian system, and the many officials, crooked or otherwise, that must be involved. He tried not to look at his watch.

Ten minutes past two, was the deadline.

With less than two minutes to go Tim could stand it no longer. The entire situation had taken on the aura of a farce, and he was beginning to feel like a third-rate actor between takes of a Kung-Fu movie. Convinced that Lan was not going to call, he angrily adjusted the crutches and swung purposefully from the boma as if suddenly remembering something important he had to attend to elsewhere, but the only thing on his mind was a desire to suffer the ignominy of defeat without an audience.

He was way out of his depth. How he could ever have imagined pulling off such a dumb stunt was beyond him. The Chinese were far more adept at this sort of intrigue than he could ever hope to be. Obviously, Lan had accurately assessed his lack of guile simply by his conversation, and knew he was not the type to kill in cold blood. By not calling back, Lan was gambling that his trump was higher, and he was right.

Tim realized there was another possibility that he had not given sufficient consideration. Lan may well be telling the truth about not having any influence with the Malaysians. He may have engineered Kelly's arrest, but since then she had become a victim of the system, and her fate was now out of his hands.

Wang's mobile phone warbled as Tim passed through the gate.

Thankfully, he was already out of view, so his clumsy stumble as he started with surprise mid-swing went unseen. He experienced a rush of exhilaration. It was not over yet. The phone was stuffed in his shirt, and he dropped a crutch so that he could retrieve it hastily, but restrained himself from answering immediately, allowing the urgent summons to repeat itself three more times while he gathered his composure, then he steadied himself and pressed the OK button. 'Yes?' he enquired, subduing the tremor with difficulty.

'Mister Smeeth.' It was not Lan's voice. 'Please listen carefully, Mister Smeeth. Someone here is going to speak to you, but you must not talk back. The person will not hear you. If you try to speak you will be disconnected. Wait please.'

Tim heard a series of clicks, then a voice that set his heart to pounding and the blood rushing to throb in his ears. 'Mister Smith, my name is Kelly Maddock. I don't know who you are. I have been told that you know me and are trying to help me.' Her voice was loud. Too loud. And studied, as if she were reading her words, and they had a distinctly nervous quaver in them. 'I have been well treated here in prison, but I will be beaten and abused if you do not do what they say. That is the only way you can help me.'

She was cut off abruptly. The line clicked again and the man came back on. 'You have heard her, Mister Smeeth. Do what she says.'

'You bastards! What the hell are you...?'

'I am going now,' the man said over the top of him. 'Another person will call you back in a very short time.'

With only the hollow sound of the closed line in his ear, Tim lowered the instrument slowly and turned it off. Hearing her voice so distinctly, as if she were no more than a few hundred yards away rather than several thousand miles, left him with a feeling of such bitter frustration he could not move. Even the taking of a single step seemed a futile action and beyond his will.

He lowered himself to the ground, leaning back against a pole, and waited for the promised call with a sense of deep foreboding. It would be Lan, he was sure, and he was also sure he would have no good news to impart. The only small satisfaction he had was the confirmation that Lan was definitely involved in Kelly's arrest.

When, after sitting idly in the dust for a full ten minutes, the expected call had still not arrived, Tim hoisted himself to his feet and made his way back to the cage. He glared stonily down at the reclining prisoner. 'Sit up,' he ordered, and prodded Wang sharply about the body with a crutch. 'Obviously your brother doesn't care what happens to you. He's playing games with me.'

Wang reacted to the prods by pushing them contemptuously aside, but the flush to his dark cheeks told they had raised his ire and apparently, loosened his tongue.

'My brother is a clever man. Much more clever than you, Mister Ryan.'

Tim glanced sharply at Elliot. 'You told him my

name?'

Elliot looked sheepish. 'I forget, sir.'

Tim gave a grunt of resignation. 'Never mind. He was stupid to let me know. Much more stupid than his brother, I think,' he said pointedly, giving Wang a few more jabs. 'Now he knows we can't let him go.'

'I kill the bastard, for sure,' Elliot growled, scowling furiously at Wang.

'Not just yet, ' Tim said. 'I still have a few games to play myself. Throw a few buckets of water on his head to cool him down and get rid of the stink, Elliot, or even the hyenas won't eat him. And you had better get something to eat yourself. I'll send Seki to keep an eye on him for a while.'

The veiled threats must have sounded as unconvincing to Wang as they did to Tim, for the only reaction he gave was a faint smirk, although he did stiffen in expectation of another jab in the ribs as Tim suddenly turned on his crutches to move away.

The call eventually came at six - four hours after the deadline - when Tim was sipping on the last of a cold beer and wondering if he could risk another. He needed it badly, but he needed an alert brain more.

'Please forgive the delay, Mister Smith,' Lan said after Tim had answered with his brusque, and now almost customary interrogative. 'I have been very busy.' He did not sound in the least apologetic. 'You had a call from my friend… and yours?' he added.

'What's your game, Lan? Your brother is very uncomfortable at the moment.'

'He is used to that, Mister Smith, but I doubt if the same applies to your girlfriend. At the moment she is being treated well, but that could change very quickly. She is a good-looking young women, I hear.'

'You listen to me, Lan. If anything happens to her…'

'Nothing will happen to her, Mister Smith, unless you refuse to release my brother. I may even make a few suggestions to some people that she may be innocent of drug trafficking and was being used only as an unsuspecting courier. Her sentence will be less, and eventually she will be freed.'

'No, goddamit! You said you had no influence there, you lying bastard! I want her free now, do you hear? Right now!'

'I hear you too well, Mister Smith. Unfortunately my influence only extends to a few minor officials, not all Malaysia. She has been formally accused and must go through the judicial system. If you are reasonable, I will help and she will be well treated. I expect to hear from my brother by this time tomorrow that he is free and safe, otherwise your friend may find herself suffering something unpleasant. At least for her it will be. This time tomorrow, Mister Smith.'

'You slimy sonofabitch...' But Lan had already gone.

***

Compared to her previous accommodation, the two rooms were luxurious, almost an apartment, but Kelly had felt safer in the cell. The female wardens there had been friendly, even polite at times, and she had never felt threatened by them or the other prisoners, several of whom were English-speaking Caucasians.

She had even met a white American woman, although not the type she would normally associate with, and there had been three Australians, one with a child. Most were there on minor drug charges, except for two Australian girls who, like herself, had been charged with trafficking in heroin and faced the death penalty if finally convicted. They had been there for eight months and were still awaiting further trial. Both were in their early twenties, but looked fifteen years older. It did little for Kelly's peace of mind.

No explanation was given for her sudden move.

Early in the morning, two female wardens she had never seen before appeared at her cell and brusquely ordered her out. When she remained sitting on her bunk, asking where she was being taken, one of them, a fat woman with a pock-marked face and the slit eyes look of a dozing cat, strode in, grabbed her by the hair and dragged her bodily from the cell. It was her first experience with rough treatment, and so unexpected that Kelly could only gasp in shock, then stumble away under the threat of a raised baton.

Prodding and herding her like an animal, they paraded her silently past the cells, then through a series of gated corridors to a group of rooms adjoining the administration block. They shoved her into one and locked the heavy door, leaving her alone.

The room contained a table, two chairs, a single bunk, and an overhead fluorescent light. The walls were bare, with no windows, although she could feel a stir of air and hear a faint hum coming from somewhere. An adjoining cubicle revealed a basin and shower. Beneath the shower, a hole-in-the-floor toilet gaped uninvitingly. Her very own en-suite.

The thinner of the two wardens returned with a threadbare towel, a bar of yellow soap, a green prison smock, and a pair of oversize baggy green bloomers. Kelly was instructed to remove her civilian clothes, which were bundled up and taken away, hopefully to be laundered, but Kelly had little faith in the domestic service. She had seen neither the embassy official, nor the promised toothpaste and shampoo. Her questions and demands were brushed aside. They are coming soon, seemed to be the stock excuse

Kelly showered and changed, then lay on the bunk to ponder her situation. Despite her earlier rough treatment, she felt encouraged by the move. It was next to the administration section, which was one step closer to freedom. Why else would they bring her here, if not to prepare her for something?

A male voice in the corridor and the sound of the door unlocking caused Kelly to sit up expectantly. The fat warder who never spoke, and to whom Kelly had given the name Keystone Kate in commemoration of the happy band of half-wits from the silent movie era, entered with a man in a Hawaiian shirt and long, slick black hair smoothed straight back, as if it had recently been dipped in oil. He carried a clipboard and what looked to be a tape recorder, which he set down on the table. He gave Kelly a brief glance, then began fiddling with the machine, unwinding cords and pressing buttons, speaking into a microphone. 'Hello? Hello?' He rewound and played it back.

Satisfied, he looked at Kelly and seemed surprised to see her still sitting on the bunk. He beckoned impatiently, as if she should have known better. 'Come,

come.' He pointed to the other chair. 'Sit there.'

With Keystone Kate looking unfriendly, Kelly complied without further delay, speaking only once seated. 'What's happening?'

'No questions, please.' He placed the clipboard before her. 'Read this. First you study, then you must speak into microphone. You understand?'

Kelly read the few typewritten sentences in disbelief. Her first reaction was to laugh disdainfully. 'Are you kidding me? What's this all about... who the hell is Mister Smith?

'No questions!' He slapped the edge of the table sharply, a quick, admonishing slap, as if smacking the back of a disobedient child's hand. 'Only speak into the microphone. Is this not what I say to you?' His voice rose and he stood to lean forward and poke at the clipboard with a stiff finger. 'Did you not read where it say you will be beaten? It is true.' He glared down at her, and Kelly stared contemptuously back. She was not afraid of him. He reminded her of a prissy teacher trying to be tough.

'Look, I have a right to know what is going on. I want to see my lawyer. I'm not reading any of your stupid propaganda.'

He lifted his hands in a gesture of exasperation, turning to Keystone Kate and saying something in

Malaysian. His tone was questioning, complaining, and the fat warder observed Kelly silently, her flat face expressionless, yet her apparent lack of interest was more intimidating than if she had snarled. Kelly shifted nervously in her chair, preparing herself. This time she would not be taken unawares.

Seeming bored with the proceedings, Keystone Kate walked past her to the shower. She removed the wet towel from where Kelly had draped it over the basin to dry, and dropped it into the toilet hole, ramming it down with her baton.

'What's going on?' Kelly demanded. 'I want to see my lawyer. The Embassy is going to hear about this.' Her demand sounded ineffectual, and went unanswered.

Keystone Kate turned on the shower and stood for a moment with hands on hips, watching the hole fill, then she dropped her baton into the basin and came towards the table.

Kelly scrambled up to move behind the chair and lift it threateningly. 'Stay away from me, you fat bitch.'

With one arm outstretched, the warder came on like a battering ram, barging contemptuously through the jabbing chair legs as if they were no more threatening than the blunt toy spears of a child's toy. Then she turned and came backwards, using her considerable weight to smash Kelly hard against the wall. She held her there with a shoulder while she reached for a grip on her hair, then whipped her free arm round to lock Kelly's head in the crook of her elbow. Ignoring the flailing fists that thumped on the top of her head, she dragged Kelly backwards to the shower.

Her hair was released momentarily as the water was turned off, then she was hip-thrown face down on the wet floor. With the wind knocked out of her, Kelly had barely time to catch half a breath before her hair was gripped once more in a bunch and her face pushed far down into the full toilet hole.

Already breathless from her struggles and fall, and the choking hold on her throat, Kelly felt her chest constrict immediately, and her entire body writhe against the overwhelming need to breathe, while at the same time her nose, her mouth, and even her eyes, remained firmly shut to prevent it. Then Keystone Kate threw her full weight across her back and the small amount of air in her lungs was forced out in rush of bubbles.

With no air whatsoever, waves of darkness washed over Kelly. She opened her eyes wide, but still they kept coming. Her upper body convulsed, the spasms pushing from her diaphragm into her empty lungs, into her tight throat, and she knew she was drowning. Then her head was jerked from the water.

Like a stranded fish, her mouth opened, gasping wide. Half-swallowed water gushed out and air rushed in. Water that was tainted and slimy, and air that was fetid with the lingering foul odours of some unseen cesspool. Her stomach rejected, and she vomited water and sour bile. Then, as she choked and gasped, her head was thrust down once more.

This time she did not resist. Could not. The darkness came quicker, then almost immediately began to recede into soft light, brighter in the centre, like a distant sun, and her mind came suddenly clear. I'm dying, she thought, and didn't care. She did not feel the heavy weight being lifted from her upper body, or the release of her hair. Dimly she heard the gurgling of water around her ears and was vaguely aware of it diminishing in volume, but felt nothing until the weight returned to press heavily down between her shoulders. It went, then came again, twice more. Faintly, she heard herself groan.

She was alone when she finally recovered. She dragged herself away from the stinking hole to crouch in the corner, resting her head in the junction of the two walls, nauseated and with a throbbing head. What little was left in her stomach she spewed up between her knees, then she reached up to turn on the water and fumble blindly for the soap.

She removed her sodden smock and washed her face and hair, lathering hard and ignoring the burning pain on her scalp from her pulled hair. She washed out her mouth, then scrubbed the rest of her body vigorously with rigid fingers, scouring away the feel of the fat warder and the rotting cabbage stench of her. She pulled herself upright on the tap to stand under the cold water until the lather had gone and she felt strong enough in the legs to move.

She was asleep when they returned. Keystone Kate roused her by prodding with her baton, and she sat up quickly on the edge of her bunk, blurry-eyed and groggy.

The tape recorder was back on the table and slick-hair was reading from his clipboard, his lips moving, no doubt rehearsing his part of the speech.

Not waiting to be summoned, Kelly rose and took her place on the chair, wanting to get it over with as soon as possible. The few sentences would only take a minute, and the contents were certainly not worth what she had been through.

She took the clipboard without looking at him and read them again. It made no sense to her. In essence, it was not that different from a ransom note. A threat to someone she didn't know, but who knew her and was trying to help. It could really only be Billy or Pop. What they were expected to do in return for her safety was a mystery, but at least they would hear her voice and know she was all right. It may even do her some good.

'When do I get to see my lawyer?' she asked. With her willingness to comply already implied but not yet completed, she saw no reason why she shouldn't do a little bargaining of her own. 'And I would like my toothbrush and other things.'

'Yes, soon, soon. After we finish. You need practice?'

'No, just tell me when to start.'

***

Tim lifted the instrument high, intending to hurl it against the slate-feature wall, but caught himself in time. His temper had already cost him - and Kelly. With a string of oaths, he tossed it onto the soft couch instead, then shoved back his chair, upending it with a clatter, and bringing a concerned Frek rushing in from the kitchen. 'Bring me another beer,' Tim barked, more to get rid of him than any need for alcohol. It would have to be a lot stronger than beer to calm him down.

He gathered his crutches, snatched up the mobile

phone, and thumped out through the door, bellowing for Elliot, and when he came hurrying in response, arriving at the same time as the beer, Tim changed his mind again. 'Give it to Elliot,' he told Frek, and swung away to Juliette's office, where he could be alone to sit quietly and think undisturbed.

But sitting still was impossible. He paced the small office on his crutches; two swings one way to the filing cabinet, a clumsy about turn, then two swings back to the steriliser to repeat the process.

His head spun with all the smart things he could have said to Lan but hadn't, and all the angry words he did say but shouldn't have. Lan the businessman had remained cool and cunning, while he had reacted like what he was; a dumb bushie more used to handling recalcitrant rhinos than wheeling and dealing, even when a life was at stake. And not just any life, but the life of a woman who had saved his.

Without her attention after Rosie's attack he would have lost too much blood, and been too weak to get to the plane. Even had he made it, he probably would have passed out in the air and crashed anyway. Now her life was at stake and he was doing nothing. His helplessness was driving him crazy. He had to do something.

The satellite phone caught his attention where he

had left it on the desk, and he eyed it speculatively for a moment, then took the card from his breast pocket on which he had written all the important telephone numbers.

He sat on the step outside and dialled John's number in Harare. John had one of the coolest heads in a crisis that he knew of, and he needed to speak to someone who would understand, who might come up with a few ideas but, as he had expected, he received no answer. John was not due back from the Zambezi Valley for at least another two weeks. Juliette was the next choice. She would understand, and Kelly was her friend. He dialled her number, but previous attempts at getting through to Cocos had proved as successful as trying to call someone on the moon, and so it was now.

Tim looked at the number for Chipimbiri Rhino Sanctuary and reached for the buttons, then he paused, letting his hand drop to the desk with fingers tapping as he considered how much of what had transpired he should tell his father. Informing him about his now worse than useless hostage would definitely be asking for trouble. Chris Ryan had done some crazy things in his life, but Tim doubted that his father would have gone this far. And he already knew about Kelly. He dialled the number and continued his restless tapping, letting his mind go blank. He would play it by ear, but he had to speak to someone.

It was his mother that answered, her voice hushed, and Tim remembered again that it was well after midnight in Australia. She would be using the bedside phone.

'Sorry to wake you, mom. I need to talk.'

'Tim?' Her voice strengthened. 'Is something the matter, son?'

'Not that serious. I can call back in the morning, if you like.'

'No, wait, I'll go through to the other phone so I don't disturb your father.'

She was gone before he could protest, and Tim spent the time wondering what he could say that wasn't too trivial. If he wanted a sympathetic ear he would never find a better one, but he could tell her even less about what was happening than he could his father.

He needn't have worried. 'What's bothering you, love?' she asked without preamble after picking up the kitchen phone. 'You don't sound your usual cheerful self.'

That was his stepmother all over, Tim thought with a wistful smile. She had always been able to tell by the tone of his and Juliette's voices when trouble loomed. He had once told her that she had the hearing of a mother bat.

'I'm worried about Jules's friend, Kelly.'

'Lord, yes. We are too. Your father has been on to the American Embassy practically every day trying to get information on the poor girl, but they don't seem to know much more than they told us in the beginning. Either that, or they're not saying. He's sure they don't believe the drugs had been planted.' She sighed wearily. 'I suppose they hear the same story from every person that gets caught with them.'

'Do you believe it, Mom?'

'Of course I do. We all do. Juliette says Kelly would never have done such a thing. What do you think, Tim?'

'I can't tell you the details over the phone, Mom, but I know for a fact she's innocent. She threatened to expose… you know who, and had to be kept quiet. Anything she says now will just be taken as something she made up as an excuse.'

'What have you been up to, Tim? Not sticking your neck out, I hope.'

Tim skipped neatly over the question. 'I feel responsible, Mom. She saved my life. I have to do something. It's driving me crazy sitting here like a bloody cripple and not being able to do anything to help her.'

For a few moments his mother was silent. When

she spoke again her tone had changed. 'Yes, I should have known,' she said positively, as if suddenly realising the important truth in something not previously taken seriously. 'I know it's none of my business, son, but did you have an affair with the girl?'

It was Tim's turn to be silent, which, apparently, was all the answer his astute mother needed.

'Are you in love with her?'

'Hell, Mom, I really don't know what I am…'

'What did you have in mind?'

'About what?'

'About helping her. You're not thinking of going to Kuala Lumpur by any chance, are you?'

Until that moment Tim had not admitted to himself that going to see Kelly was what he wanted to do more than anything else. He could do nothing at Gara Pasi. There was little he could do to help by going to KL either, but simply being there to talk to her, letting her know that she was not alone, would be a start. Then, as one thought led to another, then yet another, opening a whole new Pandora's box of possibilities, Tim experienced the familiar rush of exhilaration that usually followed when frustrating, nebulous thought showed how it could be turned into positive action.

'Tim?'

'Yes, mother, as a matter of fact I was. There's

not much I can do around here with my leg in plaster, and John's still tied up in the Valley. I can come back via Oz and help with settling in the rhino. What do you think?'

Her voice took on a wistful tone. 'I think you are your father's son, Tim. I liked Kelly. She's your sort of no-nonsense type, and if you love the girl you must do what you think is right, but I want you to promise not to do anything silly and land yourself in trouble as well.'

Tim chuckled, feeling the relief. 'You mean like Dad did in Egypt when he rescued you from the Sheikh's house?'

'We won't go into that,' she said firmly, and changed the subject. 'How do you intend getting there? I believe there is a direct flight to Hong Kong from Johannesburg. That will probably be the quickest and cheapest.'

For the next ten minutes they discussed booking arrangements and money. He should use the company's Australian credit card, his mother advised, to avoid dipping into Gara Pasi's foreign currency account. It was yet another onerous stipulation of Mugabe that whites owning large tracts of land must use it to attract foreign currency or risk being thrown off without compensation. Even wildlife sanctuaries were not exempt.

'And don't worry about your father,' she reassured Tim, pre-empting the question he had been holding back. 'I'll explain to him in the morning. Just be careful and keep us informed. I'll let Juliette know what's happening too.'

When she had gone, Tim leaned back in the chair and exhaled a deep breath, sitting there for a moment to wallow in the satisfying prospect of imminent action, then he clambered up and bellowed for Frek.

'Coffee please, changamiri,' he said, using the Shona word for friend to make up for his previous belligerence. 'And how about a steak with some of your special gem squash, hey? I have much work to do.'

The chirping of the mobile jarred Tim awake at dawn. He stumbled up from the desk and went outside to answer, managing a wheezy hello.

'Good morning, sunshine,' his mother's cheery voice greeted. 'Are you awake?'

'Not really. I suppose you're getting your own back.'

'Well, one good turn deserves another, as they say, but I thought I'd catch you early in case you went flying or something silly like that. If you can make it to Harare by eight tonight, I've booked you on a flight to

Hong Kong via Jo'burg. Other than that they're pretty well booked for the next few weeks.'

Suddenly Tim was fully awake. 'You have?'

'Well, I know how difficult it is to organise bookings from there, and Carol, the dear, managed to pull a few strings. Can you make it?'

'Absolutely.' Arranging a quick flight had been a pivotal part of the plan he had spent the night working on. A lengthy delay in getting there would only make everything more difficult, and also more risky for Kelly. Lan could not be put off indefinitely.

'Carol has also booked you on a connecting flight to KL, but you will have to make your own hotel arrangements. You won't need a visa if it's only for a few days.'

'Hell, mom…' Tim cleared his throat, not knowing what to say.

'Dad says don't forget to take the phone and keep in contact. Now, if you have a pen handy, I'll give you all the details.'

Tim found a clean sheet amidst the night's clutter of notes and sat on the step to write them down carefully. 'You're a star, Mom. No wonder I love you.'

'Take care, darling, and good luck. And please tell Kelly we're thinking of her and doing what we can.'

Lydia arrived with welcome coffee and rusks

a few minutes later, when he was sitting at the desk, staring dazedly at the phone and rubbing his ear.

As she left he instructed her to send Elliot and Frek to see him at seven sharp, then checked through his notes, smiling with satisfaction as he scored through the telephone number of the travel agency that headed the list. One down and six to go.

Next on the list was the number of the National Parks camp at Chete, where he hoped to find John Singleton. He allowed himself a sardonic smile as he reached for the phone. It was time for the dumb bushie to put his half-arsed plan into action.

***

Spying could be a very confusing business at times, Elliot thought. One had to walk on one path, yet set his trap to snare the enemy on another. It was much like marriage. A woman lured a man with the promise of her body and he failed to see the trap of children that lay ahead. But even if he did see it, as he did, the bait was so enticing that a man didn't care, as he didn't. It was a confusing thing indeed, for sure.

With his head freshly shaved by Lydia, and now attired in his white robe - which he had sworn never to wear again after the bicycle incident because it made him feel like a woman - Elliot stood waiting as Lydia knelt at his feet to repair the damage caused by the chain. To stitch it required lifting the hem to the level of his knee, and his jokes that he wore nothing beneath, and that she must not try to sneak a look, caused her to blush and giggle shyly.

'It is a thing of such greatness and beauty,' he told her with quiet, almost rapt reflection, as if describing a famous work of art, 'that to see it and not own it will cause you much sorrow.' He placed a hand gently on the crown of her bowed head and gave it a few conciliatory pats. 'But soon, when your father agrees, and allows us to marry, you will have a good viewing and will cry with happiness, for sure. Now leave the mending, my tempting woman, and summon the people. It is time to go.

Followed by a small, select group of Gara Pasi staff and family members, Elliot strode across the dusty compound to the rhino stockade. He assembled the congregation in the shade of the large sausage tree that grew beside the pole wall and bade them sit down, then paced thoughtfully to and fro with his mahogany staff, until he had their undivided attention.

'We are here to praise the Lord,' he declared sonorously.

'Praise the Lord,' the group responded faithfully.

'We must sing the praises,' he commanded, and nodded to Lydia. She began to sing the first verse of a hymn in a high, sweet voice, leading the others, and they followed in close harmony, picking up the melody with natural ease.

Elliot did not know the words either, but joined in by repeating the last few in each line, adding his strong bass. When the hymn ended he bade them all rise by making upward motions with his staff. He had a feeling it should have been the other way around, and that they should have been standing to sing and sitting to pray, but he couldn't remember for sure so let it go.

'Now we must pray for the soul of the sinner who is about to die,' he called loudly, to ensure Wang could hear every word. 'We beg you, Jesus, to forgive him his sins, and also to forgive us our trespasses in the name of justice, for does it not say in the bible that for an eye must be taken an eye?' He raised his staff to prompt, and the congregation responded dutifully.

'Yebbo!'

'And for a tooth must also be pulled out a tooth?'

'Yebbo!'

'So be it then.' Elliot signalled for them to sit, then opened Lydia's Shona bible and began reading passages at random, skipping the difficult words. That they had nothing to do with sin or revenge was of no consequence, for it was the effect he was after, and he spoke quietly.

They sang another two hymns, for it was enjoyable, then ended with a further short prayer for the sinner and a litany of amens. It was very impressive, Elliot thought.

He led the group into the boma and stopped by the cage to look down at the prisoner. 'It is time,' he declared haughtily.

Wang was sitting on his rolled-up sleeping bag, hugging his knees, and looking distinctly pale. His eyes shifted restlessly over the assembled, ogling group, and one corner of his mouth twitched spasmodically. 'What are you doing?' he asked in a tremulous voice.

Elliot ignored him, laying aside his staff to produce a key and open the lock. 'Bring the sinner out…forth,' he commanded.

'No,' Wang protested. 'Where is the white man? I want to see him.'

'Gone,' Elliot replied. 'Did you not see the aeroplane leaving yesterday? He does not wish to witness your killing.'

'No! You have it wrong. He does not wish me to be killed. That is what he meant. I know!'

It took two men to lift the iron shutter, and another two to drag the reluctant prisoner out, with Elliot rapping him on the knuckles with his staff when he clung to the bars. Once out, his hands were bound and he was shoved out of the boma to where the Land Cruiser had been parked near the shed.

As they went, the group began dispersing, taking the path to the huts, so by the time they reached the Toyota, only Elliot and Sibanda remained to bundle Wang into the back with his sleeping bag. Using the lock and chain from the cage, Elliot fastened him securely to the rear door. He was taking no risks on Wang's ability to leap out when they were underway.

He was in the driver's seat, about to start, when Sibanda, sitting beside him with the AK, suddenly groaned and clutched at his stomach.

'What is it?' Elliot demanded.

'I think I have a snake in my belly,' Sibanda wheezed, his face screwed in pain. 'A very big snake. I will have to get some muti. I think so.'

Elliot clicked his tongue in sympathy. 'Go then. It is of no matter. But leave the gun.' He turned to scowl at Wang. 'We go alone, yellow mabunu. Do not try to be tricky. I have the gun.' He lifted it to demonstrate. 'But do not worry,' he said mildly. 'It is not for me to kill you. I am a man of God, and it is Sunday. I can only shoot you a little bit on the legs if you are running.' He laughed. 'To kill you is the job of mister hyena.'

He started the engine and the vehicle jerked forward in short leaps until the speed increased and they were able to proceed smoothly along in third gear.

Elliot drove north towards the Sabi River and Mozambique border, heading deep into the National Park, following the same old track he had used after freeing the rhino and stealing the horn. If the Chinese wondered why he was being taken so far he did not ask. He remained silent, but observing him in the rear-view mirror, Elliot could see Wang carefully inspecting the chain and tailboard, and he had noticed him sneakily testing his bound wrists to see if he could squeeze himself through his arms and bring them to the front. With his short legs it did not look as if he would find it too difficult. He would have to be careful, Elliot told himself. He was a very tricky fellow, this one, for sure.

The terrain became stonier and more wooded, the track more tortuous as they reached the foothills, and Elliot brought the vehicle to a halt. 'This is the place of the hyena,' he explained. 'Now we must go by the feet to tell them we are here.' He picked up the rifle and climbed out to open the rear door. 'Lie down on your front,' he ordered, and when Wang complied and was safely stretched out and unable to make any surprising moves, he poked the barrel into his back and, using one hand, removed the padlock and chain. He stepped back with the AK at the ready and ordered Wang out.

'Walk in front,' Elliot commanded, indicating with the barrel towards a game-trail leading into the hills. He walked several paces behind, quietly humming one of the hymns sung earlier that morning, keeping a steady eye on Wang as the rocky trail descended into the sandy bed of a dry stream.

They were nearing the bottom when Elliot suddenly lost his footing. Arms flailing, but still gripping firmly to the rifle, he skidded clumsily past Wang, and sprawled headlong onto the sand.

Wang was quick. Before Elliot could recover, he spun round, scrambled swiftly back up the bank, and dived for cover.

Elliot rolled over and shouted for him to stop. He did not attempt to fire. He sat with head cocked, listening to the faint rattling of stones and rustling of bushes as Wang made good his escape. He was still sitting when, some moments later, came the sound of the Toyota's engine revving, followed by the skidding noise of its wheels accelerating over stones.

**

John Singleton yawned widely and eased his cramped limbs. It had been a hectic and exhausting twelve hours. Even now, dozing stretched out on his back on the front seat of the Landrover with his feet out the window, he could still see the endless dark road unfolding before him, its centre-line dazzling white in the headlights. He sincerely hoped it was worth it, and that he was not going to get fired for wasting his, and everyone else's, valuable time on a wild goose chase.

From somewhere outside came the faint hiss and crackle of a radio, then a few moments later the African police inspector stuck his head in the window. 'It is coming,' he said. 'Better take position.'

John sat up quickly, cocking his head to listen, then nodded with satisfaction. 'Thank God for that. I was beginning to wonder.' He slid out quickly. 'Are you ready, Mathias?'

'I am ready, sir.' Mathias rose from where he had been resting in the shade of the vehicle and brushed the sand from his uniform.

'Good. Remember, no shooting. Leave everything to the police.'

Less than twenty paces wide, the dry stream-bed with its soft sand was the perfect site for a roadblock. With John's vehicle blocking the track at the top of the far bank, and the grey police Landrover concealed in thorny grey scrub off the incoming track on the other, once inside the trap, there could be no escape. And in the event that this should be attempted on foot along the sandy bed, John and Mathias were positioned on one side and two police constables on the other.

The inspector was so confident that he didn't even attempt to conceal himself. He waited in the centre of the dry stream beside the track, with his pistol drawn but not raised, and when the green Toyota skidded to a halt halfway down the bank, he beckoned it forward casually, as if directing suburban traffic. The arrival of the police vehicle behind endorsed the invitation, and the Toyota continued on to stop beside the inspector.

With the threat passed, John sauntered up to have a good look at the man Tim had told him about on the phone. Particularly, he searched for bruises or other signs that he had been in captivity for a few days, but he appeared unharmed, and was even smiling pleasantly as he spoke to the policeman.

'…luck to find you,' he was saying. 'I have been trying to find my way to the border at Vila Salazar.' He laughed, high-pitched and girlish. 'I think I am lost.'

'You are a long way from there, sir,' the inspector said politely. 'And you need a permit to be here. May I see your driver's licence please?'

'Certainly! Of course!' He lowered the sun visor and removed a plastic licence from a pouch behind.

'And this is your vehicle, sir?'

'Yes. Except also a company one.'

'But your licence and registration is for Mozambique, Mister Wang. Do you have a passport and permission to be in Zimbabwe?'

This seemed to be a problem. Despite a frantic search through the glove compartment no passport could be found, although it did reveal a mobile phone, which appeared to puzzle the man. He examined it carefully, checking to see if it was working, and apparently it was, for his expression brightened considerably. 'I believe I must have left my passport at my friend's house in Harare,' he said with a confident smile. 'His name is Mister Marufu. A good friend of mine, and also a relative of the President. I am sure if you contact him he will settle this matter.'

'The President's brother-in-law?' The inspector looked impressed, handing back the licence and returning the pistol to its shiny holster, and John Singleton's heart sank. It was this sort of political power play he had been afraid of. He had known Inspector Maynard for several years, and the policeman had a reputation for honesty and integrity, but he was still an African, and this was now black Africa. A wrong step could earn the inspector a severe reprimand by his political superiors, if not a spell in prison.

'So, you know him,' Wang said loftily. It was a

435

statement, not a question, and his demeanour appeared to change instantly from that of accused to that of interrogator. 'Why are you here, anyway? Is there not enough crime in Harare to keep the police busy?' He laughed to soften the jibe, but without humour. To John it looked more like a sneer.

'No sir, we are here to look for poachers. Will you come out of the vehicle please?'

Wang's sneer vanished, replaced by an angry frown. 'You think I am a poacher? You are making a big mistake. Here...' He thrust the mobile phone through the window at the inspector. 'Take it. Call Mister Marufu and speak to him. Ask an operator for the number.'

'Out of the vehicle, please. We wish to search it.'

'Search it? What for? Can't you see it is empty?' Nevertheless, he swung open the door and jumped to the sand. 'Do it then. Search it. You will find nothing.' He strutted about like an angry bantam, threatening reprisals as the two constables opened the rear door of the Land Cruiser and looked in.

As Wang had reported, there was precious little, only a plastic drum of water, a padlock and chain, a few pieces of short rope, and a rolled-up sleeping bag. One of the constables crawled in to drag the sleeping bag out. It seemed unusually heavy, and when dropped to the sand it landed with a solid thump. He unrolled it with his foot, then lifted the closed base of the bag, up-ending it to deposit four rhino horns onto the sand.

Their appearance was greeted with exclamations of surprise from the constables, and also from Mathias and John, whose short laugh was tinged with relief. Anticipating the discovery, he had already positioned himself so the sun was behind, and now took several photographs, including one of a stunned Wang looking down at the horns.

Although he must have been more pleased with the outcome than anyone, Inspector Maynard's only response to the find was a faint smile. 'Can you explain these, Mister Wang?' he asked politely.

Wang could only stare at the horns in disbelief.

'Mister Wang?'

Wang finally found his voice, although it was not the same one he had been using a few moments ago. 'You are trying to frame me!' he cried indignantly. 'You put them there. These are not mine!'

'We put them in your bag?' the inspector said incredulously, looking at his constables with eyebrows raised. Was it you, Constable Tafura?'

'It was not me, sir,' Tafura replied, trying not to grin.

'Was it you, Constable Chinyamba?'

'Or me, sir,' he answered, barely able to contain an erupting snort of giggles.

'You think it is a joke?' Wang howled. 'You are nothing but an ignorant bla… you had your agent put them there when I was locked in the… in the cage… It is true! He threatened to kill me with hyenas! You don't believe me? Then come, I will show you the place.' He spun away, making for the door of the vehicle, and Inspector Maynard spoke to his men.

'Arrest him.'

They obeyed with alacrity, pouncing on the struggling Wang and crushing him against the truck, where they expertly cuffed his hands. Still threatening and protesting that he had been framed, he was locked into the wire cage at the rear of the police Landrover.

Before leaving, Inspector Maynard approached John and offered his hand. 'A good day for our rhinos, sir. After the horns have been recorded as evidence, they will be sent to you at your head office.'

'Congratulations, Inspector, you handled things very well. I hope you throw the book at the bastard.'

'You can believe it,' he said grimly. 'What do you think about him saying he is a friend of Marufu? You think it is true?'

'Probably,' John answered, although he knew for a fact that it was. 'But believe me, even if he could show photographs of the two of them together, holding hands, Marufu will still deny ever knowing him.'

'I hope you are right, Mister Singleton. Being a policeman is not easy when there is a law for the people and another for the politicians.'

'This time it will be you and the people who will win,' John said with conviction. 'By the time I have finished my report and a few copies have mysteriously found their way to the Standard, along with some equally mysterious photographs, not even Mugabe would dare intervene.'

Inspector Maynard adopted an uncertain frown. 'I'm not sure that's such a good idea, sir. Is it not against the law to leak official information?'

'Which law are you referring to, Inspector? The people's law or the politicians one?' He smiled, and the policeman laughed, extending his hand once more.

'I have no idea what you mean, sir, but good luck with it anyway.'

With one of the constables driving the impounded Toyota, the two-vehicle convoy departed, continuing on in the same direction as Wang had been going before his brief dash for freedom had been interrupted.

With Mathias for company, John drove in the opposite direction - from where Wang had been coming. He could not help but feel a certain sympathy

for the Chinese agent. He had been framed all right
- well and truly - and the irony of his situation must
be driving him crazy. No one in his right mind would
believe that he had been held captive in a rhino cage
for the past few days, especially as he had already lied
himself into a corner by saying he had been visiting
in Harare. And his idiotic babbling about hyenas only
made it worse. What that was about, John had no idea.
Maybe Wang was already crazy.

'There he is, sir.' Mathias interrupted John's
thoughts and pointed to a lone figure detaching itself
from a shady spot beside the track.

John stopped next to him and returned the anxious
frown that greeted him with a reassuring grin. 'You
don't have to worry, Elliot, it worked perfectly. Our
friend is now in police custody.'

Elliot's relief showed in a fine display of white
teeth. 'Thank you, sir. I was very much afraid for his
escape with the horns. He is a very tricky fellow, that
one.'

'So are you, Elliot. You did well. Even your
friend, James Bond, would be impressed with such a
successful operation.' He opened the door and got out,
directing Elliot in. 'Squeeze in here next to Mathias.
You can tell me all about it on the way back to Gara
Pasi. I want to know how you and Tim managed to get

Wang there in the first place. He didn't have time to tell me everything.'

As the bizarre tale unfolded, John became increasingly concerned that Tim had gone to such extreme lengths simply to have Wang arrested. He also felt vaguely disappointed that Tim had not confided in him, but guessed it was because he had not wanted to involve him in something as hare-brained as kidnapping.

He could make nothing at all of the many telephone conversations that Elliot reported Tim as having on the mobile phone. Elliot's recounting of events were confusing to say the least.

***

'But I can't afford to wait two days,' Tim protested to the Chinese travel agent. 'I have to be in Shanghai by tomorrow morning at the latest. Is there no way I can get a visa sooner?'

The woman agent seemed hesitant, and Tim took a chance.

'I don't mind paying extra for it,' he said meaningfully. His deadline with Lan had already expired by forty-two hours. Waiting around in Hong Kong for another two days would be pushing his luck too far. He was playing with cards of unknown value, in a game he was unfamiliar with, betting that Lan, not knowing what was going on, would do nothing hasty. It was what he would do in the same situation. Lan may be worried, but he knew he had the highest card and would gain nothing by defacing it without good reason. He had nothing to lose by waiting, but Tim was not prepared to risk Kelly's welfare any further.

The agent observed Tim thoughtfully for a few moments. 'There is the possibility of a two-day business visa,' she said. 'Can you give me the name of someone there who will verify the visit?' She gave a small, embarrassed smile. 'They don't usually check.'

Tim hesitated, but he had no choice. 'Yes, definitely. I have urgent business with a Mister Lan of the Golden Horn Company.'

She nodded with satisfaction. 'Good. Can you leave your passport with me and come back in a few hours?'

Tim killed the time fretting in a nearby restaurant, giving his leg a rest. He was back with half an hour to spare, reading travel brochures until the woman called him into her cubicle. She handed him his passport and ticket.

'All in order, Mister Ryan. I'm sorry for the delay. It will cost an extra fifty dollars.' She smiled. 'Our mainland cousins are quick to learn the benefits of capitalism.'

Back at the hotel, Tim lay naked on the bed under the ceiling fan and tried to sleep. As fascinating as it was, the scenic delights of Hong Kong would have to wait for another time. Both his aching leg and his tortured brain needed rest badly, and he had a feeling he was going to need both operating at full capacity in the uncertain days ahead.

He had given up worrying about Elliot and Wang. Whatever happened there was now beyond his control, and he would find out soon enough when John returned his call. Hopefully it would be with good news, but either way, as long as Elliot hadn't done anything stupid, like kill Wang - or get himself killed - it didn't really matter. Wang was out of the picture. It was only himself and Kelly now, and the unpredictable Lan Hui Ping.

He worried instead about what he was going to do in Shanghai. All he had going for him was the element of surprise, but how he was going to use it he had no idea. What he did know, and which caused him to squirm with discomfort whenever he thought of it, was that Kelly's life depended on him coming up with something good.

***

Kelly was not returned to her previous cell as she had hoped. She was kept in almost total isolation, her only visitor an old hag who brought her food and weak tea twice a day. She never drank water, and seldom ate more than a third of the food, restricting herself to bread and those substances she thought least likely to necessitate use of the hole in the floor.

Occasionally, the thinner of the two Keystone Cops brought laundry and checked to see that she hadn't been constructing escape tunnels. She didn't see the fat one. Presumably she was being kept in reserve for heavier duties. The Indian lawyer and the embassy official never made an appearance. Neither did Slick-Hair and his recorder.

With little food and no exercise, Kelly saw her legs become thin and knobbly, and the veins in her arms become more prominent. Thankfully, she was without a mirror, so could not see the hollows in her cheeks and beneath her eyes, but she could feel they were there. *Everywhere except my butt and my belly,* she complained to herself, caressing the gentle swell of her abdomen.

She had not thought of Tim in a long time. Or anyone else for that matter. With nothing to occupy her mind she felt herself slipping into morbid lethargy, her thoughts turning inward. She still could not accept that she may be hanged. The thought of a rope being placed around her neck and a hood pulled over her head was too bizarre to believe. But with each passing day in isolation the truth of her situation was reinforced, and the possibility seemed less remote. The outside world receded to a hazy place in the past, difficult to recall, its people shadowy and their lives not linked to hers. Prison was her world now. A place where hanging took place.

Making a determined effort, Kelly tried to get outside of herself. Morbid introspection, she realized, was a first step towards dumb acceptance and loss of hope, like holocaust victims meekly queuing to enter the gas chamber. She had already succumbed to intimidation, rationalising her agreement to do the recording as unimportant. Next, she thought cynically, she would be going out of her way to please Keystone Kate.

***

Sitting on the low granite wall of a raised garden that seemed to thrive exclusively on cigarette butts, Tim gazed disconsolately across the paved square to

445

the headquarters of the Golden Horn Company, and felt his spirits plummet to new depths.

Of all the grand old colonial buildings that dominated this part of Shanghai's waterfront, it was one of the most imposing. With its fluted columns, heavy architecture, and shiny domed roof complete with spire, it reminded Tim of a German officer's steel helmet from the First World War. Gold was the wrong color though, he thought, aware that he was distracting himself from thinking about the real issues confronting him; problems as overwhelming as the city that hummed and hissed around him like a disturbed nest of ants.

He felt as if he had lost all sense of reality. His being there seemed unreal, and his purpose even more so. He was an insignificant misfit with no hope of achieving anything. He began to wonder gloomily what the hell he was doing there.

Sitting on the same low wall a few scant inches away - which seemed about the maximum space one could expect to remain separated from humanity in Shanghai - a man in a faded blue jacket and floppy cap sat looking forlornly at the stained concrete before him, as if pondering the same question, and Tim pushed himself up, needing to move away. Slinging his airline bag over his shoulder, he limped across the square with forced determination.

The inside of the building was smaller than its exterior had promised, but equally impressive with its terrazzo floors and glass chandeliers. The effect was somewhat spoiled though, he thought, by the giant ceramic mural of a red dragon - sporting a single gold horn on its grotesque snout - that dominated one of the white marble walls. Large showcases lined two of the other walls, either side of a cage-type lift with bronze lattice concertina doors and an old-fashioned clock-type floor indicator.

Below the dragon, cordoned off by a reception counter, was a modern office area, in which scurried chic young Chinese girls in mini skirts, and male clerks wearing black suits, ties, and flashy Reeboks. Maybe, Tim thought facetiously, they ran to work to avoid the traffic congestion.

He gave the office a wide berth, likewise the man attired like a Chinese general who stood rocking on his joggers beside the lift. Conscious of his superior height and fair complexion, Tim played the tourist by feigning interest in the contents of the glass showcases.

They were filled with clear glass bottles containing colored powders, ornately decorated porcelain jars with similar contents, and a variety of ancient measuring devices. One contained only dried leaves, berries, and strange herb-looking substances. Another was filled entirely with bottled reptiles, insects and crudely stuffed animals. Placards beside each exhibit apparently gave an explanation, but they were written in Chinese.

Other than the exhibits, which appeared to be the components of ancient Chinese medicines, Tim could see no other clues as to what business the building housed. It may well have been a museum for all he could tell.

As he hobbled slowly from one showcase to the other, he felt his uncertainty return. He knew he was at the right place. The English-speaking driver of the taxi had assured him it was, and the name was inscribed in English as well as Chinese on the brass plaque at the entrance, but the knowledge itself was only the first step. It was what happened next, that worried him.

Somewhere inside - presumably in one of the offices above - was the man he had crossed the world to confront, yet now he was there he could not find the means to go the few steps farther. To simply ask to see Lan would achieve nothing, and would spoil the element of surprise. But within two days he had to somehow convince him to arrange for Kelly's release. He could threaten, but he had no gun to make the threat real, and did not even know what Lan looked like.

It was not in Tim's nature to be indecisive. After having wrestled with the problem for so long, and still unable to find a solution, he came to the conclusion that he had no alternative but to try reasoning with Lan. He was a businessman, and despite what had passed between them, should at least listen. He had no personal vendetta against Kelly, and once he assured him that his brother's life was not in danger, that he had been arrested but not harmed, and that no doubt he would soon be freed anyway, he would have no reason to be vindictive. He would explain his own behaviour as the actions of a desperate man. He could even say he had come to apologise personally. Losing face. That ought to carry some weight in China.

Convinced it was his only option, Tim started across the floor to the office reception, then stopped short when he saw the display of rhino horns. They too, were behind glass, much thicker glass by the solid look of it, and the display covered the entire length of the second wall.

He went closer to investigate. It seemed as if every species of horn ever known must be represented, and a sample of every product ever manufactured from them. In a recessed, highlighted display in the centre, was the preserved mounted head of a North African black rhino. Both horns were still in place. Of all the unfortunate beasts that were being hounded to extinction it was the most rare, and therefore the most valued and sought after. In Yemen, Tim had heard, a dagger handle carved from them was worth the price of a new Mercedes.

The stuffed rhino gazed lifelessly out at Tim through its glass eyes, and he stared back in outrage.

Rhino horns, and probably only horns, he realized with growing dismay, was what the business he had been unable to define was really all about. Golden Horn Company was nothing but an international horn broker; a business flourishing on greed, superstition and ignorance, blatantly thumbing its nose at everything he believed in. He could never bring himself to even speak to the man who ran such a business without taking him by the throat, let alone try reasoning with him. He had to find some other way.

A soft chime, followed by the rattle of the lattice lift doors opening distracted Tim momentarily from his dark thoughts, and he glanced across to see an old man emerging from the ancient lift with a white poodle in his arms. Tim moved away, making for the exit, and was almost there when he heard two short words being called out sharply from behind, as if a command: 'Cha-Cha!'

Tim stopped suddenly, as if they had been directed

at him. He turned to look.

The old man was still by the lift, but had been joined by the man in the general's uniform, who was attempting to adjust a child's pram, his fingers made clumsy by haste. The dog was not in sight, then Tim saw it appearing from behind the reception counter. One of the dog's hind legs was encased in plaster, and it held the leg suspended as it nimbly avoided the outstretched hands and giggling enticements of two clerks.

The old man called it again. 'Cha-Cha!' More sharply, and the poodle reluctantly hopped towards him. It was lifted up with gentle admonishments from its owner and placed inside the pram. The general's attempts to assist were dismissed with an imperious wave and, seemingly unaware that he was being silently observed by the entire smiling staff, the old man pushed the pram towards where Tim stood watching at the main entrance.

Tim retreated hastily to wait outside, the name still ringing in his ears. When first he had heard those words spoken sharply on Wang's mobile, he had assumed they were some sort of Chinese expression or oath. He would never have guessed they were the name of a dog. A recently injured dog. And the traffic noise in the background on the phone. Was it possible that he had called at the exact same instant of the dog's accident?

Tim dismissed the thought when another, more important fact, suddenly penetrated. Had his brain not been so sluggish he would have realized immediately that it was Wang's father he had been calling, so he must be this apparently senile man with the dog in the pram.

Tim did not believe in signs, portents, or any other superstitious nonsense, but this time he was willing to break the rule and go with his hunch that things were about to change. He had nothing else to go on, and just maybe the lucky Chinese dragon would smile rather than crap on him for a change.

Following the old man along the waterfront promenade should have been easy with the crowds, which slowed the pace but, handicapped by his leg, Tim was hard-pressed to keep him in sight. The pram cleared a path, but it closed swiftly once past, with many pedestrians stopping to turn and stare at the strange spectacle of a dog in a pram, and causing Tim to either bump into them or dodge around. It was made no easier in that most of the time he could only see the old man's back, and his drab blue jacket and baggy cap was identical to that worn by half the population.

It was a relief when they stopped to cross a street,

when he could take the weight off his leg momentarily. It had begun to ache again, and not for the first time did he wish he had put up with the inconvenience of bringing his crutches. He was aware that he was pushing himself, and his fractured leg, to the limit, risking everything with little chance of success, like a dog chasing a speeding car. Lan's father couldn't speak English, so even if he found the opportunity to get him alone, which seemed unlikely in this place, how was he going to explain his predicament to him?

Worrying about the problem brought about the same negative feelings of unreality he had experienced earlier, and in that respect his leg and the associated pain helped, allowing him to worry about something else instead of the futility of what he was doing.

After crossing three busy streets, one of which appeared to be gridlocked entirely with bicycles, the crowd thinned suddenly and Tim was forced to drop back to avoid being noticed. He followed the old man through wide gates into what looked to be a park, and suddenly there were no crowds at all.

The transition from mayhem to tranquillity was so startling that Tim stopped in surprise, wondering if perhaps he was entering the grounds of some sacred temple or cemetery.

A curving path ran from the gate through manicured

lawns and exotic flowering shrubs, meandered past lily-ponds and ancient-looking trees. In the distance he could see a small lake with a zigzagging wooden bridge, and on a hillock alongside, a pagoda-type building surrounded by blooming flowerbeds and a scattering of tables under red and green umbrellas.

On one of the lawns some children were flying gaudily decorated kites, watched by adults from benches nearby and, reassured, Tim continued on in the old man's wake, hurrying to catch up. He would not get a better opportunity of being alone with him.

He was still several yards behind though, and forced to pause when Lan's father stopped to talk to three men sitting together on a bench under a tree. They rose to inspect the pram's occupant with nods and smiles, as if admiring a baby, and the poodle was lifted out by its proud owner to display the plaster cast on its leg. Tim could almost believe he could hear the sympathetic comments as they leaned forward for a closer look.

The poodle was lowered to the ground, whereupon it immediately skipped away with nose to the ground, and the old man, after parking the pram in the shade, went in his turn to admire the songbirds in their small cages that hung suspended from the branches of the tree.

Tim found a sparsely shaded spot behind a shrub and eased himself thankfully onto the grass, wincing as the sudden release of pressure made itself felt, not in his leg below the knee as he may have expected, but throbbing high on the inside of his thigh, close to the groin.

It was beginning to cause him more than a little concern. If the break didn't mend properly, as the doctor had warned it might not if he didn't rest and use the crutches, he would have to go through the whole aggravating process once again.

But travelling with crutches had seemed too awkward, and so far the horse stirrup Frek had bound onto the foot section with ducting tape had held up well. Other than the aching, the only problem he had experienced was where the tape beneath the stirrup kept wearing through, adding a metallic clank to every step. And he had been forced to cut halfway up the inside leg of his best pair of jeans so he could get them on. Once that difficult manoeuvre was accomplished - usually by lying on his back - and the balaclava pulled over his foot to keep the toes clean, it was then a simple matter to pin the trouser leg together so it didn't flap.

He was checking the tape when he noticed the poodle sniffing its way towards him, and he reacted spontaneously. 'Hi, Cha-Cha,' he said. 'Find anything of interest?' The dog's head lifted sharply, ears cocked, its intelligent eyes observing Tim expectantly. It growled softly, but without menace, and cast a quick glance over its shoulder for reassurance before again facing Tim with alert interest.

'Have a bit of a leg problem myself,' Tim said conversationally. 'Care for some biltong?'

No dog on earth, Tim believed, could resist the nutritious strips of dried raw meat. At Gara Pasi he made it from game, salted and spiced with vinegar and dried in the winter sun, and he always carried a ready supply in his pocket. It was far superior to the flavourless beef jerky sold in packets at most airports, but that was all he had. He fished in his bag for an open packet, helped himself to a slice, and held out another towards the watching dog. 'Come and get it, Cha-Cha.'

When the poodle stayed back, its interest stirred by the rustling packet, but still wary, Tim tossed the slice of jerky on the grass between them, and Cha-Cha came forward to sniff cautiously at it before exploring further with a delicate lick. Finally convinced, it picked the slice up in its teeth, gave it a few experimental chews, then gulped it down.

'There you go. First time, huh? Have some more.'

After the third piece Tim had a new friend. The dog lay beside him with eyes fixed and unmoving on the rustling packet and its delicious contents. Not even urgent summoning from the bench could separate them. When Cha-Cha's anxious master came to investigate, as Tim had guessed he might, he returned what was left of the packet, closed the bag, and leaned innocently back on his elbows.

The old man approached Tim with his face wreathed in apology, interspersed with hand-clapping and stern looks each time he called to his recalcitrant pet.

'We could both be in big trouble, mate,' Tim said quietly, scratching Cha-Cha's soft underbelly with a surreptitious finger. When the old man stopped a short distance away, seeming hesitant, Tim sat to pull up the leg of his jeans and display the white plaster, pointing first to it, then to the plaster on the poodle's leg. 'Both same,' he said, smiling.

It seemed to do the trick. The wrinkled face lost its look of uncertainty, the expression changing from one of concern to one of surprise. 'Hai!' he exclaimed, 'Sum, sum.' He nodded vigorously, and came closer for a better look.

'You speak English?' Tim asked hopefully.

'Hungleesh?' He shook his head regretfully. 'No Hungleesh.' He said a few words in Chinese, also a question by the sound of it, and Tim shrugged, putting on an apologetic look.

They seemed to have reached a stalemate, the awkward silence stretching, and Tim racked his reluctant brain for a way to capitalise on the unexpected opportunity. The way things were he would be lucky to get another one. Becoming desperate, he was about to blurt out a few names, starting with Wang and Lan, when the old man turned to call out to his three companions on the bench, beckoning, and when they arrived, looking puzzled and serious, as if they were being drawn into some sort of unpleasantness, he pointed to one of them - a man with a thin, baggy-eyed face. 'Hungleesh,' he said to Tim, then spoke to the man, apparently giving an explanation.

The sad face brightened. 'Ha sa goo Hungleesh,' he boasted.

'Excellent,' said Tim. He made to rise, but the old man signalled that he was to remain seated.

An explanation was given about the strange phenomenon of the two broken legs, each plastered limb being pointed out in turn and, although Tim's leg had been clearly displayed throughout, they reacted with exclamations of surprise, as if seeing it for the first time. 'Sum, sum,' they agreed in a disbelieving chorus, then, as if cued, all broke into knowing smiles and nods at the same time. 'Sum, sum.'

Taking the initiative, Tim prodded his chest with a finger. 'Me, Tim,' he said slowly, pronouncing each word clearly.

The one who boasted he could speak English understood immediately. 'Mee Tim,' he explained quickly to the others, gesturing towards Tim, then introduced himself with a similar pointing finger. 'Zhu Yong Zhong.' He gave himself a prod for each name.

His companions followed his example, giving their names and prodding, and Tim acknowledged each with a smile and dip of his head. He had no hope of remembering any of them, even the first names, but did remember the last person's when it came, experiencing a strange sensation of deja vu when he heard it from the lips of the old man himself. 'Shen Hui Ping.'

The poodle was now reclining on his stomach with head resting on the airline bag, his aristocratic snout suspiciously close to the opening, and Tim tapped him gently on the back. 'Cha-Cha,' he said, and grinned at the old man.

It was the cause of much cackling amusement, which increased when Cha-Cha jerked his head up guiltily to observe them with drooping ears and a look of profound indignation.

They were close to the main path, and the laughter caused two passing students - a boy and a girl - to stop

459

and observe. Laden with books, they had a university look about them and, seeing an opportunity, Tim called out to them. 'Do either of you speak English?'

They exchanged a few words with each other, seeming unsure, then both came forward. 'We both learn English,' the boy said. 'Do you want me to explain something for you?' He spoke slowly with a strong accent, but succinctly, and Tim grinned with relief.

'Yes, if you are not in a hurry,' he answered.

'We have plenty time,' the girl said. 'We like to speak English. Everyone like to speak English now in Shanghai.'

'You both speak it very well,' he complimented.

'Ha sa goo Hungleesh,' the sad-faced man interjected, looking even sadder.

The students didn't laugh, or even smile at his attempts as Tim had been expecting, and he quickly subdued his own. The male student spoke respectfully to the older men in Chinese, apparently introducing himself and the girl, then he did the same to Tim. 'I am Zhu, and this is Chen.'

'My name is…' Tim hesitated. A bit of face-saving on his part too, wouldn't go amiss. 'Me Tim.'

The girl saw through it but didn't let on, only the lowering of her eyes and the suspicion of a smile. She's a smart cookie, Tim thought. And a pretty one.

'You visit Shanghai from America?' Zhu asked.

'Will you explain to my friends here as we speak?' Tim stalled. 'I have an interesting story to tell them.' Two of the men were becoming restless, as if about to leave, and he wanted them to stay. He would have to speed things up a bit. 'Please sit down.'

'Of course!' Zhu spoke to the men, explaining, and they settled themselves on the grass, their interest restored. Zhu sat on his stack of books, and the girl with her legs tucked under, as only supple girls can. She adjusted her short skirt modestly.

'We will tell them everything you say perfectly,' she assured Tim seriously. 'We thank you for giving us such an important lesson.' Then she laughed and clapped her hands with joyful anticipation. A happy soul.

'My pleasure,' Tim replied, feeling a trifle bewildered. 'First, would you please tell them that I am honoured to be in your country and to have them as friends, including Cha-Cha here.'

Her laughter was reminiscent of Chinese music, and her translation was received with gracious smiles and return comments. 'They are equally honoured,' she reported.

'I am not from America,' Tim said. 'I'm from

Africa… Zimbabwe.' He watched the old man carefully as he said the word, but saw no sign he had recognised it, even after Zhu had translated.

Tim gave his next bit of information directly to the girl. 'I am not a tourist. I am here to beg for the life of my girlfriend.'

She gasped, hands going to her face. 'Is true?' she asked, eyes wide and intense.

Tim nodded sombrely. 'She is in prison in Kuala Lumpur, threatened with death for something she didn't do, and the only man who can help her is here, in Shanghai. A very important man who knows the truth but won't speak it.'

'I am very sorry for such a bad thing to happen in Shanghai,' she said with deep sincerity. 'It make me want cry to hear of it.' She bit on her lip and turned to Zhu, who was looking uncomfortable. 'You must speak now,' she said softly.

Zhu's translation evoked all the responses Tim could have expected, except for the one he had hoped for. From disbelief to dismay, even expressions of anger, and Shen Hui Ping appeared to agree with them all. Tim began to wonder if he even knew anything about Kelly. In a way he hoped not, for he seemed a pleasant old man who obviously cared for animals, but at the same time it made his task more difficult. Maybe he was being too subtle.

Tim answered the most important of the return questions first. No, he didn't know the man, or even where to find him in such a big place as Shanghai.

'I only know him by the name of Lan,' he said disconsolately, watching the old man carefully from the corner of his eye. 'And I know he has a brother working in Mozambique whose name is Wang.'

Shen Hui Ping's head had lowered thoughtfully after hearing the first name. When he heard the second he looked up sharply. Tim pretended not to notice, stroking Cha-Cha's belly and turning to face the girl. 'I think this important man believes that his brother is dead, but I know he isn't, and if I could find Lan and tell him the good news, maybe he will help save my girlfriend.'

She translated a part of what had been told her, then became so emotional she again had to hand over to Zhu. Tim could not have wished for a better ally. Her distress communicating and causing the audience, with the exception of Shen, to shift restlessly. Returning to Cha-Cha's belly massage, Tim was aware of Shen's scrutiny throughout, and noticed that when one of the old men asked something of him, Shen silenced the man with a brusque word, quietly spoken.

Tim could do no more. Shen knew, there could be

no doubt, and that was as far as he could go. Finding a knife and threatening to kill the old man unless he ordered Lan to free Kelly - which had crossed his mind - was ludicrous. It only happened in the movies, and would land him in prison as well. He gently dislodged Cha-Cha from his bag and tried to get up, wincing, and Zhu jumped from his books to help.

'You have pain? Please, you must let me look. I study to be doctor.'

'We both study for medicine,' the girl added.

Tim submitted reluctantly to their combined examination. Sitting in one position had not helped, and the pain was worse, but now seemed hardly the ideal time. Zhu examined the stirrup contraption with a shake of his head. 'What doctor put this?'

'Doctor Frek.'

'Not good. Must use crutches. Where is pain?'

Observed closely by the girl and the now standing ring of men, Zhu unfastened Tim's belt and lowered the jeans, revealing the inflammation on the inside of his thigh. 'You have infection,' he declared solemnly.

'You must go to the hospital,' the girl said, her flawless brow wrinkled with concern.

'I have to return to Hong Kong tomorrow,' Tim explained. 'I'll have it checked there.'

She examined the scar on Tim's thigh, now

healed, but still looking a little raw in places. 'You have accident?'

Propped on one elbow, Tim adjusted the tail of his shirt to cover his tartan underpants. He explained briefly how it had happened, and was rewarded with exclamations of awe from the onlookers once she had translated.

'You very brave man,' she said.

Shen Hui Ping asked a question of Zhu, and after a brief discussion he turned back to Tim. 'Do you have medicine for pain?'

Tim shook his head, disappointed it had not been something more revealing that the old man had asked. More discussion followed, then Shen dug into one of his jacket pockets and removed a handful of small vials. He selected one and handed it to Zhu. 'He is a supplier of herb medicines,' Zhu explained. He opened the bottle to inspect and sniff at the contents. 'He says it will help with pain.'

'I will bring some water,' the girl said, making the decision for Tim.

While she was away, Zhu removed the balaclava to examine his toes. 'You can move them?'

'Not much,' Tim replied, trying to wiggle them with little success.

'You go to hospital tomorrow,' Zhu instructed

sternly. 'No delay.'

Chen returned with a Coke bottle filled with water, and Zhu, after consulting with Shen, emptied most of it out, leaving only a few mouthfuls. He poured half the green-grey powder from the file into the bottle and gave it a swirl before handing it over with an encouraging nod. 'Good medicine for pain,' he said authoritatively. 'He also give to dog.'

Tim eyed the muddy green liquid with strong misgivings. It had the look of something taken from the bottom of a swamp. He took the bottle reluctantly and raised it in a toast of thanks to his unexpected benefactor, but Shen was busy inspecting the contents of his pockets, his wrinkled face impassive. Watched expectantly by the others, Tim drank it down in one gulp and grimaced. It tasted like swamp water as well. He hoped it wasn't rhino horn.

Zhu assisted him up and handed him the airline bag. 'We help you to the gate and find a bicycle taxi,' he said.

'Please tell the men it was a pleasure meeting them,' Tim said, 'you too, of course. Thanks for your help.'

As return smiles, modest denials, and good wishes were being exchanged, Tim dug in his bag for one of his business cards. It had the Gara Pasi name

466

and emblem of a rhino head on the front, and on the back he had written his satellite number, in case he ever needed to pass it on to someone, and now seemed the ideal time. He slipped it into the half-full packet of jerky, shuffling it to the bottom.

The poodle's ears pricked up at the sound of rustling cellophane, his eyes imploring, and Tim gave him a piece then handed the packet to Shen. 'For Cha-Cha,' he explained.

Shen Hui Ping took the packet but did not return the smile, giving a swift bobbing bow of his head in its place, then he turned to walk away, with Cha-Cha hopping close behind, nose pointed towards the packet clutched in his master's hand.

With their bundles of books tucked under one arm, and Tim's elbows supported by the other, Zhu and Chen assisted their charge to the gate and along the street to where several of the bicycle taxis with their two-wheel rickshaw-like trailers were clustered near the corner. Surprisingly, the dog's water, or perhaps the rest, seemed to be helping, for he experienced little pain on the walk. He gave Zhu the address of the hotel and the budding doctor negotiated a price, then both he and Chen fussed him into the trailer.

'Hospital tomorrow.' Zhu said firmly.

'We want you to remember good things of

Shanghai,' Chen said. 'I am a Christian, so I will pray for you soon to be with your girl safely.' Her China-doll face crumpling, she turned away. 'Goodbye, Mee Tim,' she said over her shoulder.

Zhu shook Tim's hand swiftly and hurried after her, and Tim watched as they walked back the way they had come, Zhu talking animatedly to Chen, who seemed not to respond. She turned her head to look back, and Zhu did the same, but neither waved. As they continued on, Zhu put a comforting arm around her shoulders, pulling her closer, and Chen leaned against him. With her outside arm encircling her books, she surreptitiously lowered the one trapped between them to modestly tug down on the rising hem of her skirt.

***

Cha-Cha gazed lovingly at his master, his entire body shivering under the restraint of his adoration, and his mouth drooling with expectancy.

Shen extracted another shaving from the packet and lifted it to his mouth, chewing slowly on the initially rubbery, but still tasty morsel, savouring the taste and trying to identify its origin. He was almost certain it was dried meat, but of what type he could not say, although by its saltiness and spicy aroma it could well be disguised goat. Even so, if powdered, it could have some potential if mixed with medicinal herbs of foul taste.

Cha-Cha's low growling whine of disapproval tugged Shen from his thoughts and he selected one of the larger pieces for him, then sought another for himself, but his fingers touched on the card and he withdrew it to look in puzzlement at the English words. They meant nothing, but the picture solved the mystery of what he had been eating. It was disturbing. Unlike the horn, the meat itself would have no medicinal properties, but the picture inferred that it did, and therefore was dishonest. It would be worth investigating further.

Shen put the card in his pocket and gave the last two pieces of what remained in the packet to Cha-Cha, ripping it open so he could lick all the crumbs, then he carefully folded the cellophane and placed that in his pocket as well.

At the bridge of nine turnings, Shen lifted Cha-Cha from the pram and watched as he thirstily lapped water from the lake. It had been an eventful morning, and the young girl student, Chen, reminded him so much of his granddaughter. He had come for peace, but had found torment. It seemed that once again he had been forced into thinking with two hearts.

Like the bridge, the business had many turnings,

but where the bridge could be travelled both ways and taken at leisure, the business could not. And neither did all the turnings bring happiness and tranquillity to his old age as he would have liked.

Reluctantly, Shen retrieved his mobile phone from where he had stuffed it under the cushioning of the pram, and dialled Lan's private number at home. He hoped his granddaughter would answer. She was one of the happy turnings, and would guide him on what heart he should choose in this troublesome matter.

**

After a week of Kelly not seeing the fat guard, she finally returned, and with a vengeance.

She began coming early in the mornings, when Kelly was asleep, waking her by throwing aside the blanket and ramming the baton suggestively between her legs, which again made Kelly fear for her unborn child, or by pulling her hair, until Kelly was sure at least half of it had been torn out. Thankfully, the visits were brief, not lasting more than a few minutes, but Kelly began to dread the mornings, and soon found herself awake and waiting for the guard, never knowing what nastiness she would have to contend with next.

It was made worse by her not knowing the reason.

No demands were made of her, and she surmised that either Keystone Kate was bored, or was administering the abuse that had been intimated with the recording. Perhaps the mysterious Mister Smith had not done whatever it was he had been told to do.

Keystone Kate never departed without putting a hand to her throat, lifting Kelly onto her toes, and making strangling noises. The only sounds she ever made, and Kelly came to the conclusion that she was a retarded mute. It made her even more nervous.

She suffered her abuse with dumb acceptance, not resisting, and remaining as silent as her tormentor, even through the pain, denying her the satisfaction of getting a reaction. It was her only weapon.

When left alone, Kelly forced herself to think outside of the prison; of those places and people that had touched her life, to stir emotions that had become dull and lifeless under a pall of uncertainty and fear. She thought of her father, and received guilt in return. That surprised her. If anything it should have been anger, pity, or perhaps disappointment for what might have been, but it was none of those. It was definitely guilt. It was certainly not her fault that he had become what he was, but could she have tried harder to understand? Tried looking beneath the surface and not what lay on top? She came to the conclusion that she could. She had tried with Rosie, so why not her father. He had no one else and, when it came down to it, neither did she.

Thinking of Juliette brought nostalgia and longing. She was not her oldest friend, but was the dearest, and she missed her desperately. She wondered what she would do in this situation. Probably try to rehabilitate Keystone Kate back into the wild where she belonged.

And Tim. She didn't know what to think of Tim. He invoked such a plethora of conflicting emotions that she only felt confused. In many ways she felt much about him as she did her father. Like him, he had most of what she both admired and deplored in a man. He was arrogant, immature, compulsive and thoughtless, yet also caring, exciting, skilful and brave. She was not sure if she felt any love, but no longer felt any anger or resentment over what had happened. As with her father, she did feel a certain guilt, but perhaps that was for the best. He did not know - would never know - that she carried his child and, if the worst happened, that it had shared the same fate as herself.

Once again, Keystone Kate appeared, but this time late in the afternoon, when Kelly was dozing. There was little else to do in the small room.

'Hup!' The baton prodded crudely between her thighs. 'Hup!'

Hearing Keystone Kate speak caused Kelly to

hesitate in surprise.

'Hup!' She grabbed a handful of Kelly's hair and tugged her part way off the bunk. 'Take hoff clothe. All clothe.'

As she fumbled hastily to remove the smock, Kelly heard male voices in the corridor outside. They paused at her door, waiting, and Kelly glanced at the guard for some explanation, then suddenly found her fingers turn clumsy and falter. It was also the first time she had seen Keystone Kate smile.

***

Nibbling reflectively on the juicy end of a grass stem, Elliot watched the seductive swing and twitching of Lydia's plump buttocks as she walked on the path ahead of him, balancing a drum of water on her head. It was a very unfair system, he thought sadly, that required a man to pay for a wife. For sure, it should be the other way around. He would be taking on a big responsibility, whereas the old man would be losing one. And how was he supposed to take care of Lydia if he gave all his money to her father? Money he didn't have, and had no way of getting unless he went back to robbing buses. The thought prompted a sardonic smile. Maybe he could persuade the old fool to take travellers cheques.

It was an intriguing thought, but not one to be taken seriously. Having his father-in-law arrested was not a good way to start a marriage. But he had to find some means of getting the five hundred dollars demanded, and soon. Saving it out of his wages would take more than a year, and he was not prepared to wait that long. Lydia grew more appealing with each passing day, and himself more desperate. He doubted if he could remain faithful for another week.

Inevitably, Elliot's thoughts turned once again to the plan that had been fermenting in his brain for the past two days like a bad batch of beer. When first conceived on the ride back with Mister Singleton after the arrest of the Chinese, it had been in the form of a wish, but the more he thought about it now, the more he came to realize it was more than a joke, it was actually a good idea. For sure, it was the idea of a man who had drunk too much mashesh, but it was less dangerous than robbing tourists, and more suited to the skills of an experienced God-fearing spy, such as himself.

Still, Elliot demurred. He had been through a lot during the past few months, and with Mister Tim away and no chipimbiris to look after, life at Gara Pasi had become very pleasant, with long hours spent talking and lazing in the sun with Lydia. Things were progressing well between them. They spoke often of what they would do once they got married, of the house they would build with a proper iron roof, and of the children they would have to fill it. Indeed, she was becoming so receptive, that had it not been for the constant presence of her irritating younger brothers, he was sure he would already have managed to get his hands on those two quivering mounds of delectable flesh.

It was a surprise visit by Sibanda later that day, who came to boast that Miriam was pregnant, that finally convinced Elliot to go ahead with his idea. That his lieutenant should be reaping the comforts of a husband without having to pay labola, or even get married first, while he could only dream of such delights, did not sit right with him.

'A man of honour should pay for his wife,' Elliot declared haughtily in answer to Sibanda's foolish questions as to his own status. 'How else can he prove his love to her, and also to her father?'

'I think it is more to prove that he can make money,' Sibanda replied with unusual insight. 'But for me it is not a problem. Miriam's father knows I am a good man and will not beat her.'

'I think she will be the one to do the beating,' Elliot sneered, losing patience. 'Anyway, I would already be married but for you spending too much of our money. Now it is myself who must replace it and make more for us both.'

Sibanda was not offended by the unwarranted accusation. He had long since learned to discriminate between Elliot's insults that were meant, and those that were merely grumbling, but the added illogical statement of financial support caused him to frown in bewilderment. 'I fail to understand...' he began, but was cut short by Elliot.

'I have a plan to make us rich again.'

Sibanda's frown changed to a look of alarm. 'What is it?'

'I will tell you tomorrow,' Elliot answered. 'After I have returned with you to Mozambique.'

'Tomorrow? But that is not possible. There is no bus until Sunday.'

Elliot smiled slyly. 'Did you hear me say we must take the bus?'

***

The ancient patrol jeep, its faded US Army green scored by countless brushes with thorn bush and Mopani branch, and now sporting two new dents in its right front panel, coasted silently into the lane behind the Chinese restaurant and stopped in the deep shadow of the building. It was close to daybreak.

Elliot took the AK-47 from Sibanda, then slipped quietly from the doorless and topless vehicle to go as far as the corner, peering round it into the gloom of the restaurant yard. It was deserted. He returned to whisper urgently to his lieutenant. 'You must go to the front of the house. If the new truck of the Korean is there, you must make a hole in the tyre with the bayonet.'

'Uh! Will it not make a big noise?'

'Is it that you think a wheel is a balloon?' Elliot replied scathingly. 'I will show you how to do it.' He took his bayonet and demonstrated the position on the spare wheel of the jeep, holding the point against the soft part of the tyre next to the rim. 'Do it slowly by pushing.'

Sibanda took the bayonet reluctantly and disappeared into the dark, and Elliot returned to watch the yard from the corner. It was close to the empty crates of bottles from where he had spied before. It gave him an uneasy feeling, being there again, but he was much happier with the plan now. Not having a vehicle had been one of the biggest hurdles, but with that difficulty overcome, he felt confident with the rest. It should be easy. For sure, the Korean was a problem, but also an opportunity. The man had tricked him, catching him by the neck and kicking him on the knee. Now he had an AK and the Korean only a pistol. To kill him would be the pleasure denied him by the Chinese.

A soft whistle in the darkness alerted Elliot to Sibanda's return, and he went to meet him at the jeep.

'It is not there,' Sibanda reported breathlessly, smiling with relief, and Elliot grinned. It seemed revenge would have to wait, but the task would be much easier without the threat of the Korean interfering.

'Have a smoke,' he said, removing one from his pack and handing it to Sibanda. 'Cover with your hands, like how we did it on sentry duty.'

They smoked and talked quietly about the old times in the bush until it was light enough that they no longer had to shield their cigarettes. Then, with Sibanda at his shoulder, Elliot returned to the corner to await the arrival of the old Chinese owner.

He appeared about an hour after it became light, crossing the yard to the kitchen as he had before, and Elliot pulled back out of view. The uncomfortable three days spent on surveillance from within the crates had finally paid off in full.

Elliot listened to the jangle of keys and the unlocking of the back door. When he heard it open, he gave Sibanda a dig with his elbow, alerting him to follow, then slipped quickly around the corner, past the empty crates and stinking bins. He paused briefly at the open door, then followed in behind the old Chinese at the same instant as the fluorescent lights flickered on in the kitchen.

'Thank you,' Elliot said politely.

'Hai-ya!' The old man staggered back, gaping at Elliot, his toothless mouth opening and closing as if chewing something.

'Yes, it is the ghost of me,' Elliot said, taking hold of the startled man's shirt and pushing him against the wall.

Sibanda's hoarse whisper echoed urgently from the other end of the kitchen. 'The door of the fridge is locked!'

Still chuckling at his good joke, Elliot snatched the bunch of keys from the Chinese man's limp fingers and skidded them across the floor to Sibanda, then he followed, shoving the old man before him. He turned on the heavy light switch fixed to the metal wall of the cold room as Sibanda jerked open the solid door to release a cloud of fog.

It was a much smaller room than Elliot had expected, and not all that cold. A quick search of the interior revealed shelves of vegetables, milk, leftover food and other small perishables, but no frozen goods, and no tin trunks.

With the owner's shirt still bunched in his fist, Elliot gave him a shake. 'Where are the horns?' he demanded.

The man cringed, half raising an arm as if expecting a blow. 'Please… no horns here... all gone.'

'I see,' Elliot said, disappointed. It seemed they had risked all for nothing. He gave the owner another few shakes to vent his frustration, then shoved him to the back of the room into a stack of empty crates. He raised the AK. 'Then I must kill you if you do not tell where it is you hide the money.'

'No! You must not kill me! I have no money…' He spread his hands in a gesture of defeat. 'Do not shoot and I will give you the horns.'

'Uh! You lie to me?'

'I do not lie. They are there.' He pushed aside the empty crates to reveal another heavily sealed door, and Elliot bounded forward to pull it open, releasing an icy blast from within. It was the main freezer. A larger room, containing frozen meat, chickens, and one black steel trunk.

'Hold the Chinese,' Elliot instructed Sibanda, then dragged the trunk out. It too, was locked. 'Keys?' He snapped his fingers urgently. Quickly! Quickly!'

Sibanda rushed to fetch the bunch and Elliot juggled with them in his haste, wanting to be safely away now, but still needing to see for himself. He finally found the right key and flung the lid open.

The trunk was stacked full with rhino horns, at least ten, and Elliot stared at them in growing wonder. 'Je...sus!'

Sibanda came closer to gaze in, and echoed Elliot's surprise. 'Eh! Eh!'

Momentarily ignored, the Chinese owner took the opportunity to bolt. He was slipping through the door when Elliot caught sight of him.

'Catch him!'

Had the old man not made the mistake of attempting to close the heavy door behind him, he may well have escaped and raised the alarm. Sibanda caught him by the shirt and dragged him back.

'Do not be stupid with us,' Elliot admonished him mildly. 'Now we must lock you inside instead of us. Not so?'

Receiving no reply, Elliot pushed the owner to the back, then he and Sibanda dragged the trunk out to the kitchen. 'I leave the lights on so you cannot be afraid,' Elliot reassured the shivering prisoner before slamming shut the door. The Chinese was a sinner, for sure, and had recognised him, but he felt no urge to kill him. He was in a generous mood.

Elliot was sorely tempted to search the restaurant

and house for money, but aware that the staff would soon be arriving, he reluctantly decided against it. They carried the frozen trunk between them to the jeep and heaved it into the back, blowing on numb fingers and chortling gleefully as they scrambled into their seats.

Elliot had not been able to locate the reverse gear. He put it in second and lurched forward, making a turn in the yard around the crates before racing back through the lane and onto the road, bouncing through the drainage ditch, and swerving violently aside at the last moment to avoid another vehicle entering the lane.

'Uh! The Korean!' Sibanda yelled.

Elliot straightened the jeep before turning to look behind. The vehicle - a shiny new Toyota - had stopped at the entrance to the lane. 'What is he doing?'

'Looking,' Sibanda answered, then, with relief. 'Now he is going inside.'

Elliot slowed, almost bringing the jeep to a halt.

'Uh! Why do we stop?' Sibanda queried, panic sharpening his voice.

'Should we go all the time in this gear? I must drive. You must look to the gun.' He put the jeep into top gear, revved the engine, and released the clutch slowly, slipping it until they had picked up sufficient speed not to stall.

The still sleeping town had only two streets, and

only one that led out. Elliot sped along it, mindful that as soon as the Korean discovered what had happened he would come after them.

'Take the gun and sit on the tin suitcase to look backwards,' he instructed Sibanda, shouting his orders into the wind. 'If he follows, you must shoot.'

The road behind was still deserted, though, when Elliot swung off the main road and onto the dusty track to Massangena, and he began to relax and slow down, but they had progressed for little more than half a mile when Sibanda yelled an excited warning from the back. 'He is coming!'

Elliot risked a quick glance behind. For a moment all he could see was the billowing cloud of dust thrown up by the jeep, then through it he caught a flash of early sunlight reflected from a windscreen.

'We must run to the bush!' Sibanda screamed at him, and Elliot needed no further persuading. The small jeep could fit more easily between the trees than the much larger Toyota. But first he needed to change gear. He brought the vehicle to a halt and carefully selected low-range, then second gear. 'Quickly! Quickly!' Sibanda urged.

Elliot drove cautiously into the long grass bordering the track, picking up speed only when it thinned under the trees and he could be sure there were no hidden ant bear holes or boulders to snare them. Borrowing the jeep without permission was bad enough without wrecking it as well. Mister Tim would not be pleased. Also, they would not get far having to carry the heavy tin suitcase, and Elliot had no intention of abandoning its valuable contents.

Unfortunately, they were still too close to civilisation, and the stretch of bush they had entered was narrow, ending at the edge of a maize field while still in view of the track, and they had left a clear path for the Toyota to follow. It swerved off the dusty road and came roaring after them.

Elliot had no choice but to continue on into the field of dry maize stalks, ploughing his way through them with the crackling sound of a raging bushfire.

'Shoot! Shoot!' he bellowed, but before Sibanda could comply, the stalks ended abruptly and the jeep burst into the open, heading directly for a group of huts. Elliot was too close to avoid them, although he did try, his last-second tug on the wheel pointing the jeep directly towards a gap between two huts. It seemed impossibly narrow. With his foot frozen on the accelerator, Elliot closed his eyes as the jeep ripped and screeched its way through, grinding out the other side in a shower of dry mud plaster.

Squawking chickens and a yelping dog scattered

in alarm as the jeep knocked over a rack of drying pots and thumped over a cooking fire, causing a shrieking woman with a child on her back to leap aside.

A more solid thump and metallic crunching came from behind, signalling that the Toyota had not been so fortunate.

'He crash with the hut!' Sibanda reported excitedly, but Elliot was too preoccupied with trying to find a way out, his way forward blocked by a pole fence and stone cairns. He swung the jeep in a circle around the scattered fire, searching, then headed for another, wider gap between huts, taking them back the way they had come.

'Turn around now and shoot!' Elliot bellowed as he drove directly towards the Toyota.

It had apparently stalled after coming into contact with a grain hut, its bonnet buried in dried maize cobs and the windscreen shattered. The angry dark face of the Korean was turned towards him, his mouth moving as if shouting, then Elliot saw the raised arm and pistol. 'Shoot! Shoot!' he screamed at Sibanda, and ducked his head as the Korean fired and the bullet cracked close overhead.

'I can't do it!' Sibanda screeched back in panic.

'Are you hit?'

'I am fixed to the suitcase!'

'What?'

'My trouser! It is fixed to the iron suitcase!'

Elliot had no more time to figure out what Sibanda was shouting about. The Korean was scrambling out of the Toyota with the pistol, no doubt to get a better shot, and with less than twenty short paces separating them, he could hardly miss.

Crouching low, Elliot drove directly at him, and the Korean hesitated. He fired one hasty shot that went wild, then jumped aside at the same instant as Elliot swerved to avoid crashing the jeep into the heavier Toyota. A burst of automatic fire and clanging thuds as the bullets struck the Korean's vehicle, told that Sibanda had finally joined the battle. Another burst, and no answering fire, also suggested that the Korean had either been hit or was keeping his head down, and Elliot careered back into the maize field, following the now flattened path out.

There was still no sign of pursuit when they reached the main track, but Elliot was taking no more chances. A short distance away, on the other side of the track, a herd of cattle was being let out of its thorn enclosure, and he headed the jeep towards it, forcing his way slowly through the herd.

Half the cattle were already out when Elliot drove sedately into the boma and beckoned urgently to the gaping herd-boy standing inside with his whip. As the boy approached hesitantly, nervous at sight of the gun, and no doubt also alarmed by the firing he must have heard, Elliot parked the jeep hard against the piles of dry thorn bushes where it couldn't be seen from the road.

'Quickly!' he ordered the boy. 'We run away from a mad person.' He tapped the side of his head to demonstrate. 'Take your cattle over the spoor of the jeep. If a Chinese man in a truck asks if you have seen us, you must tell him we went on the road to Chimoio. You understand?'

The boy merely gaped, and Elliot shooed him away. 'Go! Go! We will stay here until you bring the cows back tonight. Do not tell anyone of us or you can be in much trouble. If you do as I say, my friend will give you ten dollars. Now go!'

The boy ran to obey and Elliot turned his attention to Sibanda, who was still sitting on the black trunk. 'Get down, you fool! You can be seen over the fence.'

Sibanda had a pained expression on his face. 'I can't do it. My trouser is fixed to the iron suitcase with cement from the ice.'

Elliot came to look more closely, then snorted with laughter. 'Take them off, you fool. Hurry!' He shook his head in amused disgust. 'Must I be the one to tell you everything? Even how to take off your trouser?'

The Toyota appeared a short time later, as the last of the cattle were trailing out of the boma, but it did not stop, which was perhaps fortunate, for the boy simply stared at it as if mesmerised. It drove slowly towards Chimoio, making an ominous clanking sound. Peering through the thorny grey branches, Elliot sighed with relief and cleared the AK.

They stayed hidden in the boma until the cattle returned at dusk, eking out the remaining cigarettes and compensating for the stench of cow dung by speculating on how much money they would get for the horns. Elliot wallowed comfortably in the knowledge that, even after paying Sibanda his share, he would still have enough to buy at least ten Lydias if he so wished.

After a few hours in the sun, the tin trunk had thawed sufficiently for Sibanda to reclaim his trousers and repair his dignity and, later that afternoon, he dug into the pocket for the ten dollars he had intended for the bus fare

'Do not complain,' Elliot said as Sibanda grudgingly handed the money to the grateful boy. 'Is it not better to drive with me than go on a bus? For sure, I should be asking twenty at least. Now we must go.'

As they were getting into their seats, Elliot gave Sibanda one more instruction. 'We have no lights,' he explained, 'so you must sit on the front and give the direction with your hands.' He sniggered. 'Because of bumps, I think it will be a good idea to stick your trouser to the jeep.'

***

John Singleton shook his head in disbelief as he viewed the contents of the tin trunk. Twelve rhino horns was a sizeable haul, and worth a considerable fortune in the wrong hands. That Elliot had contacted him, instead of trying to sell them on the black market, restored some of his dwindling faith in Africans, and Elliot in particular. He would not have gambled ten dollars to a pinch of shit that a former terrorist and poacher would have been able to resist such a temptation.

Two things worried John, though, and he was loath to mention either of them to Elliot. The first was that he did not trust his own department to pay the reward without asking a lot of questions and going through miles of red tape, and the other was that the ESPU had been planning an operation of their own to snare the Korean and the network of poachers he had obviously taken over from the Chinese.

Still, John rationalised. It was done and he had

the goods. He could get around the details if necessary. Joubert should be willing to take the horns and pay the reward in South African rand. But either way, he was determined that Elliot was not going to lose out. Honesty may be its own reward, but in Elliot's case it was going to be hard cash. He would put a call through to Joubert tonight, and also to Tim. Maybe it would be a good idea to hold off telling Tim about the jeep, though.

'I'll give you a receipt for them,' John told the anxiously awaiting Elliot. 'And I'll get you the reward money as soon as I can. Well done.' He wrote a receipt for the horns on a page of his notebook. 'I'll need a name later, but I don't believe it would be wise to give your real one, Elliot, even to the ESPU.' He paused to grin at him. 'How about I just put the initials JB? That should do it, don't you think?'

***

Its battery fully charged, and despite Hong Kong's hospital regulations, the mobile phone sat on the bedside cupboard within easy reach, hidden from official eyes by a large "Get Well" card Tim had borrowed from the bed opposite. He still worried about good reception in the hospital, with its generators and myriad other electronic gadgets, although he had already proved they made no difference by calling the travel agent to further postpone his booking to Kuala Lumpur, and to have the woman call him back.

He also worried that the Chinese American in the adjoining bed, whom he had persuaded to stand vigil over the instrument while he was in surgery had fallen asleep, although he had been assured that he hadn't.

Concern over whether or not the phone would ring was not all Tim had to keep his mind occupied. He also worried about his mobility. His leg had been reset - the fracture having shifted - and he was to remain in hospital for another two days at least, until the antibiotics had worked and the inflammation in his groin had subsided. Then he was to remain bed-ridden for another ten days, which was impossible. Thankfully, his medical expenses were covered by insurance, but even had he wanted to stay in Hong Kong, which he didn't, he could afford neither the time nor the expense. Come what may, he was determined to go to Kuala Lumpur to see Kelly, for it was now obvious that his trip to Shanghai had been in vain.

The night spent there had been the worst of his life. Unable to hobble any farther than to the en-suite toilet and back without succumbing to pain, and not knowing what was happening - if anything - with Shen

Hui Ping, he had almost driven himself insane.

Shen must surely have seen the number on the card - which he had stupidly forgotten had also included his name - and certainly he would have spoken to his son, Lan, but neither had called.

Had the old man been able to speak English he may have called him instead, and had considered calling Lan, but could think of nothing to say to him that would not perhaps make things worse.

He had made his play according to his own rules, without threats or pleas, betting that he had assessed the old man correctly as being one of the old school, with traditional values, and now all he could do was wait. And waiting was not his thing.

After much procrastination - mainly because of the fear of hearing only bad news - he called the American Embassy in KL and had his fears partly confirmed. They had not had any contact with Kelly, and had not heard or been able to contact the lawyer in over a week. They suspected she had been moved somewhere, maybe to another prison. They had promised to investigate and call if they heard anything, but so far they hadn't, and his own calls to the embassy had verified there was no change.

He felt guilty about not contacting his parents, Juliette, or even John, to let them know what was happening. With no good news, only failure and excuses to give them, he had not yet been able to pluck up the courage. To admit defeat to them, he felt, would also be admitting it to himself. He decided to give it one more day before calling Lan as a last resort.

The mobile chimed softly late in the afternoon, and he snatched it up, spilling water from the jug over the card, but it was only the travel agent, confirming his flight to KL in two days.

He barely had time to put the instrument back, sweep away the water and replace the soggy card, when the mobile chimed again. He picked it up carefully, controlling his impatience, but it was not the agent.

'Mister Ryan?' an American voice queried, and Tim's heart leapt.

'Yes?'

'This is the US Embassy in KL, sir, You were enquiring about Miss Kelly Maddock?'

'Yes?' It sounded so feeble that he said it again, more strongly. 'Yes, I was. Have you heard anything?'

'Yes, sir. I have only this minute returned from taking her to the airport. She's on her way to LA. As yet we don't know the details, we'll look into that later, and we didn't get much opportunity to talk. We wanted to get her out ASAP in case they changed their mind. Never know with these guys. If you like we can...'

Tim listened to the explanation with half an ear. He didn't need the reasons, only the results. The answer he already knew.

He thanked the man and sat with eyes closed, enjoying the euphoria of an untroubled mind, and the novelty of thinking only good things about Shanghai.

Part two

Florida Heaven Trailer Park had improved since she was last there. An attempt had been made to clean the pool, and the dead palm at the entrance had finally collapsed.

Kelly paid the cab driver and walked boldly past the caretaker's bungalow. If Freako was there he made no appearance, and she continued unchallenged to her father's trailer.

The truck was parked in its usual position between the battered palms, the driver's window open, and Kelly experienced a strange sensation of time lapse as she passed by it, as though it was only yesterday she had been there instead of almost three months.

Empty bottles and cigarette packets littered the passenger-side floor. Definitely no improvements there. The keys were in the ignition. Another key was in the trailer door, which was ajar, and Kelly smiled wryly. A trusting fellow, her father.

He was lying alone on the double bed, tucked into a foetal position in his undershorts. The covers were on the floor. The room stank of stale smoke and bourbon, and the bedside table was littered with glossy realty pamphlets, a full ashtray, and an empty bottle of Jack Daniels, in the bottom of which lay a dead moth. No improvements there either.

Kelly lifted the blinds and opened the window, leaning out to take a breath of fresh air before returning thoughtfully to look down at her father, her resolve wavering. It was one thing to plan his rehabilitation from the security of Pop Franz's shack in the Sound, when the negatives could be skipped over in favour of the larger issues, but once she woke her father, she would have to deal with them, and there would be many.

Some of them she had dealt with on the flight from Kuala Lumpur to LA after leaving the prison, giving herself purpose and direction, so she did not dwell on the miserable experience that even after two weeks, still haunted her almost hourly, day and night. She needed some serious rehabilitation for herself.

She had planned to spend a few weeks on the Sound in her beloved Bessie Bee, catching up on life and sunshine while she studied a few books on alcoholism, but it hadn't turned out that way. Bessie had been repaired and was ready to fly, but the weather was foul, and her houseboat was still occupied by tenants. In any event, Pop Franz had flatly refused to release the plane.

'No way,' he said adamantly. 'Take a look at yourself. A goddam scarecrow. You're not fit enough to fly a kite, never mind that hulk. No, my girl, you're grounded until further notice. That's an order. I have a spare bunk and a warm cabin full of good food. And besides, I want to hear what you've been up to. Goddamit, Kelly, you almost caused an old man to have a heart attack.'

But after ten days of miserable weather she became restless. She had suffered enough isolation and inactivity in prison. Pop reluctantly arranged a flight for her to Florida. She had discussed her plans with him concerning her father and he reassured her that his previous offer still stood. Two weeks on the wagon and he had a job.

Billy Steel had added his support as well, giving her a place to sleep and, perhaps best of all, took her for a flight in his newly renovated Jenny, letting her take the controls. And it was flying again that strengthened her resolve. Being in an open cockpit with the wind singing in the wires and blowing through her hair brought home to her that she was truly alive and free, and she determined that no matter what it took, her father was going to experience the same.

After a telephone call to the trailer park had confirmed that her father was still there, she had not made any definite plans or bookings as before, preferring to play it as it came. She had taken a bus to Palm Bay and a cab to the Park, and now she was there it was too late to have second thoughts.

Had the Hispanic woman been there, or had he been lying sprawled and snoring on his back, filthy, unshaven and with a bottle clutched in his fist, looking like the typical movie drunk, it may have given her an excuse. But seeing him curled into a ball like an innocent child, his clothes neatly folded on the chair, sparked maternal instincts she could not ignore. He needed her. She was all he had left, and she needed him.

'Father?' She reached out to shake him gently by the shoulder, her hand hesitant at the unfamiliar feel of his pale flesh.

He gave no response, and she moved away to inspect the kitchenette, taking the bottle and ashtray with her. It was surprisingly clean and bare. No old food congealing on dishes in a cluttered sink. And no coffee either. The combined eating and sitting area was equally bereft of clutter, other than a pile of dirty laundry on the couch. Kelly observed it thoughtfully for a few moments then, with a sigh of resignation, bundled it into a sheet and took it outside.

The communal laundry and toilet block was in the centre of the park, situated alongside a covered barbecue. Two elderly Hispanic women in curlers - obviously permanent residents - broke off their animated conversation to eye Kelly curiously as she entered with her bundle. She approached them with a smile, realising as soon as she saw the machines that she had no coins, only notes in her pocket, and walking back to ask Freako for change was out of the question. With the aid of a twenty she persuaded them to do the washing and deliver it to the trailer, then she left the park to buy a tin of coffee from a nearby convenience store.

Her father woke to her noisy clattering in the kitchenette and the sound of the turned up radio, as she had intended. He peered owlishly around the door and she greeted him cheerily. 'Morning, Father, coffee's up. Black, I'm afraid. The milk has gone sour.'

'Kelly? What the hell you doing back here?' He withdrew before she could answer, and a few moments later she heard the electric pump splashing water into a basin on the other side of the thin wall. She went through to the living area and he reappeared a short while later, wearing a pair of shorts and a sports shirt, his face red and puffy. He did not look pleased to see her. He jabbed his finger on the button of the portable radio, switching it off. 'Can't stand that goddam racket first thing in the morning.'

'It's after ten. You don't look so good, Father.'

'I work late, and you don't look so good either. Why are you here, Kelly? To give me another lecture?'

'We had a date, remember? You stood me up.'

'I left a note. Like I said. I was too busy.'

'So you got the deal then?'

He didn't answer, and she gave a small laugh. 'Uh, huh, that's what I thought.' She had promised herself she would remain cool and play it smart, but his belligerent, unrepentant attitude was too much.

'What the hell business is it of yours? I thought you'd gone back to Seattle.'

'What happened to the girlfriend?'

He ignored that question too, opening a cupboard to remove a half jack of bourbon and splashing a good tot into his coffee, then taking a defiant swig from the bottle before capping it and picking up his mug. He made to sit, then changed his mind, walking instead to the door and peering up at the sky, as if checking the weather, but even with his back turned, Kelly could see the trembling of his arm as he raised the mug to sip from it. She was not sure if it was caused by anger or alcohol.

'I went to Africa,' she said to his back. 'To a game sanctuary. I flew a biplane there… a Tiger Moth.' It was too soon to tell him about prison.

He returned to sit at the table and top up his mug from the bottle. 'So why did you come back here?' He indicated to her bag near the door. 'Not to stay, I hope. I only have one bed.'

'I told you. We had an agreement, and I mean to hold you to it. You've broken enough promises to me.'

'And I told you I'm too busy, so why don't you leave me alone and get on with your own life? Just leave me out of it.'

'That would be the easy way out, wouldn't it? I never took you for a quitter, Father… or a welcher. You need help, and I'm going to give it to you whether you like it or not.'

It was another mistake. With his initial craving satisfied and the trembling halted, he had begun to relax, but she had touched his pride. It showed in a darkening of his face. 'I think you had better get your ass out of here before I give it the wumping it should have had a long time ago.'

'Fine, if that's the way you want it.' Kelly stood to thump her mug on the table, slopping coffee, then found her freed hand temptingly close to the bottle. She swept it angrily from the table to crash against the wall. 'Drunken bum.'

Her father's once swift reactions must have slowed, but there was no evidence of it as his backhand caught her on the side of her face, knocking her back against the wall. She slid down it to collapse on her knees beside the bottle, stunned and shocked, tasting blood in her mouth. It was the first time he had ever struck her.

He stood blazing down at her, one hand raised and eyes wild, looking as if he was about to strike her again, and Kelly glared defiantly back, daring him, then she lowered her eyes to inspect the blood on her questing fingers. The dwindling gurgle of the emptying bottle sounded loud in the heavy silence. When she looked up again his eyes had changed. They shifted restlessly, searching over her as if puzzled at seeing her there, and the raised hand lowered to reach out uncertainly.

'Jesus, kid…'

Kelly ignored his outstretched hand. She pushed herself up, wiping blood from her lip onto the back of her wrist, an unpleasant vision of Keystone Kate flashing across her mind. She gave him one last cold look, then picked up her bag and went out.

***

502

'To be used in an emergency only,' Billy Steel said to Kelly with a wry grin, explaining the function of the two handles attached to the rudder cables passing through the rear cockpit of the Bristol. 'In case the pilot gets killed. It's one of the few old tandems that you fly from the front. The gunner sat in the rear cockpit facing back with a Lewis gun, and the pilot had a Vickers that fired through the prop. State of the art in its time. Fighting back-to-back, you might say. As you can see, I've turned the rear seat around to face forward.'

Kelly responded to Billy's explanations with acknowledging grunts, preoccupied with her misgivings now that the intimidating reality of the Bristol confronted her in all its faded glory. It had seemed such a romantic idea when first she had conceived it at Gara Pasi after flying the Moth. Now she was not so sure.

'What are the sandbags for? Ballast?'

'Exactly.' Billy leaned in to unfasten the restraining straps and lift out four bulging sandbags from the rear seat. 'If you're flying solo you have to substitute the equivalent weight in the back so you don't upset the centre of gravity.' He dumped the bags on the cement floor and moved to the rear of the biplane. 'Let's take her for a spin.'

Kelly stepped hesitantly from the lower wing. 'Are you sure about this, Billy? I mean, is it fully airworthy?'

'Having second thoughts, kid?'

'No... I just want to be sure it's legal. I can't afford to lose my licence. But if the FAA guy says it's okay...'

They wheeled the fighter out to the grass tie-down area, and Kelly watched closely as Billy chocked the wheels and did a pre-flight inspection. Like many old biplanes, the Bristol had no flaps and no brakes, but it did have a steerable tailskid.

'How are we supposed to communicate with each other up there?' Kelly asked, remembering the Moth. 'A chalkboard?'

Billy laughed. 'I've been meaning to rig up something, but yes, that's how it's done.' He reached in and produced a child's small blackboard with chalk pencil attached by a piece of string. 'Same as Tim uses.'

Kelly smiled. 'I should have guessed.'

'Jump in,' Billy invited. 'I'll wind her up.'

The view forward was restricted, with only a small gap between the upper wing and the engine cowling, and that criss-crossed with struts and wires. Further obstruction was provided by an old-fashioned compass attached to the trailing edge of the upper wing, immediately in front and above the minuscule

Plexiglas screen. Combined with the steep angle caused by having the nose in the air and the tail on the ground, what little view remained was blurred by the spinning propeller. To see where she was going, Kelly had to lean out to one side and weave the plane constantly. It was a lot different from the Moth. Landing was something she didn't want to think about.

'She's a bit heavy on the ailerons,' Billy cautioned as they turned at the end of the strip to line-up with the runway. 'Big engine, so watch the swing.'

Billy was right. The Bristol flew like an old truck, roaring down the runway with the tail swinging as she struggled to keep it straight, and she had barely managed that when it suddenly began hopping, impatient to be up. She felt Billy's pressure on the rear joystick and followed through, lifting them off.

It was much the same in the air. Any lapse of concentration on the stick brought instant retaliation in the form of a sudden pitching down of the nose and a diving turn to the left, like a shying horse. And, like a skittish horse, it needed a wary approach but a firm hand.

Handling notes listing the various speeds, weights, fuel capacity and general performance figures did not exist for the Bristol as they did for modern airlines. Billy had compiled his own notes - many of them copied directly from Jane's Fighting Aircraft of World War 1 - and adjusted to suit the Siddely Puma engine, as opposed to the original Rolls-Royce Falcon. Take-off, landing and stalling speeds, even endurance, was something that any reasonably proficient pilot could be expected to work out for themselves, and was simply a matter of cautious trial and, hopefully, without too much error.

With Billy sprawled comfortably in the back seat, Kelly spent an hour doing the usual stalls, steep turns, incipient spins, forced landing exercises and, once she was comfortable with the weight of the controls, and Billy had bullied her into it, three barely passable landings and take-offs.

'You've got it licked, Kelly,' Billy complimented after they had landed and she had removed the sweaty helmet. 'Let's get a drink and I'll fill you in on some of the mechanical stuff.'

Later in the afternoon, Billy sent her up alone with the sandbags strapped into the rear seat, and by then she was confident enough to enjoy it. She did not put herself through the paces, simply meandered aimlessly across the sky, enjoying the sunset and revelling in the unique experience of being alone with the old fighter.

She removed her shoes and folded her palm lightly around the worn black handle of the joystick, feeling the biplane's pulse, and wondering how many pilots had sat where she was now, sweaty hands guiding as they searched the sky for the enemy. Maybe even the triplane of the Red Baron himself.

After she had landed, refuelled, and tied the wings down in the parking area, Kelly strolled around the plane, enjoying the relief and euphoria of her accomplishment, looking at the old fighter with different eyes now that she had begun to master it and her fears.

It was ugly, no doubt about it. The low upper wing and tail gave it a squat, lurking appearance, as if crouching in readiness to pounce, and the drab chocolate with uneven patches in a lighter color, crudely painted over with the white registration numbers, didn't improve its looks.

It deserved a name, she decided, and paused to give it some thought. It was not pretty enough to have a girl's name. One of the books reported that it had been called the Brisfit, but that sounded too much like misfit. Searching for something more romantic, she came upon Bertie, and settled for that. Bertie Brisfit. It had a typically British ring to it, she thought, suitably masculine for a battle-scarred veteran fighter, and in keeping with its glamorous era.

She paused at the wooden propeller, turning it to

rest neatly in a horizontal position, then giving Bertie an affectionate pat on his pointed nose before strolling thoughtfully back to the hangar, probing cautiously with her tongue at the cut on the inside of her lip.

Now that she had proved she could handle the Bristol, her vague dream of flying it back to the Sound - an idea she had once rejected as a foolish daydream - suddenly seemed more attainable. It was all of three thousand miles, with the freezing cold of the high Rockies to negotiate, but it was not impossible. The Bristol had a good ceiling of fifteen thousand feet, and the disposable weight given was a generous six hundred and thirty pounds, not counting the fuel. Many of the Bristols had been converted to three-seat tourers after the war, so space was not a problem. She would have adequate room for baggage and warm clothing. If she could raise the loan, using the Seabee as collateral, and get Billy to go along with her scheme, she could see no reason why it shouldn't work.

***

'Floats?' Billy observed Kelly with both his eyebrows raised in surprise. 'I doubt that's ever been done before on a Bristol.'

'Any reason why it shouldn't?'

Billy was thoughtful. 'Not really… I guess. I've seen them on a Gypsy Moth, so maybe it will handle them okay. What do you have in mind?'

When Kelly told him, Billy laughed. 'Hell, kid, that's crazy.' He shook his head in amused disbelief. 'Where the hell did you come up with something like that?'

Kelly's spirits sank. 'I could think of no other way. You don't like the idea?'

'Like it?' He chuckled. 'Of course I like it. It's crazy.'

Kelly beamed. 'I knew you'd understand. When can we start?'

Billy rubbed at his thinning bald patch, eyeing the paperwork littering his desk with an expression of distaste. He pushed back his chair. 'Okay, kid, let's go take a look.'

Billy studied the Bristol at length, walking around it and inspecting from every angle, and paying particular attention to the wheel struts and that section of the fuselage where they joined. He came to stand beside an anxiously awaiting Kelly to give his opinion.

'Well…' He screwed up his face, seeming uncertain. 'It will be a first, that's for sure.'

'But it can be done?'

'I think so, but it will take a bit more looking

into, especially the centre of gravity problem. I'm not concerned about the weight, and the steel tubing of the fuselage will make it easier, but the extra drag will affect performance.'

'That I can handle. I won't be in a hurry, and I'll feel a lot more confident with the landings. Thinking of having to make a crosswind landing on a hard surface was beginning to give me the yips.'

'Be the other way around with me. Never tried landing on water. But you can still dip a wing, remember. You won't have stabilising floats.'

'Uh, uh, not me,' Kelly said. 'I'm an expert.' She grinned. 'Do you think we'll have any trouble finding them?'

'Nope.' Billy was confident. 'This is Florida. Should be heaps of spare floats around. Have to be the right ones, though. I'll give you a list of telephone numbers and you can start calling.'

Kelly lingered happily for a moment to check the ropes and give Bertie a pat on the nose. 'You're going to get a pair of galoshes,' she said. 'Now what do you think about that, then... old chap?'

Kelly's idea of fitting floats to the Bristol was not motivated entirely by her respect for crosswind landings on hard surfaces, or even her greater familiarity with water. The rhumb-line distance from Florida to Seattle was a little over twenty-five hundred miles. At Bertie's average slow cruising speed of one hundred and ten miles an hour at low altitude - which Billy estimated would be reduced to a hundred once the floats had been fitted - it did not take a rocket scientist to figure out that it was going to take close enough to twenty-five hours of flying time.

Under normal circumstances, she could reasonably expect to complete the journey in three days, even with having to stop every four hours for fuel, delays caused by diversions, bad weather and headwinds, but she was in no hurry. With floats she could land on remote wilderness lakes rather than trying to find grass airstrips, most of which would be privately owned and without facilities. The route she had worked out was crowded with waterways and wide rivers - all of them potential runways - often bordering on small villages, where she could buy fuel and food.

Rural America, with all its beauty and variation awaited her pleasure, and she was determined to enjoy as much of it as possible and make up for lost time. A time she had come close to believing had been lost forever.

***

Even with Billy's considerable expertise and web of contacts, it was a full eight, hectic days before the Bristol was ready. With Billy accompanying her, Kelly had flown Bertie to Fort Lauderdale to have the floats fitted by the same man who owned the Gypsy Moth, and who had a spare set.

'They're a bit undersize for the Gypsy,' he explained when she called him. 'They're really for the Tiger I had, so should be about right for your weight. Bring it down and I'll take a look. Be interested to see this old fighter of yours.'

The amount of interest Bertie caused in Fort Lauderdale stunned Kelly. In the three days they were there, she had several offers of purchase at more than double what Billy had estimated was its worth. She also had dozens of requests for joy flights, all of which she had to refuse. It gave her much food for thought.

While Billy worked on the floats, Kelly took time off from helping him and paid to spend a few hours learning to fly the Gypsy. Although she was used to operating from water in the Seabee, float planes, she discovered, were quite different to flying boats, sitting much higher, and being less forgiving.

Then Bertie was finished, and she found herself in the role of reluctant test pilot sooner than she would have liked.

At five in the morning, while it was still quiet and the bay was calm, Bertie was wheeled from the hangar on the float trolleys, taken down the ramp, and eased gently into the water. Perched high on his bright blue galoshes, he looked rather sporty. More like a dragonfly now than a crouching locust.

'She's all yours, kid,' Billy said to a lingering Kelly. 'Go give her a workout. I'll wind her up.'

'It's a he,' Kelly corrected, and stepped onto the float.

The two men trailed behind and off to one side in the Gypsy, matching her moves through the taxiing trials, then followed her into the air and, as if disdainful of such unnecessary chaperoning, Bertie performed his tests without a flaw.

'I think he likes them better than wheels,' enthused a flushed and jubilant Kelly as she climbed from the cockpit. 'Did you see that last landing? Not even a splash!'

They flew Bertie to Port Charlotte that afternoon, and next morning, after saying her farewells and thanks to Billy, Kelly flew to Palm Bay to complete her preparations.

***

'You want me to what?' Freako's watery eyes observed Kelly with the disbelieving expression of a circus performer being told he was to be fired from the cannon feet first. 'You crazy or somethin'? Why the hell would I want to do that? And you ain't exactly been the friendliest, have you, Chicky-babe?'

'The name is Kelly. Look, I'm sorry if I was rude before. I was angry with my father. I didn't mean to take it out on you.' Kelly forced a smile to strengthen her apology. Had there been another way, she would have taken it rather than enlist the aid of the fat trailer-park owner, but she had no choice.

'Yeah, well…' Freako wilted quickly under her bright smile, shrugging and paying nervous attention to flipping over the pages of the ledger, suddenly out of his depth and lost for words, and Kelly's attitude towards him softened. He was younger than she had first thought, probably no more than early twenties, and still with pimples. His slobby appearance was nothing but a defensive front, she decided. Like the puffed-up frills of a lizard.

'He used to be a fighter pilot, you know. A hero. And now look at him. A bum on the skids and going downhill fast. I have to try straightening him out, Freako, you understand? Anyway, I got the impression you wanted to get rid of him.'

Freako first nodded, then shook his head uncertainly, as if not knowing which way to go. 'Yeah, I suppose... but it's gotta be illegal, what you aimin' to do. I could get in deep shit jus' for helping... and what if he wakes up? I ain't got no quarrel with your old man. Leastwise, not when he's all paid-up... which he ain't.'

'It's not illegal, and he won't wake up... trust me,' Kelly said with confidence. 'How much does he owe?'

Freako consulted his ledger and scribbled a few calculations on a pad. 'Six hundred and twelve dollars, near enough.'

Kelly produced the new cheque book and pen that had been issued along with the loan she had received, and wrote the amount. She ripped it out and placed it on the counter between them, covering it with her hand. She smiled disarmingly. 'As soon as you agree to help me.'

Freako shrugged, then sniggered. 'Yeah, what the hell. It could be kinda fun getting rid of him... no offence.'

'None taken. I'll need to sell his truck. Think you can handle that for me? You can deduct a commission. Ten percent okay?'

'Hell, Chicky... Kelly? I ain't aiming to rip you off. That truck oughta be about seven, eight hundred bucks. How about I keep the truck, and I'll tear up the cheque as soon as you send me a signed transfer of ownership.'

He was obviously not as dumb as he looked, and this time Kelly's smile was genuine. 'Know something? You're a nice person, Freako. You deserve a better name. What is it, by the way?'

'It's Freako.'

'Okay, Freako, it's a deal.' She held out her hand, and he took it self-consciously, nodding jerkily in place of words, his pimples glowing several shades brighter.

***

Going back to see her father was an ordeal that Kelly could definitely have done without. She was still angry and hurt that he had struck her, and the fact she had provoked him was no excuse. She had done that many times before, and he had always simply given her his "you should know better than that" look, which had always put her in place without his having to lift a hand.

Neither did she like what she had to do when she saw him. Subterfuge was not something she had much experience in, especially with her father, but she could think of no other way.

When everything was prepared, she called Freako from her motel room, confirming that her father was there, and that Freako had removed the keys from the truck as a precaution against her father leaving before she arrived.

When the cab dropped her at the entrance to the Park, the new Freako was anxiously waiting for her, wearing a clean shirt and with his hair slicked into place. She left him with her canvas bag that was still adorned with airline stickers, and went directly to her father's rented trailer, walking quickly, with a confidence she was far from feeling.

He was sprawled on his back, snoring under the covers, which made her feel better. She left him while she went to prepare a mug of coffee, using the sachets she had taken from the motel, not willing to take the unnecessary risk of finding he had run out again. When it was made, she took it through to the living room and placed it on the table.

From her shoulder bag, she removed a half-pint bottle of Jack Daniels and placed it beside the mug. Also from her bag, she took the pack of tranquilliser capsules she had acquired from a chemist recommended by Freako. She dropped two into the coffee and stirred it, then went through to wake her father, glancing at her watch on the way. It was almost eleven. She would not get away much before twelve. Later than she would have liked.

She shook his shoulder, gently at first, then more vigorously, until he groaned and opened his eyes. 'Wake up, Father, we have to talk.'

She waited on the couch, listening to his sounds, fighting the temptation to throw the coffee out and forget the whole thing. If Freako's information was wrong, or her father had a medical condition she didn't know about that reacted badly, the consequences could be dire. This was no rhino she was tranquillising, and she hadn't the vaguest idea of what sort of antidote to use if things went wrong. Going back to prison for patricide was not a pleasant prospect.

She had reached the point of capitulation, was already standing to remove the coffee, when he came in, smartly attired in sports coat and tie.

'Hi, Kelly, didn't mean to keep you waiting.' To Kelly's further surprise, he crossed to where she stood and gave her a hug. 'I'm sorry about hitting you like that, kid. Don't know what the hell came over me.'

'Me too,' she mumbled. He smelled of toothpaste and aftershave.

'Glad you came. How about I take you out to lunch to make amends. You look as if you need fattening up.'

'That's not necessary, Father. We can…'

'Sure it is. I know a great little seafood joint.' He smiled and winked. 'Only take my best clients there. You can tell me about Africa and this health farm idea of yours. I think...' He paused at sight of the bottle on the table. 'You bring that?'

'To replace the one I knocked over... let me make you some fresh coffee.' She snatched it up before he could object and hurried through to the kitchenette.

'Forget the coffee, Kelly, I'll get some later at the restaurant.'

Kelly threw the contents of the mug into the sink and washed the cup, then held her wet hands to her face. I must be crazy, she thought.

As they drove sedately out of the trailer park, Kelly caught a glimpse of Freako's pale face staring out through his screen, and she put her arm out of the open window to make urgent signals low down against the door, out of her father's view, aware even as she made them, that they would make no sense.

'That freaky kid giving you any trouble?' her father asked.

'Oh, no... nothing like that,' Kelly replied, withdrawing her arm surreptitiously.

***

Kelly nibbled on her artfully arranged mountain of frilly lettuce without appetite, listening without interest to her father's impractical real estate schemes, and wishing she was someplace else.

It had started well enough, with some fancy cocktail he insisted she have in celebration of a big deal he was finalising that night, but thereafter, both the lunch and the one-sided conversation, had deteriorated.

On the short drive to the restaurant he had chatted amiably - almost too pleasantly - showing a glimmer of his once sharp sense of humour, and she had made up her mind to tell him about the biplane and her intended cross-country flight. She also wanted to tell him about the prison, but hadn't been given the chance.

Fast talking, it seemed, was part of selling, and he tried to sell himself to her - and no doubt to himself as well - with all the phoney charm of an uptown gigolo. It was as pathetic a performance as it was distressing, and she found it hard not to walk out. All that stopped her was that she knew it was not her father talking but his jaded pride. And she guessed that he knew it as well.

He drank steadily, becoming even more loquacious, but never asked about her trip to Africa. He did mention the health farm though, saying he was looking forward to it, and would be free to go there as soon as all the details of his deal had been completed. A week, maybe two at the outside. He must have forgotten that he had told her almost the identical story before.

That did it for Kelly. At the end of the meal, she ordered espresso for them both while he was in the washroom, not giving him the chance to refuse, then dropped the capsules into his cup along with the sugar, stirring for a long time, hoping he wouldn't finish until they had fully dissolved.

She watched carefully as he took the first sip, and held her breath as he pulled a sour face then spooned in more sugar. It must have improved, for he drank the remainder without comment, although he alternated with sips of bourbon and topped-up the cup with it when half empty.

Kelly had already caught the waitress's eye for the bill. She half expected to pay, but her father produced his wallet and, surprisingly, gave a handsome tip.

'Very nice, Father,' Kelly lied. 'Thanks.'

'Nothing's too good for my girl. Have to do...' he hiccuped, '...more often. Whatsay?' He was beginning to slur his words, but Kelly was unsure if it was the drink or the drug. 'Ready to go, kid? Have to get... work.'

'Oh, yes...' She stood quickly and led the way out, hoping he wouldn't collapse before they reached the truck. Once safely outside, she took his arm. 'Want me to drive?'

'Ya tink I'ma hova da limit?' he joked.

She laughed dutifully. 'No, I was only…'

'Good idea. Can't be too careful these daysh.'

The first true indication that the drug was taking effect came when they were halfway back to the park.

'Don't feel good,' he muttered. 'Damn shrimps. Sue the bastards… if food poison.'

'Want me to stop?' she offered, but kept driving, picking up speed, and thankfully he didn't answer, rubbing his eyes and groaning.

He fell asleep as they entered the park, and Kelly eased gently over the speed bumps. At least, she thought with relief, he wouldn't have to be carried out of the trailer.

Freako's door partly opened as she passed and she signalled for him to follow.

He arrived as she was getting out after loosening her father's tie, and Kelly halted his query before he had a chance to open his mouth. 'Don't ask, Freako. I don't want to talk about it. Watch him while I get his stuff. If he wakes, or does anything funny… like choke, call me.'

To Freako's credit he complied without a murmur, and Kelly went hastily into the trailer. Her father had pitifully few belongings, but still far too much. She pulled the two large suitcases down from the bedroom cupboard and dumped them on the bed, then crammed them both full of the clothes and other items he was not going to need, including the portable radio and a clock. She kept aside his warm clothing, including two pairs of jeans, his joggers, a pair of boots, a fleecy lumber jacket, and a cardboard file containing important personal papers. She agonised for a few moments over a set of golf clubs, then hauled them and the cases to the front door, from where a nervous Freako loaded them into the back of the truck. What remained, Kelly bundled into a blanket, then took that to the door to be loaded as well. Nothing in the kitchenette was worth bothering about.

'You drive,' Kelly instructed Freako breathlessly. 'May as well get used to it. Stop at the office and I'll switch bags.'

While Freako carried the suitcases inside, which were to be picked up later by a courier and delivered to Billy, Kelly bundled the remaining clothes into another canvas bag she had brought with her own. She discarded the blanket, having already purchased a waterproof sleeping bag to take its place.

They drove with their unconscious passenger propped between them, Kelly trying to listen above the sound of the engine to his soft breathing, and Freako staring silently ahead, trying to act as if everything was perfectly normal.

Finding a suitable mooring for the Bristol, where her father could be loaded on without being seen, had given Kelly several headaches. There were no calm secluded beaches, and she knew from experience how difficult it was to move a plane that had become stranded on a sandy beach with a receding tide. In the end she had simply moored it at one of the quieter jetties and put her trust in luck.

But luck must have departed with the tide, for the jetty was crowded with fisherman.

'Stop... stop here!' Kelly commanded urgently, and Freako slammed on the brakes, sending their relaxed passenger hurtling forward. Kelly barely managed to get an arm across in time to prevent what could have resulted in a serious concussion.

'Careful!'

'Jeez!' What you do that for?' Freako complained. 'I thought we was about to drive into the frigging water.'

'People,' Kelly explained. 'How are we going to get him into the plane with all those people watching?'

Freako observed the crowd silently, and Kelly did the same, her mind working in high pitch. The Bristol was all packed and ready to go, only the two bags and her father to be put on board.

'Back up slowly around the corner of that shed,' Kelly ordered. 'I don't want them to see us until I'm ready.'

When they were out of view, Kelly gave him further instructions. 'Now listen carefully, Freako. I want you to drive up quickly to the plane, beeping the... no! Not yet. Wait until I tell you... drive up beeping the horn, as if it was urgent, like an ambulance would. Pull up next to the plane and...'

'Was that your plane? Jeez, I thought it was one of them normal ones with a door. How we gonna lift him in there?'

'If you let me finish I'll tell you. When you stop, get out quickly and load the two bags in the rear cockpit... you'll have to take the plastic cover off first. Put them as far forward as you can, on top of the other stuff, and make sure you stand on the marked place on the wing. I don't want your big foot going through it.'

'Okay, okay, I ain't that dumb...'

'Now, give me a hand, will you? Take his coat and tie off while I get his jacket from the bag. We have to dress him for flying.'

It was more difficult than she had imagined. Her father was not a small man, and his limp dead weight made it awkward, but finally they managed to get the fleecy jacket on and zipped.

'Okay, Freako.' Kelly took a deep breath. 'Let's do it.'

With the horn beeping urgently, they sped up to the jetty and jerked to a halt, sending three fishermen scurrying out of the way in a tangle of rods and lines.

Freako burst from the cab as if it were on fire, hauling the bags down the steps to the plane while Kelly, looking helpless, appealed to the curious onlookers.

'Can someone help us please? My father has collapsed and I have to get him into the plane quickly... he needs to get to his medication.'

'What's wrong,' someone asked. 'Heart attack?'

Kelly shook her head, thinking furiously. 'No, it's something else... to do with space sickness... I think. I have to get him to the Space Centre as soon as possible.'

'He an astronaut or something?'

'Sort of...used to be.'

'Goddam! Those guys are heroes, man...'

A tanned youth in swimming trunks pushed his way to the front. 'I was about to head up that way in my jet-boat. I can get him there in no time at all.'

'No... thanks, but security is a problem. It will be

quicker in the plane... they know me there. Can you help lift him, please?'

A burly man in a vest elbowed Kelly aside to look in at her father. 'Big fella, ain't he? Never get him down them steps and into that plane. Leastwise, not in one piece.' He leaned in to clasp his arms around her father and haul him out. 'Take his legs, we'll do it with the hoist.'

The athletic young man jumped to take the legs, and together they carried him to a boom winch alongside the steps and set him down. 'Hold him in a sitting position,' the burly man instructed. With the expertise of long practice, he quickly fashioned a sling, fitted it around and under her father's armpits, then took up the slack with a few turns of the handle. 'You may have to turn and back the plane up a little,' he told Kelly. 'Get it set up and I'll drop him right in for you.'

'That will be wonderful, thank you.'

'You sure he ain't drunk?' he asked quietly, giving her a sly look.

'Yes,' Kelly answered, 'he is. That's what set off the problem.'

Dangling limply in the sling, her father was swung out on the boom and lowered expertly into the cockpit amidst enthusiastic advice from the spectators.

Kelly manoeuvred him into the seat, removed the

sling, and fixed him into the safety harness, securing the buckle with the long-hooped bicycle lock she had bought for that purpose. She had no idea what effect the cold wind was going to have, or the drug, once he woke and found himself airborne, and she was not going to take the risk of him doing something stupid like jumping out. She had already unbolted the rear joystick for the same reason.

She hastily fitted his helmet, goggles and gloves, placed a sleeping bag on either side to prop him up, then spoke to Freako, who stood by the mooring rope, looking confused. 'Hold the tail in until I've started the engine and am back in the cockpit,' she instructed. 'Then give me a shove out. And, Desmond... if you want to impress the girls, lose the crude tee shirts. You don't need them.'

Desmond Frankens blushed, his pimples glowing like a virulent rash. 'Where'd you learn my name? I kinda gotten used to Freako.'

'It's in your office, on the certificate.'

He shrugged, partly raising a hand in farewell as Kelly hurried over the wing to spin the propeller. She waved her thanks to her helpers and gunned the motor.

Its roar coincided with thunder rumbling ominously in the north - the same direction as she was headed.

***

They had been in the air for a little under an hour when Kelly thought seriously about turning back or finding a place to land. Two weeks of fine weather and now, when she needed it least, wall-to-wall clouds. Bulging grey monsters standing on their slanting pillars of rain like mushrooms in a field, and the only way through, if she had the courage, was to weave among the dark columns in a precarious game of tag, searching for the gaps while trying to avoid the stalks, and hoping all the while that it didn't close in altogether.

With only seven hours experience in the Bristol and no instrument rating - which wouldn't have helped anyway as Bertie had no instruments for blind flying - trying to push through was foolish. She would not have attempted it in the enclosed and well-instrumented Seabee. And with her father in tow it was worse.

It had been an important part of her strategy to have him come awake in the air, introducing him back to real life with a jolt, but according to her rough calculations he still had at least another hour to go before the drug wore off. If he woke on the ground the effect would be spoiled. Not only would she have to explain her actions immediately, he could become violent, demanding to be released, then simply walk away without having experienced anything more than a headache. She had hoped for another hour at least for him to sit there alone, tying to adjust and figure it out for himself.

She had also hoped to reach the first of her planned lakes near the Florida border with Georgia and Alabama, but even if she managed to negotiate the storms, her delayed departure now made that impossible. She would have to find somewhere else to put down.

With the decision made, Kelly ducked behind the tiny windscreen and banked the Bristol, going well below the cloud base and heading between the first two of the giant pillars of rain. A glance behind showed her father had slumped low in his harness, the sleeping bags having moved and his head lolling. His goggles had been knocked askew, exposing one closed eye and giving him an even more lopsided look, like a lifeless Cyclops. 'Hold on, Father!' she yelled into the wind. 'I think we're going to get wet.'

***

Major James Maddock fought desperately against

the drowsiness that threatened to overwhelm him. It had been a long day. Two missions and seemingly endless briefings and debriefings, and now into the black hole of the night, seven miles above the Pacific.

The moon had waned, and a layer of cirrus cloud obscured the stars, removing all points of earthly reference. His world had shrunk, cocooning him in the warm red glow of the instrument lights, its outer limits marked by the monotonous blinking of the flight leader's red wingtip light, some twenty feet on the other side of the Plexiglas. The faint hiss of static in the foam-rubber earphones of his helmet overlaid the thin, unceasing whine of the turbine wheels. No sense of forward motion, only a gentle vibration. A subtle invitation to sleep.

***

The columns of rain had all but joined, and the first drops slashed across the windscreen, hammering on her leather helmet and goggles with the sound of castanets in busy fingers, and with it came a buffeting turbulence that strummed the taut stay wires in a jerky flamenco.

An updraft caught them, thrusting them up, almost into the dark cloud, before the downdraft pushed them back again with gut-sinking speed. Heavy rain pounded on the top of her head, and Kelly swung away, searching desperately through her blurred goggles for another passage, worried that they would lose or damage the floats in the turbulence.

Then suddenly they were through. The rain stopped, as if turned off by a sympathetic hand, and they roared smoothly along through air that sparkled in shafts of sunlight.

Kelly twisted around to check on her father, the rear-view mirror she had fixed to her windscreen for such a purpose having proved useless due to the unceasing vibration.

He was awake, sitting upright with his goggles off and clutched in his hand, squinting out to the side with a screwed-up expression that told her nothing. Then he replaced the goggles and sank lower in the seat, almost disappearing from view. Kelly turned back quickly. The cold rain or bumping around must have done it. The first hurdle had been successfully negotiated and, for the moment, she could allow herself a small smile of self-congratulation.

But not for long. More dense pillars loomed ahead, more challenges, and she tightened her harness. As they drew near to the storm Kelly risked another glance behind and saw that her father had sunk low in his seat again, invisible under the sleeping bag, which he had pulled over his head.

She settled down to concentrate on flying as she had never flown before.

***

'Victor Lead, fuel check.'

Welcome relief; a touch of reality. He blinked, stretched his eyes wide, and moved out of formation to focus on one of the twenty luminous needles on the panel.

'Victor One, twenty-three hundred pounds.'

'Victor Two, two-zero hundred.'

The others called in at twenty-two and twenty-one respectively.

'You go first, Bobby.'

'Rog.'

'Victor Lead, descent check to level one-five-zero and speed brakes in five. Counting... four... three... two... one...now.'

Only light buffeting as the brakes thrust into the slipstream. He eased the stick forward, following the red flashing light down to rendezvous with the two KC fuel tankers below. Time to suck up and not fuck up.

***

Kelly sat on the cockpit coping with her boots on the seat cushion and her arms stubbornly folded, looking haughtily down at her father. 'You can curse all you like, but I'm not letting you out until you promise to behave.'

'Gimme that goddam key!' He jerked angrily at the straps.

'And shouting won't improve your headache.'

'Goddamit, Kelly! What the hell are you trying to prove with this stupid stunt?'

'I'm trying to prove you're still the man you used to be…the one I loved. And I'd be careful with those straps if I was you. We don't want them snapping when you're hanging upside down.'

He glared at her, the effect somewhat spoiled by the white goggle-print etched into the oil splatterings and windburn on his face 'You think this is funny? Some kind of big joke? Well I'm not laughing. I'm your father, for Chrissakes!'

'That's right, you are, and I intend to keep you. All I'm asking is that you promise not to do anything silly if I let you out.'

'What the hell is that supposed to mean?'

Kelly shrugged. 'You tell me.'

He glanced about, at the wet grassy bank on one side, and the empty stretch of water on the other. 'Where the hell are we anyway?'

'That's for me to know. And I don't mean one of those wishy-washy promises you've been handing out like they were realty pamphlets. I want a hero's promise... in exchange for this.' She held up the key to the bicycle lock.

'I can't believe this is happening. My own daughter... kidnapping me, for Chrissakes. I could have had a heart attack, waking up like that. You planned all this, didn't you? What did you put in my drink?'

Kelly ignored the question. 'Well, you had better start believing it. We still have a long way to go.'

'What do you mean... how long?'

Kelly pursed her lips in thought. Better to let him have it in small doses. 'You promised me a week at the health farm, but that's impossible now. This is the next best thing... maybe better. This way we get to see some of the country as well.'

'What?' He frowned, blinking, as if he hadn't understood.

'A great adventure, don't you think? Just you and me and the great outdoors.'

'You expect me to sit here, freezing my ass off in

this heap of crap for a week?' He laughed sardonically. 'Okay, you've proved your point, you got me flying again, now let me out of here, Kelly, I'm getting tired of this, and I have an important meeting tonight that I've been working on a long time. If I miss out I could lose a bundle.'

Kelly hoisted herself off the coping with a sigh. 'You already have.' She dropped the key into her pocket and tossed out the small bag containing the ropes and pegs, then swung her legs over. She stepped from the wing onto the float and jumped the short distance to the bank.

'Hey… where do you think you're going?'

'To secure the plane. Still a few storms around, in case you haven't noticed.'

'You intend keeping me sitting here all night?' There was a note of disbelief in his voice, maybe even a hint of desperation. Kelly wondered if it had more to do with the lack of bourbon than the lack of comfort.

'That's up to you. If you make the promise I ask, I'll set up the tents and fix you a bed.'

He laughed scornfully. 'You can go to hell, you snotty, smart-ass brat. Keep me here another minute and I'll rip the wires out of this goddam thing.'

'Go ahead. I'll fly it anyway.'

'I'm not joking, Kelly, by the time I've finished

this machine will never get off the ground. Believe me, I know what I'm talking about.'

She replied with a scornful laugh of her own. 'That makes a refreshing change. But if you do, first let me tell you something...' She glared back into his furious eyes. 'This old piece of crap, as you call it, was a gallant fighter, just like you were. The only difference is it never gave up. So go ahead, rip away, then I'll have two old fighters that can't fly. On the other hand...' She stepped back onto the plane to retrieve her shoulder bag from the front and dig inside to produce her trump card, the half bottle of bourbon she had recovered from the trailer cupboard. 'Make the promise and both these are yours.' She held up the key in one hand and the bottle in the other. 'The choice is yours, Father. Make it now and stick to it, or get the hell out of my life forever.'

In the lengthy silence that followed, Kelly felt her resolve waver and begin to crumble. What she was doing seemed suddenly to be impossibly puerile, as unrealistic a girlish fantasy as ever she had dreamed, and fated with the same unsatisfactory result. It was harder than she had anticipated. Hard to watch him sitting there, a grown man - her father - shamed and humiliated, trying not to look at the whiskey.

With sudden anger she flung the bottle away,

hearing it thud and slither on the wet grass. 'Damn you, Father. Do what you want.' She dropped the key onto his lap and jumped to the bank, concealing her despair behind a burst of activity, angrily shoving the mooring pegs into the mushy ground until they all but disappeared.

She listened to him vacating the cockpit, heard the thuds of the holdalls and camping bag being tossed out, then saw him drape the damp sleeping bags over the warm engine cowling to dry. She watched surreptitiously to see if he would go for the bottle, but he didn't, occupying himself with sorting through his clothes while emitting a string of unintelligible grunts.

Unable to stretch her simple task any farther, Kelly went for a walk into the still dripping trees. The storm had moved on, dark and flickering in the west, and the muted sunlight of the late afternoon shafted through the trees, bringing a measure of peace. It was probably futile, what she was doing, she thought despairingly. Alcoholics weren't rehabilitated that easily, but she had committed herself and would go through with it. Two quitters in the family was one too many.

She angled her return to pass the bottle. It was still lying untouched where it had stopped partly under a bush, and she experienced a brief moment of exaltation. Maybe it was not so futile.

Her father had changed into jeans and a plaid shirt, looking country, and the gas cooker was hissing purposefully under a pot. His damp jacket hung from the propeller, prompting her to think of her own discomfort, but she was not in the mood for changing just yet.

'Almost ready,' he said with forced pleasantness, and Kelly mumbled her thanks, her mood swinging once again, this time to guilty acceptance.

They ate the heated canned stew standing and in silence, Kelly dipping chunks of bread, and her father shuffling aimlessly about, staying well clear of the bottle. Kelly washed her tin plate using a clump of wet grass. 'Thank you,' she said politely. 'That was good. Would you like some coffee?'

'He nodded, swallowing hastily. 'Yes, that will be nice...thank you.'

She filled the mugs and handed him one, taking his plate. 'If you wish to call someone about this meeting, I have your cell phone.'

'Oh?' He looked surprised, then shrugged, shaking his head. 'I don't have the number.'

'Call directory assistance.'

He frowned. 'Yeah... I guess...'

Kelly dug in her bag for the instrument, then left for another short walk, taking her coffee with her, not wanting to hear. When she returned he was full of gay sarcasm.

'Well, there goes another deal all shot to hell.' He shook his head, as if at some private joke, and Kelly did not pursue it, not wanting to know if she had been the cause.

She produced a collapsible rod and box of tackle from the camping bag. 'Why don't you try your luck?' she suggested. 'You'll find some bait in the food box.'

He ignored the rod, lighting a cigarette and strolling with elaborate nonchalance along the bank, as if completely relaxed and enjoying the balmy evening.

Too exhausted and emotionally drained to prolong the farce any longer, or to bother about erecting the two small tents, Kelly spread the waterproof groundsheets and engine-warmed sleeping bags under the wings - his on one side and her own on the other - then changed into dry clothes and crawled into hers, wriggling on the hard surface to find a place for her hip. She lay still, listening to the dwindling thunder and the occasional plopping of fish, holding a hand to her abdomen. 'Sleep well, my baby,' she murmured.

Whenever her father lit a cigarette, which was too often, she could see the glow of his Zippo, and waited for the cough she knew would follow. He gave up after half an hour and grunted his way into the sleeping bag. Kelly searched for something worthwhile to say, but could think of nothing. She settled for a sleepy-sounding goodnight, to which he replied with a fake-sounding yawn.

She listened to his restlessness, and was still awake some hours later when he crawled from his bag. She saw the glow as he lit a cigarette out of her view, smelled the rich aroma of tobacco as the fresh night air carried it her way, and was about to join him, to somehow make it easier with her presence, when above the smoke she also caught a whiff of Jack Daniels.

Kelly turned her back on it with a sigh and closed her eyes, trying to force sleep. It was a long way from being over, it seemed. For both of them.

***

Kelly did not mention the overnight disappearance of the bottle. Clinging to the frayed shreds of the previous evening, she pretended not to have noticed, greeting her father politely when he crawled stiffly from his bag at dawn, roused by the smell of coffee and her noisy clattering of tin mugs.

She smiled pleasantly as she offered him a mug. 'Manage to get any sleep?'

He responded with a derisive snort, shrugging

into his fleecy jacket before taking the mug.

'Yes, It will be cold up there,' she said. 'Better dress warmly, or better still, stay in the sleeping bag.' She looked up, studying the still gloomy heavens with a confident, knowledgeable air, as if inspecting it for the first time, but she had already studied it with care when the stars were still showing. 'It's going to be a nice day though. Should warm up okay.'

He grunted again, non-committal, then hunched his shoulders and turned away, 'Have to take a pee,' he muttered gruffly.

Kelly watched as he walked towards the trees, still holding his mug. Make it last, Father, she thought, then muttered under her breath. 'When that's gone it will be cold turkey time.'

His step was a little jauntier when he returned, smoking a cigarette, and he even managed a weak smile. 'Any more coffee?'

While she filled his mug he stomped his feet and rubbed his hands vigorously, warming them. 'Okay, this is the deal,' he said decisively. 'I did promise you, so I'll go along with this crazy idea of yours, but only for two days, then I must get back.' He smiled apologetically. 'I wish it could be more, Kelly, but I have to make a living, you know.'

About to protest, Kelly hesitated. One problem at

a time, she told herself, and the first, which had been how to get her father back into the plane, had just been solved. She shrugged in mock surrender, putting on a wistful smile. ' It's not what I had planned, but I guess it's better than nothing.'

***

Bertie refused to allow the distraction of calculators and other such modern technological devices to intrude into the serious business of flying. He was strictly of the old school. Even the clasping of the joystick between knees while trying to hold down the wildly flapping chart seemed to irritate him, and he was quick to show his displeasure. Pay attention to what I'm doing, was his price for co-operation, or we could jolt you back with some involuntary aerobatics. As a result, Kelly was forced to wrestle with mental arithmetic.

Her first refuelling stop, less than an hour after their departure, was at a lake on the state border between Georgia, Alabama and Florida, where her boating guide had informed her she could refuel from a jetty. It did not mention that the supplier also owned the adjoining grocery and liquor store, but her father appeared not to notice, complying without comment to her request that he supervise the refuelling while she went to the store for a few supplies.

'Where to now?' he asked on her return.

'I've never seen the Mississippi. Thought we'd have lunch there … maybe stay overnight.'

'That far? What's wrong with right here? The fuel guy says the fishing's not bad and they have a good campsite with showers and toilets.'

And a liquor store, Kelly thought, but she hesitated only briefly. She would have to face that problem sooner or later, and staying on the good side of him, even if it was for only another day, had its appeal. Either way it meant that tomorrow he would get into the plane without argument, which was her greatest concern, so it made little difference in that respect. After that he would know they were not returning, but once they were in the air there was not much he could do about it. Except perhaps, start ripping out the cables. 'Okay, Father, that sounds great. Let's see what we can catch for dinner.'

'And you can stop calling me Father. I'm beginning to feel like a catholic priest.'

While he removed the camping gear, Kelly returned to the store and paid for a camping site, then spoke to the owner regarding the purchase of liquor by her father. It made her feel like a traitor, and was made no easier by the owner's secretive smile as she was trying to explain, but she discovered that her treachery had been justified when he pushed the cardboard carton that was sitting on the counter towards her.

'I was wonderin' what to do with this. Your father ordered it while I was workin' the gas pump. Said I was to bring it as you were leaving, or hold on to it for a while if you stayed to camp. Credit card and receipt is inside.'

Kelly opened the box to reveal a carton of cigarettes and two bottles of bourbon. She removed the bottles and dropped the card in her pocket, wondering how she had missed it. She had already checked through his wallet. Then she realized it must have been in the jacket he had been wearing at the restaurant.

'I'll keep the cigarettes,' she said. 'If you don't mind exchanging the bourbon...?'

'Sure, no problem, miss. Don't want to be no party to a man's drinkin'. Had a wife went that way.'

Kelly made up the difference in groceries, including a can of condensed milk to help disguise the taste of the capsule she intended dispensing with her father's coffee before they departed next morning. If he slept for the four hours it was going to take to reach the Mississippi, she would be one step closer. The next step she would handle when the time came. The cold turkey time.

***

Serpent-like and sluggish, gleaming under the midday sun, the great Mississippi River appeared upon the chequered flood plains.

Kelly flew along it, searching for a suitable place to put down and refuel. She had changed her mind about camping the night there. With no shortage of ready transport on the river, it was too convenient a place for her father to leave once he discovered what was happening. She needed a more secluded place for the confrontation, and her guide book had revealed one only eighty miles beyond the river in Arkansas; a wilderness lake with no facilities and only rough tracks leading in or out. It sounded the ideal place for a few days.

With her father awake and showing signs of agitation, Kelly was ready with her excuses when she taxied up to the ferry terminal. She did not have long to wait.

'What the hell are we doing here?' he demanded as the engine spluttered into silence.'

'No need to shout, Father. I told you I wanted to see the Mississippi.'

'I thought we were going home. That was the deal.'

'We'll be on our way just as soon as we've refuelled. There's a cafeteria up there. Want me to get you something to eat... some coffee maybe?'

'I need something stronger than that to anti-freeze my ass.'

'You slept most of the way, so it couldn't have been that bad.'

'Wasn't feeling good. Too much fresh air.' His voice changed, becoming less irritable and more reasoning. 'See what you can do, will you, Kelly?'

'You told me yesterday you didn't need it.'

'I don't. Just a tot to warm me up.'

'Then it will be another to keep you going.'

His smile held more desperation than humour, and Kelly went along with it, wanting to keep things smooth until they reached the wilderness lake. Surprisingly, he had not made an issue over the two bottles of bourbon, and had not asked for his credit card, which was even more surprising. Or perhaps not, Kelly thought. To make an issue would be to admit being sneaky.

He had helped clean the plane, pumping new grease into the rocker-box and wiping old grease from the cowling, fuselage, windscreens and goggles, then spent the day fishing and talking to other campers, and she had watched suspiciously, but saw no secretive passing of bottles, and smelled nothing on his breath. In every respect he gave the impression of being a perfectly normal and happy camper. 'I'll see what I can organise,' she said, not committing herself.

She returned to find him busy with grease gun and rag, still playing the part. 'I think it's only grease that's holding this old crock together,' he said, taking the Styrofoam cup and sniffing. 'Rum?'

'It was all they had.' She did not mention that it was rum essence they used for cakes, or that she had stirred in the last of her capsules, and he seemed not to notice, setting it aside to cool while he put away the grease gun, then gulping the muddy-looking drink down with a shudder.

'Yechh! They must have dredged that up from the bottom of the river.'

Kelly delayed for as long as possible to give the capsule time to work, taking her time about paying for the fuel and oil, but the Mississippi mud must have had some countering effect, or the one capsule wasn't enough, for he was awake when they took-off a half-hour later, and still alert, looking over the side at the passing scenery, when she turned west, onto her course.

It took a while for him to register. Watching his vibrating image in the mirror, Kelly saw him glance behind, then sit upright to lift his goggles and squint over her shoulder to the compass on the trailing edge of the upper wing, a few feet in front and above her head. He shouted something, his mouth moving, and Kelly stared ahead, pretending not to have noticed.

She could not ignore the chalkboard though when it rapped her urgently on the thigh a short while later. Why this way?

Kelly waved a hand in the air, making a confusing ballet of signals, then scrawled a return message. Wait.

It seemed to work, for he sat back in his seat, although he appeared to have lost interest in the countryside and turned his attention to the back of her head.

After ten minutes she changed course slightly and started to descend, skimming a few hundred feet above the wilderness forests that extended in a solid mass of green on all sides.

When the lake appeared she turned to follow its winding course through low, heavily wooded hills. It widened to reveal a small island, and she felt a surge of elation. It was no bigger than a football field, well treed and, like the surrounding lake, appeared deserted, with no sign of boats or smoke. The shortest distance between it and the mainland was a good three hundred yards, so unlikely to harbour pesky bears or campers.

The shining surface was unruffled, telling of little wind. She circled it once, then reduced power and put down with barely a splash, switching off after a quick burst to coast in towards the mossy bank. It was a good landing, but unappreciated by her father.

'What the hell are we doing here?' he demanded irritably. 'Is this another one of your childish stunts? You're full of crap, you know that?'

Kelly jumped ashore with the rope to tie off on a tree as soon as the floats grated on the shale. 'Come on,' she called over her shoulder, 'stop complaining. It's beautiful here. Let's find a good spot to camp.'

'Goddamit, Kelly, we've just been camping. I hate camping. If I never go camping again it will be too bloody soon. I told you I have work to do... Kelly? Goddamit, get back here!'

Kelly tramped the short distance through the undergrowth to the other side of the island and stood quietly to absorb the tranquillity. The air was sweet and fertile, the silence wistful, broken only by the light, lonely cries of birds and the distant splashing of a single duck taking off. She could not have found a better spot.

Now would be the perfect time to tell him, she thought. He would have no option but to listen, and it would give him something other than himself to think about.

When she returned he was still in the plane, sitting on the cockpit coping with his back turned, looking out over the water. The smoke from his cigarette drifted up lazily.

'You must admit it's beautiful,' Kelly said.

He didn't answer.

'You can stop feeling sorry for yourself, Father. We have to talk.'

'I'm done talking.'

Kelly sat on the float to remove her boots and socks. She tossed them onto the bank then rolled up her jeans, easing her feet into the water one at a time. It was colder than she had expected, and wonderfully clear. Her magnified toes looked large and foreign, like someone else's. She wriggled them into the sandy mud.

'This time last month I was in prison,' she said. 'You have no idea how much I appreciate... being here...' It did not come out as she had intended. She wanted to be calm and in control, to shock him, but the last few words took control of themselves, ending on an abnormally high note.

She heard him flick away his cigarette and shift restlessly, as if turning towards her. 'What the hell are you talking about?'

'I was...' The sniff came uninvited, '...was facing

the death penalty... Daddy...'

It was almost a squeal, and Kelly rammed the heels of her palms against her eyes in a vain attempt to stop the sudden onrush of unwelcome tears. It was not supposed to happen like this. She was supposed to be strong. She had to be strong... for both of them.

She felt the float move under her as he climbed down. 'What's this all about... what are you trying to tell me, Kelly?'

'It was in Malaysia... Kuala Lumpur... on my way back from Africa. I was arrested at the airport. They found heroin in my bag. It was...'

'Drugs? You? Are you kidding me?'

She shook her head. 'No, it was planted. I upset some African politicians on the plane.'

'Jesus... and this is for real?'

She looked up at him, regaining control. 'It's true. I was facing the death penalty. They hang you there for drug trafficking.'

'Jesus Christ...'

She had shocked him all right. His expression was frozen in it, his face pale and his eyes dark and searching, fixed on her, but looking in, seeing something else, something beyond, or perhaps behind, to the unthinkable.

'Christ,' he repeated quietly, 'why didn't you tell

me this earlier, when you first saw me?'

'Didn't get much of a chance, did I?' She smiled weakly, but it still struck him hard. His lips tightened and he turned away to stare over the peaceful lake.

But his anger was not at her. 'I'm sorry, kid.' He placed a hand on her shoulder, then more firmly on her head, stroking her hair. 'I guess I've been a big disappointment to you.'

She reached up to take his fingers and cling to them. 'I thought about you often when I was in that dreadful place. I had to stop thinking about myself and what may happen or go crazy. I promised myself that if I was given my life back I would do this trip and bring you with me, to see if I could give you your life back too. That's why we're here, Daddy. I need this. I need you.'

She squeezed hard on his fingers and he lowered himself to sit beside her and place an arm about her shoulders, and she rested her head contentedly against him. 'Thank you. I needed that too.'

'You have a lot of guts, Kelly.'

'Maybe I take after my old man.'

He laughed, disdainfully. 'You don't have to patronise me, kid. I'm a bum, and I know it. Have for a long time.'

'Times can change… can't they?'

'Maybe. Now why don't you tell me about this drug and prison thing from the beginning? Obviously it worked out or you wouldn't be here.'

'It's a long story. Maybe we should set up the camp first?'

They unloaded the camping gear and moved to the bank, Kelly stepping delicately over the sharp pebbles with her bare feet, her father squelching about in his shoes, which had been dangling unnoticed in the water.

While he went busily about clearing a space for the tents, setting up the gas stove and boiling water for coffee, Kelly dawdled uncertainly over the food box, happy to see him take charge.

She still felt unaccountably drained and emotional, hanging on the brink, yet at the same time felt strangely content. It had not gone according to plan, but had worked better than she had expected. She had unwittingly reversed their roles, making him the comforter and her the comforted, and she found herself more than willing to play the part. It was what he needed.

Sitting on the food box with her foot in her lap, picking at an imaginary bramble thorn, she watched silently as he erected the tents, arranged sleeping bags, and hammered in pegs. She hid a smile as the flimsy hammer came apart in his hands and he tossed it aside contemptuously, cursing under his breath. He never did have much patience with tools.

He thumped the peg in with his squelchy heel then, to her astonishment, stripped to his undershorts, waded in past the plane, and plunged into the icy lake.

Kelly hastily lowered her foot and stood to watch anxiously as he swam out for a short distance, then thrashed his way back in a flurry of arms and spray. He emerged blowing and puffing, shaking water from his hair. 'Hot damn!' he panted, 'that is fresh!'

Kelly rushed to get him a towel from the bag. 'What are you trying to do?' she scolded. 'Give us both a heart attack?'

He grinned at her, the crooked one she remembered. 'How about you?'

'No thanks. A bit too fresh for my liking.'

'Chicken?'

Kelly hesitated. The challenge was tempting. She wanted to share in the foolishness, and the cold did not bother her. A quick swim would be invigorating. What deterred her was that she only had a bikini, and it was not yet time for him to learn of her pregnancy. She had been keeping that shock in reserve. So far, she had managed to conceal the unbuttoned gap in the top of her jeans by wearing shirts that she could leave hanging out.

'Okay,' she capitulated, 'but I have to skinny-dip, and I'm a big girl now. No peeking.'

She was in and out quickly. It was too cold even for squeals. All she could manage were gasps. She towelled herself vigorously, until her skin was pink and glowing, then wrapped herself in the towel.

'How does my big girl feel now?' he asked, handing her a steaming mug.

'Wonderful! Isn't this just great?'

He took a cautious sip, eyeing her speculatively. 'How long can I expect to go on enjoying it... or is that a secret?'

Kelly delayed her answer, returning thoughtfully to her seat on the food box. It was going too well to risk antagonising him now with ultimatums and a heavy-handed approach. He had to know soon... tonight, but not yet. 'That's up to you, Daddy,' she hedged. 'Can I tell you my story first?'

She told him everything from the time she had left him and gone to Juliette's graduation in Philadelphia, and he listened with a frown of concentration, his only interruption an occasional grunt, an expressive shake of his head or, as was the case when she told about reading to Rosie, laughter. When, despite herself, her words slowed and became choked or husky with emotion, he looked down tactfully and waited patiently

556

for her to continue.

It was an illuminating, but also traumatic experience for Kelly, talking openly to her father like this. They had not been close for so long that at times she felt an almost overwhelming sense of unreality, as if she were speaking to a stranger, then the next instant the stranger was gone and her father was back, the reality of his presence equally as overpowering.

They skipped eating and filled up with coffee and biscuits, the story continuing under the blaze of the stars, both wrapped in their sleeping bags and agreeing to sleep out of the tents.

When she told him about Keystone Kate and her near drowning in the disgusting toilet hole, making light of it by laughing, he became agitated, muttering something under his breath.

She did not mention her last meeting with Keystone Kate, though. As long as she lived she would never forget the feeling of utter despair that the fat warder's smile had invoked in her when ordered to remove her clothes. Or, after expecting the worst, how she had been forced to make use of the evil toilet hole one more time, vomiting into it with relief after the embassy official had entered with Slick-Hair to inform her that she was to be freed. It was only then had she realized how close she had been to giving up; to losing her will to survive, and that was not something she wished to remind herself of too often.

Her relating of the tape-recorded message and her sudden release was as perplexing to him as it still was to her.

'Mister Smith sounds awful phoney to me,' he commented. 'You didn't hear his voice?'

'No. I thought it may have been Billy or Pop, but they assured me it wasn't.'

'Those bastards could have told me,' he growled.

'It's my fault. I asked them not to. Sorry.'

She heard him take a long, deep breath. 'Goddam it, Kelly…'

***

After the long silence, the sudden break in the UHF static jolted him alert before the urgently rising voice of ground radar broke through loud and clear.

'Break, break, Bronco flight, you have a pop-up at your six o'clock.'

G forces sucked as he reefed the Phantom into a hard left turn. At the same time the hairs on the back of his neck prickled. It was always like that when he couldn't see them. The MiG 21s would be coming vertically up from behind, after building to supersonic speed low down beneath the radar. Their heat-seeking Atolls would be primed and ready to launch.

He glimpsed a silvery flash up high to his left and pulled up after it, kicking in the afterburner. He rolled onto the MiGs tail, fixed it with his gun sight and flicked the auto-acquisition switch. 'Visual contact.'

As usual, he heard Richard gulp twice on the intercom as he caught and held his breath, but at least he was doing his job. 'System lock-on.'

The four seconds needed for the radar to adjust to the missile system always seemed like four hours. He fired, felt the half-ton missile leap off the rack, and saw it snaking out in front, turning sharply with the MiG as the pilot tried to evade.

The Sparrow struck in the centre of the shiny blue fuselage and the MiG seemed to stop in mid-air as it suddenly transformed itself into a ball of black smoke and orange fire, spewing debris like an erupting volcano.

'Red Corral, Bronco One. Splash one MiG 21.'

'Roger, Bronco One. He's off our scope, but you have another two turning now onto your six o'clock.'

'I see them, Jim...' Richard's voice rose high in panic, 'they've launched... break, break!'

The first two Atolls missed, but he turned too late to avoid the third, and the Phantom pitched violently as its tail exploded.

***

Kelly woke to the sound of splashing and walrus-like snorting in the lake. She eased stiffly out of her damp sleeping bag, still tired after a restless night listening to her father's own tossing and turning. He must have gone through a full pack of cigarettes. She was relieved to be up. She slipped hastily out of her baggy tracksuit pants and into her jeans.

The coffee on the gas stove was boiling furiously. She filled the mugs as her father came huffing and puffing from the water. 'Are you in training for some sort of weird Japanese game show?' she asked.

He chuckled. 'It's part of my escape plan.' He paused in his towelling to take a handful of flab at his waist and jiggle it. 'Need to lose this.'

'How did you sleep?'

'Like a baby. You?'

'Same. All this fresh air.'

He made a skirt of the towel and wrapped his hands around the mug. 'So what exactly is the plan?'

Kelly had hoped to get in first so he wouldn't have to ask, but his question made it easier. 'No plan. I thought I'd leave that up to you. What I had hoped though, was to have you all to myself for two weeks. I want to catch up on the past. I also need to think about the future. Can we do that please… Daddy?' She smiled sweetly.

He laughed.

Sensing victory, Kelly pushed on. ' Funny how the simple things you've never worried about before suddenly mean so much when they're taken away. To fly over rural America in the spring. That's all I wanted in prison.'

'And I suppose, just by coincidence, this joy-flying will somehow end in Seattle.'

Kelly pulled a sour face. 'Didn't fool you, huh?'

He shook his head. 'Not for a minute. I was only playing dumb when you slipped me a Roofie and tied me into the plane. Thought I'd let you have some fun. That's the sort of thing parents have to do you know. Let their kids tie them up so they can dance around them like Comanches on the warpath.'

Kelly laughed, happy to see his old sense of humour. 'Yes. I'm sorry about that, truly I am. I was getting desperate. But we don't have to go to Seattle if you don't want to. We can stay around here. I can't dictate your life. I only want to be a part of it.'

'Two weeks?'

'That's all. Just to get to know my hero again.'

He grinned, shaking his head in resignation. 'Sure, why not? I can use some of that myself. And who can resist such a sweet talker anyway? Seattle it is.'

Kelly squealed with delight and threw her arms around him. "Thank you, Daddy.' She gave him a squeeze, then a kiss on his stubbled cheek. 'Thank you.'

He returned her hug one-armed, holding the mug at a safe distance. 'But no flying computers,' he said sternly. 'That I don't need.'

Kelly nodded. 'Whatever you say.'

'By the way, what's happening with my truck and rental trailer? I need to contact Freako before he starts freaking out.'

'You don't have to worry,' Kelly reassured him quickly. 'It's all been taken care of. How about some breakfast? I'm starving. Bacon and eggs okay? I love the smell of bacon frying in the outdoors, don't you? It reminds me of that time in Oklahoma...'

She chatted on gaily as she went about cooking their breakfast, one reminiscence leading to another, recalling the good times. She had suppressed them for so long in her memory because of the pain associated with them. Now they came in a flood, the stronger because of it, like forgotten but once cherished gifts freshly unearthed from the attic. She was happy and wanted to hold nothing back.

'You're going to be a granddaddy soon,' she said as they squatted together at the water's edge to scour the dishes with muddy sand. 'I'm pregnant.'

He almost slipped into the lake. 'What?'

She stood to lift her top enough to expose her stomach above the unbuttoned denims. It did not look so prominent now that she was not trying to hide it. She forced it out a little farther and gave it a rub. 'Three months and three days.'

He observed her naked abdomen with a puzzled expression, continuing absent-mindedly with his scouring, as if unsure that he wasn't having his leg pulled. Then he looked up at her face smiling down at him, his frown softening. 'Hot damn, Kelly, but you sure are plumb full of surprises.'

'So how do you feel about having a pregnant, unmarried ex-convict for a daughter?'

'Don't put yourself down, kid, you don't deserve it.' He gave his attention back to the clean dish, putting on more mud. 'What I think is not important. How do you feel?'

Kelly pulled down her top and lowered herself back onto her heels beside him. 'I don't know, Daddy. Sometimes happy, sometimes scared. How am I going to fly? I may have to sell the Bee.'

'This happen in Africa?'

'Uh, huh.'

'The guy whose leg you fixed.'

'Yes. Tim Ryan.'

'He know about it?'

'No.'

'You intend telling him?'

'No.'

'Why? You don't love him?'

Kelly hesitated. 'I don't know what I feel. He's charming, daring, handsome... in a way. A born pilot... like you, and he's also arrogant and chauvinistic. He has a way with animals you wouldn't believe, especially rhino.'

'And women, by the sound of it.'

'Yes. He reminds me a lot of someone else I know.' She sniggered quietly.

Her father appeared not to notice. 'Damn knees can't take this bending any more.' He straightened slowly, groaning, then placed a foot under her buttocks and tipped her forward.

Kelly screeched and fell headlong into the lake. She staggered up, gasping, waist-deep in the water.

He roared with laughter, hands on hips. 'That's for the insults. I'll pay you back for all your other cheek later.'

'You… you…'

'Careful now, you don't want to go insulting your daddy no more.'

It happened again. It was as if she had no will of her own. She felt her face tighten and begin to screw up and covered it with both hands, but she could not prevent the sound from escaping; a series of inelegant snorts, followed by a long, thin, coyote-like wail.

'Kelly?' He was quickly beside her, taking her in his arms. 'What is it, honey?'

She clung to him.

'I'm sorry, baby. I didn't hurt you, did I?'

She shook her head against him. 'Nooo…' It too, was a wail.

'What then?'

'Noth… I'm… happeee…'

He laughed with relief. 'Me too, kid. Come on, let's get you out and dry.'

She nodded, sniffing and pulling away. 'Sorry. Don't know what came over me. Silly bitch.'

'You'll feel better now? Not hiding any more surprises?'

She shook her head.

'Christ… that's a relief.'

'We can do it, can't we, Daddy? We can beat it together… this alcohol thing. We'll help each other.'

He was silent for a few long, agonising moments, then he sighed. 'We're sure going to give it one hell of a try, kid.'

He did try. And Kelly tried to help him. She was ill-suited to playing the role of helpless pregnant female, but did her best. It was the only weapon she had remaining.

'Ouch!'

'What?'

'How are you supposed to tie these fish-hooks?'

'Not like that. Pass it here.'

She pretended not to notice his unsteady hands as he turned aside to do it. She stooped with a groan to probe reluctantly amongst the bait. 'This stuff has gone all squishy. And the smell. Yuck! I don't think the baby likes it much.'

'Must be having a girl then.'

And later, as they were preparing Bertie for departure the next morning, going through the seemingly never ending task of pumping new grease in rocker-boxes and removing the old from the windscreen.

'Can you do the top ones, Daddy? The reaching up... don't know how I'm going to manage when it gets bigger.'

He relieved her of the grease gun. 'That's the trouble with these old radials.'

'The Seabee is even worse,' she said. 'The Franklin engine goes through nearly a quart of oil an hour. Sprays it all over the fin, and you know how high that is. Have to use a ladder…'

He was not sleeping much, and what little he did have was restless and twitchy, filled with groans and whimpers, as if he were having bad dreams. During the day his mood swings were frequent, and she tried to keep him occupied, but was fast running out of ideas. If she could only get him to fly again, maybe it would help.

'Ouch! Ow!'

He lifted up quickly from where he had been, head down, stowing and securing the camping gear onto the floor of the rear cockpit. 'What's wrong?'

Kelly placed her right foot gingerly on the ground. 'Ow!' She hopped to the float and sat to lift and cradle her ankle. 'Damn!'

Concerned, he climbed down beside her. 'What did you do?'

'I slipped…' She screwed up her face, 'twisted my ankle.' She rocked back and forth.

'Let's have a look.' She submitted to his examination bravely, with only minor flinching.

'I don't think anything's broken. Probably a sprain. Have we got anything to strap it with?'

She pointed to the white first-aid box sitting on the bank in readiness to be loaded. 'In there... elastic bandage.'

He strapped it firmly. 'There. Best keep the weight off it for a while.'

She took a deep breath and lifted herself gamely on the strut. 'If you can help me up to the front...' She took a hesitant step. 'Ow! I'm sure it will be okay...'

'Forget it, kid. You can't work the rudders with a sprained ankle. It looks like we'll have to stay a bit longer.'

'Damn! I'm getting sick of this place. I was looking forward to getting to Missouri today. I don't suppose you...'

'He laughed. 'I was a jet-jockey remember? Haven't flown a piston since Korea, and never a float plane.'

'So? It's still like a bicycle or a horse. And you taught me in the Stinton. Now it's my turn. I'll have hand-rudders in the back for emergency, and if you like we can replace the rear stick. The rest is easy. I can talk you through it.' She gave him the most expectant, endearingly helpless look she could muster. 'Please... just for me?'

'Hell, Kelly. I'm not that much of a has-been. Just give me a run-down on float technique, then a smack on the back of the head if I do anything wrong. And you had better let me do the prop swinging from now on. I don't want no grandchild growing up with one arm longer than the other.'

No head slapping was necessary. The take-off run was a little shaky, and he held Bertie down longer than she would have, but her doubts were dispelled the moment they lifted off and her father did a low turn - barely twenty feet above the water - to follow the course of the lake.

Kelly felt the same tug of disquiet that she had experienced with Tim. She would never have had the courage to turn so low in a strange plane - especially Bertie - after so long a time without any flying.

It was a fleeting resentment though. Her father had a few thousand hours more experience than she did, and had flown Mustangs and Phantoms in combat. She could never compete with that. She settled down happily to enjoy the novelty of sitting in the back and watching him fly, congratulating herself on her own success.

She had achieved more than she could have hoped for, and in a much shorter time. She had expected it to be uphill all the way, with anger, deceit, even violence.

That wouldn't happen now that everything was out in the open, and she was confident he would find the strength to see it through. He would still need her help though, she thought. The battle was going well, but it was still too soon for the victory dance.

***

Country America was doing its springtime best to impress, brazenly revealing its bright new undergarments of multi-patterned green. Not as impressive as the autumn regalia of oaks and aspens, but viewed through half-closed eyes and oil-splattered goggles, it still rivalled the most inspired works of Monet.

Farms unfolded beneath like the slow unrolling of a canvas, revealing arrow-straight roads and chessboard fields that looked smooth enough to land on. They flew over the toy villages with their Matchbox cars, and skirted round the larger centres. Blue lakes ahead brought relief to the landscape, and also to Kelly, who waited for their arrival with confidence, then viewed their passing with unease, but the beat of the engine remained steady.

They were not the only ones in the sky. Other small planes came to scrutinise the stranger from the past with its goggled occupants, flying alongside to exchange waves and signal encouragement with rocking wings, and it was the same on the lakes when they landed. Boats appeared from nowhere, and so did people, to ogle and question.

At a lake in Kansas, Kelly received an unexpected boost to her rehabilitation program when the operator of a tour boat pulled alongside as they were refuelling.

'Hey, buddy,' he called out, 'what sort of airplane you got there?'

'Bristol F2b Fighter,' her father answered.

'Mind if I have a looksee inside? Kinda interested in antique airplanes.'

'Sure.'

'Had they charged a dollar for a look inside it would have paid the fuel bill for the entire journey.

He came to stand on the float and introduced himself. 'Tom Lincoln.'

Her father wiped the grease from his palm to accept the handshake. 'Jim Maddock. My daughter, Kelly. This is her baby.'

'Nice to meet you folks.' He observed her father thoughtfully. 'Say... you wouldn't be Major Jim Maddock now, would you?'

'Once upon a time.'

'Well, I'll be...' He grinned widely and pumped

her father's hand for a second time. 'Knew you from Bien Hoa. Sergeant Lincoln. Armaments. Used to load you guys with Sparrows.' He chuckled in reminiscence. 'You, more than most. Ten splashes if I remember. Never forget the big aces. Well I'll be...'

'Nine,' her father corrected. 'A long time ago...'

Former Sergeant Lincoln inspected Bertie enthusiastically, shook her father's hand for a third time, wished them both a safe journey, then returned to his tour group, still shaking his head in disbelief. As the boat chugged away they could hear him talking on the cabin speakers to his passengers, giving them a run-down on the Bristol, and on her father. '... Major Jim Maddock USAF. A real live double ace. Give them a wave, folks. Don't see too many around like him no more.' He beeped his horn and the passengers waved dutifully.

'Wave back, Daddy?'

He followed her example self-consciously, looking embarrassed, but also pleased.

'See? I'm not the only one who thinks you're a hero.'

He laughed scornfully.

'Don't put yourself down, Daddy,' she said, recalling his own words. 'You don't deserve it... not any more.'

***

It became colder as they moved north through Nebraska, the news that it was spring travelling more slowly, and it seemed not to have reached Wyoming at all. On the high plateaus it was still knee deep in winter, the peaks gleaming white against the sapphire sky. And with the rising elevation they had to fly higher, which made it even colder. More often their gloved hands sought warmth from the exhaust that ran the length of the fuselage outside the cockpits.

They pushed harder, flying longer and stopping less. At her father's suggestion, they turned west to pick up the highway across the Great Divide Basin, and with the scarcity of lakes Kelly began to wonder if fitting Bertie with floats had been such a good idea. With wheels they could land on the highway in an emergency, and although floats may have been better on snow, it was not something she would like to attempt. She was glad it was her father doing the flying over that section.

Her ankle sprain had made a remarkable recovery after only one day, due mainly to the fact she had forgotten to limp, and they shared the piloting, but her superior eyesight when it came to reading maps that vibrated and fluttered in the wind like a trapped bird made her more useful in the rear.

Kelly was flying the next day, though, after a cold night in a reservoir and a late start, due to having to hitch a ride in a pick-up to get fuel from a gas station some twenty miles away.

She followed the Oregon trail through the Rockies and South Pass, Bertie struggling through an icy headword at nine thousand feet that at times seemed to be pushing them backwards. Then they were through, and winging their way down below the white peaks and over jagged canyons like a soaring eagle, Bertie's nose pointed towards the lowering sun and the as yet unseen recreation lake where they would spend the night.

Kelly relaxed. The worst was over. In two more days they would be at the Sound, and home. She began thinking of what she would do once they got there. Pop Franz would have to be the first stop. He would be delighted with her success, and the thought gave her a thrill. It didn't matter that her father hadn't been dry for a full two weeks. Nine days was close enough, and he didn't want the job anyway. Her own plan was better. Sound Sea-Air could do with another pilot now that summer was just around the corner, and her father's name and flying reputation should make an impact.

Then Bertie hiccupped.

From her hunched down position to escape the worst of the icy wind, Kelly sat bolt upright. She stared at the few instruments in shock. They told her nothing. Everything seemed in order. The fuel gauge showed they still had a quarter of a tank - more than enough to reach the lake, which she expected to see at any moment.

She was still staring at the gauge when it flicked twice against the pin. The engine hesitated, picked up again, then stopped.

The silence was profound, filled only with the rush of wind and ominous moaning of the wires. It couldn't happen, but it had.

Kelly stared helplessly at the spaghetti-like arrangement of tubes, cylinders and taps that comprised the complicated fuel system. Everything seemed in the right place. She worked the brass plunger of the fuel primer while the propeller was still windmilling, but it did no good, and she turned to look and raise a questioning hand at her father, but he returned an eloquent shrug, equally perplexed. He pointed down, and Kelly returned hastily to her duties, her training on forced landing procedure prompting her reluctant brain into action.

They had little altitude to work with, barely two thousand feet and, when she needed it most, no lake.

She lowered the nose to hold what Billy Steel had told her was probably the best gliding speed and held it there as best she could. Bertie considered trimming devices as merely another new-fangled gadget.

Fighting the urge to panic, Kelly searched desperately amongst the rugged landscape for a place to land. Water glinted below, at the base of steep cliffs, but it was only a twisting mountain stream full of white rapids.

They were well below the peaks now, losing altitude steadily, and with nowhere to go but straight ahead. There too, seemed hopeless, with nothing to see but more jagged rock and no opening, giving the frightening impression that they had entered a blind canyon.

But the stream had to go somewhere. Kelly followed it hopefully, the tumbling rapids now clearly visible. A straw in a sea of rock.

Then the canyon turned. From what had seemed a solid wall a gap appeared, growing wider, and through it she could see a broad valley opening out, and in the valley, running for its entire length, the most wonderful shimmering lake. Buildings, tents and trailers cluttered one side. It was the lake where they were to stay the night.

Kelly's heart leapt when she saw the welcome

expanse, then sank equally as rapidly when she realized they did not have the altitude left to reach it.

The stream she had been following plunged through one last cataract, then disappeared into a swampy area crowded with tufts of grass and rushes that widened and gradually diminished as it became the lake proper, but the deeper water was a long way ahead.

Then she saw the cattle and the fence. It cut right across the swamp, directly in her path, and the cattle grazed near it on the green tufts, standing in water up to their hocks.

Kelly had no option. It was the swamp or nothing. She held the speed well above the stall to keep Bertie straight and steady. To go in nose first would be disastrous.

She jumped as her father leaned forward to bellow in her ear. 'Take the fence head on!'

She touched down with the nose high, ten yards into the first sign of water, thumping, hopping and skidding over tufts, one float catching and slewing them so they hit the fence at an angle, but it gave way easily, pulling over the posts, and the strands brought them to a halt close beside the flashing hooves of a startled and hastily departing cow.

'Well done!' her father complimented, and Kelly

collapsed into nervous, hysterical laughter.

***

Their involuntary arrival had been seen from the camp. Within twenty minutes a flotilla of small boats and canoes came to their assistance, noisily towing them to the camp jetty.

A close inspection of Bertie by herself, her father and several willing helpers, revealed that apart from a few scratches from the fence, and a liberal splattering of mud and cow dung, he seemed to have suffered no visible damage. The cause of the engine failure proved to be dirt in the fuel, and they guessed it had come from the old drums they had borrowed from the gas station.

To celebrate their lucky escape, they accepted offers of hot showers, thick and juicy barbecued Wyoming steaks, and attended a country-style dance at the camp recreation hall.

With liquor freely available it was a worry for Kelly. Made worse by the shortage of eligible women. Wanting to stay close, she instead found herself rounded-up by several grinning cowboys with big Stetsons and bigger hands, all intent on boot-scooting her outside for a breath of fresh air. She lost contact with her father early in the evening, and when she eventually managed to break away, found him sitting innocently in a corner with a group of old-timers. Some were drinking but, to her immense relief, he was not.

'You go enjoy yourself, honey,' he told her. Your daddy can look after himself.'

'I wish I could say the same,' she laughed breathlessly, and was herded back to face the music before she could say any more.

But when the dance finally ended she could not find him.

They had erected their tents in the camping area, and she checked there first, hoping he had gone to bed, but his tent was empty. Alarmed, she scoured the entire area, even going to the extent of enlisting the aid of one of her cowboys to check trailers and cabins in which lights were showing and laughter could be heard, but without success. She recognised one of the old-timers and asked him, but there too, she drew a blank. He had left about halfway through the dance, she learned, and they believed he had gone to bed. She even checked the plane.

Angry and disheartened, Kelly returned to her tent and crawled into her sleeping bag. But as tired as she was she could not sleep. She tried to convince herself that she was wrong, that he had not gone back to drinking, but she knew in her heart that he had. She had failed, and so had he. Everything they had accomplished was for nothing. In some ways they were both worse off than before, because now they would have to live with the failure always between them.

He returned to his tent in the early hours of the morning, stumbling over guy-ropes and muttering incoherently.

Lying awake in the dark, Kelly wished that he had not returned at all.

***

The ejection sequence was automatic. Richard was a little ahead, clearing clean, but he was not so lucky, his ankle catching the canopy, and something crashing against his helmet.

He came to at three thousand feet, when the chute opened, also automatically, and he clung to the risers, drifting towards a rice paddy.

The sky was empty. So was the paddy field. A group of charred huts smouldered at the edge. It was late afternoon.

He landed on his back with a squelchy splash. Richard helped him up. They dumped the chutes and Mae Wests, hiding them as best they could in the stinking mud. The locator was muddy, but undamaged.

Light-headed dizziness came as he removed his helmet.

The field was too open, he said. Charlie would see them. They had to move away.

Stooped low, Richard helping, they started for the raised path leading to the burned huts, then he saw the girl on a bicycle.

It was too large for her. She straddled the crossbar, swaying from side to side to reach the lower arc of the peddles, pushing hard on them, casting anxious glances in their direction. On the back of the bicycle was a bamboo cage containing two chickens.

Richard waved his pistol, shouting, and she wobbled to a halt, the bicycle falling sideways until her foot reached the ground. Large almond eyes in a heart-shaped face, flat chest heaving with nervous exhaustion.

Can't let her go, Richard insisted. She would run straight to Charlie.

Richard released the squawking chickens and pushed the bicycle off the path into the paddy. He waved his pistol, signalling her to walk in front, back to the huts from where she had come.

Quick, nervously willing steps and hasty backward glances, oversize threadbare dress slipping off one shoulder. Thin legs and bare feet. A frightened child.

One hut with no thatch to burn had partly survived,

the mud-plastered pole walls canted over, offering some shelter and concealment. Hard to focus on his GI watch. The girl sitting obediently, hugging her knees. He sat too, his wet flying suit cold and stinking. He removed his boot to relieve the ankle, but did not look. He closed his eyes against the dizziness.

When he opened them again he was alone. No girl. And no Richard.

***

Kelly left her father to sleep it off and spent the morning doing joy-flights. She made them short and remained within easy landing distance of the lake, but with clean fuel in his tank, Bertie performed without a hiccup.

She stayed away from the tents all day, not ready for the confrontation she knew would have to come. In the afternoon she cleaned and refuelled, ready for an early departure, then called Pop Franz, knowing he would already have left his office. She was not ready to admit her defeat to him either. She left a message, letting him know that she would be there in two days, and giving no other details.

It was dusk when she finally plucked up the courage to get it over with. Then, once again, she couldn't find him.

'Thought I saw him a while back,' one of the old-timers informed her. 'Looked to be goin' by the busted fence. Maybe he's aiming to mend it. Waistin' his time though. Posts all rotten anyways.'

'Did he look drunk to you?'

The man looked bemused. 'Not so as I noticed, honey.'

She found him sitting on the edge of the marshy area, smoking and watching the grazing cows. His back was to her, and she approached uncertainly, prepared to retreat if he was drunk or drinking, but she saw no sign of a bottle. She coughed lightly while still some distance away to announce her presence, not wanting to be the first to speak. He turned briefly, then resumed his study of the cows.

'I guess it must be lecture time,' he said.

'No, Father, not any more. From now on what you do is strictly your own business.'

'So, we're back to formality, are we?'

'Yes, and this is where we part company, I'm afraid. I'll give you the money to catch a plane back to Florida. One of the men here will give you a lift to Cheyenne. You'll have to buy another truck, by the way. I gave yours to Freako in exchange for the rent you owe him. I'll give you the money for that too, then we're all square. I don't want to see you again.'

She wanted to say so much more, to let him know that she had been so sure he could do it, and how bitterly disappointed she was, but she could not stretch herself that far. She turned away. 'I'll leave the money with the camp secretary. Goodbye, Father.'

'Sit down, Kelly, I have something to tell you.'

She kept walking.

He came after her, took her gently by the arm. 'Please, kid. Not this way. I need you to listen. After that... well, maybe you'll still want to leave, but at least give me the chance.'

'Listen to what? Excuses? Apologies? More promises?' She pulled her arm away. 'It's too late for any of that, you've hurt me enough.'

'Yes, I have, and for what it's worth I do apologise. I love you, Kelly. You're the one person in the world I shouldn't be hurting.'

'Why then, Daddy? I loved you too. Why did you have to do it?'

He sighed deeply. 'That's the hell of it, kid. I didn't. I found that out last night.'

Too distressed to keep still, Kelly kept walking slowly, and he walked beside her, silent and thoughtful, and she waited for him to continue, not knowing what to think, but strangely relieved that it hadn't ended as she had intended.

'Drinking didn't help. It never did, but at least it helped me sleep. Not last night though.' He laughed without humour. 'Last night was hell, and it's all your fault.'

'Mine?' She stopped to look at him in disbelief. She opened her mouth to demand a reason, but the words would not come. It was the first time she had looked into his eyes since finding him sitting there, and she was shocked at what she saw. They were sunken and red-rimmed, but they had been like that for a while. Now there was more; an expression of anguish and despair, like the eyes of a man lying helpless on the ground with a sword poised above his head.

He looked away. 'This week with you has been sheer hell, but also the best thing that has happened to me since Vietnam. It showed me that there are still things in life that I want, and that I can't run anymore. I know how it sounds, but also for what it's worth, whether you stay or leave, the drinking is over.'

'Run from what?' Kelly asked quietly.

He took a deep breath, as if coming to a painful decision. 'You asked me some time ago if I blame myself for your Uncle Richard's death. The answer is yes. I killed him.'

'It was war. You said it yourself. He took his

chances like everyone else… like you did. You don't have to take the blame for being shot down. You could just as easily have been killed yourself.'

He shook his head. 'No. He wasn't killed when we took an Atoll as I reported. We both bailed out. Richard was perfectly okay. Better than I was. He landed in a rice paddy without a scratch. I busted my foot and took a knock on the head. I killed him, Kelly. Blew his goddam brains out.'

Kelly stared at him in horror. 'What are you saying?'

He couldn't look at her. 'There was a girl…. about the same age as you were then. She had some chickens on the back of a bicycle, taking them away from the burned huts. God, Kelly… she was only a child… a frightened little girl on a bicycle that was too big for her, could hardly reach the pedals… just like when you… God…'

He stopped, turning to face the lake so she couldn't see his face, and she laid a hand softly on his arm. 'Go on… I don't care what happened. It was a long time ago. Tell me.'

'Richard threatened her with his pistol. Said she would give us away. She didn't try to run, only wanted to save the chickens. She couldn't understand what we said, but obeyed our signals quickly… too scared not to. She sat quietly in the hut with us. We were going to keep her until the choppers arrived. I felt dizzy from the crack on the head and went to sleep.' He paused again to light a cigarette, taking a long time.

'Go on, Daddy.'

'When I came around she was gone, and so was Richard.'

'She escaped?'

'No. While I was unconscious, your sweet Uncle Richard took her outside and raped her.'

Kelly gasped, her hand flying involuntarily to her mouth. She stared at him above her fingers in numb shock, and he looked back at her with his lips twisted strangely, as if at the taste of something unpleasant.

'When I went looking for them I found her dress. It was all she had… nothing else… just that raggedy old dress. Then I saw Richard. He was drowning her in the filthy water. Lying on her. Holding her face under.'

Kelly could not take her eyes off his tortured face. 'Oh my God,' she whispered.

'I tried to help her, but had to hop on one foot, and by the time I got there it was too late. She had stopped struggling. When I asked Richard what the hell he thought he was doing, the sonofabitch had the gall to smile at me. "Just another moose", he said.'

'Uncle Richard…? Oh my dear God, Daddy…'

'I went for him. Hit him in the face while he was still trying to zip his pants. Threw him on his back in the water, and he pulled his pistol on me. I dived on him as he lifted it, knocking it up, and it went off under his chin. Killed him instantly.'

Kelly was speechless. She sat on the grass and he sat with her, both of them without words strong enough to express how they felt. He lit another cigarette and blew the smoke out forcefully between tight lips, and Kelly took his hand.

'I left him there, Kelly. Nothing I could do. I carried the girl back to the huts. She weighed nothing. Just a baby. The bastard had used my bootlace to tie her wrists. I took it off and put the dress back on her. Left her there and walked out of that place. The choppers picked me up from the path a few hours later.'

'Poor Daddy,' Kelly whispered.

'You can see why I couldn't stay with your mother. How could I tell her that I had killed her brother? And when I looked at her, all I saw was Richard.'

'Yes… I wish you had told me. I would have understood.'

'I couldn't. I just had to get the hell out, away from the war, the brutality, and everything that reminded me of it.' He sighed. 'Doesn't work like that, kid, does it?'

'No, it doesn't, but it's over now. So you killed

him, but it was an accident all the same. You can't blame yourself, and I certainly don't. That poor girl. I think I would have felt the same.'

'That's the worst of it. Even had it not been an accident, I know I would have killed him anyway.' He laughed bitterly. 'That's what war does to you.'

'I never did like him much,' Kelly said. 'He was always too nice, if you know what I mean.'

'Oh? I thought you did.' He paused. 'He didn't try anything funny with you, did he?'

'No, nothing like that, but he sometimes made me feel uncomfortable because he bought me too many nice things.'

'He was a weak man, Kelly. He resented me because I was his CO, and because I took him out of the front seat and put him in the back. He didn't have what it takes to be a combat pilot.'

'How about you, Daddy? Do you still have what it takes?'

He found a weak smile. 'I'm trying, kid. I'm trying real hard.'

***

To welcome her, and not to be outdone by the mainland, the Sound put on as brilliant a display of fine weather as Kelly had seen there. The peak of Mount Rainier rose on the horizon to sparkle in the afternoon sun like a lantern in a window, guiding her unerringly towards the labyrinth of island-dotted waterways she called home.

Swooping low, she buzzed Pop Franz's shack then circled, waiting for him to appear before coming in to land. With the engine shut down she drifted confidently in to the jetty, not waiting to touch before standing on her seat to wave her helmet and goggles and call a greeting. 'Permission to come aboard, Colonel.'

Pop Franz flashed a welcoming smile as white as that of the mountain. 'Only if you're good looking.'

'That means you first, Daddy,' Kelly said, sensing his uncertainty at meeting his old friend after so long a time, and after what had passed.

She needn't have worried.

'You old bastard, Jim.' Pop grinned. 'I ought to put you on a charge for giving me such a hard time.'

'Up yours, Colonel.' Her father returned his grin, and Kelly swallowed as the two old friends shook hands and thumped shoulders.

When her turn came she submitted breathlessly to a long hug in silence, Pop unable to speak for several moments. It was an emotional homecoming. Kelly couldn't remember a better one.

But after a few hours of excited reminiscing over the trip, she got the impression she wasn't that welcome.

'Got a bunk fixed up for you, Jim,' Pop said, 'but wasn't sure if you'd be staying, Kelly. Your tenants are out and I gave the place an inspection to make sure everything was in order. Stocked the refrigerator and had Maisie freshen up your bed.' He smiled. 'Thought you'd need that after a few weeks of roughing it on the ground, and that's about all I got here. Oh yes,' he added quickly. 'I also had one of the men fly the Seabee over. She's checked-out and ready to go.'

'You guys wouldn't be trying to get rid of me now by any chance, would you?' She said it jokingly, but felt a stab of disappointment. Her father too, had a strained smile.

'Hell, Kelly,' Pop said. 'Of course not. You're always welcome, you know that. It's only that we have a lot of catching up to do, and you don't want to be listening to all our war stories. Trust me.'

Kelly sighed theatrically. 'Okay. I know when I'm not wanted. But I'll be back tomorrow.'

They came down to swing the prop and see her off, and she gave them both a hug, taking the opportunity to whisper in Pop Franz's ear. 'He's dry, Pop. Keep it that way.'

Once she was in the air, Kelly found that she really didn't mind leaving them alone all that much. They could talk more freely without her being there, and she was definitely looking forward to her own bed, some time alone to think, and to enjoy her thoughts for a change without any pressure. It had been so long since she had been able to do that.

The first indication that things were not as they should be came as she was taxiing up to her houseboat in Fridays Harbour. The lights were on and the door open. Her beloved Bee was moored alongside as Pop had promised, but she paid it scant attention as she switched Bertie off and drifted in, casting anxious glances between the spare mooring post and the open door of the houseboat. It seemed that the tenants hadn't moved out after all.

She stood on the float in readiness and jumped to the jetty before it touched, the rope already in her hands. She secured the front, and was bending to do the same to the rear when a voice said from behind: 'Why, howdy there, stranger.'

Kelly recognised the phoney western drawl immediately and spun round with a shriek of joy. 'Jules!'

***

Juliette Ryan groaned as she leaned forward to apply more sun-lotion to her legs. 'God… Is it just my imagination, or is this boat moving?'

Kelly laughed. 'One glass of Champagne too much, I'd say.'

'Your fault for making me drink your share.'

'Blame the baby. I still can't believe you're here, Jules.'

Sunbathing topless in the privacy of the minuscule after-deck of the houseboat, they were catching the warm midday sun and recovering from the mild after-effects of a bottle of Champagne and little sleep. It had been a night to remember. A night of tears, Kelly remembered with a smile. Tears of joy, nostalgia and laughter. Champagne tears.

'And I can't believe you're pregnant.'

Kelly grunted again. 'Thanks for reminding me.'

'I still think you should come back with me to Australia.'

'I thought we went through all that last night.'

'I don't remember last night.'

Kelly sighed. 'You're going to tell him, aren't you?'

'I think my nipples are getting burnt. How about a swim?'

'It's too cold. You'll come out with icicles for nipples. Answer my question.'

Juliette was thoughtful, rubbing cream on her breasts. 'Think about it, Kelly. We're friends. We'll be keeping in contact. You may even visit. How do you expect to keep it from him? I can't lie to him. Sooner or later he's bound to find out, then we'll both feel bad. And don't you think he has a right to know?' She replaced the cap on the tube then leaned back on her arms. 'Yep, the way I figure, you ain't got no option, pardner. And you don't have to worry. Tim will do the right thing.'

Kelly sat up to join her, looking out over the harbour to her favourite mountain glistening in the distance. It always seemed to be there when she needed it, but it couldn't give her direction in this instance. On this one she had to find her own way.

'That's what bothers me, Jules. I don't want him to feel obligated. It was as much my fault as his, and because I'm pregnant is no reason to get married.'

'How about love… isn't that a good reason?'

'I suppose, but I'm not sure I feel that way about your brother. I like and admire him, of course, but it's hard to love someone who had sex with you simply to prove whether or not you were a lesbian.'

'The idiot.' Juliette gave a long-suffering sigh.

'Mind you, he's only a man. You can't expect too much. Anyway, he thinks differently now.'

'Maybe, but he doesn't love me, and that's all that really matters.'

'Are you kidding? Do you think he went all the way to Hong Kong just so he could have his leg reset? Of course he loves you. Maybe he doesn't know it yet, but I do.'

Kelly laughed. 'My friend, the misguided matchmaker.'

'If the fool hadn't messed around with his cast he would have seen you in KL, then maybe things would have turned out different between you two.'

'I still have to thank him for that. He didn't have to feel responsible. It was my big mouth. Anyway, he wouldn't have been able to see me. I wasn't allowed visitors. I hardly got to see the stupid lawyer. By the way, did I tell you about the tape recording?'

'You mentioned something about it. Some propaganda that you refused to do, which is why you had to go through the toilet thing. God, what a bitch. I'll be surprised if you don't get terminal constipation. So what about it?'

Kelly had no problem remembering what it was she had been forced to say. The words still ran through her head at times like an irritating song. She recited them again, and saying them out loud brought the memory unpleasantly close. 'I told my father, and he thinks Mister Smith is a phoney name. What do you think?'

Juliette didn't answer right away, looking at her with a thoughtful, intent expression, then she said quietly: 'Well, well, well.'

'Well what?'

Juliette shifted around to face Kelly, pulling her slim legs into an almost lotus position. 'I may be wrong, but listen to this.' She leaned forward to place an attention- getting hand on Kelly's knee. 'Tim won't tell me the details, acts all smiley and secretive, but from what he said, and from what I managed to get out of John, I have a feeling this recording has something to do with what he and Elliot cooked up between them, and if ...'

'Elliot? The same one who died in prison?'

'Hah! We have got a lot of catching up to do. He escaped. Pretended he was dead. Can you believe that? He's planning to marry Lydia.'

Kelly sat upright to clap her hands and squeal with delight. 'I love it. Tell me more.'

Juliette filled her in on the little she knew, and Kelly listened avidly, recalling the unlikely spy with affection. It seemed he had achieved the impossible after all. Forest Gump the second.

'Anyway,' Juliette said, bringing the conversation back to where they had left off. 'John told me that Tim and Elliot captured that Chinese agent in Mozambique. Elliot was going to kill him, but they handed him over to the police.'

'Good!' Kelly said emphatically.

'And,' Juliette said knowingly. 'Tim said that he had used the man's satellite phone to call the Golden Horn Company in Shanghai. Said he wanted the satisfaction of telling them their agent had been caught. And you know what else?'

'What?' Kelly asked quietly, as if about to hear something scandalous. Juliette's secretive manner was making her breathless. It must run in the family.

'He used a phoney name.' She sat back with a satisfied look. 'Said he needed to protect Gara Pasi. Didn't want it getting back to Mugabe's henchmen.'

Kelly felt even more breathless, and a certain light-headedness that had nothing to do with the wine. 'Did he say what name he used?'

Juliette shook her head, but her expression didn't change. 'No, but my brother doesn't have much imagination when it comes to that sort of thing, and he's used it before... several times, in fact. Usually when he got into trouble. I wouldn't be surprised if he had a passport in the name of Smith.'

Kelly snorted with laughter. 'Hell, Jules, so do half the people in the world.'

Juliette was unabashed. 'Okay, we'll see. I'll call him tonight and ask.'

'Any bets?'

Juliette grinned. 'How about... if you lose, you come back with me to Australia?'

Kelly shook her head. 'Uh, uh. I was thinking more in terms of ten bucks or a bottle of Champagne. Now tell me about Rosie and Bamba Zonke.'

'First a drink... not Champagne. Orange juice. Lots of ice. I saw some in the freezer. And while you're there you'll find some Panadol in my bag.'

'Yes madam,' Kelly answered meekly, mimicking. 'Why don't you just call me Lydia, madam?' She hurried in and returned with clinking glasses and a sealed envelope in her teeth, which she handed to Juliette along with the tablets, after first taking out two for her own consumption. 'I found this in your bag. It has my name on it. You buy me a gift?'

'Oh, yes. Sorry, I forgot.' Juliette handed it back. 'It's from Tim.'

'Oh?' Kelly sat to rip it open. It was a color photograph of Rosie and Bamba Zonke, with the message We miss you scrawled across the bottom corner. She smiled as she turned the photo to show Juliette. 'I miss them too.'

'Looks like something is written on the back,' Juliette said.

Kelly flipped it over. Only two short sentences. She stared at them.

'So?' Juliette asked. 'What does my darling brother have to say?'

'Did you know about this, Jules?' Kelly asked quietly, still looking down at the words. 'I mean, you came here only to see me... right?'

'What are you getting at? Of course I came here to see you. What does...'

'Are you certain Tim doesn't know about me being pregnant?'

'How could he? I didn't know myself until last night... what's he been up to now? Give here. Let me see.'

Kelly handed her the postcard and Juliette pushed her sunglasses up to read. She returned the card wordlessly and leaned back on her arms with eyes closed and the suspicion of a smile on her lips. Then she gave a deep, long suffering sigh of resignation that was as phoney as her western drawl had been. 'Oh, shit.... now I suppose we have to go through all that soggy, snivelling crap again.'

***

Rosie snorted, blowing a fine spray of mucus over Tim's arm.

'Thanks, Rosie.'

Pushing the persistent Bamba Zonke aside with his good leg, Tim removed another bunch of carrot tops from the bucket, holding them low in the flat of his palm, and Rosie's long upper lip curled gently over and pulled them into her wide mouth. 'That's your lot for now.' He glanced at his watch, then along the path leading to the buildings. It wouldn't be long now.

Keeping the bucket out of reach, he pushed himself up from the log on which he had been sitting and tucked the single crutch into his armpit then, followed closely by Rosie and the calf, hobbled the short distance to the gate, squeezing through and shutting it quickly behind. He left the bucket of vegetable scraps out of sight in the shade, glanced at his watch again, then turned to peer through the foliage. Rosie and the calf were walking slowly back to their favourite shade-tree, Rosie still with a limp, but much less now. 'Good girl,' Tim breathed.

The path was still empty. He picked up the bucket to check again that the turnips were at the top, standing with them in his hand for a moment, undecided, then he shoved them back and dropped the bucket to the ground with a grunt of irritation. 'Settle down, dimwit,' he chided himself.

Juliette was playing her stupid games again, he was sure of it. She had used that same, do as I tell you because I know better than you, tone when she called, the same as she had with the card. It should have been a letter. He could have said a lot more in a letter - explained a lot more. But no, it had to be a card. Keep it short and simple, she had insisted, spelling it out for him as if he were a moron. And, as usual, he had given way, just as he had now, standing here, hiding behind a bush. Maybe he was a moron.

Half an hour, she had said, that's all. After half an hour of polite conversation with Mom, she'll be wondering where you are, getting nervous, then I'll send her down alone and you can do your thing. Don't screw it up.

Remembering, Tim gave a derisive snort, then checked the time again. The half hour had been up three minutes ago. If Jules was wrong she was going to be in for it, good and proper. No messing about this time. Kick her arse all the way back to Gara Pasi.

Then he saw her.

She was wearing jeans and a loose shirt, walking

casually, looking down, and his pulse began hammering. She looked thinner, but her figure was as good as he remembered. He made himself look busy, stooping over the bucket, clanking it noisily, then picking it up to move slowly out of the shade onto the path, stopping there to look and wait, as if just seeing her. He fixed a smile, feeling as if his face had been sprayed with wet cement. 'Hello, Kelly.'

She looked up to smile and partly lift a hand. 'Oh, hi, Tim.' She said it as if surprised to see him there.

'How are you?'

'Fine, thanks. And you? How's the leg?'

'Better, thanks.' He shifted uncomfortably on the crutch. 'Another two weeks... about.'

'That's good.' She stopped a few yards away, smiling, looking as nervous as he felt, which made him feel a little less so. It was not going well.

'It's great to see you, Kelly. You look good. You've lost weight.' He cursed his stupidity.

'Prison diet.'

'It must have been a bad time for you.'

'Yes. I've had better.'

He nodded, suddenly lost for words. It was too early to talk about that, or to bring up the card. Then he remembered. 'I have a surprise. Come, I'll show you.'

'Oh?' She brightened. 'Can I carry the bucket for

you?'

'Thanks.' He fumbled clumsily with the handle.

They walked in awkward silence for a few moments, then both started talking at the same time. She laughed. 'You first.'

'Look... over there.' They had reached the gate. He stood on one leg to point with the crutch. 'Under the tree.'

'Oh... Rosie?'

He grinned, opening the gate. 'Come.'

'Inside? We're going inside?'

'Yes.' He went in and she followed hesitantly. 'Don't worry.'

'Are you sure?' She gave a short, nervous laugh. 'I'm not...'

'It's quite safe.' He took the bucket from her and dug in it for the turnips. 'Do you remember the fluttering sound you used to make, trying to get her to come? Try now... over there on the log. Sit down and hold these behind your back.'

'She stood where she was. 'I don't know about this, Tim. I think I'd rather watch...'

He put the bucket down and took her hand. 'Come. You'll see.'

She came reluctantly, holding back. 'Tim?' Her voice was alarmed. 'She's getting up.'

'Yes. Sit down and make the noise. It's okay, I'm right with you.'

She sat as directed, gave a nervous little cough, then wet her lips and made the fluttering, horsy sound. She started to giggle, then stopped abruptly as Rosie pricked her ears and started walking towards them, pace quickening, and Kelly made to get up. 'Tim?'

'Don't move. Lean forward, hands behind back. Don't give it to her until I say.'

'Oh, God… are you sure she isn't charging?'

'Look at her tail. It's limp. Make the noise again… softer this time.'

She did as instructed and Rosie's pace quickened, ears pricked. 'Oh, shit…'

'Don't worry.' But Tim was a little concerned. Rosie was coming faster than usual. 'Do it again,' he said quietly. 'Softer still.'

Her lips must have been dry, for it came out more as if she were trying to blow out candles.

Rosie stopped a few paces away to lift her head and sniff. She blew softly then, with her head still raised, stepped closer.

Looking down at Kelly sitting there as rigid as a statue, the turnip leaves shaking in her hand like a tree in a gale, Tim felt something indefinable rise in his chest. He had not been completely sure until that moment. Now he was certain.

Then he became aware of what Rosie was doing and felt something even more profound. Something that sent a shiver of awe up his spine. Rosie had never done this with him before either. With her head extended forward, almost to the point of overbalancing, she softly nuzzled Kelly on the chin with her long upper lip.

Bamba Zonke broke the spell by clattering the bucket, and Rosie lowered and turned her great head to look.

'Give her the turnips now,' Tim instructed. 'Hold your hand out flat.'

Rosie took and chewed on them appreciatively, then strolled away to see what delights were left in the noisy bucket.

Kelly looked up with her eyes shining and her face flushed. 'Oh, Tim... did you see that?'

He smiled at her, the feeling of awe still with him. 'She missed you. No doubt. If that wasn't a kiss I don't know what is.'

'That was the most wonderful... the most... I don't know how to describe it. I feel like... Oh, Tim... how? How did you tame her like that?'

'Me? It was you who did it. I only finished off. She's never done that before.' He shook his head in lingering astonishment. 'She remembers you, Kelly. No doubt at all.' He offered a lifting hand. 'Come. Well done. You're a brave girl.'

'Thank you, Tim,' she said meekly, still overwhelmed. 'That was the most wonderful surprise. I still can't believe it.'

He squeezed her hand to still its trembling. 'Animals learn to forgive more easily than people.'

She was silent until they were out through the gate, then turned to face him.

'Tim. I have something to…'

'No. Me first. Kelly, I…' He stopped, his courage wavering. Her face was thinner too, and her eyes were fixed intently on his, so green in the sun, and still shining with wonder from her experience, as they had done that day after her loop. She was beautiful. He looked away, self-conscious. 'You got my card…'

She nodded, eyes steadily fixed.

'Well, in case you're wondering,' He took a deep breath. 'I want you to know that I meant it.'

'All of it?

'Every word.' It's going all wrong, he thought. Damn Juliette and her interfering. If I continue on like this I will screw it up. He took another deep breath and grinned. 'I'm sounding like a dork, aren't I?'

The eyes narrowed, smiling, and her lips followed,

but she remained silent, waiting.

'The truth is, I can't remember every word.'

'Oh?' A slight crease showed between her eyes.

'I remember saying I miss you... right?'

'We miss you,' she corrected.

'Yes... and er... I love you... right?'

'Yes...' Her eyes were softening... smiling.

'It's the last bit I can't remember exactly.' He frowned. 'I know I asked you the big one, and I mean it, but I can't remember how I said it, exactly. Damn!'

'Please marry me.'

He grinned. 'Okay, if you insist.'

'You bum!' She laughed, eyes sparkling. 'Now you're sounding more like the Tim I remember. You had me worried there for a while.'

'So what is it? Do I have to go down on my knees? Kinda awkward with a broken leg.'

'First tell me if you like children.'

'Can't stand them, but if they were ours I guess I could learn to put up with the noise and stuff.'

'Do you like them already made?'

'You mean adopt?'

'No, I mean already made.' She lifted up her shirt to reveal a smooth round belly, giving it a pat, and Tim felt a sense of deep disappointment creep over him. It must have shown on his face when he looked at her, for she smiled sympathetically. 'Not much good at arithmetic, are you?'

'You mean…'

She nodded. 'I think he's going to be a pilot too. Sometimes I'm sure I can feel his arms flapping.'

He could think of nothing to say, could only stare at her smooth rounded stomach in wonder, the feeling of awe returning, but different this time. And love. He knew it was love. He could think of no other feeling like the one swelling within him like an uplifting balloon. Or the child growing inside Kelly's womb. His child. Their child.

'Well?'

He saw her small frown of uncertainty and was quick to stop it. 'That's terrific, Kelly.' He gulped. 'That's really great.' But it was not enough to express how he felt. He dropped his crutch to reach for her. 'Hell, Kelly, that's Bloody *excellent!*'

The End